The Return of the Obeni

Other Books by Leon Allen Bryan

★ *Tales of the Obeni*
★ *The Progeny of Misinterpretation*

The Return of the Obeni

Leon Allen Bryan

Writersandpoets.com

Published by: Writersandpoets.com

Book Design: Earl Cox

Cover Design: @Alexa_Eliza

Back Cover Photography: Leon Allen Bryan

Printed in the United States of America

First Printing:

Publisher's Note:

ISBN 10: 0-9762710-6-0
ISBN 13: 978-0-9762710-6-2

Writersandpoets.com

Dedication

This book is dedicated to Pamela Bryan, a lifesaver.
You were the only woman besides my mother who was concerned
about my relationship with God. It can't be easy living with an author
who uses his finger to write on invisible sheets of paper.
At times even finding him having a dialogue with no one.

Except for the days my children were born,
you are the best thing to happen to me.

PS. There are no refunds!

Acknowledgments

I give thanks to God for each day of life.

To my granddaughter Rachel, when I needed names for characters, you always provided them, thank you.

To my editors Ms. Angela Fritz, and Mrs. Debra Gaston, for seeing what I could not, thank you. To everyone who encouraged me to keep telling stories, thank you.

Once again, to those who were around to cause confusion, you continue to make me stronger, thank you.

Lastly, I urge you to listen to some of my favorite artists and read *This Is My Story* by First Baptist Church-West.

Never a day / The United Tenors

Noah's Ark / Najee

Invisible / Black violin

A Reason, A Season, A Lifetime / Tia Fuller

About the Author

Leon Allen Bryan was born in New York City and grew up in the Sugar Hill area of Harlem. He attended Manhattan Community College, and York College. He lives with his wife Pamela in NC, and is the author of *Tales of the Obeni*, and *The Progeny of Misinterpretation*. His next book will be about family legacy.

Chapter 1

My father told me many stories about his life and mine to inspire me and build my character. Benjamin Reeves Sr. wanted me to know how hard life was growing up in the south in early 1900, and the hardships he'd overcome. As a black man in America his greatest wish was that I seized the most out of any opportunity.

From an early age he taught me to pray before I went to sleep. He told me God sees and knows all, and there was nothing you can hide from the Creator of all things. By listening to my dad's testimonies I believed what God thought of me was important. I tried to make my actions pleasing to God but at times I fell short.

Like most young children who lied to their parents I did too, but I had a boundary. There were days I said I'd just be down the block and wind up across 110th Street, or in Central Park riding my bike with Ronald and my other friends. When we sat down for dinner and my father asked how my day was I told him anything but where I really was. But I never deceived him when it came to the truth about my prayers.

When I was in bed for the night dad would ask if I'd said them. There were times I was almost asleep and wanted to tell him I did, when it wasn't true. But I'd be honest then pop would say, "Bennie get up and give thanks."

Even now as a grown man if I'm in bed and forget to give thanks before I go to sleep, I must get up and do it. It's as if my father's hand is pulling me by the leg like he did when I was small and hadn't moved fast enough.

My mother felt the same way about wanting me to be productive and believing in God's influence. From her perspective she enjoyed serving the Church as a member of the Usher Board. It was my mom who made me realize God had a purpose for everyone including me. Shortly after I went to high school I began to wonder what my mission was. It seemed as if God were placing obstacles in my way to make me stronger. He was honing me like a metal tool forged in fire and shaped for a specific task. One day I would be required by The Creator of All Things to take an assignment that would be difficult, and like Noah, I could not refuse.

One spring evening in 1965 when I was a child, my father and I were leaving his sisters Maude and Marion's house on Gates Avenue. We were almost at the entrance to the Brooklyn Bridge headed for Harlem when Pop realized he'd left his pistol behind. I was between five and six years old when I offered a solution. I told him if it were possible for my arm to stretch I could reach back across the winding streets to retrieve his gun. All I had to do was unlock the latch on the black iron gate in front and ring the bell. When the door opened my arm would continue stretching inside to recover the pistol from the dresser drawer. That way he wouldn't have to go back.

At that age I knew it was impossible, but I was just thinking out loud. His response made that a day I will never forget. Instead of telling me how silly my idea sounded or getting frustrated because we had to return he just smiled. He turned that 59 Chrysler around and soon stopped at a light. Then he placed his hand on my shoulder and said with confidence and pride, "Bennie you are an abstract thinker!"

He sounded pleased with my suggestion then clarified what abstract thinking meant. Pop explained it as an ability to theorize a problem using unconventional methods. Even if it was not possible to use my arm that way it showed I had creative thoughts. I was young and didn't understand those big words, but he explained. That day my Pop made me feel significant and smart. It was one of the many reasons I loved him so much. I became convinced there was nothing I couldn't accomplish if I set my mind to it. All I had to do to succeed in life was use my head to come up with a solution.

Now as an adult I was in a bind. My life had been turned upside down and twisted inside out. I'd lived through the most unbelievable adventure, and it was going to take more than abstract thinking to solve my problems this day. A witness to an experience that was easier to declare fiction than acknowledge the events as truth. I was the victim of a surreptitious trauma suffering from survivor's guilt and didn't realize it.

I was a young black man and co-owner of a successful laundry business in Harlem, confused as hell about the direction I was heading. The franchise Ronald and I started several years ago was doing well; it was my love life that was a disaster. Like most men my age I had a healthy appetite for women, but I was confused. I went from one lady to the next sampling the pleasurable sensations they offered. At the time I equated manhood with the number of women I'd slept with. But deep down I wanted a lady I could gaze and smile at the way my father did when he looked at my mother. The one I needed to love, marry, and have children with. I sought the day when I could tell my son or daughter, they had the gift if abstract thinking, and encourage them as I had been.

After a few failed relationships and several weekenders, the dust settled and I found someone. Terri Anderson was a brilliant attorney I met on her way home one day in the Bronx. She was attractive, professional, and intelligent. Her shapely body and lighter skin complemented mine when we lay close. Terri had all if not most of the qualities a man looked for in a mate, and we began to have an exclusive relationship for a few years. During that time I found it difficult to tell her I loved her because of her odd behavior, and suspicious nature. After some time despite her quirks and short temper I did anticipate a moment I could tell her the words she wanted to hear. Regretfully that day never came.

While Terri and I were together my uncertainty grew worse, so I decided to get away for a while without her. I went to Africa and while vacationing in Egypt during the spring of 1986, I did meet a woman and fall in love. The break up that followed between Terri and me was disturbing. For a time I wouldn't know how lucky I was to have gotten away with just a few angry looks and curse words.

My new acquaintance was a lady by the name of Whende who became the ultimate desire from a fantasy that could never be improved. She had large embracing eyes and dimples when she smiled. Her skin was dark like mine but beautiful like she was gently bathed by the sun. She wore her hair in locks with small decorative shells and beads woven within. Whende could've been comfortable as the CEO of a large corporation, or the general of an army. This strong black woman could only complement a worthy and virtuous man because she behaved like royalty. She wasn't able to leap tall buildings with a single bound, but she was full of courage and humor. I was confident she could accomplish anything she set her mind too.

Her 26-year-old mind held an old set of values which gave me new ideas when I looked at my life. Every time I watched her I craved her mind and body. This feeling intensified after the first stormy night Whende and I were lovers. Just the scent of her skin made me to lose my cool. I had to protect and possess her because she was precious. I was in love with The One and there was nothing I could do about it.

A tragic accident left Whende afflicted with a form of amnesia. She'd lost all knowledge of our affection and to make matters worse she wasn't able to speak or walk. The love of my life now had an empty mind in a beautiful black woman's body. She was a bed ridden vegetable helpless and unaware, and I felt duty bound after the mishap to care for her.

To get her out of Africa and back to my home in New York, a new identity was created. I claimed her as my sister and gave her the name Linda Reeves. Her mental capacity was evaluated before we left Egypt, and the doctor believed she would never get better. A few days later we were in Harlem and for the first few weeks Linda was fed milk and juice from a bottle because she couldn't chew. Her every action was that of a new born baby coming from the maternity ward. She required adult diapers and constant supervision. Weeks later Linda began to make gurgling sounds and was somewhat aware of her surroundings. As the days progressed I found out the doctor who first examined her had been very wrong. Her mind had merely been erased like chalk words from a black board.

The ancient papyrus scroll regarding the Obeni was translated to say, "Death to all that is known," but it had been misinterpreted. The death referred to the knowledge within the mind not the physical body. So each day Linda got smarter while regaining her motor skills. She went through the mental stages of development five to six times faster than a normal child would have. So I began to foresee she would one day remember who she was, and the love we shared.

A few months later Linda had gone from crawling and walking to bolting around the house. Her crying and undecipherable mumbles became the speech of a three-year-old. I was glad to see her progress however the lie I told about a sibling connection between us had to constantly be reinforced. Not just to my family, and neighbors, but her new doctor and home attendant. The most difficult person to preserve the deception was I.

This deceit made me feel like two individuals grasping separate memories. The right hand held the love we had, while the left was the brother I now pretended to be. Reinforcing the belief I was Linda's brother was the only way to stop the shameful temptation growing within me. Less than three months prior we were in each other's arms, and it was hard to forget.

Sometimes I found myself watching Linda and remembering how good she'd felt that one and only night we'd slept together. The way our brown skinned bodies complimented each other in rhythmic motion.

Often I reminisced of the adoring way she looked at me as we embraced, and the sweet smell of her hair. Only the love and respect I had for her combined with the high moral standards of my parents stopped me from the unthinkable. Until the day she was able to recall our love my intention was to stay celibate.

With each week of Linda's improvement came another crisis and more lies to create and maintain. I discovered she was carrying my child and couldn't tell anyone. The moment I'd looked forward to from the time I was a teenager had arrived. I was going to be a father but it was a bitter sweet moment. For a time I was depressed but the hope she would regain her memory gave me optimism.

As time went on Linda's mind seemed to grasp information quicker because she was soon to become a mother. Six months into the pregnancy her mind was that of a teenager. And with her new ability to reason she asked so many questions it was hard to manufacture believable stories. She wanted to know when our parents died, and what day she was born. Why there were only pictures of me when I was a kid but none of her? Still I continued to deceive the one I loved and that was hard to accept.

Linda's rationale was fine tuned to a point where she'd look at me with disbelief when I answered her questions. Her probing nature and intellectual mind worked constantly. In the morning I'd awake afraid of what she may ask next, or how long I could keep this farce going. There came a point when her inquiries were so numerous I had no choice but to turn her loose at the library on 136th Street and Lenox Avenue.

Once inside Linda reacted to books like a child in a toy store. The first book she read was on human birth then math and history, followed by western religion. Two weeks later while Linda and I were sitting in the kitchen eating dinner, out of the blue she asked if I knew the father of her child. The fork inches from my mouth I froze, only my hand shook for a second, and she took notice. Still I looked into her trusting eyes and lied by telling her I didn't know, and then ate. Before she could ask another question I changed the subject to taking her shopping in the morning. Her confused stare gave way to silent agreement. But I knew the day was coming when she wouldn't let me get away with such a diversion from her inquiries.

Shortly after that on mostly rainy nights with lots of wind, Linda began to have recurring nightmares about an unknown man. She wouldn't go to sleep with a coat on a hanger in view, or a jacket draped over the back of a chair. They had to be inside her closet with the door shut, or she'd think someone was in the room if she awoke. Even with those precautions every so often Linda's fear would overcome her. I'd hear a knock on my door sometime after midnight. Between the claps of thunder and flashes of lightning the door would slowly open. A tall shadowy figure spoke in a tearful but panicked voice,

"Bennie, I'm scared!"

"What's wrong Linda?" I'd ask groggily.

"The squiggly man is trying to get me! He almost…"

"You gotta slow down I can't understand what you're saying."

"I said he came again… the squiggly man. He's trying to get me!!"

"The what man?"

She fought to relax still holding the arm of the stuffed monkey she took to bed with her. Then Linda looked around my room to make certain she wasn't followed. I'd forgotten she'd given a name to the villain in her dreams. Trying to sound calm I said, "the squiggly man again? You just had a bad dream, he's not real. Go back to sleep nothing can hurt you, you're safe okay?"

"But I think he's gonna get me! He keeps following me… reaching for my hand to grab me!"

When the bad dreams first began Linda described the figure as a silhouette made of black smoke or dark liquid, with no distinguishing facial features. But something was different when she spoke about it that night.

Linda jumped up and down to make sure I was listening and said, "Bennie… he almost caught me this time for real!!"

"He did? Tell me what happened? And talk slower."

"I was running… down a grassy hill behind our house…but the house looked different," she said moving her arms in a running motion.

"What was different?"

"Our house was not as tall and all by itself," she answered sounding confused.

"Linda I don't know what you mean when you say by itself?"

"I mean well…it felt like my house. Like I knew where I was, but it didn't look the same. The ceiling was real high, all the furniture was different and the rooms were too. The fence was gone in the backyard, and…and the house was not connected to the others, it was just the one house."

"Really," I said, knowing the house she referred to.

"Oh! And there was a pool in the back yard."

"Wow!" I said understanding Linda was dreaming of her home in Egypt.

"And…and the first time the squiggly man was standing on the hill watching me. Then he started running towards me. Then the next time I dreamt about him he was in the house. He chased me down stairs and around the pool!" Linda said sounding upset.

"So what happened this time? And try to relax; you're safe."

"Ok, this time I…I was sitting in the backyard reading. I stood up and when I walked by the pool he was under the water. Then he reached up to pull me in. But I started running…then he ran after me and I woke up."

Now she came closer poking her bottom lip out and said, "I don't want to go back to my room. Can I sleep in here tonight? Please!"

"You're getting too big for this Linda."

"But I'm really scared!"

She held the monkey chest high so their faces were almost side by side. The desperation of her voice took me back to the days when I was small, had a nightmare and asked the same question. And when my parents told me yes, there was a feeling of security I never forgot. In my desire to one day become a good father I would inevitably say yes to her.

"Alright come on."

Lifting the covers Linda would run to the other side and plop on the mattress with a huge smile and sigh of relief. We'd turn back-to-back and soon she would be sleep leaving me to lie still but restless. There was no doubt Linda was running from a fear I caused. The squiggly man who pursued her at night in her dreams was me. And with each nightmare he got closer.

When morning came I left her sleeping and didn't see her until after work. After that I wasn't surprised she was reading a book on dreams, and what causes them. When she finished she started reading between three and four books a week. The nightmares had not returned and by the time she was ready to give birth Linda had read more than three hundred books on more subjects than I can count. Her reasoning caught up to her physical age but still she showed no signs of remembering her real identity.

I could say without a doubt she still loved me but not the way I needed. The sibling bond I concocted with Linda had hardened like wet cement. With each passing day I felt as if I'd signed a contract I couldn't break. I began to chastise myself every time she called me brother. My frustration and resentment caused me extreme stress. As a result I'd often get to work late and be rude to the customers. Soon after I distanced myself from friends and called my real sister Demetrice, and Aunt Dot less.

Besides being strained I was horny as hell and my libido was steadily rising. At times it was hard to control…literally. When I got home or on my days off I'd sneak into the bathroom and lock the door. While Linda was down stairs I'd sit on the toilet and masturbate as if I was a teenager. The nights began to get worse to the point that my hand could no longer satisfy me. I'd never gone so many months without sex and something had to give.

Sometime before Linda went into the hospital to give birth I met Thomasina. Just a few years prior I never would have given this woman a second look because she was married. Now she had all the qualifications I wanted. She was bold, very appealing, and extremely submissive. This small but voluptuous woman was missing a top front tooth that made her smile sexy. My thinking was with a married woman there could never be a strong attachment between us. We could just meet, have sex and at the end of the night she had to go back to her husband. Plus when the time came for my life to return to normal I'd have none of my feelings invested in a relationship. It turned out I was wrong about the effect this woman would have on me.

Thomasina was four years my senior when we met in the grocery store. After we began to date she told her husband Derrick I was her older sister Angie's child. This made me very uncomfortable, but I went along anyway. It was a case of one head having control over the other. And given I was already frustrated; Thomasina received the coldest side of me. I made sure she felt only the pleasure she came for and little else. As far as I was concerned we were just having sex. Then I'd give her a few dollars for her kids or whatever she asked for.

The pretense was I'd pick up Aunt Thomasina from her house, say hello to her husband Derrick from my car then wave bye as we drove off. Most of the time when we were together I never listened to a thing Thomasina said. And when she wanted to talk about how simple and lazy her husband was I had the remedy. I'd stand in front of her while she was talking and unzip my pants. She'd stop speaking to look at me. Then I'd tell her I didn't want to hear that bullshit and remind her of why she was there. I made sure I treated her just like she treated her husband, and she loved it. But you can't treat people wrong and not have it come back to you, and in a few months that's just what would happen to me.

When it was close to the time for Linda's baby to arrive I broke off the affair with Thomasina. She didn't take it well at first, but I knew she'd get over it. On the 26th of March 1987 Linda went into labor and was taken to Harlem hospital. She gave birth the next day to a baby girl and named her Tiffany Reeves. It was the happiest and saddest day of my life. I held an extension of myself in the flesh and was forever changed. An overwhelming sense of responsibility for these two lives was my only concern. I held my baby girl next to the bed and rocked her until she went to sleep. The hard part was giving her back to the nurse and not being able to express the joy I felt at becoming a father.

A few days later when Linda came home it was not easy to get her to listen to me. She was 27 years old and finally the age was equivalent to her mature intellect. I'd raised her to be smart and independent the way my parents had done for me, and my efforts came to fruition. When I tried to reason with her my ideas had to make perfect sense or she rejected them to follow her own mind. The woman that loved to play and jump rope in the backyard with our dog Mister was gone. A lady stood before me ready to assume responsibility for her life.

Linda was adamant about what path she wanted to take and didn't need or ask for help from me. She decided when and what she ate, the clothes she wore, and how to take care of her baby. She began to make her own doctor's appointments and left the house many times without letting me know where she was going. I began to wonder was this what parents go through when their children start exercising their freedom? And did the headaches and knots in the stomach ever go away from worrying about them?

The thought that gave me constant fear was Linda discovering I'd been lying to her. If she did find out I wasn't her blood brother with no original memory of her own, she'd never believe how we met. How could anyone accept the circumstances of our first meeting, or the unexplained way she forgot our adoration? There wasn't a soul in the world I could speak to who could relate. There was a time I could have talked to my best friend and business partner Ronald, but our relationship was changing. Discussing my personal problems with Ronald was like talking to him and his wife Lorraine.

Not long after Linda came home with the baby she began to have blackouts when she saw her reflection. I believed the loss of consciousness was the result of her real memory trying to return. I just didn't give the healing process enough time. One day Linda came out of a daydream and spoke to me in her native language. They were words I waited more than a year to hear; too bad I wasn't a bit more patient.

That day she looked into my eyes like the first night we made love, and I was thankful. Her memory returned and she knew who I was. I touched the side of her cheek, smiled and said, "Whende?" She smiled and hugged me. We started to kiss, I held her closer than I had in a very long time. Our hands explored each other's bodies as we moved to the couch. Never taking our eyes off one another we laid down. Kissing her feverishly I paused to look at her and she said, "Neir abeir Bennie, neir abeir."

Those words meant I love you in her language and they were sweet to hear like the taste of her lips. I caressed her breasts enjoying the moment. Suddenly she tensed and withdrew a bit. As quickly as her old memory came it was gone, and I was her brother again. Linda's body recoiled from my embrace, and she was repulsed at the sight of me. It was a look of horror and betrayal I will never forget. She ran stumbling upstairs crying and refusing to let me explain. She locked herself in her room with the baby and would not answer when I spoke from the other side of the door. It was my intent to give her time to calm down. The next morning I got up early walked past her room and left for work. When I came home later Linda and Tiffany were gone. That was Monday evening April 27, 1987, and now a year later I still hadn't seen or heard from her.

During the year she was missing I took weeks off from work to look in any city Linda ever mentioned or saw in a travel magazine. I spent two days in San Francisco, since more than once she talked about wanting to eat at Fisherman's Wharf. The next day I was in Los Angeles, and then I flew to Dallas. After days of aimless searching I began to doubt I'd find her in Dallas. Still I knew Linda wasn't in New York and I didn't want to go home.

From there I went to New Orleans, Atlanta, then up to Buffalo and Toronto. Jet lag wreaked havoc on my sleep and my nerves. To make matters worse, somewhere between New York and Canada I lost my father's gold watch. It was one of a few precious items he'd left to me before passing away. I took it off to change the time to this zone and put it on the bathroom sink before washing my hands. I finally noticed it was gone while on the short flight to Canada. Pops wore the watch only on special occasions, and that's why I had it. Wearing it gave me hope, and now it was gone.

When evening came I found myself at a hotel in downtown Montreal. Somewhat mentally drained I sat on the bed with a small glass of cognac. The television was off and the silence soothing. My thoughts swung back and forth like a pendulum from Linda to the watch, Linda and the watch, then back again. Without her or that small piece of jewelry depression became my constant companion. Just a year or so ago I was happy and living in a home with love, and now I was alone.

Struggling with not knowing her whereabouts or if she was safe, was a new sensation. Then it hit me after almost twenty years of misunderstanding, the message was clear. A revelation comes in each person's life when you finally see why your parents chose a course of action or said a particular thing you didn't agree with. I put the glass down smiling as I pictured my mother's face. It took almost twenty years but now I realized why she kicked my ass when I came home four hours late from school.

It wasn't planned for Vincent and me to ride the train together after our fifth grade classes were over, but we did. On that spring day he invited me to his home. My thought was to stay just fifteen minutes and leave. I'd see where Vincent lived and the next time he could come to my house after school. When we got there Vincent's mother let us in. I was greeted by their dog, a chestnut-colored boxer who begged to be petted. He followed us to Vincent's room and stayed next to me licking my hand while wagging that stubby tail.

The next thing I knew Vincent showed me all these cool toys. He had a model of the Land of the Giants space ship with a working door. On his dresser were figurines of Batman and Robin standing next to the Batmobile. He had a toy plane with blinking lights and sound. He had board games and puzzles, and toy guns that shot small plastic sticks with suction cups on the end. We both had the same GI Joe with fuzzy hair and beard, and we had the same space capsule GI Joe sat in. But Vincent had the green army jeep and more accessories to go with his GI Joes.

After that he got behind his bed and I hid by the edge of his dresser, and we played cops and robbers. Then we shot a nerf basketball into a small hoop above his door. His dog tried to participate so we worked him into the game as the referee. I was laughing and having more fun then I'd had in months. That day was every little boy's dream. Then Vincent played with a foot long red racing car with chrome rims, and I had that big yellow Tonka Dump Truck I'd wished for but didn't get last Christmas. Everything I wanted was right in that room, a friend to play with, toys, and a dog. Later his mother brought us fried bologna sandwiches with lettuce and tomatoes on a plate and cherry Kool-Aid. I was so comfortable it was like being at home. We ate the food and played some more and the next thing I knew it was twenty minutes after six.

I'd lost track of time and stayed too long, but I assumed my mom would understand. I got close enough to my house to see the blinds move on the first floor and I knew she saw me. I was still happy and excited when I walked past her and then she let the door slam. Standing with my book bag in the living room I started to explain why I was late. It turned out all the stuff that was important to me wasn't the same to her. And to make matters worse it didn't sound like I was sorry for being late.

When she came back with the belt I was surprised. I didn't see how she missed the part where I was having fun and accidentally lost track of time. Her arm raised and I said, "Ma, I won't do it again ma, I promise! I just forgot what time it was that's all!"

She wasn't listening and I felt the belt hit me across the shoulder and I kept repeating, "but ma, he had a dog. I was playing with the dog!!" She could have let me off with a warning and I never would've done it again but she didn't. So I stayed mad with her for a very long time after that. Only until this moment do I see how worried I made her. But if Linda came home safe no matter what she'd done I'd welcome her with open arms.

The next morning I left Canada and went back to Harlem disappointed. The problem was there were too many places to investigate on my own. So I placed ads in the personals for the entire month of March in several newspapers in the cities I'd visited, and the ones on my list I didn't get to. In each paper the message was the same, **Linda, I'm sorry please come home**, and that was all.

I waited for several more weeks for a response from the ads but there was none, and I became miserable. Linda was gone and abstract thinking wasn't helping me locate her. At my wits end I hired a private investigator, Wayne Queen to assist in the search. He was a detective for the New York City Police Department recently retired on disability. I don't know how successful I expected him to be when most of the information I gave him about Linda and her real identity was false. And if I told him the reason she ran away he probably wouldn't help me at all.

At first the search had him looking for old acquaintances and affiliations Linda couldn't possibly have. Soon Mr. Queen discovered she had no history of employment or childhood friends. Linda never had a summer job, or applied for working papers when she was a teenager. There was no record of her attending any elementary or high school in the Tri-State area. The only thing she had was the bank account she emptied the day she left, a library card, and a social security number.

After less than a week on the case Mr. Queen called me sounding disgusted. He commented how odd it was Linda didn't exist until only a few years ago. He reminded me that withholding information would make the job harder. Still he pressed me for an explanation as to why I never filed a missing person's report with the police. I made up a story about the money Linda taking wasn't all hers and not wanting to get her arrested. After a moment of indecision he took some more money to keep looking, but he was becoming suspicious of me.

By now depression walked with me everywhere. I'd told more lies in less than three years than in my entire existence. Not just little white lies, very big important lies that altered lives. Frequently I relived seeing Linda's face and the disgusting way she looked at me before she left. It bothered me her last thoughts were of me as a pervert. There wasn't a day I wished I'd been more patient and understanding, but the damage was done.

As weeks piled into months and the holidays approached, the possibility of not seeing Linda became genuine. I was solely responsible for the changes to her future. Because of my intervention she had none of her real family around, and by now they were surely dead. She could live her whole life not knowing the truth, and I was one of a few who could explain. If she one day forgave me and came home she'd never comprehend what really happened. I believed it was necessary to leave some proof behind in case I had a fatal accident.

Linda deserved to know we were not related, and Tiffany was my child. I shook my head in despair then went for some paper and pen. Off the top of my head I wrote what I thought was most important. The next morning I added a small part about her accident. I labeled the episode a drowning and the rest of the words were an apology for not being more tolerant. At first it was three and a half hand written pages I kept in a sealed envelope with Linda's name on it.

The same day at work I thought she deserved to know she was born in Egypt even if I didn't know her actual birth date. So when I got home I added this information. Before I put the paper down I wanted to write how Linda and I met, but that story was unbelievable even for a sane person.

A few days later I took Mister for his afternoon walk. He was the Rottweiler Linda and I had from a pup. When we got to the park it seemed I hadn't said enough in the letter about Linda's accidental drowning and memory loss. So when I returned home I got some more paper and added more details to the letter. Then I figured I might as well mention how she got to America, and why I changed her identity. Now since I revealed that, I had to tell her, her real name. Linda introduced herself to me as Princess Sakatet Whende, born from a royal family. Like Haile Selassie who could trace his ancestry hundreds of years back to the time of King Solomon and the Queen of Sheba, my love was an actual Princess from Africa. Linda's families were direct descendants of Egyptian Kings and Queens.

The next week I had off, I spent half the time writing to keep despondency away. With each word and sentence I wrote weight lifted from my heart. By the end of November 1988 I'd written a declaration of the true circumstances that was almost fifty pages long. The document grew too large for an envelope, so I made two copies and placed them in folders. In case one was lost there was another in a safe deposit box at the corner bank.

One day just after my birthday in January of 1989 I decided to make our story public. So everything around the time before and up to meeting Linda was placed within the sheets. I changed the names of some people including my friends and eight months later, the letter was over three hundred typed pages. Then I disguised my confession as a book and called it Tales of the Obeni. I considered placing Linda's picture on the cover but quickly decided not to. My hope was Linda would stumble upon it, read it and regain her memory. At the very least if she didn't believe the entire story she might accept my apology.

Luckily there were less than a handful of individuals who knew Linda's past. One was my real sister Demetrice, and the group of individuals who helped me get Linda out of Africa. I didn't waste time convincing my best friend Ronald and his wife Lorraine of Linda's true origin even though they were in Egypt with me before Linda's accident. It seemed easier to keep them guessing since our friendship was becoming strained.

After the book was published, I jumped every time the phone rang, or someone was at the front door. This was a time in my life when pathetic was the best way to describe me. I didn't go out except to walk the dog or shop for food. Social events were a thing of the past and my aunt Dot, and sister Demetrice never saw me. I was a single moderately handsome thirty-year-old man whose only date was with some lotion, and my right hand.

One night after 10pm, I was in my bedroom about to kneel and pray. A storm was brewing outside and the rumbles were getting louder. Between the thunder claps I could hear the light tapping from Mister's paws walking on the tile in the downstairs kitchen. Then I heard him run up the stairs to stop by Linda's room. Soon he came into mine then stood at the foot of the bed. It amazed me that he checks the house every night like a security guard, and nobody taught him to do it.

"Is everything okay Mister?" I asked. He stood there waiting for me to complete the kneeling position. My arms rested on the mattress, then I put them together and bowed my head. With eyes closed I inhaled deeply and prayed.

"Dear Lord… Creator of All Things, thank you for this day you've given me. Thank you for loving me and keeping me safe. Please protect my family and friends."

I paused eyes still closed looking into the darkness of my mind, until I could hear myself breathing then I continued, "Please dear God, keep Linda safe, please…Amen."

When I looked up Mister walked to me. I rubbed his head and patted his chest. He was an amazing dog. Mister even knew to wait until I finished praying before he came to say good night. It was also funny he knew when I came from the bathroom with the lotion he had to sleep outside my room.

A muggy breeze came from under the cracked window just enough to make the curtain ripple. I got in bed then turned the light out. This was the time I contemplated the pain I caused us both. She'd been gone two years, five months and 18 days and every night I had the same thoughts. The lightning flickered and I considered when Linda's mind was like a very young girl afraid of the thunder. She'd knock on my door frightened and ask could she sleep with me. Ironically the first night we made love in Egypt the wind was blowing the curtains in her room and the night was warm like this.

All my life I wanted a woman to love and when I found her I fucked it up. Linda was somewhere in the world, and I could only hope she was still praying before she went to sleep like I'd taught her. If she was still talking to and trusting God I could feel some measure of comfort. Also when I prayed at night I asked God to keep Linda safe, and to bring her home. Then I'd lie down and think how good it was when she was here, and all we'd been through. Then inevitably back to that last evening she was home. I got in bed knowing Linda was just down the hall very upset. I should have made her listen to my story and not waited for the morning.

After many years of feeling helpless I tried to reach Linda with another book. I continued to write about my tortured days from the time she left to ease my pain, preserve my sanity, and curb the anger. If the first book didn't reach her hands a second should increase the chances of her reading our story and forgiving me. Keeping most of the same guidelines as Tales of the Obeni the only real names I used were hers and mine. I refused to believe we'd never see each other again. Like a recurring nightmare I wished I'd never gone to Egypt because when each morning came I was still alone.

Chapter 2

A tall slender brown skinned man in his late thirties was one of many walking up the subway stairs across the street from the corner bar. It was after 4 pm and the sky was darkening. He stood out of the crowd's way to fasten his coat as they hurried up past him. It was Monday two weeks before Christmas 1989 and what was rain when Mr. Queen got on the train now turned into sleet and the ground was dusted with ice crystals. The aroma from the famous fish-n-chips spot on St. Nicholas was recognizable and stroked his hungry stomach. Mr. Queen's eyes followed the long line of people waiting across the street braving the weather, which further reminded him how good the fish was. His only hope was the line would be shorter when he returned after finishing his business.

He tilted his hat to face the wind then crossed the street. When he got down the block to the next corner his mood had already changed. As a private investigator when he first took this case there was a good feeling. He would be reuniting the family of a man who had helped rebuild his Harlem neighborhood. But as time went by Mr. Queen was thoroughly convinced that man had been lying to him. His skills were wasted for months chasing a ghost when he could have been getting an innocent woman out of jail.

This time he was going to treat Mr. Benjamin Reeves like a suspect and get to the truth. As a former police detective it was hard to believe in coincidences. When the wife is found missing or murdered you start asking the husband questions first. When the kids don't come home you ask the last people who saw them and that's how it goes. But when two cases where people disappearing are linked to one individual, that's where you start.

Approaching his destination he stopped under the tree in front of the house to have a smoke and choose his line of questioning. Mr. Reeves wasn't the type of guy you could grab by the collar and intimidate. He had to be played like a chess game until he was cornered and decided to lay his king down. As he lit another cigarette one thing became clear he was not leaving without the right answers.

Two smokes later a car rolled down the street and slowed near the tree, then parked in a space further down the hill. A younger man slightly shorter and darker in completion got out of the car. To his friends and family he was known as Bennie, and he joined Mr. Queen under the tree.

"Were you waiting for me?" the man asked reaching to shake hands.

"As a matter of fact I was."

Mr. Reeves got anxious, still holding Queen's hand he asked, "Did you find her!?"

"No not yet, I'm still working on it. But I had some questions… was in the neighborhood so I came over. I hope that's okay?" he asked in a sly tone.

"You're kidding right? Sure it is, come on… we'll talk inside. I see you grew a mustache. I almost didn't recognize you."

"Yeah I had to try it for a minute."

"Just watch yourself on these steps. As a matter of fact I gotta throw some salt down now cause it's slippery out here."

"Yup people can slip up," Mr. Queen said in the same sly way he'd answered previously.

"Huh?"

"Nothing, after you," Mr. Queen said smiling.

The men went inside the house and were greeted by a large Rottweiler walking from the living room. The dog watched both men for any strange behavior.

"Hang your coat here and…there's my boy," Mr. Reeves said cheerfully. Then the dog came wagging his stubby tale and licking his hand.

"He's okay Mister…He okay," Mr. Reeves said rubbing the dog's head. Mister smelled the stranger's leg then looked back at his master.

"I forgot you had a dog. Is he friendly?"

"Once I introduce you he is. Go ahead you can touch him."

Mr. Queen rubbed the dog's head then said, "He's nice."

"But tomorrow if you come I have to introduce you again, or he'll act like he doesn't know you," Mr. Reeves said firmly.

"Get out of here!"

"That's right, you're, good for today."

"No kidding?"

"I'm telling you the truth, so just go in the living room and make yourself at home. I'm gonna sprinkle the salt. And trust me he won't bother you," Mr. Reeves added pointing to the living room.

Then he grabbed the small bag of salt by the door and went outside. Within a few minutes he was back, and his guest wasn't in the living room. Instead of calling out he walked to find him. Mr. Queen was standing in the kitchen looking out the window into the backyard. Mister lay on his pillow with his head on his paws watching both men.

"You want a cup of coffee or something to drink?" Mr. Reeves asked standing by the other window.

"No I'm good."

"So what brought you over here?"

"I wanted to ask you about Beverly Simmons?"

"Beverly who?"

"Simmons, Beverly Simmons?" Mr. Queen repeated slowly.

"The name doesn't sound familiar. What does she do?"

Then Mr. Queen abruptly changed the subject. "That's a big backyard. You plant anything out there in the spring time?"

"No, I'm not into taking care of grass and flowers. I was thinking of cementing the whole thing one day."

"There's enough space back there to bury stuff," said Mr. Queen with a little chuckle.

There was an awkward silence then Mr. Queen said, "You ever bury anything out there?"

"Are you messing with me?"

"Now why would you say that? You been straight with me all along… right? I'm just saying that's a big backyard that's all, just relax."

"Sorry, sometime ago I found a dead cat and I buried it in the corner by the fence," he answered pointing to a spot outside.

"And how long ago was that?" Queen asked while touching his mustache with his fingers.

"Look, I know you didn't come all the way over here to ask me about some fucking cat!! So what's up?"

At that moment the dog stood from his bed. Mr. Queen turned and opened his jacket to expose his sidearm then kept his hands by his side. In response Mr. Reeves took off his coat draping it over the back of the chair to show Mr. Queen the gun tucked in his waist band. The two men stood still like a scene from a western movie but it was the homeowner that broke the silence.

"Mister it's alright," he said with a commanding voice, "you wanna go outside? Come on let's go outside boy."

Mr. Reeves walked around the table and the dog followed. Mr. Queen listened to footsteps go down to the next floor and soon he could see the dog in the back yard sniffing around. Mr. Reeves returned with a calmer attitude. He sat at the kitchen table and asked Mr. Queen to join him. Mr. Queen sat with one hand out of sight while Mr. Reeves sat with elbows on the table and both hands in a ball under his chin.

"Why don't you just ask me what you wanna know?" Mr. Reeves said as if he were tired.

"Will I get a straight answer?"

Since he'd withheld some important facts the comment was taken like cod liver oil chased with hot sauce. Mr. Reeves rubbed his head then looked the detective in the eye and said, "Yes."

"Well…I'm here about Terri Anderson?"

"Terri?"

"Yes Terri, do you know her?"

"Terri Anderson?" Mr. Reeves asked as if he were hearing the name incorrectly.

"Yeah, Terri Anderson."

"Yeah, I know her!"

"So you admit you know her?"

"If it's Terri the lawyer, light skinned, cute yeah I know her but…"

"How well did you know her and, what was the nature of your relationship?" Mr. Queen probed.

"The nature of our relationship? What's going on…why you asking me about some old girlfriend?"

"I'll let you know."

"She has nothing to do with me anymore! Didn't I tell you it's been a long day! Now you show up out of the blue and start asking me about a woman I haven't seen in years. I don't have to tell you nothing about her! As a matter of fact this…"

Mr. Queen cut him off loudly while pointing across the table and said, "No, this is what's gonna happen! First I'm gonna stop working on your case cause you been bullshiting me from the start. Then I'm gonna to do some investigating of my own, and it's gonna get nasty. I'm sure the police are gonna want to know where you got the fake passport for Linda. And after that they'll start looking at bank accounts and your financial records. Shit, they might even come over here and dig up your back yard!"

The two sat quietly until Mr. Reeves gave in and said, "I don't know why you want to ask me about Terri but go ahead. Just don't stop looking for Linda please!"

"Let's start with the last time you saw her?"

"The last time I saw Terri was in a bar on the east side."

"And when was that?"

"Maybe and month or two after we broke up I guess."

"Go on," Mr. Queen urged.

"She came in with some friends and…"

"Was a man with her?" Mr. Queen asked quickly.

"No, two women. One of them was a co-worker. I think her name was Tina, or Trina something like that."

"Keep talking."

"They came in…Terri saw me, looked at me like she was really pissed then they went to the back of the bar."

"Why was that?"

"I guess she didn't want to see me, I don't know. After that me and Ronald finished our drinks and got the hell out of there, and that was at least two years ago." Reeves said.

"And you're sure that was the last time you saw her?" Queen probed with disbelief.

"That was the last time I ever saw Terri!"

"Now, why did you two break up?"

Mr. Reeves tapped his fist lightly against his mouth but wouldn't speak. The questions opened old wounds that hadn't healed. Not only had he blamed himself for Linda running away but the hurt he'd caused Terri too.

"Did you hear me?" Mr. Queen asked.

"There's some stuff I left out."

"I know," Mr. Queen said sitting back in the chair to relax.

"This is what really happened. The first thing I should say is Linda isn't my sister. Not by any blood relationship or anything. We're not first cousins, or second cousins, or nothing. I met her on a trip to Africa and we fell in love. As a matter of fact I wasn't even gonna come back to Harlem, that's how serious it was. But she did have the accident and lose her memory. All of that was true."

Mr. Queen sat still without changing his expression. Some part wanted to believe what he was hearing since the two had gotten off to a good start when they first met, but then he had a question.

"I know about the loss of memory and the blackouts, but why claim her as your sister?"

"What can I say, it made sense at the time, but it's bothered me ever since."

"And the passport?"

"I got help with her passport and new identity in Egypt."

"Who helped you do that?"

This bit of truth he wanted to keep to himself so he lied, "I don't know… but I'm lucky we got away from those thugs and back here safely, believe me."

Because a professional investigator couldn't find Linda, Mr. Reeves wondered if she was assisted by the same organization that helped him get her out of the country. They had the money and contacts to do it but there was no way of knowing for sure. Mr. Reeves resumed his explanation,

"Now this part is hard for me to say cause I messed up bad. During one of Linda's blackouts I thought her memory returned so I kissed her, and that was the worst mistake of my life. She left the next day and I haven't seen her since."

"Damn! I don't know what to say," said Mr. Queen placing his other hand on the table.

"Don't say anything until I finish. When we first got back from Egypt there was a time when Linda could barely walk much less take care of herself. I think I told you about that."

"Yes and her doctor confirmed it."

"Well Terri came here while I was washing Linda in the tub a few days after we got back from Egypt. When she saw that… she wasn't too happy. She said we were finished and not to bother her any more. And that's why we broke up even though it was gonna happen sooner or later."

"Why was that?"

"Because I just didn't love her. Terri is a good woman… but she wasn't the one," he answered sadly.

"Really, you're telling me she's a good woman?" Queen repeated.

"She sure is, so what was I saying? Oh so that's why Linda doesn't have a history in this country it's because I lied. I should have told you before but I didn't think you'd help me if you knew the real reason she left," Reeves said stopping short of mentioning the Tales of the Obeni publication. He figured since Mr. Queen was a detective he'd find the book, read it, and have a whole other set of questions, but not right now.

"So tell me more about Terri. What kind of person was she?" he asked.

"Are you going to tell me what this is all about?" Reeves asked nervously.

"I will, but right now I'm asking about your relationship?"

"What can I tell you, she's like any other woman. She's got her dramatic moments, but Terri is caring and sensitive. She's smart, attractive, and has a good job. Everything a guy could want."

"I know what you mean," Mr. Queen said remembering the day he questioned Terri.

"I don't know what else to tell you. She treated me good and while we were together it was serious. She had keys to my house; she'd come over clean up sometimes or make dinner for us. When we went out she'd pay for dinner now and then. We did stuff couples do and I thought she'd make a good mother someday."

"Really?"

"Yeah of course."

"And did you have keys to her apartment?"

"No."

"Why not."

"I never asked her for a key, she didn't offer and that was fine with me."

"But you've been to her place?"

"Yeah a few times, but we mostly stayed here," Mr. Reeves added.

"Now where did she live?"

"In Tracey Towers in the Bronx near a high school. I forget the name right now."

"Was that the only place?"

"What do you mean?"

"Nothing, did she ever tell you about her past?"

"She never talked about her past much."

"How about where she grew up… or where she went to school, what her parents were like?"

"All I know is she was born in Virginia and both her parents are dead. Her father died when she was a young girl, and so did her mother. I forgot where she said she went to school," Reeves answered honestly.

This time it was Mr. Queen who sat at the table with a puzzled look. After being somewhat deceived for a long time he found it hard to believe in this twist of fate, but he was about to play this game of chess to the end. With his next move Mr. Queen was going to find out what he wanted to know.

"Mr. Reeves before I tell you why I'm so interested in Terri can you think if there was anything different about her, anything a little strange?"

Reeves thought for a moment smiled and said, "She could be a little distant and sad but then there were times she knew just what I was thinking before I could say it. What else did she do?" Reeves said looking up at the ceiling for more to say. After snapping his finger a few times Reeves said, "Oh yeah I remember something, Terri was a runner. She liked to run and we ran around Central Park some weekends. She said she ran track in college. I think she was a good lawyer, but she never talked about the details of her cases when we were together."

"Okay," said Queen rubbing his chin.

"And one thing I remember about her was when we were outside it was like walking with a private security guard." Reeves said smiling.

"What do you mean by that?"

"Terri made me feel if something jumped off in the street she wouldn't be scared…you know? Like one night we'd just got out of the car. We were walking to the house and she saw a guy sitting on the stoop before I did. Yeah, she is very observant; you couldn't sneak up on her and I've tried. You know like if we out I'd go down one aisle and she goes somewhere else. I've walked up on her and just as I was about to touch her she'd turn around every time."

"I guess that makes sense."

"So tell me… is Terri in trouble?"

"Not any more… she was murdered. Someone shot her in the stomach and three times in the head execution style. It was…"

"Terri's dead?" Reeves said sadly.

"Yes, she's been dead for years and you're acting like you didn't know?"

"I didn't know…I really didn't. I had no idea!" Reeves said defiantly.

"Well Terri's dead, and here's the thing. The crime was staged to look like a break-in, but robbery wasn't the motive."

"What makes you say that?"

"Well there were no B and E's in high rise buildings in that area at all, and no signs of forced entry. The time of day was all wrong. She wasn't killed coming home at night; she was done in on a Sunday morning when people are going to church. Plus there's a door man in the lobby. So Terri must have opened her door for someone she knew, you know what I mean? Then the killer after firing the first shot stood over her after she fell… then shot point blank three more times in the face."

Mr. Queen demonstrated by extending his arm and pointing to the floor and continued,

"And you're telling me she was very observant so that means it had to be someone she knew."

Mr. Reeves had a blank expression on his face as he leaned forward to get his coat from behind his chair. He reached in his pocket for cigarettes, and then went to the counter for an ashtray. On his way back to the table he raised the window a few inches to let some fresh air in then sat down. Normally he'd ask if the smoke bothered a guest but this time he didn't care. Striking the match took a long drag then blew in the direction of the window.

The news of Terri's death was like a brick slapping him in the mouth. There were no words to express his grief. Terri and he hadn't spoken since the day she was last at his home. There were many times he thought about calling her to say how sorry he was that the relationship didn't work. But he respected her wishes and left her alone. Still she was the only lady he'd come close to saying I love you. Sure Terri had a few quirks but there was never a doubt in his mind she loved him. Now this beautiful young woman was dead. Not only did he feel quilt for what happened to Linda, but Terri's death as well. His eyes began to swell but he did not want to give Mr. Queen any clue to his emotional state. He gathered himself then stared at the trail of smoke in the air and asked, "Did you catch the guy?"

"Not yet…but there's no statute of limitations on murder, and this is the first time I ever saw you smoke."

"Yeah I know."

Mr. Reeves smoked when he was a teenager then quit after many years but started again. The way he saw it he had a choice of drinking or smoking, and drinking seemed the riskiest.

"Well I'm just gonna say it since you're here, I didn't kill Terri. I would never hurt her," Reeves blurted out after another deep drag.

"Would you submit your gun to a ballistic test?"

"Sure, you want it now?"

"No, not yet and so far I think you been straight with me. Why don't you keep doing that and we might get through this," Mr. Queen said warning him.

"I will."

"So tell me what happened with you and Terri?"

"We just weren't compatible that's all. You know how things start out good in the beginning, and once you see the real person you have to make a decision. I had to make one myself, but I did care for her, I really did. I never met anyone like her and that's the truth. Shit she was the only woman who ever had keys to my house."

"You told me that already."

"That's right! There was a time I thought she was the one. And even though she's dead I never wished something like that for her," Reeves said daring to be contradicted.

For a time Reeves sat at the table a bit distraught from the news. With a small measure of sympathy Queen said, "I got something I need to tell you and I think I'll take that drink now. What do you have?"

"I got vodka, brandy, rum and beer," Reeves said standing up.

"Let's have a shot of the brandy."

"I'll get it but first I need to let Mister back in."

It was dark outside now. Mr. Queen got up from the table to look in the back yard when his host left. Soon after only a sliver of light shined from the open basement door when the dog ran in then the light was gone. Mr. Reeves decided to leave Mister in the basement until they finished their conversation. Minutes later the two men sat across for each other and raised glasses. Mr. Reeves took one last drag then used the ashtray.

"Here's to Terri, rest in peace sweetheart," Reeves said sadly.

He paused looking at his drink before he tasted it.

"Cheers," Queen said reluctantly then continued, "Well there was a reason Terri's death wasn't a big news story. And now that I see how you felt about her this won't be easy, but I'll just say it. You know when I started talking about coincidences?"

"Yeah."

"I met Terri Anderson when I was a Detective in her office downtown. I went there to question her about a man named Eddie. And before you ask me I'm gonna tell you this was more than four years ago in May of 84. You didn't know her then did you?" Queen hastily asked.

"No not then. Well let me explain cause you're asking about some dude in May. Terri's birthday is, I mean was in April, I can't remember the exact day. I kept asking and she let me take her out. So if she was still seeing that guy in May I didn't know, but we just went out and that was all. It was later, probably June when we started dating or July I think. We took it slow and then it became exclusive, I'll say it like that," Reeves said.

"So you said that was in 84 right?" Mr. Queen probed.

"Yes... in 84," Reeves replied with irritation.

"Did she ever mention her last boyfriend Eddie?" Queen asked trying to get a spark of jealousy.

"No, I never asked her about old boyfriends, and she never asked about my past relationships. So no I never heard about Eddie. As a matter of fact once we got together, she never talked about her past."

"Okay… so like I was telling you I was at her office in May of 84 because she co-signed a car loan for this guy Eddie. Eddie left work Saturday night which is actually Sunday morning in the month of April 84," Queen said stressing the date then he continued, "A witness told me he thought he saw Eddie get into a dark colored car about a block away. After that he was never seen again. A couple of people I interviewed told me Eddie was running away from baby mama drama, but his new girlfriend and his mother don't agree. They swear he was pleased with the news of becoming a father. His mother is absolutely convinced her son met with foul play. I mean this was a guy who never missed giving his mother a card on Mother's Day, or bringing her a present on her birthday and Christmas. A guy who loves his mom like that doesn't just stop talking to her… right?" Queen said.

"You're right, so what do you think happened?"

"I think he's dead! Eddie was living with his mother, and he never said he was going away, or told her good bye. He never took any of his clothes, or personal belongings. A man running away doesn't leave his car at work for days when he can drive it somewhere and dump it. He'd been to Macys looking at baby cribs with his girlfriend and he had over six hundred dollars left in his dresser. So my question is how does a guy skip town without his car and no money?" Queen asked after taking another sip.

"So you think he's dead," Reeves said with indifference.

"This is what I think, or rather what I know. I know Terri has been surrounded by a lot of murdered people, and that can't be ignored. All the evidence is circumstantial but shit! There's so much of it, she has to be involved! Just let me tell you a little bit about the only woman who had keys to your house. Did you know Terri was with her mother when she died in a car accident?"

"No. I told you she didn't talk about her past," Reeves replied.

"It was just the two of them, and in less than a year Terri's father died in his car inside their garage. Mr. Anderson's death was ruled an accident but guess who found him?" Queen asked with his face frozen and waiting.

Reluctantly Reeves said, "Who Terri?"

"Exactly! And you say you didn't know any of this?" Queen said smiling.

"No I didn't. She found her father dead...that must have been traumatic. Now I wish I'd pressed her more about her life and how she grew up," Reeves answered sympathetically.

"Alright, well after that Terri's boyfriend at college was bludgeoned to death by the KKK," Queen said swiftly trying to remove any compassion for Terri. Then he continued,

"Yup, his name was Clinton Adams a nice young man, and a fine student from a good family. Clinton's father is still the Pastor of the church in his home town, and Clinton planned on becoming a doctor. One morning he went running...with Terri, and that was the last time he was seen alive and ..."

"Wait a minute now; you just told me the Klan did it!" Reeves interrupted.

"Yeah but again, Terri was the last one with him, understand? Are you getting my point? They never convicted anyone for Clinton's murder, the case is still unsolved!" Queen said looking for validation.

"That doesn't mean anything!"

"Well tell me this, how many people have you been with, and you were the last to see them alive?"

"I can't think of anybody."

"I'll wait..." Queen said sarcastically.

The two men shared an awkward silence again until Reeves spoke, "Alright no one!"

"Well that's my point, I just named three and I wasn't finished. When Terri came to New York she had a secret affair with a co-worker named Danny. Danny was later involved in a hit and run in Brooklyn while riding his bicycle home. He was dead at the scene and the car that hit him was stolen not far from his house, and then abandoned a block from the train station. But it doesn't stop there. After she stopped seeing Eddie who disappeared there was a man named Trent from the Bronx, Terri dated him. He was stabbed so many times the coroner lost count! That's at least six deaths connected to Terri I know of, and that's not... a... coincidence!" Queen said slowly.

"What are you trying to say?"

"What am I trying to say? What am I trying to say? You must be in denial! I'm telling you there was something very wrong with your girlfriend. And if Terri wasn't a murderer, she had to have an accomplice because the bouncer Eddie was over six feet and muscular. He was use to handling rowdy people. And I just can't see that little woman over powering him without some help."

"I can't believe this, I just can't. There has to be an explanation, something you're missing," Reeves said in disbelief.

"I've been over and over and over it, and most of the evidence leads back to her. Now are you sure you can't think of anything cause now is not the time for secrets. You already kept information from me that might have helped me find your sister, I mean Linda. Now another young lady's life is on the line so help me, and I'll continue to help you," Queen said.

"There is something I left out. The day Terri and I broke up she came here and found me washing Linda in the bathroom and got mad. Like I mentioned before when I first brought Linda here she'd lost motor skills and she had an incontinence issue. I hired a nurse a few days later but before that, I had to be the one to do it. So anyway Terri saw that, and she wasn't happy," Reeves stuttered.

"Will you just tell me what happened?"

"When Terri came in the bathroom she…she thought I was cheating when she saw Linda and went after her. I pushed Terri back and she was pissed. She went downstairs and came back with a knife, and I thought it was gonna get really nasty up in here! I thought she was gonna stab me, but she didn't. Instead she told me never to call or speak to her. Then she went downstairs poisoned my fish and left," Reeves said as if a weight had been lifted.

"And you don't think that was important?" Queen asked.

"Not really given the circumstances. There are women who've caught men cheating and didn't kill him so no."

"And I've worked on cases where women have and trust me, I think you were lucky. With some serial killers there's usually a victim that gets away and…"

"Serial killer?" Reeves interrupted.

"I know it's not what you want to hear, but every now and then a murderer forms a special bond and finds it hard to take the life of a particular person. It's possible you Mr. Reeves just never pushed the right button for Terri. It's possible too many people knew you were dating, or maybe she just never got the opportunity…who knows. Remember she kept an affair with her co-worker Danny a secret from the rest of the office. Whatever the reason, just be glad you're still here. Oh and there's one more thing," Queen said with a huge smile.

"What now?" Reeves asked, wondering with all the news about Terri, what Queen had to smile about.

"Sorry I always think about Columbo when I say that. Did you know Terri had another apartment in the Bronx on Jerome Avenue?" Queen asked watching Reeves suspiciously.

"I didn't know that…no, are you sure?" Reeves answered sadly shaking his head.

"Mr. Reeves just so we're clear you're telling me you've never been in that apartment?"

"I'm sure. I've only been to her apartment at the Towers," Reeves responded with some hostility not caring if he was believed.

"Well let me tell you this place was a hide out. Everything Terri had was in one dresser drawer. Three bra and panty sets, one black dress and one pair of jeans with a grey hooded sweat shirt. There was one pair of dark sneakers, one face cloth and one towel. In the same drawer was an unopened bar of soap, a toothbrush, and a new box of tampons. Everything and I mean everything she had in that room could fit inside a shopping bag. Terri also had a credit card, fake passport, and driver's license under the name Beverly Simmons. We found those taped to the back of a dresser," Queen said glancing at his watch.

"So that's why you asked me did I know somebody named Beverly," said Reeves sitting back in his chair.

"Yes…so I want to ask you one more time. Is there anything else you can think of about Terri that was out of the ordinary? Anything at all… did she talk in her sleep?" Queen asked hastily.

"No."

He really wanted to tell Mr. Queen that most of the time Terri was very quiet, but strangely attentive to him. She seemed like a person who was new to laughter but when she did it was genuine. Like the night he and Terri were sitting in his living room watching Re-animator on video. There came a part in the movie when the re-animated body was holding its own severed head. All of a sudden Terri laughed so hard she rolled off the couch onto the floor. He thought it was funny too, but she was hysterical. Terri held her stomach while twisting into a fetal position. When she composed herself a bit she asked for that little part to be rewound over and over again. After the part was rewound for the last time, she said to Bennie, "You know what would have been funnier?"

"What?" he asked giggling with her.

"If while the guy was holding his own head he said…" Immediately Terri stopped talking.

"What baby, what would have been funnier?" Bennie asked urging her to continue.

She crawled close to him from the floor wrapping her arms around his leg and resting her head on his knee never finishing her sentence. She just stayed like that on the carpet until the movie was over, then they went upstairs. As Bennie remembered, Terri never said another word that night. The last sounds she made were soft moans from pleasurable sensations received before they went to sleep.

Drawn back to Mr. Queen's voice Reeves heard, "And what about Linda, is there something more you need to say about her?"

"No I can't think of anything, that's it."

"I can see you're upset so when I tell you I've covered all the bases… I have. And the only reason this story hasn't been all over the news is because it's an embarrassment to the City of New York," Queen said reaching for his drink as he continued.

"You can't have a serial killer defending, or prosecuting suspects. The District Attorney, among others, would have to go back and review all of Terri's cases. That might be cause for dismissals, or at the very least, retrials. City Hall has to keep what she's done quiet, but I can't let that happen. There's a young lady depending on me for justice," Queen said standing up.

"Who's that?"

"Her name is Leeanne and she's serving time for a murder, and I know she didn't do it. Terri dated Trent after you and he's dead and I mean it was brutal, you hear me? There was hardly any blood left in Trent's body because the mattress soaked it up like a sponge," Queen said not wanting to reveal how Trent died in case Reeves knew more.

"So I need evidence because an innocent woman is sitting in jail and your girlfriend did it!" Queen said staring at Reeves.

"She's not my damn girlfriend anymore!"

"Well your ex-girlfriend then. So I've got to do something, you hear me? I've got to do something. People are disappearing around you too, and I can't afford to waste time, understand!" Queen yelled back while standing up.

"So that's it?" Reeves answered as if he didn't care.

"That's all I have for now, but I'll be talking with you."

"What about my piece? You want to take it now?" asked Reeves pushing away from the table.

"That's a 38 right?" Queen asked watching intently.

"It is."

"Terri wasn't shot with a 38 so no, I don't need it."

Reeves put his jacket on closed the window and walked with Queen to the front door. He opened then closed it behind them and Queen said, "I thought you were in for the night?"

"I'm almost out of cigarettes so I might as well get some now," Reeves answered walking with him up the street. He had another pack upstairs, but he needed some fresh air after the bomb that was just dropped on him about Terri.

By now it was dark and the ground was slippery in spots. They walked up the hill and around the corner without talking. Reaching the corner by the train station Mr. Queen saw three people in line waiting outside to get into the Famous fish joint on St Nicholas Avenue. He shook Mr. Reeves' hand and told him he'd be in touch then left. Mr. Queen walked slowly to the train station entrance then past it another twenty feet or so to stand behind the last person in line for food. Once there he immediately looked over the shoulder of the man in front to see Mr. Reeves walking across the street into the store.

Mr. Queen began to separate the facts and evidence from the circumstantial. He'd already checked Mr. Reeve's pistol permit with his former partner who was still a Detective. Mr. Queen understood when he got off the train Mr. Reeves' gun and the murder weapon weren't the same caliber, but he tested Reeves to see how much he knew. Mr. Queen was also aware that Reeves had the same 38 for the past six years. Still Reeves could've bought a different gun on the street if he'd wanted to. Then all he had to do was report it stolen but hold on to it as a throw away. While this was only a theory he took a step closer to the counter and thought about the next piece of the puzzle.

Because of other cases the former Detective had to accept as fact that a person could live with a serial killer and have no idea they're murdering people. Terri was connected to at least 5 deaths before she knew Reeves unless he was lying about when they met. Combine that with Linda's disappearance, who isn't really Reeve's sister looks suspicious. If it wasn't for the neighbor across the street who witnessed Linda get into a cab with her baby, Mr. Queen would seriously be looking at Reeves in connection with Linda's disappearance.

But what really didn't make sense was that bullshit story about Reeves falling in love with a woman he just met from another country. It was pretty unbelievable to think a man could go on vacation in Egypt of all places and fall in love. Then like some kind of a bad dream the woman has an accident, forgets who she is, and that she ever loved him. That's straight out of a soap opera, Mr. Queen thought as he placed his order. Suddenly forgetting where he was Queen blurted out in disbelief.

"No way in hell that's the truth!" Queen said annoyed for letting that slip.

"What was that my brother?" asked the man behind the counter.

"What…oh nothing, I was thinking about something else," Queen said paying for his food.

Queen left with fish and fries feeling extremely disgusted. He walked to the curb with his arm in the air to catch a cab. Reeve's story didn't make sense like a badly written episode of Good Times. Thelma meets that pro football player and just when the family is about to get out of the ghetto, he got injured. Can't play anymore, he's broke and has to move in with her in that small apartment. It just doesn't happen in real life that way, Queen thought opening the door of the cab.

The whole time Queen never saw Reeves leave the store, so he gave the driver ten dollars to wait. Minutes later Reeves came out and headed back home then Queen told the driver to leave. When Queen got home he'd made a decision. He was going to use the forged passport against Mr. Reeves like he'd done with snitches and informants. It didn't matter whether it was by the book or not, whatever it took to get Leeanne out of jail.

Without knowing Reeves crossed the street in front of the very gypsy cab Queen was in. When he opened the door Mister was waiting as the only reminder of trust and affection he had left. Mister followed Reeves to the kitchen intently watching him place all but one beer inside. Reeves opened the can leaned with his back against the counter and drank half the can before setting it down. He'd taken a huge risk with a fake passport for a woman he'd just met. Now someone else knew he'd committed a crime and dangled the threat of prison over his head. He went upstairs to take a shower leaving the unfinished can on the counter. Two incidents happened in this bathroom with the last women he'd ever cared about. Linda was gone and Terri was dead and gone.

After the shower Reeves tried to keep it together but his mind was in chaos. The only thing left to do was pray so he kneeled by the bed. When he finished he looked out the window for a minute then turned out the light. It took forever to get comfortable but within moments Mister was yawning in the dimness. Reeves stared at the ceiling mentally whipping himself for every mistake.

Queen had to have some of that information about Terri wrong. As far as he was concerned Terri was a good woman. If it weren't for falling in love with Linda he might have eventually married Terri. It's not like the thought hadn't crossed his mind. But then if Queen was right about Terri being this vicious killer she must have loved him more than the others. He could have been the one who helped her escape the misery. All Terri needed was a man she could trust who didn't back down whenever she got besides herself.

Now the question on his mind was why she let him live? Was it because he opened the car door, or brought her flowers on occasion to show affection? He turned on his side, then his back, and to his side again. Still trying to relax Reeves remembered how every time Terri looked at small children playing on the street she'd smile, then squeeze his hand and look at him with such love. Terri was truly happy when they spent time together, and there was no doubt she wanted children. Looking at the shadows around the room Reeves remembered thinking she'd be an excellent mom to their children too.

So what was it? Why couldn't he see any signs of how vicious she could become. He began to think of Terri as the lion and he the tamer with the whip. Only the whip was between his legs, and he controlled her violent behavior with passionate days and sinful nights. Making sure she was satisfied before she went to sleep probably saved his life he thought. Whatever the reason, the truth was he missed her.

In the subsequent days ahead an unforeseen transformation occurred. Reeves began a regimen of punishment with polluted memories. Psychologically he battered himself with guilt and sadness, coupled with anger. Starting from that time he stole five dollars from his father's pocket. He'd think of more mistakes until the depression came. He'd messed up Linda's life and took responsibility for Terri's misfortune too. As a result of accepting blame he would soon become a bitter person. The rock he'd rested his soul upon would be beaten with thoughts of the past he could never change. Each hurtful memory acted like a small drop of water wearing down his foundation over time. Even the adoration he held for women was soon to change, and it would be so gradual he'd wake one day and not recognize who he was.

Chapter 3

Saturday the 17th was eight days before Christmas. 1990 was just around the corner and Benjamin Reeves still did what came normal when faced with crisis. He'd prayed the night before and in the morning tried to find an answer. Without having breakfast he took Mister out early for a long walk. Although it was chilly enough to see their breath, Bennie felt Mister had been cooped up in the house long enough.

They walked down the block past the funeral home and the playground on St. Nicholas where he and Mr. Queen first met. Next they went up the hill and around the corner to Alexander Hamilton's house on Convent Avenue. He stopped for a moment to look at the porch and tried to visualize people walking around and doing their day-to-day chores in the 1700s.

Hamilton's house had been moved from its original location and now sat just blocks from City College. Mister sniffed a tree in front of the property while a small dog began to bark as his owner approached. Mister sat down uninterested until the dog was gone. Then Bennie's mind drifted to an article he'd read in the City Sun newspaper. He remembered seeing what they claimed was the original picture of Hamilton without the usual wig men wore in those days. The article said Hamilton was born in the West Indies, the child of a mulatto woman. The newspaper had two pictures side by side. One had Alexander Hamilton's hair a salt and peppered afro next to the one on the ten-dollar bill. At the time the picture and Hamilton's race was called into question. Some were saying it was a hoax and Hamilton wasn't of African descent. As far as Bennie was concerned he didn't care one way or another, but if it were true why not let it be known?

Because The City Sun and The Amsterdam Newspapers appeared to have the most objective viewpoint, he began to read them every week, particularly after watching Glory with Denzel Washington. At the end of the movie it was stated Fort Wagner was not taken by those brave black soldiers, and he accepted that as truth. Later Bennie read in the City Sun that Fort Wagner was in fact captured. Not taking the Sun's word he went to the library and found the newspaper reported correctly. Following that he tended to have a little more faith in what they printed.

Leaving Hamilton's house the two continued walking up Convent Avenue past the Baptist Church towards home. Later that afternoon Bennie and Ronald would meet, and it had nothing to do with the laundry. Their long overdue gathering was simply to ensure the friendship remained strong and healthy like the business.

A few doors from home Bennie stopped to glance across the street at a familiar stoop and had another thought from an earlier period. He smiled imagining a day in 1973 when all the guys sat there as kids. He could see Reggie bending down tying his Pro-Keds next to his brother Ray Ray, who leaned on the rail by the sidewalk. Ray Ray was at least four years younger than everyone and we knew Reggie couldn't come outside unless he took his little brother. Mark and Donny could be sitting at the top in front of the entrance to the building. A few steps further down he imagined himself at one end and Ronald on the other side drinking some cola.

It was perhaps a day they'd come from the basketball courts. Dennis, the oldest, still bounced the ball tempting anyone to take it. Then he began to show us he could make the same spin move Earl the Pearl Monroe made last night against the Lakers in the finals. He asked if we saw the Pearl do it with a voice so loud you could hear him from across the street. Because Dennis was loud, when we were outside and wanted to call someone to the window, we'd ask him to do it.

That was the same stoop they watched the neighborhood winos fight four houses up the block, and Beulah came out and beat up two men. It was a time when they were all the happiest. An instance when teenagers didn't have a care in the world. Nobody thought about the problems of maturity like bills or broken hearts. That day none of the guys knew the future would separate them from adolescent bliss.

In a few years Reggie's family moved from Harlem to Queens while Donny went into the Marines. Mark stayed around but withdrew to a new group of friends that liked stronger drugs than the joints they smoked. Dennis was the first to become a father and drift in and out of depression because he couldn't put the bottle down.

It was shortly after that Ronald and Bennie's friendship developed. There came a time if Ronald left his house and didn't see the other guys he rang Bennie's bell first, and if Bennie came out before the others he rang Ronald's. After a while they were almost inseparable even to the point of planning mischief.

Bennie and Mister stayed a little longer staring at the empty stoop of that now abandoned building as the memories continued. He thought about the day he and Ronald were outside and the subject of this boy, whose name he couldn't remember came up. They were tired of this kid always asking for a sip of soda, or some of their potato chips. But when you saw him he made sure he ate fast so nothing was left to give you.

They hatched a plan while sitting on that very stoop to put an end to the begging. While the rest of the guys weren't around they looked through the trash until they found a can, then Bennie pissed in it. After almost an hour, the kid came up the block while Bennie held the can. Sure enough the kid asked for some so Bennie handed the can to him. The look on his face when he spit the piss out was the funniest thing he and Ronald had ever seen. They must have laughed about that for weeks, but the kid never asked for anything else. As a matter of fact he stopped coming around altogether.

Because neither of them grew up with siblings at home, the two got closer than the rest of the guys over the years. Every now and then it was just Ronald and Bennie outside on the stoop. That was the time they conversed about subjects the rest had no interest. Like how many stars were in the universe? Or how deep the ocean was, and how the bottom looked? What it would be like to have a family like Dennis? And of course how stupid their fathers could act at times. It didn't matter if they were out on a warm summer day or in the cold with their gloves on. They shared the pains and frustrations of growing up with each other, and the confidence was never broken.

Like the day Ronald told Bennie he broke his mother's eight track player because he kept listening to Pass the Peas by James Brown over and over. The tape got so tight it popped in the machine. Then Bennie reciprocated by telling Ronald he took twenty dollars from his father's pocket while he was in the bathroom brushing his teeth.

Then there were the more serious discussions, like if they had a chance who would they like to have when they played run, catch, and kiss, crazy Cheryl, or Indian-looking Cheryl? They could never agree because both girls were cute. After that their conversations moved to who was finer, Shelia Reed or Karen Baton. Then they'd think about it, silently look at each other and say Karen at the same time. But that wasn't the end; these two didn't hold anything back. They talked about the curve of Karen's butt versus the way Shelia's chest bounced when they played handball.

By the time they got to their twenties they shared a deep brotherly love. It became a custom to treat each other on their birthdays, either a week before or after. It was always the birthday boy's choice and most times they ended up at a strip club, or a sports bar. It seemed like the natural thing for men of their age to do. Have a few drinks and look at a half-naked woman dancing on stage. Too bad Lorraine didn't see it that way. Truth was it is sinful behavior, and it would take many years before Bennie would realize Lorraine was right. He shouldn't have been asking her husband to go with him. Bennie's problem was that Lorraine held him more accountable than Ronald.

This year Bennie let Ronald's birthday slip by because he'd been preoccupied looking for Linda. Still he missed his old friend and wanted their relationship to remain uncomplicated like the good old days. Back then they chewed bubble gum then pressed it between poker chips to make tops to play skellies.

With a smile and reminiscent sigh Bennie continued home trying to hold on to good memories. Over the years their trust weakened after they went into business and Ronald hooked up with Lorraine. By now Bennie was growing weary of the partnership and wanted to dissolve it. Every business decision made had to be run by Lorraine, and each time she made it her mission to disagree with Bennie. So at some point when they talked today he had to find out did Ronald have enough money to offer him a fair deal for half of the business.

With his share from the four Kleen-it stores Bennie planned to see another of his dreams come alive. The name R & B Investments had to be changed but the idea remained the same, to emulate the Korean Merchants Association. By encouraging the dwindling black-owned businesses to consolidate a small amount of money each month they could make other investments. At the very least they would have capital to make loans to themselves instead of high interest loans from the banks.

The way Bennie saw it every culture on the globe including tribes deep in the Amazon jungle with no running water still invested in their own progress. He never saw Chinese, Italian or other groups spend money with the Black community as much as we spent with them. It was a fundamental rule of economics and Black people broke it every time.

Once home he took Mister off the leash then made a sandwich and tried to think more pleasantly. All morning his mind had been a Roulette wheel of different thoughts and it was not easy to stop it from spinning. He turned on the radio and looked in the backyard while he ate. Since hearing the news of Terri's death he hadn't discussed it with anyone, so he called his sister Demetrice. She sounded busy when she answered the phone at her salon. In a few sentences Bennie told her Terri was dead, and that she was a suspect in at least five murders. Her response was silence at first then she told him he always liked the crazy ones. She was about to recite a list, but she had to rinse the perm out a woman's hair and get another from under the dryer. Before she hung up Demetrice said she'd call back a little later. Bennie knew her comment was meant to make him laugh and he found himself smiling at the window because it was true.

A familiar song began to play on the radio when he was eating. It was the Temptations' Silent Night, and he couldn't help but sing along. After that they played Someday at Christmas, then a Nat King Cole classic. When time came to meet Ronald Bennie was feeling pretty good and had some of the Christmas joy. All he needed now was a large cup of hot chocolate from the corner store.

Shortly past noon Ronald walked up the hill from Eighth Avenue on the park side by the empty pool. He looked forward to talking with his friend and finding out what he'd been doing. However Lorraine had specific questions she sent Ronald to ask. He had to find out who Bennie was dating, and why he missed taking her husband out for his birthday? If he was sleeping with another stripper Ronald was to make sure Bennie knew not to bring her to their home for the Christmas party. And last but not least he was to find out who the tall man was Bennie gave an envelope to a few months ago.

When Ronald turned the corner Bennie was sitting on a bench half way up the hill. As he got closer Bennie saw him and stood up sipping hot chocolate. They greeted with a smile then Ronald said, "that's what I should've got, some coffee."

"It's hot chocolate buddy," he answered shaking Ronald's hand.

Ronald looked the same except the mustache was gone and the sideburns too. He'd also cut his hair very short and put on about ten pounds.

"You been waiting long?"

"No… just a few minutes," Bennie replied as they stood face to face.

There was an awkward silence then Bennie said, "I was coming down the block today and I thought about Beulah. You remember that day she was out there fighting?"

"Sure do, she was a tough woman, and you know who she reminds me of?"

"No."

"A young Tina Turner."

Bennie thought for a second then said, "Those sexy thighs, right?"

"Yup," Ronald replied then he placed his hands in his pockets to keep warm. He could tell Bennie's attitude was more upbeat than last they spoke. Then Bennie asked, "Ron who was that dude we gave the soda can with the piss in it. What was his name?"

After a moment Ronald snapped his finger and said, "His name was Ricky."

"Ricky…I never would have remembered that."

"And we didn't give him a can of piss…you did," Ronald said jokingly.

"I thought you gave it to him."

"Nope," Ronald answered.

"So whose idea was it?"

"Yours."

"You sure?"

"Yeah I'm sure. You thought it up, you found the can, you pissed in it and you gave it to him," Ronald said all the while pointing his finger at Bennie.

"So what did you do?"

"Laughed my ass off when he made that face," Ronald said chuckling.

"What ever happened to him?"

"I don't know, he lived over on Bradhurst. I never knew where exactly."

While Bennie was riding the wave of good feeling from the past all of a sudden he said,

"When's the last time you were down by the rock?"

"The rock…the rock down there?" Ronald asked pointing into the park.

"Yeah!" Bennie answered as if there were another.

"Shit it's been years."

"Let's go down there."

"When …now?"

"Yeah why not, nobody's gonna fuck with us! Let's go down and see what it looks like," Bennie asked with eagerness.

"You're serious?"

"Yeah unless you forgot where it was?" he said tauntingly.

Soon they were climbing over one fence then another until they walked on a twisting dirt path. In a few minutes the men reached that place they hung out as kids overlooking the pool. Ronald and Bennie stepped slowly over the broken glass and empty beer cans until they stood on a small patch of dirt next to the rock they use to sit on.

The passage of time can do funny things. It can turn a dumb person into an intellectual, and the ugly girl everyone teased into a beauty queen. The years can also do the opposite. They can make the most likely to succeed a dope fiend, and the popular girl a dried-up woman with a purse full of regrets.

Indeed their spot was nothing like it use to be. Ronald kicked a few bottles into the bushes to make a clear place to stand. There were old rusty syringes, and condoms spread around. The ground was littered with food containers, dried up chicken wing bones, crack vials and human feces.

"You ready to go?" Ronald asked.

"Hell yeah!"

Sadly they walked away taking a seat on a bench just outside the park on Bradhurst Avenue. Bennie lost his taste for the rest of his chocolate and tossed the cup into the garbage. After that day neither man would ever go back to the rock.

"That was a trip," Ronald said.

"You're not kidding, it was nasty up there."

"And you know there are rats running around too."

Somewhat let down Bennie said, "so what else is going on...? How's Lorraine?"

"She's fine; getting ready for the Christmas party. By the way, you bringing anyone?"

"Nah just me," Bennie answered still thinking about the mess he just saw.

"You sure? Cause Lorraine needs a head count," Ronald asked watching Bennie light a cigarette.

"It's just gonna be me buddy."

"Why?"

Bennie was about to tell him he wasn't dating then changed his mind said, "it's just gonna be me," then quickly asked, "So you heard from any of the fellas?"

"Well I saw Dennis. He came in to do his clothes about two weeks ago. And of course he didn't have enough money, so I gave him ten," Ronald said.

"Same old Dennis, I saw him a couple of days ago and he tried to hit me up for five dollars. I figured he was just gonna buy some liquor, so I told him no. Shit we gave him a job and he worked four days and left, so I'm not giving him anything anymore. He's still my boy… but I'm not doing it."

The blues began to choke the holiday spirit. He looked a Ronald hoping he could talk to him like back in the day. Bennie paused and said, "I got some jacked up news to tell you."

"What's up?"

"Ron, you the only person I'm telling understand?" he said staring at him.

"Yeah I know what you mean, now what's going on?"

"Terri's dead… after we broke up somebody killed her."

"Really that's messed up, and it was right after ya'll broke up?"

"Yeah…I forget the date, but she's been dead a couple of years," Bennie answered.

"Wow… I'm sorry to hear. What happened?"

"Somebody shot her inside her apartment, and they never caught the guy. And I feel real fucked up about it but…"

Bennie found it hard to look at Ronald wondering would it be a mistake to tell him the rest. He looked down the street then in the opposite direction until finally he said, "that's not the worst of it."

"What else man?" Ronald asked sensing reluctance. Bennie tossed a butt near the curb. After a heaving sigh he said, "Terri's killed at least five people. Some of her ex-boyfriends, and maybe her momma."

"Get the fuck outta here!" Ronald said looking for a smirk from Bennie.

"I'm not joking!" Bennie said steadfastly.

"No way!!" Ronald said standing up.

"Yeah… it's true Ron."

"I can't believe it, I just can't. Are you sure?"

"Yes I checked it out and it's for real!"

"Wasn't she working for the city?"

"Yup and that's part of the reason the story about her murdering spree was kept quiet. The city doesn't want her cases reopened and maybe overturned," Bennie answered.

Ronald took a seat and Bennie told him all the details from Mr. Queen. He also answered some questions Ronald had. Now there was nothing left to say except the issues closest to Bennie's plagued heart. Part of his suffering may have been survivor's guilt or a feeling he could've changed Terri. And the worst was having a relationship for that length of time and not knowing what she was capable of. Now Bennie stood up to smoke again, and then started to speak.

"I feel responsible somehow and I wish I could've helped her."

"Helped her do what?! You're lucky the way I see it! You could have messed around and got yourself killed; you know that?"

"I don't think she would have hurt me. Terri just wanted to be loved for who she was that's all. But I couldn't do it, I just didn't love her," Bennie said with a hanging head.

"When was the last time you saw her?" Ronald asked.

"The last time was… at the Wren's nest. You were there remember?"

"Yeah I do and the way she looked at you made me look over my shoulder for a week!" Ronald said loudly.

"I know there was a cold look in her eyes I'd never seen before."

"Well I'm just glad Terri didn't get you buddy. But tell me… you think it had anything to do with when you went to Egypt that year? I know ya'll broke up right after you got back."

"Nope."

"Cause Lorraine called Terri at work, but she'd never return her calls," Ronald said.

"Okay."

While Ronald talked Bennie's mind drifted to what happened in Egypt. How Ronald and Lorraine followed him just to spy for Terri. During that trip Ronald and Lorraine met Linda in Bennie's hotel room. Because of the subsequent mess that followed, Bennie almost wound up in jail overseas. It was shortly after that Bennie fell in love with Linda and she lost her memory.

When Bennie brought Linda back to America he made sure to keep her away from his best friend and his wife. Subsequently Bennie and Ronald's personal relationship suffered. They didn't hang out anymore unless they met outside, and Ronald never was invited to Bennie's house while Linda lived there. Bennie also stopped going to their Christmas parties and social get togethers too. They never spoke of what transpired once they returned home, but Bennie knew for years they were dying to ask.

Now sitting in the cold Bennie was not going to rehash the Egypt incident. As a matter of fact it made his ears burn for Ronald just to say the word Egypt. He stood up with his hands in his pants pocket. This was enough talking for one day, and if he could trust Ronald he'd be glad to talk about more of his pain.

Bennie looked at his watch then said, "I could never figure why Terri did anything, and it might be good she didn't get in touch with Lorraine. You know what I mean?"

"You're probably right. You ready…"

"Yeah I got some stuff to take care of, but it was good to see you Ron," Bennie said taking a few steps until Ronald followed.

They walked to 145th street and stopped when they got to the corner. They shook hands then Bennie said, "This is gonna sound kinda strange, but I want you to know um…"

"What's up?" Ronald asked.

"You know you're like a brother to me and I…I just want to say if someone ever got the jump on you… and I found out who it was, I'd take care of them."

Ronald looked puzzled so Bennie continued, "I mean I know you can take care of yourself; I'm just saying if someone gets you… I'm gonna get them, and that's a promise!" Bennie said with a stern look.

Ronald was astonished and responded, "Okay."

The men shook hands again then went in opposite directions. Ronald walked down the hill not knowing what to make of their last words. He would have rather his buddy talked about the woman he wasn't allowed to meet when he and Lorraine got back from Egypt.

At the same time Bennie stopped at the corner store for the newspaper. He hoped Ronald understood the level of fondness he felt for their long-time friendship, and the risk he was willing to take. And in a few months and some short conversations if he felt comfortable, Bennie would sit with his best friend to get more off his chest. Amidst his hurt was the knowledge of having a child he loved but couldn't be with, and not able to tell anyone. So after leaving the store with the Amsterdam News there was some frustration because at that moment he had more faith in a newspaper than his best friend.

After that the days went by quickly and before long Bennie was on the Long Island Expressway headed to Ronald and Lorraine's house for the Christmas party. They'd moved from the Bronx a year and a half ago and this was the first time he would see their new home. Still he was apprehensive going to Ronald's party. It was like having a friend in denial about the vicious Mini Doberman they kept. You expected any reasonable person to keep the door closed so you didn't get bit, but they never did. Lorraine's gnaw could come in the form of a silly debate just to be annoying, or questions about Bennie's personal life to make him uncomfortable. And the worst part was he couldn't hit her with a rolled up newspaper or make her just sit.

By the time he arrived at their home it was early in the evening just before the sun went down. Bennie was determined to ignore his anxiety and enjoy this time of year. For the sake of his best friend Ronald he was going to put aside his opinion about Lorraine. The past was in the past and now he wanted to relax with friends, and just have a few laughs.

Their home was a two-story resting on half an acre with a large bay window in the front. The image of a lighted Christmas tree was visible from outside. Bennie rang the bell and Ronald answered wearing an elf's hat with large ears on the side.

"Glad you made it," he smiled.

"Yeah me too," Bennie said happily.

"Come on in man, come on!" Ronald said, taking a sip from a red plastic cup.

"I brought ya'll some vodka, and a bottle of zinfandel," Bennie said walking through the door.

Ronald took the bag from Bennie then led him to a sunken living room where everyone gathered. Two of Lorraine's girlfriends from high school, Veronica and Sharon were sitting on the couch. Lorraine's sister Carol and her husband William sat in the love seat on the other side. Carol's daughter and son sat on the floor playing with some toys next to Ronald's Uncle Smitty. With his peripheral vision Bennie saw Lorraine in the kitchen wearing red pants, a red sweater, and a Santa hat.

After greeting everyone he followed Ronald to the kitchen. When Lorraine put the baked ham down Bennie gave her a hug and said, "Hi Lorraine, it's good to see you."

She'd lost a few pounds since the last time, and he hoped her outlook changed too. Her body was stiff, and when they parted Lorraine answered with a frozen smile like a person with a wired jaw.

"Glad you could finally come and see the house. What took you so long? I was starting to think you didn't want to see us."

"Nah… that's not true," Bennie said looking at Karen.

Karen hugged him with genuine joy. They'd known each other from growing up on the block. The few times they played run catch and kiss, Bennie always tried to catch Karen but wasn't fast enough.

"I'm so glad to see you. You're looking good boy," Karen said.

"And so are you Karen, so are you. How's your mom?" he asked.

"Retired and getting on my nerves, but mom's good," she said.

"That's great, tell her I asked about her."

"So who'd you come with," Lorraine asked before he and Karen could speak again.

"What?"

"Who'd you bring in my house?" Lorraine asked with the same frigid smile.

"It's just me, why you gonna hook me up?" Bennie asked jokingly.

"So you can dog my friends out… Hell no!" said Lorraine.

It was quiet for a moment then Karen said, "This is a beautiful home… I like what you've done with the upstairs master bed room. Wait till you see it Bennie."

Quietly Lorraine walked out the kitchen then Ronald said, "I'll take you up in a minute but um…what you want to drink?"

"Let me have a beer to start. I don't want to get to tore up cause I saw cops pulling cars over everywhere."

"Yeah I saw a report in the news about the check points."

The three remained in the kitchen talking while Bennie drank. After a short time Lorraine came back and silently resumed her work.

"Come on buddy I'll show you the rest of the house," Ronald said.

"I'll talk to you in a little bit," Bennie said to Karen.

The guys left abruptly and that seemed to make Lorraine angry. The beans and rice were done but all she could think about was wishing Bennie never came over. The nerve of that asshole thinking she'd hook him up. "He must have lost his damn mind," she thought.

Shortly after Karen went to the living room to join the others so Lorraine felt some kind of way about that too. I do all this work so everyone can have a nice time, but I'm not given any credit. They must think I'm a fool who don't know what's going on, she thought.

Lorraine continued working and sulking while Ronald and Bennie were upstairs. I bet my husband is gonna take Bennie out for his birthday even though he was too busy to take Ronald out for his. Truth be told she was relieved Ronald didn't go the last time. Usually when Bennie brought her husband back home he was drunk, smelling of cheap perfume and pussy. Why did he drag Ronald to a strip club to watch those nasty women? They could have gone to a movie or went shopping like she and her friends did.

As a matter of fact the last time Ronald hung out with him it wasn't anyone's birthday. That night Ronald came home at three in the morning, and he smelled like he'd been in one of those places. Lorraine snatched a pot holder so hard the hook came out the wall. She imagined Ronald sitting in front of a stage enjoying looking at other women's bodies and touching them. In the back of her mind she wondered if he had done more than touch. If he hadn't he would sooner or later if they kept going.

To Lorraine it was obvious Bennie was trying to break up their marriage and she wasn't going to let it happen. Before the night was over she was going to take Bennie down a peg.

After everyone had eaten it was time to put the last decorations on the tree. Ronald went first then Carol then Uncle Smitty. Lorraine called Bennie when she went to the tree with two decorations in her hand. She gave one to Bennie then she hung hers on the tree and said, "Thank you for my husband and our new home. I'm so glad to have you in my life."

"I love you too baby," Ronald said, then they kissed by the tree.

Immediately Lorraine motioned Bennie to come closer and go next.

"It's your turn Bennie. Tell us what you have to be thankful for," she said.

"Shoot… I don't know um… I guess I'm grateful and looking forward to the next year, and I'm glad to have good friends," he said looking at everyone. Then he hung the small reindeer on the tree and was about to step away when Lorraine said, "Is that all? You got more than that right?"

"I don't know what else um…" he said.

"How about your life, aren't you lucky to be alive?" she asked.

"Oh, yeah well of course," Bennie answered looking at her oddly.

"I mean cause that girl was gonna kill your ass sooner or later but somebody got to her first right?" she exclaimed.

Bennie glanced at Ronald who looked at the ceiling then the walls. Someone from the direction of the couch said, "What y'all talking about!? Who was gonna kill who?"

"Yeah what are you talkin about?" Bennie asked Lorraine.

"I'm talking about Terri," she said emphasizing the name.

"Terri…Terri you remember Terri… the killer!"

Now everyone in the room was quiet with eyes on Bennie. Only the Christmas music played while Bennie's jaw dropped.

"And I can see why you'd blame yourself for what happened to Terri. You treated her like dirt running around behind her back seeing other women!"

Bennie couldn't believe what he was hearing. It was like watching a bad movie ten times expecting it to get better. Then like clockwork Lorraine started again.

"Why you think she killed all those people huh? I'll tell you why, cause you fucked her mind up that's why! And since she did those other men I know your turn was coming! You were next so you better be feeling grateful right…right Bennie?" Lorraine said with a smile and black girl neck motions.

"You don't know what the fu…hell you're talking about!" Bennie said with a stone cold expression. If she were anybody else it would be easy to tell her where to go, and just how to get there but this was his best friend's wife.

"Then tell us about it," Lorraine prodded.

Bennie stumbled to the corner like a guy hit by Tyson. All eyes were on him except Ronald who rushed Lorraine from the room back to the kitchen. Bennie took a drink and put a smile on his face. He deflected a few questions and when there were no more he said his good byes.

On the way home Bennie removed the holiday cassette from the stereo and threw it onto the highway. There wasn't shit jolly or merry about what happened tonight. His temples throbbed and he felt foolish expecting Ronald to be different from who he was. Never again would he tell Ronald anything that was personal. The little boys that sat on the stoop years ago were just business partners from now on.

When Bennie got home he was furious. He went outside with Mister in the back yard. While he stood waiting for the dog to finish he thought about Mr. Queen and his comments about hiding a body. He tried to relax but it was hard, so he walked back and forth until Mister was ready to go inside.

In the house Bennie walked around the kitchen and living room two or three more times talking to himself and cursing his decision to go to the party. After that he went upstairs to the next floor to walk some more. By the time he got to his room he had a massive headache, so he laid down. He wanted this night to be over, but he tossed and turned. Discontented thoughts were like Chinese water torture, and tonight was no exception. Now there were new problems to wear him down. Terri was dead and it was his fault. His best friend couldn't keep his mouth shut but the blame was his. If he hadn't told Ronald about Terri he wouldn't be going through this now. It's a good thing he didn't say anything about looking for Linda. And for the life of him Bennie couldn't understand why Lorraine acted the way she did, and that was another torturous drop.

With eyes wide, sounds outside were amplified. Doors opened and closed; footsteps were heard amidst muffled conversations. During this time he tossed with no relief. Bennie had a daughter he couldn't see, and he worried about her constantly. Linda, the only woman he ever loved ran away, and that was his fault too. He was alone in a home that was blissful in the past. He looked at the clock then remembered he'd lost his father's gold watch and that he was alone. His mother and father were gone, and he was alone, and that was another painful drop.

The promise Bennie made to abstain from sex until he reunited with Linda was the hardest drop of all. Women were everywhere and when they showed interest it was abnormal to act unresponsive. It was like being hungry while walking past food. The strong unbending will was crumbling in front of him. Sick of relieving that tension himself he grew more aggravated with each passing month.

Terri's shapely figure almost got him killed, and rushing his desire for Linda before her memory was fully intact caused his loneliness. As he tossed in bed more than once wondering was Linda sleeping by herself while he was alone. The thought of another man touching her was upsetting. He rolled over on his back once more and for the next few moments thought of all he hadn't warned Linda about. Like staying away from three card Monty, or never taking her eyes off her drink unless someone was watching it for her.

But that didn't seem to be enough hurt and pain. Bennie went back years to when he was eleven sitting on the bus by the back door. An older kid snatched his burgundy apple jack hat off his head then ran off the bus. He wanted to go after him, but he was scared, and embarrassed so he rode past his stop then walked home.

These persistent thoughts subsided around midnight and as he was falling asleep, the phone rang. If it was Ronald calling to apologize for Lorraine's behavior he didn't want to hear it. Lorraine antagonized and criticized him from the day they met, and once she married his best friend it never stopped. He'd forgiven her time and time again but not for this. By the third ring his resentment was boiling over. He was tired of his buddy telling his business and pissed neither Ronald nor his wife could keep a secret. With the next ring the machine would pick up but by then Bennie decided, no matter what Ronald said, Lorraine was gonna pay for that shit she did tonight.

He lay still but it was Mr. Queen's voice. Bennie answered immediately hoping it was good news about Linda.

"Mr. Queen I'm here, what's going on?"

"I thought you weren't home."

"No I'm here," he said nervously.

"I know it's late Mr. Reeves but um…"

"Why don't you just call be Bennie."

"Sure ah Bennie…well I figured you'd want to know what I've found out. I was waiting for this last bit of information before I called."

"It's no problem. What did you find out? Is Linda okay… Did you find her?"

Bennie asked sitting on the bed with his feet on the floor. His heart pounded like a race horse before the gate opened.

"Well…Yes I have but it's not good news," Mr. Queen said cautiously.

Bennie said nothing so Queen added, "you know I never would've solved this case if it hadn't been for the Anderson case too," Queen said.

"What are you talking about?"

"Well I believe Terri…"

"Terri…I thought you were calling about Linda! I don't give a shit about what happened to Terri!"

All the hours it took for Bennie to find peace were wasted. It took one telephone call and he was back to the upper levels of pissedifacation.

"You believe Terri what! What!" Bennie said furiously.

"I think you need to calm down."

"I am calm man, what do you want to say?" Bennie yelled.

"I spoke to Yvonne the nurse you hired…"

"Yvonne, are you serious?"

"Yes the nurse you hired for Linda. I spoke to her when I first started this investigation, and just recently I went to see her again to show her a picture of Terri."

"What the fuck are you doing? She don't even know Terri! Shit we were separated by then," Bennie said louder this time.

"Okay hold up, watch who the hell you're talking to! You hear me!?" said Mr. Queen.

"Yeah alright."

"Now where was I, oh so when I showed Terri's picture to Yvonne she recognized her as Beverly Simmons.

"What!" Bennie said as his hands started to shake.

"And she was very sure! Yvonne told me a woman casually walked up and started talking to her and Linda while they were headed to the park. It was a week or so after you and Ronald saw Terri and her girlfriends' downtown. Anyway Yvonne remembers Terri talking to Linda. Once they got to the park Yvonne noticed the same woman staring at Linda while she was playing on the swings. This time she had sunglasses on, but Yvonne noticed her clothes were the same, and she had no children with her."

"Well if it was Terri I think she has some kids," said Bennie hoping it wasn't true.

"No she doesn't. Terri was never married, and the coroner confirmed she's never given birth."

"I thought she had some kids, but still that doesn't mean..."

"Bennie she killed Linda and the baby. I'm sorry but it's true. I've been working with a profiler from the FBI. He says Terri is an ingenious stalker who waits, plans, then executes. Furthermore if it weren't that I believed this woman Leeanne who's in jail now for Terri's crimes I may have never caught her," Queen said.

"But we broke up so long ago. It doesn't make sense," Bennie said sadly.

"I know but remember it was several months later Eddie the bouncer disappeared. It's not unreasonable for her to follow Linda then kill her and I have proof. Now given that her victims were killed in different ways made the murders hard to connect. I'm thinking Terri killed her father too, then made it look like a suicide. Hell it's possible she caused the accident that killed her mother cause she was at the crash," said Queen convincingly.

"Are you sure you're right about this?"

"Yes...I started checking missing persons and all the Jane Does from the last day of her known whereabouts...I'm sure."

"What did Terri do to the baby?" Bennie whispered.

There was a long silence so Bennie said, "Mr. Reeves did you hear me?"

"Yes...I heard you, I'm looking through the file, just bear with me. I know this is rough," Queen replied amidst the sound of papers shuffling.

"I'm gonna start from the last time we know..."

"I want you to tell me what happened to them before you say anything else, please!" said Bennie.

"Alright then... the cause of death is unknown, but their charred remains were discovered in an abandoned building at 2111 Crotona

Avenue in the Bronx. A two-alarm fire was reported at 4:33am on the 17th, and it says here Jane Doe and baby Janie Doe weren't discovered until the 19th of August, but the bodies were in the building before the fire," said Queen.

"If Terri did it and she's been dead for a while when exactly are you talking about?"

"It was August 19 of 87."

"87! That was years ago. How…I mean why did…?"

"That's what I'm trying to tell you just hold on," Queen said.

"Sure."

"Shortly after you hired me I found out Linda and the baby stayed with her friend Sonya Dixon on 128th Street and Morningside Avenue. From there Linda went to realty agent in the Bronx to look at apartments. By the 13th of May she left Sonya's and that's when her trail went cold."

"I don't remember you saying anything about a realty agent?"

"That's because you were lying to me so I didn't tell you."

"So where did she go from there?"

"I don't know, but as I investigated Terri, it led me back to you, and another disappearance. I just put two and two together," Queen said.

Bennie's hand started to tingle while his throat swelled. Then Mr. Queen said,

"Ok I found it! An anonymous call was made to 911 reporting a fire August 17th on Crotona Avenue. The report says the fire was started by squatters who fled the scene. During the Fire Marshall's investigation the bodies of a woman and female baby were found in the basement. The coroner's report as to the cause of death was inconclusive although it leans toward smoke inhalation. The bodies were in late stage of decomp anywhere from six to eight weeks before the fire was started. During this time you were the only one who reported two persons fitting that description missing," Queen said.

"Are you sure it's Linda… I mean it could be anybody."

Mr. Queen opened a manila envelope took out a plastic evidence bag and placed it on the table.

"Do you recognize anything in there?" he asked.

Bennie stared quietly through the plastic for a minute then said, "This looks like the ankh Linda wore with this chain around her neck. And these are her ear rings and I know this flat bangle. It was her favorite. She never took it off."

"I'm sorry, I really am," Queen said.

"So tell me what happened to their remains? I mean where are they buried?" Bennie asked with eyes swelling.

"After the autopsy I believe they were cremated," said Queen as Bennie cleared his throat.

"Thank you for finding out what happened to them," he said sounding a bit more emotional.

"I also came across a copy of your book Tales of the Obeni. I understand why you wrote it. Too bad Linda never got a chance to read it," Queen said waiting for a response that never came until finally he said, "I'm sorry for your loss. Good night Mr. Reeves, I mean Bennie."

At this point he didn't care how Mr. Queen addressed him. Bennie ended the call without saying a word. For a while he sat on the edge of the bed with tears streaming down his cheeks, until his neck was wet. The phrase he tried so desperately to disregard played over and over like a record skipping. Their charred remains, charred remains, charred remains, over and over, until he buried his face in the pillow so his screams couldn't be heard.

Bennie speculated what had he'd done so awful in his entire life to deserve such hurt. Soon Mister licked his feet until he sat up and composed himself. He rubbed the dog's head then took Linda's picture from the nightstand. It was taken in front of the library across from Harlem Hospital before she'd given birth. She forced her smile because she'd just finished complaining about not wanting her big brother to pick her up all the time. The funny thing was Bennie knew Linda didn't want him to meet her. But where was that 6th sense when Linda and the baby were about to die. There were no whispers in his ear or tugging in his soul guiding him to their rescue like John Shaft.

If God was forging him for greatness by administering unbearable and relentless pain he couldn't comprehend the Creator's motives. Bennie tabulated the value of his irresponsible behavior and considered trading places with the ignorant ass acting folks. No more Mr. Nice guy he thought, stretching on the bed.

By 5 am there was comfort in not caring about friendship, or love, or doing the right thing anymore. All the miracles he'd witnessed were forgotten, and his faith in God was gone. If his parents were alive they would not be pleased. His mind, however, was made up. No more blessing his food or praying before bedtime because The Creator wasn't listening. And the next day when Bennie woke in the afternoon, the man I used to be was gone.

Chapter 4

In the following days anger and resentment rushed through Bennie like icy air from an open window. That lack of concern manifested in his physical appearance as well. He hadn't shaved, cut his hair, nor had he bothered to wash. His stinking grungy ass gave in to the sweetness of rage and indifference. Throughout that brief time no calls were returned to preserve the slight residue of sanity he had left. His only outside venture was letting Mister in the backyard to use the bathroom. Bennie had become dissatisfied with God and refused to talk to him, so he stopped praying. Even the distant voice of his earthly father couldn't persuade him back on his knees.

It was two days before the New Year and Ronald hadn't called to apologize, not that it would have made a difference. There was nothing he could say to repair the damage he and Lorraine had done. It was as if her words were arrows piercing Bennie's heart without breaking the flesh. But there was something Bennie could do to ensure it would never happen again. He wasn't going to tell Ronald shit about his personal life any more. And come next week, he'd speak to a lawyer and financial adviser to dissolve their partnership as soon as possible. If that arrangement was in Ronald's favor so be it, as long as he could get out of the laundry business.

Meanwhile, Ronald and Lorraine weren't on the best of terms because of what she'd done at the party. When Ronald shared that conversation from the park with his wife he knew one day she'd drop hints to Bennie because it was her nature. But that night Ronald was stunned she did it so quickly. In addition, she had to know her action would put a strain on Bennie and his friendship.

That's why Lorraine spent the remaining days treating her husband like a king to make amends. She fixed his favorite meals and smiled every time he spoke until he wore down. And that was the same strategy he'd use on Bennie. First he'd stay out of his way until his old friend cooled down. But instead of making his buddy food he'd take him out for his birthday. It was a perfect arrangement since the conflict was Lorraine's fault, she was in no position to object. So, a couple of days after New Years, Ronald called Bennie and they agreed to hang out.

When the weekend of Bennie's birthday came, Ronald drove to meet his buddy in Harlem after six in the evening. He got out of the car to find Bennie leaning against the cement pillar at the bottom of his stoop. They shared an unnerving hand shake then walked back towards the car. It was then Bennie remembered a similar moment of agitation between them.

It was a day like any other when the boys flocked to the stoop after coming from the basketball courts. As they relaxed Dennis, in his usual loud voice, started cracking jokes. This time it was about Ray Ray's sneakers and soon the guys were taking turns snapping on each other. When Ray Ray heard Mark laughing he started talking about Mark's weight. And when Dennis laughed, Mark called him a yellow monkey. Then the subject changed to who had the nappiest hair, and whose house had roaches. The jokes didn't need to be true they just had to be funny. So when they got tired of roaches and hair they switched to sisters, brothers and other family members.

That day they laughed and smiled having harmless fun then Ronald told Bennie he was so dark his nickname was midnight. Bennie laughed cause it was funny then he fired back with an even better one. Bennie told Ronald his mother sounded like Lurch from the Adams Family. He told the guys he'd knocked on Ronald's door last week and his mom answered in a low voice, "You rang?"

The burst of laughter sent everyone running from the stoop in hysterics except for Ronald. As a matter of fact he looked as if he was ready to fight Bennie. Instead he sat quietly for a moment then went home. The problem was Bennie forgot Ronald's mom was released from Harlem hospital two days earlier and her voice was scratchy from the tube they placed down her throat. If Bennie thought about it he never would have said it. It took a few days, but Ronald got over it and they were friends again. As they got into the car, Bennie knew forgiveness was in order, but that was easier said than done.

Most of the ride was silent except for a few comments about traffic, basketball, and what went on in the news last week. About an hour later Ronald parked across the street from a club on Hillside Avenue in Queens. They drank rum from small cups as Bennie's discomfort increased because Ronald still hadn't said anything about the Christmas party.

Bennie debated whether to bring up the subject and risk being incensed by his buddy's quibbling behavior, or just let it go. Before he could decide women started arriving. Three got off a bus not twenty yards behind the car while two got out of a cab at the corner. All made their way to the red metal door of the club and went inside.

About that time Ronald gave Bennie the flyer from a lady who used the Amsterdam Kleenit around 2pm every Tuesday afternoon. It promoted the event as a Capricorn strip party tonight only with more beautiful girls per square yard than any club in the city. It advertised a special show, private dances available, and a buffet. On the other side a picture of three women posed so enticingly Bennie had to smile and for the first time he wasn't pissed off. But an action was going to take place tonight that would begin to make Bennie uncomfortable in an atmosphere he'd grown to enjoy. Unbeknownst to him in a place of lasciviousness, he was still being forged.

They sipped again looked over and now a dozen more women were waiting to get in. After that guys lined up near the entrance Ronald and he crossed the street to wait. It was dark now and much colder than when they left Harlem. This time Bennie noticed his buddy put on black gloves with the finger tips cut off. It wasn't the first time Ronald had worn those gloves and tonight Bennie asked why? The reason was simple, so Ronald could hind his wedding ring. And all this time Bennie thought the gloves were some kind of fashion statement.

The next group of ladies went in accompanied by men wearing shirts with the word security. By now Ronald figured around 24 strippers were inside and the line of fellas was growing too. Minutes later, two women got out of a cab wearing baggy blue jeans and bomber jackets. Even with the boyish clothes they were still cute like the girls from that new group TLC. The darker girl touched Ronald on the hand telling him she'd see him inside. Once they left Ronald told Bennie that was the woman he was talking about. He also said she went by the name Mercedes and her friend called herself Diamond.

Fifteen minutes later the guys poured in, and the party was on. Ronald and Bennie sat at a crescent shaped booth at the end of the aisle not far from the stage. They ordered some beers and waited as the room filled with gorgeous women. Their attention was drawn to the back of the club as two women came out wearing black fishnet cat suits. Diamond and Mercedes moved through the crowd in a snake-like synchronous procession with their hips swaying slowly to the music. They stopped in front of the table and Ronald put down the beer. These ladies wanted to be admired and with ease they turned a full 360 degrees until they were facing Ronald and Bennie again. The transformation from the women outside to the ones standing in front of them now was unbelievable. A closer examination justified their attire as delicately bordering nakedness and artful seduction.

The ladies climbed inside the booth towering over Ronald and Bennie crotch to face. Diamond was beautiful, enticing, and felt superb to the touch. Bennie watched her gyrating legs envisioning the paradise they led to. It was like old times he thought as he touched her body. The rigidness soon followed, and she took complete advantage of that weakness by whispering seductively to him. Her suggestions of pleasure with lips lightly touching his ear were like an offer of crack to a recovering addict. Diamond told Bennie he was the king, so he made a royal command decision. He was going to fuck this woman tonight because she said he could.

From across the table a familiar voice called, "Happy birthday buddy!"

The ladies chimed in as Ronald held up his beer to toast. Then Ronald went back to feeling Mercedes' bosom while she giggled. Diamond took that opportunity to turn around and reposition. Bennie leaned back for a better look at Diamond's butt which felt blissful rubbing up against him except there was a mounting problem. He tried not to think about those damn gloves, but the moment was ruined. Bennie's erection was snatched away like heavy wind on a cheap umbrella. Absent from any signal the enjoyment was gone and Diamond didn't smell so good anymore. Still he pressed to take pleasure in the woman he held as the questions kept coming.

Why hadn't he figured out Ronald's reason for having those gloves before? He'd worn them in Manhattan at The Wrens Nest while they talked to Jenny, and the night Terri came in with her friends. As a matter of fact Ronald had them every time they went to The Goats in the Bronx. Hell he was wearing them the day they met Paula stripping at the Goats! Did Ronald think he was stupid was the question that forced Bennie to break away from Diamond for the bathroom. But before he left Diamond dropped another bomb on him. She said it was time for her to mingle and she knew he'd understand because he'd dated a dancer before. Then she continued saying he needn't worry because at the end of the night she and Mercedes were leaving with them. Any other day Bennie would've been pleased with Ronald but not now.

By the time he reached the bathroom his mind was made up. He had no intention of staying at the club with Ronald another minute. Bennie washed his hands while trying to make sense of it all. Ronald could be trusted with thousands of dollars he just couldn't keep his mouth shut. So when Bennie returned he found fresh beers and a new darker woman giving Ronald a lap dance. As Ronald indulged, Bennie sat holding his head with an agonized look. When the woman left, Bennie told his buddy he was taking a cab home because he wasn't feeling good. Ronald eyed him skeptically but insisted on taking him back. Ronald had a little more beer and they headed for the door. Abruptly he turned back telling Bennie to wait outside.

Shortly Ronald returned and they walked to the car. He took off the gloves and shoved them between his leg and the seat before they got on the expressway. By the time he passed through the toll booth he'd looked at his watch again. At some point Ronald did believe Bennie had a headache because they had a good time when they spent nights like this. But now the only thing he wanted to do was drop his friend at home.

A little past midnight Ronald double parked at Bennie's house. They shook hands then Ronald asked for an uncomfortable favor. He wanted Bennie to tell Lorraine when she called in the morning he fell asleep on the couch. If she asked to speak to Ronald Bennie should say he'd just left. Dumbfounded but without hesitation Bennie agreed. Ronald looked at his watch once more and as soon as the car door closed he left. From the sidewalk Bennie watched Ronald speed away until he turned the corner at the end of the block. Unbelievable, Bennie thought, the nerve of this dude to ask for an alibi.

Later on Bennie stood by his bedroom window smoking a third cigarette. For the last few weeks setbacks consumed his mind but not tonight. When he was done smoking he got in bed envisioning Diamond's sexy curves. Her perfume loitered along with the feeling of her lips whispering in his ear. She said he could do this, and he was gonna get that too. It was the anticipation in a woman's eyes he hadn't seen in years that excited him the most. Less than an hour ago her firm breasts were inches away from his face. He sniffed his hand wishing Diamond was there until a firm image appeared. He reached for the lotion inside the night table, and Mister instantly left the room. The dog's silhouette vanished into the hall with the reverberation of paws tapping in the distance. Hesitation festered in frustration until even the dog's gesture of retreat was a compilation of all that went wrong tonight.

Bennie put the lotion back then called for his dog. There would be no more whacking himself before going to sleep. He'd denied his needs for too long without reward. He sat up to rub Mister's head and told him he could stay. Mister walked to the foot of the bed and Bennie laid down refusing once more to pray, but still he was being forged.

The next morning, just before 7am Lorraine called looking for her husband. She was impolite as usual, expecting answers. With wounds of Christmas still fresh he decided to tell her the truth about Ronald. The words were on a precipice behind clenched jaws; instead he stuck to the script. He told Lorraine what Ronald instructed and nothing more. Then anticipating Lorraine hanging up on him Bennie told her he had to go, ending the exchange. Instantly it rang so he reached to turn off the answering machine. After almost twenty rings Bennie stopped counting. He wished he could put the phone on busy like his mom use to do when she didn't want to talk by dialing the home number with the home phone and leaving it off the hook. Instead he turned the ringer off and got out of bed declining to get involved in their marital affairs.

The following Friday the 13th was Bennie's birthday and Ronald was the last call of the evening. Bennie pictured Ronald standing in his living room with Lorraine close by as they conversed. His birthday wish was brief and strained of dialogue, so Bennie didn't ask about last Saturday. When the call was over Bennie laughed out loud in light of the situation. It was one of those stories you couldn't make up, he thought, and if he ever wrote again he might make a character based on Ronald.

It was too early to go to sleep. He walked to the stack of rented videos but was sick of watching movies. There was an idea floating in his mind the past few days and he was going to try it. Bennie grabbed the car keys in denial and went for a drive. If he told himself it was just a ride it didn't feel so bad, but in the back of his mind he knew if the opportunity presented itself he would pick up a woman with no attachments.

Soon he found himself under the elevated train driving down Park Avenue. The prostitutes raised their hands like students wanting to answer the teacher. Bennie kept driving doubling back a few times for a better look. The inner voice that nagged him from home kept telling him this was a bad idea. Ignoring common sense he drove another hour. Finally he left the area only to return after being ten blocks from his house. This time a woman recognized his car and made her way to the window. Her jeans were filthy, and she scratched her hair too much. The next lady was very skinny and appeared sickly. Even at night the red blotches showed on her neck and hands. Finally he saw one he might want but by the time he circled back she was gone.

Eventually he did leave only to head uptown past Yankee Stadium to the Bronx Terminal Market. When he was a boy his father would buy watermelons there in the summer. As the years passed the number of vendors decreased, and still a few shops opened during the day. But at night from alongside the Bronx House of Detention and through the Bronx Terminal Market, the ladies walked.

On the second pass he stopped without hesitation picking up a short heavy-set woman. She was pleasant looking and friendly at first, so they drove around the next corner and parked. Once the car shut off the woman acted nervous which made Bennie edgy too. He thought about being set up to be robbed or busted by the police and winding up in the pages of The Amsterdam News. Despite reservations he paid for her cold hands and rough mouth. She rushed and kept stopping to look around while complaining he was taking too long. After a few minutes of what would be a hopeless unsatisfied ending, he dismissed her and went home. After a shower Bennie sat in the chair by the bed to watch TV. This wasn't the life he imagined for himself, but tonight's disappointment wouldn't stop him from going back to the market another time.

A few days before Valentine's Day Bennie went to the Amsterdam Kleen-it to restock the supply room with detergent and fabric softener. He went inside the office to do some paperwork then left an hour later. When he got home and unpacked his groceries the bread was there, but the roast beef and Swiss cheese was left in the office fridge. So Tuesday Bennie went back as Chris was leaving to go the doctor.

Chris was one of their most trusted employees who started in 1983 when they opened the first store. His parents were both second generation Puerto Rican, but his father could pass for black. Yesterday Chris was sick and today he didn't look any better. His face was gaunt, and his light skin was dry like paper. There was a dime sized spot on his neck, and another below his Adams apple that looked like a hickey. Chris was going to the doctor, and he let Bennie know Ronald was in the office, and he wasn't alone. The last person Bennie wanted to see was Lorraine. So when Chris left Bennie walked each aisle glancing at every machine. With nowhere left to go he went to the office door fumbling with his keys until a buzzer sounded.

Inside Ronald sat behind the desk while a young woman wearing a black scarf and baggy Adidas track suit sat on the couch. With pinky raised the lady delicately rolled a slice of cheese around some roast beef. Before she ate she looked at Bennie and simply said, "Hi."

"How are you?" Bennie answered watching her eat his sandwich meat.

"We missed you last time," she mumbled while chewing.

Somewhat perplexed, Bennie glanced at Ronald then looked at the lady's face closely.

"You missed me?" asked Bennie.

"Yeah…see Ronnie, I told you he wasn't gonna recognize me," she said chuckling eating the last bit.

"Where do I know you from?" Bennie asked.

"It's me silly… Kayla," she giggled.

"Kayla?" Bennie responded then watched for a clue from Ronald.

"The party last month…We was trying to celebrate ya birthday and you got sick remember. Ronnie took you home after you threw up in the bathroom. You can't drink and not eat you know," she said chuckling sarcastically.

Bennie looked at the face again then said, "Mercedes?"

"Yeah it's me," she answered standing to hug him.

The way Mercedes looked now opposed to the last time was like the flip side of a coin. Today she was frumpy and unattractive, nothing like the sensual wonder woman from the strip club.

"You look different," Bennie said sadly.

"I know," giggling then continuing, "Cause I ain't at work but it's all under here right baby," she says profiling for Ronald.

"There's an Aquarius party this weekend. Me and Diamond gonna be there. You gotta come. They gonna have food and Diamond really wants to see you," Kayla said.

"Oh she does?"

"Ronnie… wasn't she looking for him when it was over. You had my girlfriend ready for some real fun and then you just left her hanging. But she's cool like that so it's all good right Ronnie, you know what I'm saying?"

"Uh huh," Ronald said.

Oh he's Ronnie now Bennie thought then asked, "Where's it gonna be, at the same spot?"

"Uh huh, and we got some new outfits, some real sexy shit but classy. So you guys coming right? I know you're coming," she said giggling at Ronald.

"It sounds good, I'll see what I can do," said Bennie.

Mercedes threw the paper in the trash then stood by Ronald. She touched his shoulder dragging her hand across to the other side while walking past and said, "I'm gonna get my clothes out the dryer and I'll talk to you later ok honey?"

"Fine," Ronald said after she kissed him on the lips then walked to the door.

It was the first time he'd seen Ronald kiss a woman other than Lorraine so how serious was this? Bennie also become aware Kayla walked dumpy and slew- footed. Nothing like the slow tantalizing stallion swagger she sported at the club. She put her hand on the knob then said, "Hope to see you this weekend Benjamin, I know Diamond wants to…"

Kayla phrased it like a question for him to fill in the blank.

"I'll see what I can do," said Bennie.

"Fine," she said snickering as she left.

Bennie's brow raised when he looked at his friend then shook his head. Not to jump to conclusions he walked to the fridge and as he suspected his roast beef was gone. Then they both watched Mercedes on the monitor take her clothes from the dryer to fold. Then Bennie said, "Dude, are you serious? You're playing it close man! What if Lorraine…"

"It's cool I know where Lorraine is. She's getting her hair braided then she's going shopping. She'll be busy until this evening," he said calmly.

"Oh…Okay," Bennie answered with indifference then said, "So you see how Chris has been looking?"

"I know, I'm glad I came through, and when I saw him I made him go to the doctor. His skin looks all ashy and he lost some weight."

"I noticed it last month too. If I didn't know better I'd think he was messing with that crack," Bennie said jokingly.

"He's just got a bad case of the flu," Ronald answered.

"I know."

"When Chris gets home he's gonna call. That's when I'll tell him to take the rest of the week off and we'll still pay him… that cool with you?"

"Not a problem, but the last time I brought up sick days Lorraine talked you out of it," Bennie said finally sitting on the couch.

"Yeah well she was wrong about that! Chris had been with us from the beginning. He always comes to work, so we got to look out for him," Ronald said defiantly putting some papers in the drawer. He cooled down to watch Kayla tie her bag and shove it down in the cart.

"You know I went back," Ronald said watching her slip on her coat.

"Yeah I figured."

Finally she pushed the cart towards the door to leave. Just a few seconds after Kayla was gone the words rushed from Ronald's mouth like water over Niagara Falls. He leaped from his seat and said,

"Dude…I knocked her boots off! …you hear me?! I had her like this," he said demonstrating as if Kayla were on the desk, "Then I flipped her over and…"

For the next ten minutes Ronald rambles off his account of that night.

"After I dropped you home I went back to Queens. The party was over at midnight, Kayla came out with Diamond, and a girl named Cinnamon. Cinnamon was all right, old as hell, but she had some big ass titties. And…and listen… Diamond wasn't gonna work anymore that night if you had been there. But anyway I took her and Cinnamon to Brooklyn and dropped em at some club near the Navy yard then I went to Kayla's house. She lives on Amsterdam and 149th Street close to City College. We got in… she took a shower… came out wearing a towel and… oh she had a cat. Then she dropped that towel, and it was on dude. When I finished with her I was dripping with sweat you hear me! And… and she was like this!!"

Ronald put his thumb in his mouth and closed his eyes to demonstrate, then he said, "Swear to God Ben that's what she did! Oh and we sniffed some cocaine, and I hit it two more times!"

Ronald explained the evening with the same intense expression as when he made a basket at the court. Then he continued, "In the morning she left me in her bed and went to the store. She came back with two bacon egg and cheese sandwiches and coffee. Then I hit it one more time, took a shower and got the hell out of there."

That massive flow of info was enough Bennie thought. It was like Ronald wanted to see how far he could stretch their friendship. Maybe a subtle hint would bring Ronald out of his filibuster, so Bennie went in his pocket for a cigarette. Then Ronald said, "And when I got home Lorraine was waiting at the door mad as a muther fucker!! She was yelling, did I know what time it was? Why did I have to sleep at your house? Then she said you hung up on her. Why'd you hang up on her? She was madder at you hanging up than at me for a minute. Then she…"

Bennie had enough and began to interrupt Ronald.

"Ron I got some stuff I gotta do," he said standing up with the cigarette in his mouth.

"Sure but let me tell you what she did. First we went food shopping and when we put the food away she said we had to look at some curtains and other stuff. So she kept me out all day and then we went to eat. I didn't get back home till ten something," Ronald said with amusement.

"You see I knew she was gonna do that so I'm glad I slept a little bit," he said while Bennie walked past.

"I'm glad it worked out for you buddy," he said finally opening the door.

"Hey, are you going this weekend cause Diamond is looking for you…we could ride together, hell we could even pick them up. And if we did, Kayla might get us in for half price," Ronald asked in a lower tone since the door was open.

"Yeah I might, I'll let you know," Bennie said turning to leave, then he heard Ronald.

"Oh wait there was something I wanted to ask you um…oh yeah have you heard any more about Terri, like any more dead bodies?"

"No, nothing," Bennie answered somberly and kept walking. Even if there was he'd never tell Ronald.

So when Ronald called Saturday morning Bennie told him he wasn't going. Then as the day dragged into evening an irritation developed. By now his buddy was having a great time while he was stuck in the backyard waiting for his dog to use the bathroom. Inside the house Bennie had come to the conclusion, Diamond couldn't be trusted, and he wasn't gonna bother with her.

He filled the dog bowl with water then looked out his kitchen window. The stillness inside gave way to that recurring pattern of pity held within. He thought about Lorraine and the Christmas party disaster for the umpteenth time until his head felt tight. Then after a bit Bennie went into the living room to sit on the couch and think about Linda. It was here he'd played That's the Way of the World. The melody they shared before her memory loss. He hoped hearing it would jog her memory, but it never happened.

He crossed his leg over his knee visualizing rubbing Terri's feet as they watched television. Back then being a gentleman and treating a woman like a lady the right thing to do; now loneliness and anger was the reward. From now on he was done with chivalry and modest signs of affection. As painful droplets of reflection were poised to generate another headache, Bennie opted for a different kind of aspirin. There was a woman somewhere who'd use her mouth without talking much. She didn't need the car door opened and he didn't have to pretend to be interested in her problems.

So the decision was made and that evening he let those nagging feelings of being caught by the police or robbed go away. He was ready to make his second attempt in the Bronx Terminal Market. That night his venture turned out acceptable, but not flawless. He had to find one skillful with Thomasina's patience, and Terri's technique. So each week subsequent to acceptable he searched, until one rainy night he found Angie.

It was after midnight on the last Friday in April when Bennie left his house, and the rain turned to a light drizzle. He drove over the bridge into the Bronx until he saw a prospect and slowed down. She was one of the previous disappointments, so he quickly moved on. Just past the Bronx House of Detention where he usually made a right turn a dark-skinned woman with curly hair waved at him. He slowed down noticing she was wearing sun glasses. The lady walked towards the car, but he rolled away. He thought it unusual she'd wear sunglasses on a dark wet night. Still curiosity got the better of him and he went back, but she was gone. He found her in the next block leaving the area so he went to get her. They rode for a minute then settled in a parking space on the overpass.

When she removed her glasses her left eye was missing. Only the sunken eye lid covered the socket. Her face wasn't bad and the more she talked the less Bennie cared. Before he could go into his pocket a police car pulled up and two officers, one black the other white in uniform got out. The driver shined a flashlight in Bennie's face while the black guy went to the passenger side. The woman put the window down and nicely said,

"It's me Angie… with the one eye?" as if he wouldn't know.

It turned out her face was a get out of jail free card. The other officer looked at Bennie's driver's license, gave it back and they left. Now the only question was did he want her to keep the glasses on or off. Off seemed logical and when she was done he'd found the woman he'd been looking for. From then he became Angie's regular using her services two or three times a month.

During that time Bennie would bump into Ronald and Kayla around the neighborhood and at the laundry. Ronald acted like he'd lost his damn mind where Kayla was concerned. His carelessness during the affair caused Lorraine to call Bennie one or two mornings looking for her husband.

At the same time Chris got a little better but he didn't put that weight back and it was obvious he struggled at work. For a man 25 years old it became clear he had more than the flu. He appeared distant and dismal, even his wife stopped coming by with his lunch. Customers whispered questions about his condition like, did he have that new thing going around worse than herpes? Time would eventually bring truth to the surface regarding Chris and Ronald. In Bennie's case forces were in motion to rid him of those contented late-night rendezvous.

As the summer drew to a close Bennie couldn't find Angie in August through mid-September. He found himself riding past the girls so much they stopped trying to flag him down. This particular night he decided to find Angie and met resistance in many forms. It was near midnight but two hours ago he sat in the kitchen drinking two beers. In between those two were five shots of vodka. He should have taken it as the first sign when he knocked the shot glass over not once but twice. Then he had an upset stomach so he couldn't leave when he wanted. When that passed he went downstairs but left his house key upstairs even though they were in his hands seconds before. All that time Mister followed him to the point of blocking his way to the front door once he was leaving. If the dog could talk he would have told him not to go. Once outside there was another delay. The car in front and the one behind his were parked too close. It was an exasperating struggle, but Bennie still got out then headed for the market.

Like many nights before Angie wasn't around. By three o'clock he was tired and made up his mind to go home. In the distance walking toward the bridge into Harlem was a woman wearing blue jeans with a gray hooded sweat shirt. She had brown skin, slim and wore her hair in a ponytail. Taking a chance he slowed down to pick her up. After Bennie told her what he wanted she shyly agreed while looking out the window. He found a safe place opened his zipper and the woman quietly performed. After the deed was done he told her he was going across the bridge and did she want to be let out there. The timid lady agreed, never looking at him just out the window. But in Harlem was where his dilemma began.

After getting out she finally made eye contact before closing the door. Bashful was substituted with a confident bye and that was the problem, the voice was deep and masculine. That couldn't have been a man he thought sitting frozen and confused. Without delay he replayed the encounter in his mind. From behind she looked like a woman, but Bennie never got a good look at her face. Then there was the voice soft till the end and always looking out the window. Damn it he had to make sure because if a man tricked him, he deserved to get his ass kicked. He looked up the street, but the person was gone. Humiliation festered until he felt like vomiting from the idea of a man's saliva on his private possession. With the urgency of a rape victim, Bennie rushed home to take a shower, but of course all the parking spaces in his block were filled. Forced to ride around feeling disgraced he settled on a space five blocks away, reaching home after 4:30am.

When he got inside Mister didn't greet him at the door. Instead the dog stayed upstairs in the hallway only watching with sympathy when he walked by as if to say, I tried to stop you. Irritated, he emptied his pockets allowing the money, keys, and wallet to fall where they may. Then he tore his shirt off, balled the underwear with the pants and threw them in the corner. In the shower he furiously scrubbed his crotch with soap then looked down to see his socks were still on. Finally the skin was clean, but his mind was forever soiled. When he got out of the shower Bennie snatched the curtain so hard half of it ripped from the rod. Then he snatched the old clothes and put them in a plastic bag and tossed them into a garbage can next to the bed. Tonight was one more drip to add in a pitcher of disappointments.

For some time in the days to follow Bennie thought about going back for revenge but the fault was his own. Plus, if he got caught beating someone up the whole world would know what a fool he'd been. Tonight his reckless pursuit of pleasure was paid for from his self-respect and dignity account. But before the week was out during one of those sleepless nights Bennie stared at the ceiling. He vowed never to go back to the Bronx Terminal Market, or pick up any more prostitutes. And if he had it to do over again, he would have listened to the dog and stayed home.

Chapter 5

A warm breeze wafted through an airy room with white alabaster walls. Outside the spacious balcony overlooked a Mississippi sized river. From the hilltop, men pulled oars on the large wooden boats below. Wind filled sails steered boats over a waterfall into the mist. The recognizable face of a Negro woman in her sixties told her everything would be okay if she loved him. The dreamer first recalled the face of this woman as a memory in the park when Tiffany fell months ago. Now the old woman floated from the balcony into the house and vanished.

Instantly the dreamer was in a boat on the river below surrounded by fishing vessels. A Negro man dressed in a burgundy robe with locs like hers sat alongside her. Patchy strands of grey hair sprouted from his goatee. His smile was warm like the heat of the sun on her face. There was a feeling of trust and safety as he pointed to the water and parts of the boat as if he were a teacher, and she the student. He called the dreamer a familiar name not spoken in thousands of years.

From the boat she found herself walking towards a stable where a Negro boy spoke. He handed her reins to a beautiful black horse. The horse sniffed her hand watching her with large submissive eyes. Now she was inside her house as a parrot flew towards her. Just as she reached out to accept the bird on her finger she woke up with a name on her lips. The old woman from her dream was called Yoba Ismeti.

It was morning first week of October 89, in the small town of Woodbridge, New Jersey. Linda tossed on the edge of her bed very much alive. She and the child Tiffany who would be four in December never died in a basement fire. But Linda witnessed that blaze in August of 87 from the next block weeks after her apartment was robbed of clothes and jewelry. Back then it seemed every time she read the newspaper there was a murder or fire in that area. So she moved away to Yonkers, and farther from her brother.

Fourteen months after living in Yonkers Linda moved again. This time because her best friend Sonya said a man named Mr. Queen came to her Bronx apartment asking questions about her and the baby. Because of that she instantly moved farther from Harlem to a two bedroom in Woodbridge, NJ, just off Roanoke Street.

Sadly, after a year in Woodbridge, Linda still had dreams that made no sense. She lay in bed reflecting on this latest before Tiffany woke up. The balcony, people, and surroundings were all familiar, like hearing a song she'd forgotten. In reality she had no memory of being royalty, speaking her native language, or being raised her entire life in Africa. When Bennie brought her to the United States after her accident he knew none of her customs. But as time went on the recollections slowly began. Fortunately the serendipitous joy of raising her baby made the confusion bearable.

At the moment Linda found peace knowing Sonya was coming to spend the weekend. From the day she and Sonya met they became close. Sonya was about the same age though somewhat darker and not as tall. Still Sonya demonstrated the true measure of a friend by taking Linda and the baby in when she ran away from Bennie, but her assistance didn't end there. Sonya helped with the move and went as far as to give Linda her driver's license, so she had ID which allowed Linda to get the safe deposit box that held most of her money. There also came a time four months after Linda moved to Woodbridge Tiffany came down with pneumonia. Sonya drove to New Jersey at 2am to sit with Linda in the emergency room. So Sonya coming was more than a visit; it was like family coming for the holidays.

Near arrival time mother and daughter sat on opposite sides of the couch looking out the front window until Sonya drove up. Outside the three embraced in a lengthy group hug then went upstairs. Forty minutes later they were looking for a parking space at the mall in the city of Wayne.

The women got their nails and toes polished while Tiffany sat in the adjacent chair coloring. When that was over they shopped, got Tiffany some juice, then headed back to Linda's. Later that evening they had Chinese food delivered, then sat in the living room in their pajamas and watched TV until the baby fell asleep. Sonya scooped Tiffany up and put her in bed. She returned walking past the living room to the kitchen pausing to say,

"Linda, I want to have a baby so bad, but Jeff isn't ready."

She continued to the fridge opening a bottle of Zinfandel then came back to sit on the floor. Linda took a glass and after tasting said, "Sonya I'm so glad to see you."

"I'm glad to see you too sister. But you heard what I said about a baby? I think he's scared to have a child with me cause his baby's mama gives him a hard time. I know that's what it is. That bitch always, always, always has something to say when I'm around her son! And I have nothing but love for the boy cause its Jeff's, you know what I mean?"

"Yes I think so," Linda answered sympathizing with her.

"So what do you think I should do, cause I feel like it's time you know? I'll be thirty in no time," said Sonya taking a sip.

"Well let me think, does Jeff want more children?"

"He said he does but not right away. And you know something… I noticed every now and then he'll ask me if I've taken my birth control pills. And when I say yes he gives me a strange look like he don't believe me. He gets on my damn nerves. Really sometimes I can't stand him, but I love him so much," Sonya said with a smile.

Linda's mouth was wide open, then they laughed, and Linda said, "I don't know what to say about that."

"I know it sounds crazy, but I do love him I swear, that's my heart. There are times I want to hit em with my cast iron skillet. You know the one we fried chicken in that my momma gave me…that one. Right upside his hard ass head," Sonya laughed then said,

"Oh shoot I almost forgot! Girl… I was waiting for the baby to go to sleep so we could talk. Guess who came to see me last month? I ain't even gonna make you try cause I see ya face, and no it wasn't him. It was that detective that came looking for you a while ago and you moved. Queen… you know I told you he came by looking for you?"

"Yeah I do remember, so what did he want?" Linda asked anxiously.

"Wait let me tell you it's good news, trust me. Okay so listen, I got home from work, and I thought I saw him, Queen sitting in a car in front of my building when I walked past. But I didn't think nothing of it so I kept on, and when I got upstairs there was a knock at the door. So I look through the peephole and it's him right. And remember I told you the man was fine. Let me tell you he was looking good like Shaft from the movies. You know Richard Roundtree who's the man that would risk his neck for his brother man, Shaft."

"Who's Shaft?"

"Girl stop playing! You never saw the movie Shaft?"

"No I never seen it," Linda answered impatiently holding her glass of wine.

"How about the song…I know you heard the song. Who's the man that would risk his neck for his brother man?" Sonya insisted.

"No girl, would you just tell me what happened please?" asking somewhat frustrated.

"Okay but wait I'm gonna tell you, but I'm gonna get the video and we gonna watch it next time I come over. So anyway um…He's on the other side calling my name and I told him to go away cause I ain't seen you. Then he says he knows that, and he had some news about you. So I'm scared now right. So I snatch the door open, but I don't let him in. Now I'm thinking he found you right, so I'm about to go off on him you know and say, why can't you and that crazy ass brother of hers leave her alone right!"

Sonya got loud and looked in the direction of Tiffany's room then lowered her voice.

"Linda I was about to cuss him out you hear me, but I held it together and let him talk. So all I said was what do you want? Then…then he says he was in the neighborhood and thought I'd want to know what happened to you since we were once good friends. The man told me you and the baby got killed in a fire years ago, but he was just finding out. Now I don't know if he's testing me, so I covered my mouth like this to make sure I don't say anything. But the thing is he really believes it."

That's when Sonya touched Linda's arm as a gesture to see that she was flesh and blood, then Sonya asked, "So you want to hear the rest?"

"Of course girl you better finish!" Linda said feeling relieved.

"Ok so let me tell you…where was I?"

"I'm dead remember," Linda said talking in a deep voice while putting up her hands like a walking Zombie.

"Look don't start no stuff up in here, zombies are real! My grandma told me she saw one walk out the cemetery when she was a little girl, so don't play. And how you know about Zombies, and you don't know Shaft?"

"Cause of Halloween, I know about vampires, witches and those scary looking pumpkins you put candles inside," Linda said getting a high five.

"You go girl… So anyway let me finish, Queen says you and the baby were burned in a fire on Crotona Avenue. Then he said there's no record of you all's deaths and they weren't gonna exhume any remains. Now here's the best part! Queen told me as far as anyone was concerned there wasn't gonna be a death certificate. Your brother thinks you're dead so he's not looking for you anymore," Sonya said taking a drink.

"Sleeping dogs lie, I don't get it. What does that mean?"

"You a trip sometimes girl, you know that. It just means no one's looking for you anymore cause they think you're dead! Now you can go on with your life honey! Celebrate a little and cheer this place up… please! Get some curtains for the windows and…and get rid of these funky blinds! They was here when you moved in. And…and put some bright colors around here, especially in the baby's room, and start being happy again like you use to be when we met, you hear me!" Sonya said pointing around.

"There were times you'd smile so big I thought you had like four more teeth than everybody else…remember? Now you smile like you had a stroke," Sonya said jokingly.

"It's been so long I…"

"I know you been going through some bad times but I gotta tell you, life is like a roller coaster. You do know what a roller coaster is?"

"Sonya I've seen a roller coaster."

"Okay so you know they go up and down just like life. You have to stick it out when you're down cause the up is not far behind. Matter of fact the up is here now cause you don't have to look over your shoulder, no one is looking for you. You are free girl freeee! So here's to your coaster going up!!" Sonya said extending her glass for a toast.

"Absolutely," Linda said assertively as they drank.

For a few moments they sat quietly with the TV playing. Linda's body melted with relief into the corner of the couch staring at the soft pink color of the wine. Sonya was glad her friend took time to savor this moment and it wasn't until she heard a shallow sigh of relief from her did she speak.

"I never told you the funny part," said Sonya.

"Yeah…what happened at the end, after he told you I was burnt up? What did you do?" Linda asked crossing her legs.

"I started crying. Listen I was crying like I lost my mind girl. Crying like I should've gotten an award, you hear me? I put my hand over my mouth and hollered and was stumbling around like I couldn't stand up good. I started crying like…like Celie in The Color Purple when Mister took her sister away, you remember?"

"The Color Purple?"

"Wait a minute Linda come on you're kidding me right? Whoopi Goldberg…Oprah Winfrey."

"I think I seen Oprah…"

"You don't know who Oprah Winfrey is?" Sonya said in disbelief.

"What does she look like? Okay wait a minute I know who Oprah is, but I never got a chance to look at her show,"

"If I didn't know better I'd think you were from another planet I swear. The next time I come I'm gonna have The Color Purple, and Shaft on video. Damn it, you don't have a VCR. You know what honey, that's alright I'll bring one next month. It'll be an early Christmas present, and we'll watch some movies when the baby goes to sleep. So any who, you took all the fun out my story girl cause you don't know how pitiful Celie looked when she couldn't see her sister anymore. But I put on an academy performance for Mr. Queen. And I purposely didn't call you in case it was a trick, that's how I almost forgot to tell you."

Once Sonya finished laughing at the end of the story Linda couldn't help but cry. Sonya put her glass down then rushed to sit next to Linda on the couch. She hugged then rocked her until she calmed down. Then Linda said,

"I can't thank you enough, I don't know what I would do if I didn't have you in my life Sonya. You're my best... my only friend."

"I'm here for you girl, it is gonna be okay and I know you don't want to wake the baby so please try to calm down and take it easy."

"I know I know," Linda said on the way to the bathroom.

Quietly she closed the door then stood in front of the medicine cabinet mirror looking at herself for only a second or two. She wiped her skin and swiftly looked away repeating the process until she finished. This habit of looking periodically at herself was born from her fear of having the blackouts return. When Linda composed herself she came out and sat back down.

"How you feel?"

"Better girl much better, how do I look?"

Sonya watched with silent skepticism. She'd never pried into Linda's life but as the months went by and the friendship grew she felt obligated to break her silence.

"I know you'll get through this," Sonya said encouragingly.

"Yup...but I want to talk about something else. Can we talk about something else for a while? I'll be fine trust me."

"Um... excuse me sista but no you're not! You're not all better! You're a hot mess," Sonya said pointing her finger at Linda continuing.

"I want the woman I first met years ago. The confident beautiful lady who told me I could do anything I set my mind to. Linda you had a presence that filled the room when you walked in like you commanded dignity and grace. You inspired me, that's why I went back to school. So as your friend and a person who loves you I want to help, I'm here for you… Will you let me help you?" Sonya pleaded.

Linda looked in Sonya's eyes and began to cry and she couldn't stop. She grabbed a cushion and buried her face while Sonya held her. When Linda was able to speak, agonizingly she wheezed, "I don't know what to do… I feel like I'm going crazy… I'm lost and…and I don't fit in anywhere. I just don't know what to do!"

"It's okay girl I got ya, we all have some hurt to deal with and you're gonna be alright!" Sonya said shaking Linda's hands firmly then said,

"But baby you have to admit something is wrong, then believe you can fix it! It's just like David and Goliath. David had to believe he could defeat the giant! That was the first step so make your problem Goliath and know you can conquer it!"

With tears exhausted and bloodshot eyes Linda reached for the wine, but Sonya stopped her from drinking and offering her water instead.

"Right now this is better for you."

Linda drank then asked, "What do you think I should do?"

"Let's start with something positive like um…You are a great mother, and you love that baby right?" Sonya said urging Linda to talk more.

"With all my heart," Linda said boldly.

"Of course you do and what else… you're a woman and we're fantastic cause we got an edge on men, life comes through us. What else um… you think of one. Tell me something about yourself that's good!" Sonya asked cheerfully.

"I like to read and… my health is good," Linda answered shyly.

"Come on girl brag about it; put some power to it like when we met, come on! Say it like this! I am a gorgeous black woman. I got these hips and this face and when I walk they stop and check me out. I'm beautiful. Say something like that!" Sonya demanded.

"I'm beautiful!"

"Say it again and call yourself strong too!" added Sonya.

"I'm strong and beautiful!"

After Linda said it Sonya had the courage to say, "Linda I never asked you why you ran from your brother because it wasn't important at the time. All I knew was you needed help so that's what I did. But will you talk to me so I can help you?"

"What do you want to know?"

"What did your brother do?"

Following a suspenseful pause Linda answered with her head down, "He got fresh."

"What did he do girl, you can tell me," Sonya urged.

When Linda wouldn't say anymore Sonya responded, "Well you're safe now. You never have to see him again right?"

"You're right never again," Linda said sadly.

"So tell me about your accident, what happened to you to make you forget your life?"

"I don't know but I think I almost drowned and my brother blamed himself."

"That sounds suspicious to me, it really does. And you say he blames himself huh?"

"Yes," said Linda and the next few questions she answered the same way.

"Do you know when it was?"

"No, I don't."

"How about your mother and father, you remember them?"

"No, I only know my parent's faces from pictures but I'm not in any photos with them. Bennie said they got ruined somehow," said Linda pensively.

"Honey that don't sound right. Not one picture of you with the family, even when you were a kid! How about a birthday party, remember any of those?"

"I just remember one, I don't…"

"Well just tell me this, what day is the baby's birthday?" Sonya interrupted.

"December the 12th."

"And yours?"

"I'm January the 26th, says it on my passport somewhere," said Linda quickly.

"So you know the day, but you only remember having one party in all these years. That's unbelievable… I don't know what to say. What about the baby's father, who is he?"

"I don't know, I can't remember him at all. I don't even know when we had sex or where. But I do remember my babysitter taking me to the park around the corner. Her name was Yvonne."

"That's good, she might have some answers honey, what was Yvonne's last name?"

"I don't know," Linda answered abruptly.

"Do you know where she lives?"

"No, she said one day she was going to take me to see where she lived but we never went. I think she called it Flatland or Flatbush, something like that."

"Okay Flatbush, I know Flatbush is in Brooklyn about an hour on the train."

"I know she use to ride the train to come over," Linda blurted out.

"You see that's good news. So what did she look like?"

Linda paused for a moment tilting back her head and closed her eyes. Puckering her face as if tasting a sour candy she put her hand on her chin. Then as if a lightbulb went off in her mind Linda snapped her finger then said,

"Yvonne was about your complexion. She was older than us, maybe in her 50's I think. Oh, and she spoke with an accent, I think she was born in Jamaica. As a matter of fact I'm sure because she always talked about missing home and that was in Jamaica. I can see her face. Now if I saw her I'd know who she was."

"So at least you have a piece of the puzzle. And what about Tiffany's father, has she asked about him?" Sonya asked delicately.

Linda's smile was replaced by an attitude of indifference simply to mask the hurt. Then she said, "No she hasn't but let me tell you what else I can't remember! I can't remember having a birthday party, or my mother's and father's faces. I don't know the name of my first-grade teacher, or any of my school teachers for that matter. I don't even remember going to school or sitting in class. The only person I have a good memory of is Yvonne and my brother.

"My brother taught me to read Dr. Suess books you know, One Fish Two Fish and Green Eggs and Ham. He taught me to do fractions and gave me spelling tests. Oh, and he taught me a lot about African history and Egyptian stuff. Did you know they were the first great civilization?"

"I didn't know that."

"Yes they were. African people been sailing all over the world long before Columbus. Now that I think of it maybe I was home schooled that's why I don't remember going to class," Linda said gaining her composure.

"Okay," Sonya answered seeing how Linda's emotions swayed back and forth.

"I got to ask you something and it's kind of personal," Linda said biting the corner of her lip.

"What girl…what?"

"Well how old were you when you got your first…period?" Linda asked halfheartedly.

"Wow…let's see, I was in the fifth grade, and we were near the end of lunch. I was feeling different when I sat down, but I didn't pay it any mind. I walked over to the trash then I heard, I don't even want to say his name cause I hated him after that. Anyway I was standing by the garbage when I heard him say eeew what's that in your chair, all loud. Everybody in the cafeteria started pointing at the back of my skirt. Miss Moore came running out the kitchen with a towel and wrapped around my waist. I never saw what was in my chair, but my dress was soaked so I can only imagine. Linda that day I was so embarrassed I didn't want to go back to school," and after a brief pause she continued.

"Thank God it was a Friday, and I had a few days to deal with it, but that was the first time it came in the damn lunch room in front of everybody," Sonya said hoping Linda would laugh or something.

"Sonya you've got to be kidding," Linda said with an open mouth.

"Girl you can't make up shit like that, but I got over it. Why'd you ask?"

"Because the first time I remember having my period was weeks after Tiffany was born. I was still staying with my brother, and I'd put Tiffany down for a nap in my room. I was feeling a little odd you know, but I didn't think anything about it. Then I went down the hall to the bathroom to pee and when I wiped, the paper had blood on it. Sonya, I wanted to scream. I thought I cut myself or sat on something until I remembered what the doctor told me at the hospital."

"Honey, I don't know what to say," said Sonya shaking her head.

"Now this is something else that's gonna sound strange. As long as I can remember, I've had breasts… always. I wish I had had pictures when I was five, but I never found any. Just ones of my brother with mom and dad when they were on vacation," Linda said walking to the window.

"Did you ask your brother about it?"

"You mean the pictures? Sure I did," Linda answered walking back.

"He said they were burned in a fire, and one time he said they were stolen when he forgot he told me they were burned up. So that's why as far as I know, I always had them," Linda said cupping her hands in front of her breasts.

"Girl…I never heard of anything like that in my life."

"You can't make up shit like that," said Linda briefly lightening the mood.

They smiled as Sonya played with her earring, Linda got serious and continued,

"Sonya I don't remember ever going through stages, you know like wearing my first training bra, or even growing into larger clothes. It dawned on me a couple of weeks ago when Tiffany told me her feet hurt, and I took her to the hospital."

"You never told me she was at hospital, what happened?"

"I never mentioned it cause I felt stupid. When I picked up Tiffany from daycare I saw her limping to the car, so I asked her what was wrong, and she said her feet hurt. So you know I took my baby to the hospital right, and you know what they told me? We didn't even get to see a doctor; the nurse told me her sneakers were too small. Cost me eighty-three dollars for somebody to tell me, can you believe it? With all I been going through I meant to buy her some the first time she said they were tight, and I just forgot. My point is, of course her sneakers got small just like her clothes get small, she's growing!"

"I don't know what to say honey but you're right, you need to find out what happened to you," Sonya answered shaking her head with astonishment.

"So like I was saying, I don't remember something as simple as growing up, and I definitely don't ever remember having sex. I think I'd remember letting a man stick his thing in me. And you know Tiffany's father could walk past me on the street, and I wouldn't know who he was. It's like the empty space on her birth certificate where it says father, that blank scares the hell out of me," Linda said crossing her legs cupping her toes.

"I don't know what to say girl, but it is gonna be alright that's all I know."

"Sonya, see this scar on my ankle, I don't know how I got this, and I almost don't care!"

Sonya interrupted cautiously to say,

"This has got to be frustrating for you but…"

"Frustrating? Honey if it wasn't for that girl sleeping in the next room I 'd have lost my mind a long time ago. She's the only person who loves me," Linda said firmly.

Immediately she realized what she'd said and took hold of Sonya's hand.

"I didn't mean that, I'm sorry I didn't mean you; you know that?"

"I know that's not what you meant… and I wasn't trying to act like I know what you're going through," said Sonya caringly.

"You're my only friend. I couldn't have made it without you, I'm so sorry," Linda said, crying once more and when tranquility returned Sonya said,

"One day that little girl is gonna ask you who her daddy is? It's coming girlfriend and you'll have to give her an answer. But more importantly you need to know for yourself! I mean you do want to know who he is, and what happened to you right?"

"Yes, yes I do, but I don't know where to start," Linda said looking for Sonya to respond.

"Well I do, and the answer is the Lord!! He can fix anything, but you must have faith, that's the key. Just have the faith of a tiny mustard seed."

"Sonya I been praying my whole life, and nothing changed so I stopped," Linda said honestly.

"A lot of people feel like that and guess what… God forgives you."

Figuring this was the perfect time she went in her overnight bag to give Linda a Bible. Linda opened it, reading the inscription aloud, "To Linda from your sister Sonya. May the words in this Holy Bible forever guide your footsteps the rest of your life."

"My spirit's been telling me to get this for you."

"Thank you," said Linda.

"Now I might not say this right, but I know with God it's not the words in perfect order that impresses Him. It's your heart He's listening to… you feel me?"

"Yes."

"Well then repeat after me… Father God I ask you to forgive me of my sins. From this day forward I will follow your will only and accept your Son Jesus Christ as my Lord and Savior."

After a short silence Linda said, "Is that it?"

"Well I could've said in Jesus's name or amen, but the important thing is do you mean what you say? Is it coming from your heart?"

"Yes it is."

"Then that's it; because Linda some people will say you must be standing inside a church or in front of witnesses. But when you start reading this book you will see God talked to people when they were alone one on one, so you are good. You believe and accept Him and that's all that matters!"

"That makes sense, it does, it really does. So what do I do now?" Linda asked nervously.

"Now you're plugged in spiritually and He is already working the problem out for you. But I still gotta say your faith is the key. Linda honey, you must believe that you can and will rise above all your troubles. And keep in mind faith without work means nothing! Do what your heart… no I mean what your spirit tells you, and The Lord will do the rest. So right now you're gonna start talking to Him again. And it doesn't need to be at night, even though being on your knees is the total act of submission. If you at the bus stop and you want to pray, you don't have to kneel on the sidewalk to speak to Him. But you do have to read this Bible. Commit to reading a page a day or every other day. Knowing how you like to read if you want to read more, do it, just don't feel pressured to do it. He wants your free will and your love okay?"

"Yes I understand, and I will, thank you so much," Linda said holding the Bible with new admiration.

"And the last thing I'm gonna say is find a church with a good pastor and join. It doesn't have to be right this minute, but it is necessary, at least I think so."

"I will, I really will," Linda said.

"Okay unless you have any other questions we gonna just chill right now and rest in His love. In the morning whatever your mind tells you to do, do it and God will take care of the rest, in Jesus name Amen!" said Sonya holding both hands above her head.

"Amen," Linda repeated.

For the remainder of the night their conversation flowed with laughter and pain. They looked in magazines for ideas to spruce up both their apartments, while making fun of the skinny models. On one page Sonya showed Linda the two-carat engagement ring she dreamed Jeff would give her when he finally proposed. Linda spoke about a man she met at the library who attended Rutgers. She thought he was attractive and very polite, but she constantly refused to go out with him on a date. That exchange prompted Sonya to share a piece of her past.

At fourteen Sonya's body developed while she held a crush for the man in her building on the second floor. Naiveté lead her to trust and be groomed for almost a year into having sex with a forty-year-old. She confided in Linda telling about the first time she let the man touch her body. That day he gave Sonya a bracelet and said it was their secret. When they finally had sex the man gave her a gold chain to wear making her promise to take it off before going home. From then on when Sonya went to his apartment, and they finished, he'd give her fifty dollars and sometimes more. He told Sonya that's how a real man shows he cares. It wasn't long before she honestly fell in love, and that was the day he changed.

He stopped giving her money and threatened to tell Sonya's mother she was a prostitute. Mortified and helpless, the secret was kept but the arrangement was altered. Now Sonya was required to be at his house after school once or twice a week. One day as she was about to leave his apartment he told her she was expected to prove her love for him by having sex with other men next week. Two days before that meeting was to take place, he was shot and killed around the corner from JT's supermarket. Sonya told Linda she never thought to ask for help because she felt dirty, and to this day her mother doesn't know about her first.

Deep acrimony in her relationship was the result of Sonya's heartbreak. It took time and the loss of a few good men until she recognized they weren't all the same. Sonya wanted to drive that point home for Linda in the event she might start dating again. So they talked some more, and cried some more, until yawns replaced tears and finally they swapped goodnights. Sonya got comfortable on the couch and Linda went to her room with a healthier outlook. So special was tonight that when Linda's head touched the pillow she was compelled to get on her knees and pray.

When morning came Linda awoke with a happiness she had not felt in years. Missing capability and conquer ability surged within her. She'd decided two things last night before going to sleep. First she was going to fight for the happiness of her child by finding help for her condition. Then she was going to find out who Tiffany's real father was.

The following Tuesday evening Linda made herself comfortable in the living room with a pile of books to research after Tiffany went to sleep. It didn't take long to diagnose her form of amnesia as retrograde because her new memories were retained. She took retrograde as a blessing instead of having Anterograde Amnesia. With Anterograde she could've forgotten her own name, her daughter's face, or where she lived.

As Linda read, two books stated Retrograde Amnesia could be brought on by a traumatic incident, head injury, or developing brain tumor. So she had to rule out the tumor by finding a doctor and getting that checked. If there was no tumor she would work on exactly what kind of accident she'd been through. Two weeks later Linda's test results came back negative for brain tumors, encephalitis, and cancer. Now she had to find a psychiatrist to sort out her disorder.

The first doctor she visited made her feel uncomfortable by invading her personal space. He stood so close puffs from his words were felt on her face. Then he couldn't talk without touching her wrist and forearm whenever he asked a question. The last straw was when he took five minutes on the phone to discuss another patient's problem in front of her. He made no apology for the interruption only a gesture with his hand for her to continue speaking.

Next Linda went to a woman doctor in Edison who listened to her for twenty minutes while filling out a prescription for depression. Linda told the doctor she wasn't sad, but excited with the prospect of regaining her life. Still she forced the prescription in Linda's hand telling her the elation would pass, and to come back next week. When Linda left her office she went to pick up Tiffany from day care. Along the way she tore the prescription into tiny pieces as if leaving a bread crumb trail. The two objectionable encounters did not stop her and in a few days she rang the bell of Dr. Samuel Q. Goldstein.

His office was on the first floor of his split-level home on Main Street, not far from where she lived. Over the intercom he asked who was there then told her to have a seat in the waiting room. Soon after Linda heard someone leaving from another exit then the doctor came out inviting her to his office.

Dr. Goldstein was a tall slim man with glasses in his early fifties. His hair was brown slightly curly, and receding, but his smile was pleasant. Linda sat on the edge of the couch across from him. Once a few preliminary questions were out of the way the session went better than expected. Dr. Goldstein genuinely cared about her condition and expressed empathy. He answered and asked most of the questions from the research books she'd read so they agreed to a return visit the following week.

During the second visit Dr. Goldstein concluded based on negative findings for tumors and other afflictions that Linda's problem was psychological. So in this session he strived to uncover the nature of Linda's trauma and if it was related to whom her baby's father was. He also posed the question; did the child's father have anything to do with her accident? Linda looked down at her hands in silence. Anticipating that reaction, Dr. Goldstein told her he believed she would ultimately make progress, and that they would work together. Hearing those words made her sit up confidently and make another appointment. This time he gave her assignments to exercise the part of the brain used in recollection.

Linda had to write her dreams, and memories down, particularly any inquiries she might think of for the next session. Dr. Goldstein told her questions act as fuel to make the brain stronger. Next was to get a deck of ordinary playing cards separating the reds from the blacks. Work with one color at a time placing them randomly face down. If the first card was a red six and the next pick wasn't the other red six Linda had to put them face down in the same spot. Twice a day she should do this until the pairs were gone. Lastly she had to answer three questions about the previous day. What clothes she wore, what she ate for dinner, and finally two places she'd been.

Dr. Goldstein asked if Linda needed paper to write the instructions, but she said no. Happily touching a finger to her head as a gesture she wouldn't forget. On that note he cautioned her not to get annoyed if she couldn't complete any assignments. It was good to associate instances of amnesia with progress instead of disappointment. Linda agreed and when the secession was over, the Doctor escorted Linda to a different door that let out in the driveway.

Afterwards she walked to the supermarket near her home. Tonight mother and daughter would have meatballs and spaghetti for dinner, with chocolate ice cream for desert. She made sure to get the cards, note pads, and a new coloring book for Tiffany then went to the register. On the way she passed a bin of stuffed animals. Next to a shark was a green parrot with yellow markings like the bird from her dream. Simply holding it caused her to grin, so she threw it into the cart.

After dinner Linda anxiously called Sonya to say she'd found a good doctor, and what he recommended she do. Sonya listened as Linda went from room to room with the phone on her shoulder and told her about her second visit. Linda told Tiffany to get her coloring book and Sonya finally got a chance to talk. She reminded Linda she'd be there the weekend of Tiffany's birthday then they said goodbye.

Linda sat at the dining room table with the cards and Tiffany with her book. Tiffany was so interested in what mom was doing she never opened her new coloring book. She watched Linda separate the cards into two piles then pick one. In a few minutes Linda finished and of course Tiffany asked if she could play too. So Linda explained the rules and gave her five pairs to start.

Instead of two games Linda played six then got the baby ready for bed. Tiffany stood on a stool next to her mom in front of the bathroom mirror. Linda passed the tooth paste and they began to brush. Afterwards Tiffany smiled to the reflection of clenched teeth and asked if she would be pretty like her mom? Linda told her yes and much smarter too. With somber expression beyond her years Tiffany told her mom she wanted to be just like her before she got under the covers.

Those profound words from one so young made that one of the best nights in Linda's life. On bended knees Linda asked the Lord to help her be a good mother. To heal her for her child's sake, and to give her power to overcome the stress she carried. After Amen, Linda stayed in the same position pondering what it would take for her to be happy. Would she like to get married and have another baby, a boy this time? Maybe she'd move again, and after that who knows. Finally in bed she knew one thing for sure, she wasn't going to stay stuck in fear.

In early December Linda's next visit to the Doctor was on a day most people would've stayed home. It was cold, rainy, and the wind blew broken umbrellas up and down the streets. Still she arrived at the office early wiping the rain from her face. For some reason Linda never used an umbrella. To her they were burdensome, blocked her vision and didn't keep her from getting wet. Instead she and Tiffany had yellow three-quarter length rain coats with matching hats.

When it was her turn Linda sat on the edge of the couch clutching her journal. Dr. Goldstein sat across from her opening his pad and said,

"It's nasty out there?"

"No not really, at least it's not snowing," she answered cheerfully.

"You don't like the snow?"

"No I like the snow too. I just mean I'm glad to be here, I don't care that it's raining that's all."

"I'm glad to hear it. So Ms. Reeves tell me how you've been?" he asked lifting his pen.

"Well let's see um… I played with the cards more than you said. I hope that's okay. And Doc I didn't ask how you were, so how are you doing?"

"I'm good thanks for asking, and it's ok to play more than twice," he said waiting for her to continue.

"It takes me a few minutes to finish a game that's why I play a couple of them. And my daughter plays with me sometimes when she's finished her homework," Linda said happily.

"She does, what grade is she in?"

"Tiffany, oh she hasn't started school yet. I just work with her using flash cards and coloring books," Linda said proudly, at the same time neglecting to mention one thing. Helping her daughter brought memories of her brother Bennie teaching the ABCs and math to Linda.

"Good to hear, so tell me about the rest of your assignments?" he asked while scribbling.

"Fine, but before I tell you about that a few days ago I had a dream about a bird. It landed on my shoulder and said neya berriee, or something like that. So now I keep this journal with me when I go to sleep so I can write down stuff right away. So what was I gonna say…oh I have no problems remembering what I ate, or wore the day before," said Linda looking away from her journal.

"That's good to know. So let's see, what's on your mind today?"

Linda flipped a few pages and sat back on the couch to relax then said,

"I want to talk about my blackouts or more specifically, why I don't have them anymore. What made them stop?" she asked looking at the doctor for an answer.

Dr. Goldstein seemed perplexed, then opened a folder from his desk to look inside then said,

"This is the first time you're mentioning blackouts. You checked no next to dizziness," he said looking puzzled.

"Well that's because I don't get dizzy when it happens. But it's been so long since it happened I kinda forgot, but it never made me feel dizzy."

"Okay tell me about the blackouts."

"It's like falling asleep on my feet in the middle of the day and I have no control whatsoever. And here's the funny thing Doc, it only happened when I saw my reflection in a mirror or window pane."

Dr. Goldstein looked at the mirror on his wall and before he could speak Linda said, "the smaller ones never affected me. One time I stopped to look at a dress through a window on Broadway. The next thing I knew someone was asking me if I was alright. Then another time I was about to cross the street, a truck pulled in front of me and I looked at my reflection. Then the driver was asking me to get out the way so he could take the glass pane off the truck. And one time rain drops falling on my head brought me out of it."

"Really? Rain drops falling on my head," he said grinning.

"Yes it started raining and…"

"No that's a song, rain drops keep falling on my head and that doesn't mean my life is,"

you never heard that song before?

"No, and that's another thing it seems I don't know common knowledge stuff like what you just said. So the last blackout was the worst," she continued unable to find the humor.

"I'd just moved to the Bronx; I was wiping a mirror on the inside bathroom door. The next thing I knew the baby was crying, and it was evening. I still had the paper towel in my hand pressed against the glass.

I'm just glad I wasn't cooking I could have started a fire. So after that I covered up the mirror, but it never happened again."

"That's incredible and you've had no more episodes?"

"No not one."

"And it only occurred when you saw your reflection?"

"Right."

"And how long ago was the last one?" he asked writing down responses.

Linda thought for a minute and said, "Doc it had to be two, almost three years ago, that's why I forgot. But you see I'm talking about it."

"I want you to look at your questionnaire again then put your initials next to any changes you make," he said giving her the form.

Linda gave the paper back and the doctor pleasantly said, "What else do you want to talk about?"

She opened the book quietly staring down, reading one line over and over to herself. When she didn't talk he prodded, "What is it Ms. Reeves."

She exhaled shaking her head all the while looking at the paper.

"Whatever it is we will work through it!" he said with authority.

As if releasing lasting suffering with one sentence, Linda looked at the doctor and whispered, "The Squiggly Man."

"The who man?"

"The Squiggly Man, I've had dreams about the Squiggly Man since I was a child," she said a bit louder. Unfortunately Linda had no idea the instances she referred to almost five years ago happened when she was a grown woman recovering from the accident.

"The Squiggly Man," Dr. Goldstein repeated abruptly looking at his watch.

He stood asking Linda to wait while he left the room then returned momentarily.

"We need to discuss this, so I told my next patient I was running late. Now tell me about this Squiggly Man?"

"Doctor when I was a little girl that dream always scared me. I'd run to my brother's room, or he'd stay in mine and read a story until I fell asleep."

"So where were your parents when this was going on?"

"Dead...it was just me, my brother, and Mister my dog. Mister was our rottweiler," she said fondly.

"Tell me what this man in your dream looks like?"

"The best way to describe it is he looked like dark grey smoke in the shape of a man. He always squiggles like a snake so that's why I started calling him the Squiggly Man. So in my dream he'd come towards me reaching to get me. But I noticed he doesn't look the same. The last time his body was thicker like mud, or Jello."

"That's very interesting! You say the man's form looks thicker?" he said hoping she would see the connection.

"Yes I guess you could say that."

"And what did you say the Squiggly Man does in the dream?"

"He reaches for me. He's trying to get to me then I wake up."

"Are you still having that dream?"

"No."

Dr. Goldstein finished writing then said, "Ms. Reeves it's very possible your brother could shed some light on your accident you know, fill in missing pieces of your memory. I think we should…"

"No!" Linda blurted.

"But Ms. Reeves I believe…"

"No! I won't do it!" she said louder.

"Ms. Reeves what happened between you and your brother? Is it some crime that we need to get the police involved?"

"I said no!" said Linda adamantly standing facing the door.

Quickly Dr. Goldstein said, "Alright if you don't want to talk about it now we won't but please sit down."

Linda sat down staring at her hands while he continued. "I must tell you holding on to painful memories will hinder your progress. Not releasing your pain is like having a stopper in a drain and the stagnant water can't get away. So not now but at some point you'll need to deal with what happened in the past so you can move forward… understand?"

"Yes I do," she said reluctantly.

"Great! So here's the good news," he said waiting for her to look up.

Once Linda did he said optimistically, "Ms. Reeves I believe absence from the blackouts, specifically in connection with your reflection, represents a strong indication of recovery. And when you speak about the Squiggly Man becoming more solid, that's a good sign too. So we're going to modify your assignment."

"Okay Doc," said Linda feeling more confident.

"First I want you to continue with the cards. You can play as many times as you want as long as it stays fun. And if you skip a day don't worry about it. Next… twice a week I want you to do this. On Thursday I want you to write two things from that past Monday. Where you were at 10:00am and what you were wearing. Then on Sunday I want you to do the same thing for the past Friday at let's say 7:30pm. What were you wearing and where you were… got it?"

"Yes I can do that," she said finally making eye contact.

"Now about what happened today, I want to remind you everything we discuss in this office is confidential. I can't tell anyone without your consent, so you understand that?"

"Yes I do it's just that I don't want to talk about my brother," she said rubbing her thumbs together.

"Alright."

"Not this time. I will at some point if it is going to help me, but not this time."

"Fair enough. So do those assignments and I will see you in the New Year and maybe we can see if you're a candidate for hypnosis," he said as they both stood up.

"Hypnosis," Linda answered with skepticism.

"Yes there have been cases with successful results but that's a long way off. We'll talk more about it Ms. Reeves," he said walking her to the door.

"Thank you Doc and I'll see you next year," said Linda opening the door to find it just drizzling. Her next stop was to get Tiffany then go home, but first thing tomorrow she'd be at the library reading up on hypnosis.

By the weekend of Tiffany's birthday Linda's joy overflowed as the icy wind blew. But that couldn't stop them from piling in Sonya's car to go shopping at the mall. Sonya was excited about the change in her best friend, and apparently Tiffany was too. When they got back to Linda's apartment Sonya hooked the VCR to the television. Then Linda put some music on the radio while they took turns modeling the new outfits. Afterwards they sat at the table to polish their nails. And because it was Tiffany's birthday, Linda let her try on makeup and lipstick.

Later that evening Tiffany blew out all four candles then opened the rest of her presents. After ice cream and cake they played a few games of Hungry Hippos. Linda decided Tiffany could stay up as long as she wanted but soon the four-year-old was asleep between them on the couch. While Sonya went to the bathroom, Linda put Tiffany in bed. They met in the hallway where Sonya started speaking about that time she lost her virginity.

Sonya told Linda when she left after the last visit a couple of days later she remembered something. At home in front of her dresser Sonya tried to put on her charm bracelet and suddenly recalled forgetting to take off the one the man gave her before going home, and that's why her mother asked her about it. Standing in the hallway Sonya told Linda her mother questioned her about where she got the money for the new purse in the bottom of her closet too. Sonya told her mom she found the bracelet and some money, but her mom didn't believe her. Then one night Sonya woke up to hear her mom screaming on the phone, "You better do something before she winds up with a baby, you hear me!"

About a week later Nelson was dead, and it was the first time Linda heard Sonya use his name.

Linda covered her mouth while Sonya looked down at the floor to continue. Sonya told her after Nelson's death she'd spend every other weekend at her father's apartment and for the first few weeks he'd pick her up from school. Linda peeked inside to see if Tiffany was sleeping, then asked if Sonya thought her father killed Nelson. Sonya simply shrugged her shoulders in response as if to say she didn't know, and then said she didn't want to know.

As abruptly as she started talking about her situation, Sonya stopped and went to the kitchen to make popcorn. She dumped the bag into a bowl and told Linda she was okay then went to the living room. Linda sat on the couch reaching for some popcorn, but Sonya playfully moved the bowl. She wanted Linda to choose the movie they were going to watch first. Linda looked at the cassettes deciding to see the oldest one first then Sonya passed the popcorn.

When the movie started, Linda recognized 125th Street even though the stores weren't the same. Eagerly Sonya slapped Linda's leg when Shaft came out of the train station. Bouncing on the couch at the same time sighing, Sonya pointed to Shaft telling Linda that's how Queen looked. Then she asked Linda again if that song sounded familiar. Linda took some popcorn, acknowledging without being serious she may have heard it.

Chapter 6

The worst thing a person can do is swap their goal for relaxation into wretchedness. That's what Bennie did after his last encounter at the Bronx Terminal Market. By early October of 1990 he followed up his foolish activity by consistently opening the Amsterdam store late and being charged with a DWI. Luckily Mr. Queen used his influence within the police department to make the charges go away. Just a week after that Bennie felt obligated to look the other way when three officers handed out a beat down on Convent Avenue. A black man in his early twenties accidentally bumped into a cop spilling beer on him. Despite the fact he apologized, he was slammed to the ground and pummeled with their nightsticks. The victim screamed for help but Bennie walked away towards St Nicholas Avenue. The man who once considered himself a righteous black warrior was just like the rest of the niggers who he gave up and took a seat.

This defeated soldier tore up his research for creating a Harlem merchant association along with plans for his mortgage company. Drunken nights caused the loss of a lot on 145th Street where Bennie planned to open a car wash. So for pity's sake he remained partners in a strained relationship with Ronald, which got worse when Chris walked in to explain how sick he really was. That Saturday after being absent two months Chris came to the office walking gingerly as if stepping on hot coals. His effort to sit on the couch made it obvious his health was worse. His face had reddish blotches that spread to the neck and hands, plus his hair was thin like he'd aged thirty years.

Bennie moved away from Chris to stand next to Ronald, who sat behind the desk. Sadly Chris told them he had that thing that was going around. Ronald asked what Chris meant so he responded by saying he had AIDS, and then stated he wasn't a homosexual. Compassionately Ronald said he was sorry to hear it, while Bennie said nothing. Instead, he backed away from their longest working employee as if he didn't want to breathe the same air. Then Bennie supplemented the awkwardness to ask how Danielle, Chris's wife was. Chris pulled up his socks trying to cover his discolored ankles, then said Danielle had it too, and they were separated. Embarrassed by his partner's conduct, Ronald told Chris he didn't need to explain but Bennie's simmering hatred for his personal state of affairs made him insinuate Chris got sick because of his wife. But Chris said Danielle didn't give him the virus because he knew who did. When Bennie asked who it was, the answer momentarily hit close to home. Chris told them it was from a black woman with an emphasis on black. He said it that way to get back at Bennie for being insensitive, and it worked, especially after Chris said she used the Eighth Avenue Kleenit.

The room was so quiet Bennie heard Ronald swallow. To cover nervousness, Ronald opened the desk drawer looking for anything and nothing. Instantly a solution to Bennie's business dilemma materialized. Ronald might get sick like Chris and in a year from now he would be free of their partnership. So eagerly Bennie asked again for a description of the woman while Ronald sorted paper clips and threw junk mail in the trash. Again Chris responded as if he didn't hear, choosing instead to explain why he stopped using condoms. He believed the lady couldn't get pregnant but months later she met him at work with sad news. She was a carrier of the virus without showing signs of sickness.

Twisting on the couch Chris relived each day he left the unopened condoms in his pocket, subsequently changing the lives of his family forever. He went on to say last week while passing this laundry in a taxi he saw the woman leave and she looked fine. Kayla came to see Ronald last Tuesday so this time he asked Chris what the woman looked like. Seconds oozed like cold molasses until finally Chris's description made it evident Kayla wasn't the woman. Bennie stopped listening until he heard Chris ask to borrow four thousand dollars and Ronald say yes.

Relieved, Chris hobbled over to shake their hands. Happily Ronald said he could pick the money up in the morning. As soon as Chris closed the door Bennie washed his hands, then stood over the couch where Chris sat. Before Ronald spoke Bennie gave two reasons not to give Chris any money. First they hadn't discussed it before Ronald said yes, and the other being Bennie couldn't see making a loan to a dying man.

Gradually Ronald found it hard to accept Bennie's erratic behavior. He'd heard increasing customer complaints of late openings, to running out of detergent and dryer sheets. Hell, they were in the laundry business, how does Bennie run out of detergent Ronald wondered? No doubt his friend was getting worse, and Ronald also thought about ending the partnership, an idea his wife was in favor of from the time they opened the second store.

Ronald listened then reminded Bennie it was his idea to start a health plan for the employees in the first place. Unmoved, Bennie replied to Ronald that he'd let Lorraine talk them out of offering benefits so if he wanted to give Chris money, he'd do it from his share. When Ronald said nothing Bennie walked and stood outside. He had a smoke then went down the block to the corner store for some potato chips, orange juice, peppermint balls, and four cans of Vienna sausages that were two cans for a dollar. Then he walked back to the laundry staying outside eating from the can with his fingers. That taste brought back memories of getting sausages from mom when he was a kid. Suddenly he felt ashamed for wishing Ronald would get sick. Nothing his old friend had done merited a death sentence. So when Bennie finished a second can he went back in the office and told Ronald he'd give Chris half the money. That day ended with in agreement but the next time they'd meet anger would be present again.

That day was Halloween night when Bennie joined Ronald and Lorraine to walk in the parade. One reason Bennie went was to recapture that sensation of joy from eating canned Vienna sausages. The other was by showing up for Halloween meant Lorraine couldn't say he acted unsociable when he missed their upcoming Christmas party. It was the perfect opportunity to kill two birds with one stone.

So Lorraine's sister Carol, her husband William, Carol's girlfriend Veronica and her new man Devin plus Sharon met in SoHo. Ronald dressed as a homeless man on skates with a sign around his neck that read, "Will skate for food." Lorraine wore Minnie Mouse ears while Carol came as Catwoman and her husband, Batman. Veronica and her friends didn't wear costumes since they came at the last minute. Just days before Bennie made up his mind to go, he made it simple. He went as the Wolf Man with a beard and rubber hands with claws.

Bennie hugged Lorraine then stood as far away from her as he could. Soon they headed towards the parade, stopping at the corner for the light. Casually looking to his right Bennie found Lorraine standing next to him. She smiled asking why he'd been opening the store late, and why he'd been drinking so much. Bennie answered by removing a glove to reach in his pocket for a quarter pint bottle of vodka. Grinning at her he took a swig and said he didn't drink that much. Before Lorraine could respond the light turned green and Bennie walked away wishing she'd stay next to Ronald.

The next time they stopped Lorraine stood by Bennie without smiling. This time she meant to aggravate him by inquiring about the pregnant woman who lived in his home after he and Terri broke up. Lorraine wanted to know if she was a family member and whose baby was the woman carrying.

Actually Lorraine was referring to Linda whom she should've recognized from Bennie's hotel room when she and Ronald followed him to Egypt a few years ago. But Lorraine didn't stop there. She also wanted to know why he'd been hanging out with Ronald every other weekend. It was an awkward question since the last time they hung out together was Bennie's birthday last January. Bennie wanted to tell Lorraine he hadn't seen Ronald; but instead he responded the same way as before, with a swig and a smile. If this evening compared to Vienna sausages it was a spoiled can with maggots, but something good was coming before the night was over.

Finally they reached the main rally point for the parade and the crowd thickened. People moved shoulder to shoulder and still Bennie kept watch over Lorraine. Then the most wonderful thing happened. When they got to the avenue that was closed off for the parade, the crowd split their group just when Lorraine stopped to ask a street vendor about a tee shirt. Ronald skated on and no one saw her except Bennie, who let everyone continue walking. Ronald did wait to see if everyone was together, but it was a minute too late, and his wife gone. In a crowd of hundreds Bennie watched Lorraine from fifteen or more yards south of them. He was about to wave his arm and yell when he thought about her conduct at the Christmas party. So instead he smiled in her direction and took a swig.

Carol and William suggested they spread out to find Lorraine while Veronica said if they did that they'd all be lost. The group stayed still while Bennie watched Lorraine's head bobbing like drift wood in an ocean of bodies until it was gone. About that time Veronica suggested that Lorraine might have gotten ahead of them, and they should go north with the flow of the parade, so they did. When they got to the end of the parade an hour later, Lorraine wasn't there so they headed to the Dallas BBQ, and that's where she was.

Bennie stood back listening to the reasoning for her absence, but it was Ronald who bore the brunt of her scolding. Lorraine insisted it was us who lost her which made no sense because we were all still together. Then she asked Ronald to rub her feet until the food arrived. As circumstances would have it Lorraine's food came out last and the order was wrong. It could've been the way she spoke to the waitress, or a coincidence she got fries instead of onion rings. At once Bennie offered to trade his onion rings for fries but Lorraine quickly refused. Everyone ate while Lorraine sat watching and grumbling. It turned out to be a fun night and the best stack of onion rings and baby back ribs Bennie ever had in his life.

The following Friday Ronald conducted one of the finer points of bad behavior by using Bennie for an alibi to spend his first weekend at Kayla's apartment. Ronald lied, telling Lorraine Bennie found a car in Pennsylvania and needed help picking it up. Depending on paperwork and traffic Ronald said he might not be home till Sunday. In reality it was Kayla's birthday and he'd promised to spend the night with her. There was some truth to the story about a car; it's just that Bennie wasn't buying one.

For a birthday gift Ronald got Kayla a used Honda Accord because he worried about her leaving those clubs late at night and asking customers for rides. So he took forty-five hundred dollars and made it the best birthday present she ever got. In turn, she thanked him in every way imaginable. From the time he got there Kayla treated him like a king by means of pampering and romance. She fixed him a drink while making dinner and before they ate Kayla pleasured the royal scepter with an ice cube tucked in her cheek.

After dinner she continued fulfilling his every wanton desire until she fell asleep naked on top of him. Caressing her body Ronald let her sleep until she rolled off, then he went to the bathroom. On top of the hamper was a towel, face cloth, tooth brush and a new bar of soap. He washed in the sink and on the way back to the bed blew out two candles then turned the radio down. As soon as he got under the covers Kayla pressed her body against his side and went back to sleep.

There was one problem that wouldn't go away, and it wasn't lying to his wife. Ronald thought about how Chris looked like he was headed for an early grave when they met to give him the money. Now here was Ronald making the same conscious mistake, abandoning condom use after the first few encounters with Kayla. What would he do if he made Lorraine sick too? It scared him that he was taking a chance on a woman who danced butt naked in front of hundreds of men for money and he couldn't stop himself.

The next morning Ronald woke to the smell of bacon frying. He reached for his watch and on the nightstand next to his wallet were keys to the apartment. He stood next to the bed still naked, wrapping himself in a blue terry cloth robe Kayla had for him and went to the bathroom. The toilet flushing brought her to the bedroom when he came out and she said,

"Ronnie baby, stay in the bed. I'm making you breakfast. When it's ready I'll call you to the kitchen okay?" she said with giddiness.

"Ok baby," he answered turning on the television.

Kayla hurried to the stove removing the bacon to start the eggs. She hadn't been this happy in a long time. Ronnie was good to her and she'd do whatever it took to satisfy him. But like her last serious relationship this wouldn't last if she kept stripping.

Finally breakfast was ready, and she called out,

"Ronnie... come on honey, everything's ready!"

"I'm coming," he said making his way to the table. Before he sat down she said,

"How does the robe fit?"

"It's nice I like it," he answered sitting down.

Kayla smiled setting a glass of orange juice in front of him. Then she put her hand on his shoulder and kissed his cheek then spoke close to his ear,

"Ronnie you knocked me out last night baby you know that?"

"Yeah?"

"Oh yes!"

"Well that's how I do it baby," answering boastfully.

"I know I know, you had me every which way didn't you?" she giggled still hugging him around the neck.

Setting the plate down blissfully her smile was authentic, so different from being on stage. The more he looked he found Kayla was actually pretty and always cheerful. In fact Ronald only saw her angry once because she didn't make any money and the customers were raunchy.

"I made you bacon and eggs, some grits with buttered toast, and here's some jelly if you want," she said opening the jar with pride.

"Do you want anything else?"

"No this is good," said Ronald picking up the fork.

"I don't cook much but I can when I want to. Oh! I put some cheese in your eggs cause I know you like cheese. You like them?" she asked.

"Yeah baby the eggs are good and so are the grits. I never had grits like this," he remarked with food in his mouth.

"It's my aunt's secret recipe and I'll make some for you anytime you want. All you have to do is tell me," she said chuckling while walking to the bedroom.

"Kayla, you're not gonna eat?"

"I can't eat now I want to get dressed. We still going to walk in the park today? I want to see the different colors in the leaves on the trees. They look so nice this time of year."

"Yes, it's your birthday so it's your call," he said before drinking some juice.

"Thank you baby, I'm gonna get my clothes together and take a shower, you eat your breakfast and leave the plate on the table," she said closing the bathroom door behind her.

As Ronald ate Kayla showered, visualizing a better future. Last night she held him while he was asleep and with a soft voice said, "I love you Ronnie." A good man was sitting in her kitchen and even though she'd been the other woman before, this was different because she had a plan for success. Kayla was going to patiently comfort his mind like an old school pimp. Every time Ronnie came to her she'd send him back so drained he'd have no interest in sex for days. Eventually his wife would find out and he'd finally belong to her.

In the afternoon Kayla drove her car downtown finding a space on the west side, then she and Ronald went into Central Park. It was a crisp day and the trees turned autumn colors. The couple found a bench facing the pond then sat close so Kayla could rest her head on his shoulder. She took a calming breath then said,

"This is a wonderful day. I just love when the trees change colors don't you?"

"Yeah they look nice, it's a nice spot."

"Ronnie could we make this our place? This bench right here. Can we call this our spot like when people have a special place no one else knows about? You know, like in the movies when people say I'll meet you at a particular time at our spot, can we?"

"Sure why not," speaking as if he didn't care.

At that moment Ronald wondered how long he'd have to listen to Lorraine complain and what she was gonna have him do once he got home. Kayla, sensing his attention wavering lifted her head to say,

"Ronnie, we need to talk."

"About what!" he snapped.

"Ronnie!" Kayla said hesitantly.

"What you want to talk about now!?" he asked standing up in front of her.

"Why you acting like this. I just want to talk to you. Why you so mad at me, what did I do?" she asked almost crying.

"What did you do?" he said to a question without an answer. Then he continued ranting,

"Shit, I don't need no problems Kayla! You knew how this was gonna work, you knew the deal from the door! I got a wife, we just hanging out that's all, nothing more!!"

Kayla lowered her head, twirling her fingers as Ronald waved his hands like a referee signaling out of bounds.

"I know that, and I would never mess this up. So why are you talking like this honey, you didn't even give me a chance to finish."

Ronald had no idea who he was dealing with. Over the years Kayla's had drinks thrown on her, costumers calling her a bitch among other names. They've laughed at and insulted her for no reason other than to feel better about themselves, so her skin wasn't as thin as she had him believe. He was dealing with a woman who knew how to stroke men's egos.

"Just tell me what you want?' he asked a little quieter.

"Never mind, you're right. Forget about it… I'm fine. Let's talk about something else," she said looking down forcing out a chuckle.

Then she pulled his hand until he sat down leaving a gap between them. She stared at the empty space and said, "I don't want you to go yet. Can we stay a little longer to look at the trees please?"

"Sure," Ronald said as if he didn't care.

"You still gonna stay with me a little while?" Kayla asked in full submission. It was the first time Ronald noticed a scar behind her left ear.

"What did you want to say before?"

"You're not gonna yell at me?" she asked puppy eyed.

Ronald said he wouldn't and without looking up Kayla sighed then said,

"I want to be straight with you and what I'm doing with my life. I don't ever want you to have to guess that's all, and I made some decisions. There's nothing wrong I… I care too much about you to ever mess this up ever. I would never hurt you Ronnie… never okay. Anyway there's something you need to know, actually two things. I wanted to tell you face to face. First…I'm not dancing anymore; I just can't do it… I can't Ronnie."

"What?"

"Yeah that's right," said Kayla moving closer waiting for his reaction.

"If you're not dancing what you gonna do?" he asked as if she was asking for money.

"Wait a minute cause I know what you're thinking, but let me finish please. I don't want anything from you," she said while Ronald stared at her waiting for the punch line.

"I got a job. I'm in training but it's a permanent job… So you wanna know what I'll be doing?" she asked smiling a bit.

"What you doing?" he asked grudgingly.

"I'm gonna be a bank teller," she said with satisfaction.

"A teller, you're working in a bank?" Ronald said sarcastically.

"How about that, I still can't get away from holding those dollar bills," Kayla said laughing then went on.

"I've always been good in math. Shoot math was my favorite subject in high school, I got all A's. That's why when tax time comes around I do tax returns," she bragged.

"You do taxes."

"I told you I do peoples taxes before. Hell I been doing taxes longer than I been dancing."

"Get the fuck outta here, for real?"

"That's right, so I started thinking, why am I still dancing when I don't want to… so I quit. I got no record, I've never been arrested, my credit could be better but that's what I wanted to tell you Ronnie. I started training last week. I have one more week to go and I'll be working on Broadway near 72nd Street," she said gleefully.

Ronald couldn't believe his ears. Then she said, "And if you noticed I stopped using cocaine so if I took a drug test I'd pass! Oh and I'm going back to school this spring semester. Just two classes for now until I get my feet wet then its full-time baby. I missed September enrolment, but it'll give me more time to settle in at work. So I haven't decided if I'm gonna be an accountant, or get a math degree but I'm going to do something!"

Ronald still surprised said, "Well good for you Kayla, I'm happy for you."

"You are? I hoped so."

"Yes I am, I really am," he said pulling her closer then kissing her.

After the news sunk in Ronald felt like a fool for yelling at her and that's what Kayla wanted. He'd had the hook yesterday from sex. She just fed him the line, and now the sinker was coming.

"There's one last thing I have to say and that is… the only person I want seeing me wit out my clothes on is you Ronnie. We just being straight with each other like always. I know you got a wife, I'll never come between that. But you made me want a different life and I'm grateful honey, you have no idea. You made this a birthday I will never forget and as long as you want me I'm here… okay baby," she said kissing him briefly.

"Yeah Kayla I hear you.

"Now you have your own key so you can come whenever you want. But Ronnie don't have no women in my fucking house! Ronnie I swear to God… I know… I would lose it… walking in my house… seeing you… with someone else, ahh hell no!" she said patting her feet on the ground. "Okay baby, I'm just saying we being straight, don't do that to me Ronnie!"

"I won't, I won't Kayla, relax," he said grinning.

"Well all right then," she said kissing him then walking to the pond's edge so he could get a front row view of those hips. After striking some poses she turned around and said,

"Baby, we don't need to eat at City Island. I just wanna spend time with you. I want to go home pick up some Chinese food, and get a video. Plus you know you gotta give me some more of that good lovin, so let's make it an early night okay?"

"That's what you want to do baby?"

"Yes that's what I want baby."

"Well that's what we'll do," he said not caring about the consequences.

The next month in mid-December boredom coupled with the chance to relive that joyous moment Lorraine got lost on Halloween, led Bennie to their Christmas party with confidence. The usual crowd was present and for the first time Veronica's new man Devin. Bennie greeted Lorraine, warmly salivating with anticipation like Pavlov's dog for the first of her insults. Eagerly he waited to deliver a suggestive response he'd seen her walking in the wrong direction that night, and then let her suspicions take over. But after an hour Lorraine said nothing offensive so he tried enticement. Playing the role of a Grinch Bennie grumbled because there were no shrimps or mac and cheese on the menu. Then in a joking manner he'd say, Bah Humbug after anyone mentioned the holiday. With all his prodding Lorraine remained quiet and unresponsive, taking the fun out of why he came. So when it became apparent there'd be no confrontation between them Bennie left with a heart thirsty for payback.

On the drive back to Harlem Bennie wondered why Lorraine wasn't acting her usual gnarly self. When he couldn't figure it out his resentment shifted to Ronald's day of reckoning. It was only a matter of time until Lorraine found out about Kayla. All Bennie had to do was be patient and inconspicuous until that opportunity came like the night of Halloween. And when it did it would be as easy as tilting one domino and watching the rest fall down. However, an answer to Lorraine's unusual mood became clear on Tuesday when he went to the post office and bumped into her sister Sharon.

Bennie was behind Carol on line and when she walked by, she said she'd wait outside. Carol worked as a dental assistant and her husband William was a conductor for New York Transit. They'd been married eight years and Bennie was happy for them. If it weren't for Lorraine and Carol being sisters he would have taken a chance on a relationship with her.

Finally Bennie came out stood next to Carol and she said, "It's good to see you Bennie. You taking care of yourself?"

Her question was genuine nothing like what her sister would ask. Maybe it was because they had different mothers, he thought.

"Carol I been good," Bennie said as they walked closer to her car.

"I wanted to know if you talked to Ronald about what happened at the Christmas party?" she asked.

"No, I talked with him yesterday he didn't mention anything, what's going on?" Bennie asked, looking concerned.

"Let me tell you William and I left right after you did because Devin was acting like an ass. He was talking loud, cursing in front of my kids, and it got to be too much."

"You've got to be kidding," Bennie said skeptically.

"I wish I was and it's hard to feel sorry for Veronica when her man acts like a fool. Bennie…Devin is one of those people who shouldn't drink. He's like little Anthony. Remember how Anthony would get drunk and start trouble? Devin is just like that. You know what's messed up is me and Lorraine have known Veronica since high school, and she always falls for the wrong man I swear! This is what happened Bennie; everyone had just gone in the kitchen. The kids were sitting on the floor in front of me watching TV. Veronica and Devin sat down on the couch. Devin put his arm around Veronica, looked right at me and said, I can't wait to get some of that pussy baby."

"No he didn't," Bennie said abruptly.

"Yes he did! That son of a bitch said it in front of my children Bennie! Then he hurried up and said oops, like he was sorry and started laughing."

"I don't know what to say Carol, I just…" but she interrupted to say,

"And Veronica didn't say a word to him. He just sat there brushing the side of his head with the brush he carries. So after that crap I knew it was time to leave. I made believe I was sick but when we got home I told William what happened. I had to stop him from going all the way back to Long Island. I wasn't gonna have my man wind up in jail because of Devin's bullshit," Carol said with agitation.

"I'm sorry Carol I didn't notice."

Suddenly Bennie realized because he was seeking payback he never saw his buddy's wife in distress. Then Carol said, "but that wasn't the worst of it; let me tell what else Devin did."

"There's more?"

"Oh yeah, before you got there Lorraine pulls me into the bedroom and says Devin hugged her from behind real tight, like all up on her behind, you know."

"What!" Bennie said, then taking a few steps backward.

"That's what Lorraine told me; he humped her behind when they were alone in the kitchen. Then after you got there I saw him feel her butt! Yes he did, he felt her like this, and she slapped his hand away, and I saw that with my own eyes!" she said, demonstrating as if someone was standing next to her.

"Get outta here! Are you serious? That boy needs his ass kicked for real, I'm not playing! So what did Ronald do?"

"I'm not sure he knows, that's why I wanted to talk to you. Ronald hasn't said anything to you about it?"

"No he didn't, but Devin did this while I was there!" Bennie said getting angrier by the minute.

"Yes I looked for you and Ronald but y'all were in the garage. I told Lorraine I was going to tell y'all, but she said she'd tell Ronald herself. Then next thing I knew you were leaving and then that thing happened with my kids, and we left," said Carol while Bennie looked puzzled.

"Damn that must've been when Ronald was showing me the generator in case the power went out. Okay that's why Lorraine was so quiet afterwards."

"You noticed that too."

"Yeah and now I know why. I don't have to tell you me and Lorraine don't get along sometimes, but I would never let somebody hurt her. That's my buddy's wife!" said Bennie proudly.

"I know I know."

"I'm gonna talk to Ronald and see what's going on."

"Fine and I'm going back to work. We got two patients coming for root canals this afternoon so it's gonna be a long day. By the way, when was the last time you had a checkup? And don't lie." She said looking at his mouth while opening her car door.

"It's been three years almost four," he said clicking his teeth together.

"Then you'd better go," Carol said holding his hand from inside to say her final goodbye. When she turned the corner he went home to call Ronald. Loyalty and friendship outweighed past bad feelings, Devin was messing with family, and he had to be corrected.

Inside the Eight Avenue office Ronald sat at the desk reading a magazine when the telephone rang. He picked it up and said, "Eight Avenue Kleenit."

"Ron what's up, how you doing?" Bennie asked.

"I'm cool just reading this magazine about something called a DVD and a CD player. They're gonna take the place of records and tapes," he said enthusiastically.

"You telling me I'm not gonna be playing my records?" Bennie answered pressing the phone to his ear as if it would change what he'd heard.

"That's right; they're starting to put music and movies on these little plastic discs. Instead of the needle on a turntable playing a record a laser reads a disc, it's new technology Ben. You remember the first time we watched a movie on Beta Max at the Center and now everybody's got a VCR, remember that? And what about antennas on top of the TV, they got replaced with a cable box."

"Yeah so."

"Well this is the new thing, no more music or movies on tape," said Ronald swiveling in his chair from side to side.

"You're telling me my albums and all my videotapes I got are going out of style?"

"It's just like reel-to-reel tapes you don't know anybody that has one cause they phasing em out…hold on a second," Ronald said answering another call. When Ronald switched back he said,

"Yup it's gonna happen, you'll see. So what's going on Ben?"

"I called cause I saw your sister-in-law today. Why didn't you tell me you had a problem with Devin," said Bennie trying to figure if Ronald knew.

"Problem…you mean Devin getting a little loud, or when he bumped into Lorraine?"

"Bumped into her, is that what you think he did, bump into her?"

"Yeah that's what Lorraine said. He got a little drunk, stumbled up against her so she put him in his place and that was it!" Ronald said getting annoyed.

Bennie decided if Ronald asked he would tell, and if he didn't he'd leave it alone.

"What did Carol tell you?" Ronald asked sitting still, placing his elbows on the desk.

Now the ball was in Bennie's court. He went for the compassionate drive to the basket but drew a foul by adding more than Carol actually said.

"Carol didn't say Devin bumped into Lorraine, she said he was feeling on your wife's ass, and titties, and stuff! Carol said homeboy humped on Lorraine's butt then squeezed her breast. Then she said when we were in the garage looking at your generator she saw Devin put his hand all on Lorraine's ass! Now that's what she said she saw him do!" Bennie said, waiting for Ronald to respond, and when he didn't Bennie continued.

"That's what Carol said she saw if I remember it right," in case he needed to retract. Ronald stood up but didn't speak right away so Bennie said, "Ron, say the word and we'll go kick this nigga's ass, bust his knee caps, or something so he's knows never to do that shit again!"

"I'll call you back," said Ronald finally.

"At the very least Devin can't come to your house anymore right?"

"Ben I'll call you back when I find out what's going on!"

"What?"

"I wanna know why Lorraine didn't tell me what happened! So I'll call you back!" Ronald said impatiently.

"Okay I hear you buddy let me know what you want to do."

Ronald never called back that day or the next, so Bennie stayed out of it.

After the last episode from the Bronx Terminal Market Bennie never went back, or picked up women walking the street late at night. As his sexual needs grew the choice was clear, he had to start dating again. So for the next two years Bennie got involved in a series of uncommitted relationships replacing trauma and pain, with anger and orgasmic relief.

The most recent conquest was Susie, a school bus driver he met one afternoon before Christmas vacation. Bennie and Mister were waiting at the corner for the light when a school bus stopped. The doors opened and a woman favoring Dionne Warwick spoke from the driver's seat. She said Mister had a beautiful coat, then asked if he was friendly. Bennie told her the dog wouldn't bite her, but he might. Susie Thibodeaux smiled as she left the bus double parked to pet Mister. They had a brief conversation and a few days later met for breakfast. While they ate Bennie learned Susie was born in Louisiana. When she was pregnant at seventeen she and her mom moved to New York. Susie's son was 22 and she'd worked the same job for seven years. Amusingly when Susie spoke she stuttered one word which was "and." She'd say, "And…and…and…and I want sausage with my eggs and…and…and wheat toast with butter."

More intriguing was the French slang called patois she could speak and the main reason for getting her in bed. For almost two months Susie's erogenous words excited Bennie immensely, however her behavior began to leave a sour taste.

It began one weekend after Susie got in the car with a major attitude. She was fed up having to loan her son money after he blew a job at the Board of Education by failing a drug test. So Bennie asked how her son could afford a new car and Susie proudly said she was making the payments. When Bennie suggested Susie stop paying for his car she got mad and stopped talking. They continued in silence while Bennie thought no sex was worth the aggravation he was going through. A song came on the radio and just as he started to bob his head Susie turned to the news. She told him he needed to keep up with what's going on in the world. At that moment Bennie wanted to turn around and take her back, but he said nothing. The next weekend they got together Susie found ways to criticize his driving. She'd say he was going too slow, or to stop when he had time to make the light. It made him wonder did the ten-year age difference make her feel she could boss him around. Whatever her issue, Bennie quickly forgot upon insertion as Susie rewarded with spoken word,

"Je voudrais que bebe, ne s'arretent pas, ne s'arretent pas!"

By now it was the middle of January and Ronald still hadn't spoken about Devin touching Lorraine. That night Bennie picked up Susie for what would turn out to be their last date. They drove to a Cajun restaurant in downtown Manhattan for some Louisiana style food. Bennie parked in the lot then shut off the car when Susie asked him to park in the next row. Bennie asked was something on the ground, but she wouldn't say so he took a look. Seeing nothing, he refused to move and for that Susie barely spoke the entire time they ate dinner. After dinner she had one of those, you're not getting any headaches and asked to be taken home. Bennie walked her to the door and hugged her, knowing he didn't want to see her anymore.

The next day he took the car for an oil change then went to the supermarket. The day after that, Bennie took Mister for a rabies shot and when he returned home Susie called. She sounded confrontational like he'd hoped, making it easier to play his get out of jail free card. Now he referred to the arrangement they made that first day over breakfast. Susie told Bennie she only wanted a friend not a serious relationship and that was music to his ears. Anyhow Susie called just before time to pick up the kids from school.

"Why haven't heard from you, your fingers broken? I was gonna come by your house and…and…and…you didn't call me. Now it's too late. Where you been? I called you two times," she said standing by a payphone near her bus.

"Well hello to you too, what's going on?" Bennie said cynically and Susie ignored him.

"I not talking bout that, I said I haven't heard from you and…and… and I don't like that. Where were you, I wanted to stop by and…and…and now it's time for me to pick up the kids. So you need to call me every day from now on, you hear me?" she said scolding him.

Bennie didn't answer, he wanted Susie to drive more nails in her coffin.

"Just don't do it again and…and…and I'll come by tomorrow."

"No I don't think so, don't come," he said calmly.

"What did you say?"

"I don't want you to come by. As a matter of fact I was thinking about that day you and I had breakfast and you said you just wanted a friend, remember?"

"Yes I remember, so what!"

"Well this ain't working out Susie," Bennie said plainly.

"You saying you're breaking up with me! Is that what you're telling me?"

"Yeah that's what I'm saying Susie."

"Why, what happened? I was tired last time after dinner that's all," she said sounding humble.

"Last time, oh we good honey I wasn't upset. This has nothing to do with anything. It's just…just me not you. It was you who told me when the ride comes to an end we'll split. That's what you said, and that day is here, that's all, you didn't do anything!"

There was a long silence and a sigh then Susie said, "I got to go and…and…and pick up the kids so I'll call you later ok?" She hung up before Bennie could answer and never called again. Before the month was over Bennie met Ganelle in the Spanish restaurant across the street from Yankee stadium.

That night the snow melted leaving a dingy black mixture of dirt and salt over the sidewalk. Bennie stood at the counter ordering rice and beans, roast pork, with fried plantains, when the heavyset woman ahead suggested he add some crispy pieces of pork skin to his meal. Ganelle was a beautiful butter scotch colored Vanessa Williams despite her weight. Smiling, Bennie took her advice then asked for her number at the cash register. He told her he wanted to let her know if he liked the skin but really he was curious to see what it was like to be with a large woman.

Ganelle told Bennie her boyfriend wouldn't like that, so he said they didn't need to tell him, and they both laughed. Instead, she wrote down his number saying she'd be in touch. One evening a few days later she called while her boyfriend was sleeping. Mostly she complained about her job as a token booth clerk and that her man watched too much television. A few more calls with the last ending in sexy conversation made Ganelle set a date. Two days before Valentine's Day at the train station around the corner from Bennie's house they met. She walked out asking where the smell of food was coming from. Bennie showed her the Famous Fish spot on the corner, and she had to have some. They stood in line just like when they met, then took the food back to his house to eat.

Bennie learned Ganelle wasn't used to being treated like a lady. She was surprised by gentlemanly courtesy like holding doors, and pulling out her chair when she sat down. So they ate and talked at the kitchen table until Bennie found out Ganelle's father was born in the Dominican Republic and her mother was from the Bronx. Hearing of her father's Spanish background Bennie hoped for the same lingual capability he heard from Susie. To his disappointment Ganelle spoke only a few phrases in Spanish. But one he would come to enjoy was her calling him her Negrito sausage.

When they finished Bennie took her to the living room for a night cap and soon they were kissing. As Ganelle's tongue searched his mouth and Bennie grew excited, a few chunks of shrimp and fries went down his throat. Even that wasn't going to stop him from getting between Ganelle's big pretty legs. They stood up, Bennie ready to take off his pants, but Ganelle pushed him back. She wanted to freshen up taking her bag upstairs to the bathroom. Bennie took a Ronnie Laws album and played it, mocking Ronald's prediction that records were going out of style. Then he sat on the couch unbuttoning his shirt and taking off his shoes. He removed condoms from his pocket and set them on the end table. Ganelle returned wearing a red lace bra with matching panties like they'd talked about over the phone a few days prior. She posed by the door touching her breasts while he looked at her big pretty thighs. They never made it to the bedroom and still he got to hear her shout aye!...aye!...aye!

When Bennie met Ganelle the next time he found two sides to her. She had the skill of Linda Lovelace with the tears of a clown like Pagliacci. After sex Ganelle would tell more about her life than Bennie wanted to hear. Lying next to him she told how her uncle molested her when she spent the summer in the Dominican Republic at twelve years old. Her father's younger brother Ramon came into her room the first week. It went on for months until she came back home, and she never told her father. She said Ramon told her he couldn't help it because she was so cute. And when she wasn't talking about her uncle, Ganelle would put herself down. She called attention to fat under her arms and stomach, none of which Bennie cared about. He refused to be her therapist when she had a man at home for that. Tired of being sucked into her pool of sadness, Bennie stopped seeing her and moved on.

The next week Ronald met with Bennie on Riverside after the stores closed. They took a bench facing the Hudson River where Palisades Park use to be. First Ronaldtalked about Chris getting out of the hospital then got to the point about Lorraine and Devin.

"Lorraine didn't want me to hurt Devin, that's why she didn't tell me what he did," Ronald said looking at his watch.

"Okay I can see that. But did it happen like I said?" Bennie asked looking at his buddy then lighting a cigarette.

"Yes she told me it was more than what she said the first time, yes, so that's all there is to that," he said somberly looking for agreement.

"Alright Ron let me ask you something? When everybody went home why couldn't she tell you then, or even the next day? And him cussing around the kids...c'mon what's up with that?"

"I understand and it doesn't make sense, you're right."

"What about Devin...have you talked to him cause we can roll over there right now, you hear me!" said Bennie loudly.

"No not yet, Lorraine straightened Devin out so there won't be any more problems."

"I still think that nigger should get his ass kicked, seriously, and I'm not messing with him anymore, I can't do it Ron... I can't. And by the way, what's up with brushing his hair, that shit is annoying. The dude is always brushing the sides of his head, what's up with that?" Bennie asked trying not to laugh.

"I don't know, he thinks he's cute I guess," Ronald said amusingly.

By now the woman walked up and said, "baby… can you spare a cigarette?"

Bennie guessed she was in her forties and nice looking enough to ask what she was up to, plus he just wanted to get away. He gave her a smoke and she cupped her hand to his for the light then said, "What yawl up to this evening?"

"Well he's about to split and I'm gonna hang out with you baby," Bennie said boldly.

"Oh you are," she answered playfully turning to the side showing off her figure.

"Yes I am, just hang out for a minute. So we'll do something, maybe have some hot wings, I don't know," Bennie said standing up like he was ready to go.

"Yeah let's do that buddy," Ronald said smiling at the woman while shaking Bennie's hand.

"My car is over there honey, let's go."

"Can we stop at the store I'm thirsty," the woman asked.

"Sure there's one right up the street," Bennie said waving to Ronald when he drove by. This woman was a welcome distraction from his growing anger, and when they got in the store he made sure she was all woman. He got a six pack of beer while she got orange juice and some peppermint balls. They stood at the counter when Bennie said,

"I need two boxes of rough riders with this,"

"Why you buying condoms, I got some," she said quietly in his ear.

"I still need some baby," he said feeling confident they were going to have sex.

After they left the store Bennie wasn't going to take her to his home, so he drove to the toll booth and went on Randall's Island. By the time he shut the car off he'd forgotten her name. She had a fifteen-year-old daughter and was a grandmother already, and that was the attraction for Bennie. He'd never slept with a grandmother before. They did eventually have sex that night in the car and Bennie thought it was safe to bring her to his house the next time, so he gave her his number. A week later she called but he was busy, and she never called back.

By the spring an old friend took notice of the women Bennie was bringing home. He'd known Gloria from childhood because she lived four houses away with her mother and father. One night Bennie returned after dropping Ganelle off, Gloria unexpectedly asked when she was gonna have her chance to ride him? While it made Bennie feel uncomfortable, he took her out to eat then they made a date for her to come to his house the following Friday. At stages in his teenage years Bennie had fantasies about Gloria because she was older than him, but that was fifteen years ago. Presently there was unpleasant pressure to have sex with her when he didn't want to. Her bossy nature and his aggravation towards women weren't going to mix. So Friday when Gloria called to say she'd be over after she showered Bennie decided to leave. It took twenty-seven seconds from the time he closed his front door and got to his car. Half hour later he was sitting in his sister's living room in the Bronx. Demetrice laughed and poked fun that he'd run away from a woman, but he didn't care. Then after midnight Bennie left to go home. Days later when he saw Gloria she didn't say anything about that night and he didn't either, but she never flirted again.

The rest of the year into the next felt like one long day split between hanging out with Ronald once a month to a few women whose names he never committed to memory. Even worse, Bennie modeled his sick employee Chris by playing Russian roulette with these women by wearing condoms sometime. Starting with one he met walking past the KFC off Lenox Avenue and 145th Street. They drove behind the bus depot and parked. He tossed his chicken in the back and reclined his seat. She teased him with her mouth by bringing him close and stopping to ask if he wanted more. Finally he let her straddle him without protection where she preceded to call him a bastard over and over until she came.

The next no name was a woman was a woman he met after leaving Demetrice's house. She was a prostitute with a pad and a pencil because she couldn't speak or hear. They had sex in her apartment after which she kept slapping the top of her head and grinning. When Bennie left she wrote on the paper and tore it from the pad. Outside her building he unfolded the note that said he could come back on Tuesdays and Thursdays.

Then there was the one he met while he and Ronald were talking outside the Chinese restaurant where Eighth Avenue and St Nicholas meet. He and Ronald were waiting when the woman walked up and started talking about how she needed something to do, and she wanted to do it with them. She was nice looking and let Bennie rub her behind when no one was looking. She said he was the king and whatever he wanted to do was fine. She was prepared to go with them but there was an uneasy vibe Bennie felt, like with Gloria, so he asked for her number. He told her he'd be back in a few hours, and they would hook up. She gave him her number and a pocket Bible which was strange.

Bennie looked at the number then said, "Baby… there's a lot of sixes in your number. 212 566 7666, what's up with that?" Bennie said emphasizing each six.

She responded with an eerie smile then walked away.

"You gonna call her?" Ronald asked.

"Hell no, you see all these sixes in this phone number no way, that girl is weird as hell. She kinda gave me the chills I'll pass," said Bennie balling up the paper and shooting in the trash can by the corner before they headed to the bar.

The next woman was one Bennie couldn't forget because her behavior forced him to rethink how he was living. Gwen lived in a three-bedroom home off Sutphin Blvd in Queens. She had five kids and a husband who worked for the city as a bus driver. Her problem was like so many others, she'd become a victim of the growing crack epidemic. Gwen looked good because she hadn't been an addict for long, but she'd do anything for money.

Bennie's first invitation to Gwen's home came in the afternoon while her husband was at work. A boy of three and his sister maybe a year older ate lunch in the kitchen while a six-month-old in a baby seat sucked on a pacifier. Bennie sat on the couch with the baby looking at him. Gwen came from the kitchen to say,

"Before I forget, if my husband comes home you're a friend of my mother's and you stopped by to let me know her car isn't ready, that's all you have to say."

"Are you sure he's gonna go for that?"

"He's working right now. I'm just saying if he came home that's all you have to say. My mama's car ain't ready and I'll take care of the rest," she said walking back to the kitchen.

That dress flowed over her cheeks like the curves on a Jaguar XKE and he was gonna take her for a test drive. From the kitchen Gwen said, "You all go in the room and play, and don't come out until I come and get you hear?"

Gwen closed the door, walked back to the living room pulled the curtain back and looked outside, then turned to face him. Her lips were shapely like the family picture on the wall behind her. She walked closer and said, "you ready?"

"You sure this is okay Gwen?"

"I'm sure, it's fine," she said removing her panties from under her dress.

"What about this one?" he asked pointing to the baby watching.

"What about him?" she answered in a sexy voice kneeling in front him.

"He is right here with us!"

"Listen…those two in the room, they can talk… he can't talk so it's fine," she said with eyes on his crotch.

He gave her thirty dollars and she unzipped his pants and went to work. It was uncomfortable to see mom while the baby sucked his pacifier, but she kept at it and things began to change. In the midst of pleasure she went to the window to look out again. This time Bennie walked behind her with a loaded condom, opened the door to that Jag and drove her around the track.

The next time Bennie saw Gwen she revealed no sexual or moral limitations. After they had sex she went to the bathroom then straight to the front door. Gwen told him she had to go out for a minute, and he had to stay with the kids. Before he could say no, Gwen was down the front steps and out of sight. The door slamming echoed like the sound of bars to a prison. Trapped, he sat on the couch across from the baby who always watched. Gwen didn't bother to tell him what to say if her husband came home, or if the kids asked for her. A few minutes later he wondered what would happen if she never came back or got hit by a car. Then the baby turned his head away from the window and started to look at him and laughed. It was odd, as if the baby's expression let Bennie know how stupid he was. That abstract mind Bennie's father praised was working overtime. He wondered if the baby was thinking about screaming so his siblings could come out and cry because their mother wasn't home.

Bennie looked apologetic at the family photo on the wall, wondering was a piece of ass worth all this drama when there were so many other women. Then he heard a crackle from the kitchen and went to investigate. On the front burner was a pot of SpaghettiOs bubbling so he turned it off then went back to the couch. Gwen never asked him to keep an eye on the stove. What if he decided to leave and the house caught fire. The baby looked at Bennie as if to say, are you getting the message now?

Petrified and broken he looked towards the ceiling and said,

"Father I know I shouldn't have come here and I'm sorry. If you get me out of this I'll never come back here again Father…never! And…and I'm gonna slow down with these women and act right!"

A few minutes later Gwen came back went right into the kitchen, came back out, and said,

"I forgot to tell you to turn off the stove, but you did…thank you."

Without letting on he was aggravated Bennie said, "I got you baby. You see your kids are fine, and those two never came out so they didn't know you were gone. And little guy here, he just sat there looking around."

"That's cause he's got an old man's soul you know, like he knows what's going on sometimes. Yup, that's my little man so you wanna do anything else?" she asked pulling back the curtain to look out the window.

"No I got to get going,"

"Well then I'm gonna feed my babies and clean up. When I'm gonna see you again baby?" she asked looking at the clock.

"Next week, I'll call you," he said walking to the door.

The same way he counted the seconds leaving his home before Gloria got there, Bennie was inside the car and driving away in less than thirty. Once home he remained thankful for a couple of days, but like most that are granted a favor, relax after the benefit is reaped. True to his word Bennie he did make changes. He never called Gwen again. He stopped picking up random women, and going to strip clubs. In addition he vowed not to date old acquaintances, and women from the neighborhood. It would take a dysfunctional case of embarrassment to get his attention the next time.

Chapter 7

There came a weekend Ronald and Bennie went to hang out at the Wren's Nest, but it was closed. Max, a former bartender from the Nest opened his own place three blocks away so they went. Max was a slim, charismatic man from Somalia, with looks that attracted ladies, especially rich ones. It was probably how he was able to open a place in his name. When Max saw them he yelled their names like they were celebrities making introductions around the bar until he stopped at two women who were there for the first time. Cynthia and Camellia were bartenders from Moe's Caribbean who worked with Max in the past. Ronald shook Camellia's hand wearing that glove to hide his ring while Bennie introduced himself to Cynthia. Cynthia had silky auburn hair flowing past her shoulders while her neckline was just low enough to show the hint of her breasts. The women invited them to sit so they ordered a round of drinks. Reminded of being trapped with Gwen's kids Bennie steered the conversation to what he wanted to know. Both women had no children and lived alone. Cynthia didn't even have a cat to get in the way, so he was happy to order another round. Sometime later with her permission Bennie nibbled on Cynthia's earlobe until he was invited to her place. Bennie accepted, leaving Ronald and Carmella at Max's.

He held Cynthia's hand until the cab came and they got in the back seat. Throughout the ride they caressed intimately until arriving at 106th Street on the Eastside. Anxiously Bennie gritted his teeth as they took of each other's clothes and made it her bed. It was time to punch the clock and go to work pleasuring her with the full package strokes. Ready to mount, missionary man assumed the position then Cynthia said, "Are you sure this is what you want?"

No she didn't utter the same phrase as Terri, he thought.

"What did you say?" asked Bennie, freezing like a mannequin.

"I'm ready baby come on!" Cynthia said pulling on his waist.

"No, what did you say the first time?"

"All I said was I know what you want baby come on," said Cynthia inching closer.

"No you didn't, you said is this what you want!" he said with suspicion.

This was Terri all over again, and that thought terminated his erection like an ice cream cone in the desert.

"What are you waiting for?" she asked becoming annoyed.

"Nothing," said Bennie backing up looking for his underwear.

"Wait a minute… are you leaving? I know you're not leaving!" Cynthia said sitting up watching him dress.

"Yeah."

"What did I do?" she asked, covering her breasts with the sheet.

"Nothing…you didn't do anything."

"You know what…there's something fucking wrong with you. I'm over here waiting and you're fuckin playing games, and I don't get it! You're putting on your clothes. What kinda man turns down some free pussy?" she said stretching the word man.

"Look this ain't gonna work out, I'm sorry" Bennie said feeling more confident once his shoes were on.

"Oh you sorry, I know you sorry, real sorry. Look don't say nothing else… you fucking faggot! I can't believe I'm wasting my time with your stupid ass. You know what…get the fuck out of my house, sorry bastard!!" she said running past wrapped in the sheet to open the door.

He left, walking down the hallway to the elevator but decided to take the stairs. That's when she said before slamming the door, "You know what, you're pitiful; you're a sad excuse for a man!!"

If Bennie was hesitant before, he was ready for that long overdue sabbatical now. His call for the Lord's intervention became an indicator to his Spirit to make a stronger connection and he listened. So he cut down on drinking liquor and stopped neglecting the business. He promised he wasn't going to have unprotected sex, or deal with married women again. For a time he felt the need to be still and concentrate on a better life. That meant not going to the Halloween parade, and skipping Lorraine and Ronald's Christmas party. The holiday music with Veronica's boyfriend Devin being invited was enough to stay away.

New Year's Eve was lonely like the last one except he cooked a traditional meal consisting of black-eyed peas a pork roast, and greens. Then he and Mister sat in the living room to watch the ball drop while listening to sporadic gunfire echoing for the first few minutes. Then he went to bed with an understanding how people can be sad enough to end their lives.

Kayla on the other hand was doing great, and looking forward to 1992. She'd settled into her job, made new friends at the bank, and within eight months was offered a supervisory position. After that Kayla got rid of everything that reminded her she'd been stripping. She stopped snorting cocaine, changed her telephone number so promoters couldn't call, and replaced her outlandish outfits with practical lingerie a housewife would wear. A new outlook started her wanting to own a business-like Ronald. With tax season coming, if she had a staff more returns could be filled, and maybe one day she'd have her own company. One thing she didn't let go of was her friendship with Diamond.

Months ago Kayla wanted to tell Ronald her good news for his birthday. She sat by the phone with a watch purchased from Cartier, but he never came. He called the next day to apologize then came by for a quickie during the week. Kayla chalked her disappointment up to problems with being the other woman and moved on. But this Friday two weeks into the New Year Ronald was going to make everything up by taking her to hang out with his friend. They were going to have a few drinks, and afterwards he promised to stay with her until Monday. For a long time Kayla dodged advances from her one of the male tellers, the bank manager, the token booth clerk, and men just walking by on the street. For the time she was with Ronald he was the only one, so she couldn't wait to see him. This time he was outside double-parked waiting for Kayla after work. She came out with co-worker Joan, introducing Ronald as her boyfriend. After Joan left Kayla posed so he could see how professional she looked in her grey business suit. Without thinking, she leaned in kissing him until she began to sweat. Everything was fine as far as Kayla was concerned, Ronald was here and that was all she cared about.

Shortly after, they walked into Max's to find Bennie at the end of the bar. Kayla stood between them as Bennie admired her new look and said, "Kayla…I could have walked right past you I swear, you look so different."

"Do I? And what do you think, is it good?" she asked really wanting Ronald to take notice.

"You look great Kayla, very professional! But you didn't have to dress up for me," said Bennie.

"I didn't. I dress like this most days except casual Friday," said Kayla adding her usual giggle.

"Casual Friday…what are you talking about?"

"At my job silly, you know at the bank."

"You work at a bank?" Bennie said believing she was still stripping.

"Yes… I been working at the bank more than a year; didn't Ronnie tell you? Why didn't you tell him Ronnie?"

"I told you a while ago… remember?" Ronald said.

"Yeah…yeah he did, um I just forgot; I've had a lot on my mind. But that's good to hear," Bennie said covering for Ronald.

"Well guess what, I got more good news. I just got a promotion. I'm a supervisor now, can you believe it! And it's all because of you Ronnie. You made me want to do better and I am, so the next round is on me," Kayla said happily jumping up and down. She was about to whisper in his ear when he asked suspiciously, "how did you get to be supervisor?"

"How?… never being late, having perfect attendance, and never having my cash drawer come up short that's how. Next thing I knew my manager just asked me and I said yes. He told me he liked the way I handled this rude customer that came in one day," Kayla said proudly smiling at Ronald.

"That's great but I'm shocked, I gotta tell you," said Bennie congratulating her again.

She hopped up and down giggling, then after hugging Ronald said,

"Ronnie did you show him the watch I got you for your birthday?"

Ronald put his arm on the bar pulling his sleeve back a bit.

"I wanted to get it engraved but I didn't… its nice right? That's straight from Cartier!" Kayla boasted while rubbing Ronald's hand.

Bennie took a drink and jokingly replied, "Damn that is nice. You got one for me?"

"Sorry, just for my baby. You got to get your own my brother," she said laughing before kissing Ronald on the side of his mouth. It was turning out to be the most fun Kayla had had in a long time. Then she whispered in Ronald's ear how hot she was, and described briefly what she was going to do when they got home. Minutes later the couple sitting next to Bennie left. He pointed to the chair, but she was happy to stand close squeezing Ronald's hand through those black gloves.

They'd been there about a half an hour when Ronald put his beer down. He abruptly removed Kayla's arm from his shoulder as if he'd seen a ghost. Then turned to Bennie and said, "Lorraine's here, she's here!"

"What…where?" Bennie asked spotting Lorraine walking inside.

Kayla stared into her drink as Ronald pushed her closer to Bennie then scooted his chair away. As his wife made a bee line in their direction

Ronald created further distance from Kayla by pushing her against Bennie's leg. Then he whispered to Kayla,

"I don't know what she's doing here baby, but don't say anything… please!!"

With time running out and one second left on the clock Kayla held her jaws tight and leaned cozily onto Bennie. Two or three years ago leaning against a man wouldn't have been an issue, but this was Ronald making her feel dirty. Nonetheless Kayla accepted her situation, forcing a smile for Ronald's sake.

"So this is where you guys are hanging out now," Lorraine said policing the area.

"Lorraine what are you doing here?" Ronald asked wondering how much she witnessed before he'd spotted her.

"Me and Veronica wanted to get out, so we came down to go to the Wren's Nest, found out it was closed, so we rode around. That's when I saw our car parked up the block and I figured you all were close. How long has the Nest been closed?" Lorraine said looking closely at Kayla before letting Ronald kiss her.

Those lips were supposed to be on her body tonight Kayla thought. Still she continued playing her part resting her hand on Bennie's thigh. Lorraine noticed and asked,

"Bennie, aren't you going to introduce me to your friend? Never mind, you too slow. Hi, I'm Lorraine, Ronald's wife, and you are…" Lorraine said extending her hand showing off her two-carat wedding ring.

Kayla was slow to speak so Bennie answered,

"Lorraine this is Kayla, Kayla…Lorraine."

"Nice to meet you," Kayla answered in a chilly voice.

"Kayla that's a nice name…funny Bennie never mentioned you. You're a tiny little thing. How long have you two been seeing each other, and why didn't you bring her to the Christmas party Bennie?" Lorraine asked standing close enough that Kayla could feel her breath.

"He wanted to, but I was working late," said Kayla thinking about the last woman that tried to intimidate her because she was taller.

"Oh okay, so what do you do Kamila…what?" Lorraine asked hoping to catch Kayla's last name.

"I'm a supervisor at a bank, and it's Kayla. Just call me Kayla," she said proudly asking Bennie to order another drink before she left for the ladies room.

Inside Kayla closed the stall door heartbroken, humiliated, and apoplectic. She struggled to calm herself, but after seeing Lorraine she couldn't understand how Ronald would choose that woman over her. The polish on two of her nails was chipped, and her hands were huge and ashy. I look way better than that bitch Kayla thought.

Once again she'd given her all to a man who was pushing her aside. If it weren't for the people she would have screamed at the top of her lungs. The worse part wasn't Ronald's arm around his wife, or being ignored. She thought that day might come when she'd need to pretend, those were the rules of the game. The agony was how easily he pushed her away, and then turned her over to Bennie like she was worthless. Still Kayla refused to cry. If this disgrace had to happen for Ronald to recognize her value, it would be worth it.

So Kayla boldly left the stall and stood in front of the mirror to fix her face. Yeah even upset I'm better looking than his wife she thought, touching up her hair and straightening her clothes. Then she washed her hands, threw the paper towel in the trash like it was a basketball, took a deep breath and marched back into the lion's den.

Bennie and Lorraine were arguing about Mike Tyson when Kayla resumed her position.

"All I'm saying is the woman was clever that's all. And if she gets some money out of the deal that's good for her, that's all I'm saying," Lorraine blurted as Ronald looked out the window.

"Wait a minute if the woman filed a false accusation on Tyson for rape and he didn't do it, that ain't right. That ain't never gonna be right that's all I'm saying, now let's drop it!" said Bennie watching Kayla go into her purse.

Kayla drank her shot, placed the empty glass on a hundred-dollar bill and told the bartender to give everyone another round. Until Kayla knew how Ronald was going to get rid of his wife she decided to mute her humiliation with liquor, while remaining cozy with Bennie. As Kayla read the labels on the bottles behind the bar Lorraine touched her on the shoulder and asked,

"Kayla, what do you think about Tyson?"

"I heard both sides of the story and to me what they say he did, it just doesn't add up. I don't think he raped her. He always been a little touchy feely with women and that's it. Plus, to tell you the truth, it's not about the money, it's about how you live your life and how you treat people. I would never accuse a man of something he didn't do so I could get paid," she said looking in Ronald's direction.

"Well if you keep hanging out with him you'll change your mind one day," Lorraine said referring to Bennie.

After that remark Bennie was about to lose his temper with Lorraine, and he knew just what to say to shut her up. He only had to ask Lorraine if she'd seen her sister's husband William lately, or how he was doing. Depending on her answer he'd ask if Willian ever apologized for getting drunk and rubbing her ass at their Christmas party. Then Ronald would come to Lorraine's rescue instead of asking her to stop making trouble. Incidents like these were precisely why Bennie believed their friendship was strained.

At that precise moment Kayla looked at Bennie then raised her glass. It was as if someone hit the pause button on his temper and he smiled for Kayla. Yes for her sake he'd let this one go, but the next time he felt this way he wasn't going to look the other way.

"Lorraine, I said I don't want to talk about it anymore. You said what you had to say, I said what I had to say so let's drop it! This is my birthday!" said Bennie.

"You're right, so here's to you buddy…cheers," Ronald said taking a drink looking warily in Kayla's direction. Annoyed Bennie stood up and said,

"Kayla, I'll be right back."

"Sure sweetie hurry back," she said sounding distressed.

As Kayla took his seat Bennie whispered in her ear,

"It's gonna be alright."

The further away Bennie walked Kayla's chest felt tighter like the onset of a heart attack. But when Kayla saw Ronald heading in the direction of the men's room too she actually became lightheaded, like the first time she danced in front of an audience. Now the mission was to fight her female instinct of jealously and have a civil conversation with her man's wife. By doing this she would show Ronald true worthiness by protecting him.

Before the bathroom door could close Ronald came in behind Bennie. When he saw who it was his jaw dropped and with a chaotic look Bennie said,

"Dude, you left them out there alone… are you nuts? What if Lorraine finds out?"

"How she gonna find out? Trust me Kayla isn't gonna say anything," he answered with amusement standing in front of the urinal. Then he took his gloves off and put them in his pocket.

"Oh you got it like that" Bennie said standing in front of the sink.

"Yes buddy, I be knocking her socks off, you hear me. That bitch ain't gonna say nothing cause she knows if she does it's over. Plus I'm not gonna let Lorraine ask all kind of questions till she finds out either. So all I need you to do is hang back for a bit after me and Lorraine leave and I'll handle the rest later," Ronald said conceitedly.

"All right playboy, you the man, handle your business," Bennie replied hoping to hear a fight if it broke out from the men's room.

"Okay here I go. I'll call you tomorrow, if not, Monday the latest," Ronald said looking in the mirror before leaving.

Less than five minutes later Bennie returned to find Ronald and Lorraine already gone.

"Kayla what happened, where did they go?" he asked, not thinking Ronald would leave so quickly.

"They left...there they are," said Kayla pointing outside at them crossing the street.

"Well what did he say?" Bennie asked.

"Ronnie said and I quote... Kayla it was nice to meet you. You take care of yourself, and tell Ben I'll talk to him later. Lorraine said...It was nice to meet you, hope to see you again," said Kayla looking utterly disgusted.

"That was it?" he asked with disbelief.

"Yup that was it. He said it was nice to meet me, then he left! Nice to meet you, hope to see you again!" she repeated irately.

"I'm sorry Kayla, I don't know what to say I..."

"You don't have to apologize, really it's not your fault. Let me have two more please," she said to the bartender, and then looked down at her shoes.

Silently Bennie stood next to Kayla until the drinks came, then he felt obliged to talk,

"So tell me about your new job. How you like working in a bank?"

"It's just like my last job except I can't take the money home with me," she said sadly.

"What do you mean by that?"

"Nothing, "said Kayla.

"Okay now I'm not used to seeing you like this. You're always smiling and laughing, don't lose that for anyone you hear me. Now how's the job for real?" Bennie asked sounding tough. She look pissed off at him but decided to answer,

"I like what I'm doing I really do, and the people are nice. Sometimes you get an angry customer but that goes with the job."

"You surprised me you know that. I'm really happy for you…really,"

"Thank you, you want another drink? Do people ask for your last name when they meet you I mean really, why'd she do that? Why does she need to know my last fucking name?" Kayla asked.

"I don't know and no I'm good, this drink is it for me," Bennie said.

"Just have one more with me and I'll make this my last one please. I don't really drink, but I need this right now," she asked putting on a pouty face.

"Okay I'll have one more but this ones on me," he said.

"Nope, sorry I can't let you do that. It's your birthday so I got it. Let's have another," she said pointing to their glasses.

During the awkward silence Kayla wondered how stupid Ronald thought she was, hiding his wedding ring under those gloves whenever they were out. She saw his ring the first time she went in the laundry to do her clothes. She finished her drink then said,

"Thanks for staying with me for a little bit. I'll see you again I guess and enjoy your birthday Bennie."

Then Kayla stood up to take her change off the bar. She hugged Bennie, this time keeping the proper distance until she breathed a sigh of relief. After that Bennie said,

"Kayla you know I'm not gonna let you go home by yourself."

"Wait a minute let's get one thing straight! It's true I'm feeling some kinda way about what went on tonight, but I'm not drunk, and I'm not going home with you, sorry can't do it," she said putting a stick of gum in her mouth.

"Oh really… well that's not what I meant. I never said you had too much to drink, and I wasn't asking you to come home with me! I was trying to say we're both going uptown we could share a cab, but that's cool you do you," Bennie said ready to walk away.

"Wait…I feel so stupid, I'm sorry, that makes a lot of sense. I should've known that's not the kind of guy you are, I'm sorry, it's been a rough night. Can we just leave?" Kayla said humbly.

"Sure, so we'll drop you off then I'll take the cab the rest of the way."

"Fine when you say it like that it makes sense, let's do that," Kayla said with her usual giggle.

As the blocks passed by the window of the taxi Kayla felt more foolish. Ronald had the nerve to say nice meeting you then left with the watch she bought him. The idea she was going to spend another night alone irked her more as the liquor influence grew. At the next stoplight Kayla looked at Bennie, remembering the night they first met. Ironically it was his birthday being celebrated that night also. Bennie had a chance to have sex with Diamond and turned her down, something men rarely did. If Kayla did decide to seduce him it would be a stimulating challenge.

"I just thought of something funny," said Kayla chuckling.

"What?"

"Two years ago when we met, you were celebrating your birthday remember?"

"You know you're right I sure was, and it has been two years. Time sure does fly, I can't believe it," Bennie said smiling.

"Don't say it loud, but do you remember the name of the place?" Kayla asked slapping him on the arm.

"No, I really can't but I remember that night. How's your friend what's her name?"

"You're talking about Diamond."

"That's right her name is Diamond. How's she doing?"

"Honestly I don't know. We don't talk much since, you know, I stopped, and got a job. She'll be calling me soon to do her taxes. You want me to tell her you asked about her?"

"Nah that's alright, but what you mean when you say you gonna do her taxes?"

"Sweetie I been preparing returns for years and I do good work. Tax season is when I make a little extra money and that's because I always enjoyed numbers, it just comes natural to me," she bragged.

"For real?"

"Yup, I like it so much I decided to make math my major!" she giggled.

"Kayla you're certainly amazing, I mean it, you've come a long way."

Finally their taxi turned the corner and began slowing down until he was told to stop. A group of teenagers were sitting on the stoop when Kayla said, "Bennie you see that guy in the dark coat next to the fat one?"

"Yeah I see him, is he giving you problems?"

"Every now and then, so would you mind walking me upstairs and staying just for a few minutes please?" she asked placing her hand on his.

"Sure, I'll go up with you."

"Thank you Bennie," she answered sounding relieved.

Kayla insisted on paying the driver then Bennie followed her to the entrance. The boy in the dark coat moved to the side speaking politely to her when they passed by. Once she unlocked her door Bennie said, "alright Kayla I'll talk to you later."

"No, no wait just… come inside, for a minute please?" she said softly.

Curious about this fragment of Ronald's life, Bennie allowed Kayla to pull him inside while turning on the light.

"Bennie, thanks I appreciate it, just have a seat, I'll be there in a minute. Turn on the TV, the remotes over there," she said pointing to the couch before going to the kitchen.

Kayla's apartment wasn't what he expected at all. Instead of clothes lying about, the living room was neat. She had a painting on the wall of a couple lying on the floor next to the fireplace. Suddenly Kayla's cat brushed against his ankle then went under the couch.

"Kayla your cat is out here!" he yelled to the next room.

"Her name is dog," she answered back.

"Dog, you're joking right!"

"No I thought naming my cat Dog would always make me laugh and it does. It's funny to call a cat Dog," she said from the other room.

Then Bennie said, "I see you got a picture of Malcolm and King over here."

"Thank you, I always liked that photo of the two of them. I used to wonder what would've happened if they'd more time to know each other better?" she asked removing her shoes at her bedroom door.

"I think after Malcolm came from Mecca he had different ideas about Elijah Muhammad. I think, like all of us, he had to grow but never got the chance," Bennie said looking at his watch.

"You're right we've all got to grow that's for sure, including me. But just sit for a minute these shoes are killing my feet and I been in them all day," Kayla said closing the door.

One of Kayla's bathroom doors opened to the living room and one lead to her bedroom. Bennie heard the shower come on and wondered what she was doing. In the bed room Kayla removed her makeup, stripped off her suit, throwing the bundle in the bottom of the closet, then got in the shower.

Afterwards she put on lotion and the new rose-colored nightgown Ronnie was supposed to see. Kayla was about to put on perfume then changed her mind. Why waste it when she wasn't going out. She put the bottle down then put on an oversized plaid chenille robe, and pink bunny slippers. Before she went out she kept the shower cap on her head for effect. Kayla figured Bennie had seen her at her sexiest, this time she simply wanted to use a different costume. When she walked out Bennie said, "oh shit!"

"What?" she asked.

"Kayla, are you serious?" he asked with wide eyes.

"What, this is okay. I mean I think this is appropriate while you're here right?"

Bennie noticed her slippers and started laughing.

"What's wrong?" she asked.

"Nothing, I just never saw you like…"

"This is what I wear when I'm home… mostly, what else would I have on. Now I know you don't think I'd wear what I had on when we met, do you?" she asked chuckling.

"No, of course not, it's just every time I see you, you look different. But your slippers are the bomb."

"I'm glad you like em as a matter of fact I have some for you."

Kayla went back to the bedroom grabbed the picture of Ronald she kept on her nightstand, and threw it on top of that pile of dirty clothes in the closet. Then she stood on her toes to reach a shoe box on the shelf.

"Happy birthday this is for you… enjoy."

Inside was a pair of brown slippers shaped like Teddy Bears. Kayla got them for Ronald weeks ago but if she had her way Bennie was going to get much more, then she went to the kitchen.

"I can't take this Kayla," he said shaking his head.

"No, I got those for your birthday, its fine. You can wear them when you're at home; no one has to know. Now I want you to eat some of these chicken wings before you go, and relax we're good. Bennie you been straight up with me from day one, you really have, that's the truth. And you know what else I noticed about you?" she said continuing the flattery while giving him a plate.

"What?"

"You're a man who's not scared to say what he wants and, what he don't want. You know how I know that? Because the night I met you, you could have been with Diamond. I don't know but I just guessed you were going through some stuff. I respect you for going your own way. Diamond said something was wrong with you, but I told her you had more important things on your mind, and that it had nothing to do with her, that's all I mean," said Kayla.

"Yeah you're right," he said taking a bite.

"You wanna know what else she said about you?"

"What?" he answered not really caring?

"So this is what she said to me. She said the brother was touching me just right. I was feeling him, then he just stopped."

"Damn she sure did have it all together for real, how's she doing?" asked Bennie while chewing.

"Oh she's got it all together huh? Well thank you that's what I need to hear right now," she said waiting for him to change his words.

"You looked good too Kayla," he said quickly.

"Yeah um whatever…you know I'm just messing with you boy," Kayla said walking back to the kitchen.

Still wanting to say something nice Bennie sat back on the couch. "These wings are good Kayla, thanks, they hit the spot."

"You said they hit that spot Bennie…good. So that means I can ask you a question, and I ain't trying to start nothing. I just want to know do people you just meet ask you your last name? Be truthful now, cause I don't ask nobody their last name when I meet em do you?" she asked placing a beer on the coffee table, then sitting across from him.

"Well I don't, but sometimes I have."

"Okay cause like for instance when you found out my real name you never asked what my last name was. Seriously Bennie do you know my last name?" she asked waiting patiently.

"Nah, I don't know it."

"See that's my point. You don't know it and you've seen me a bunch of times, that's all I'm saying. It don't make sense," she said taking a piece of chicken for herself.

"I see your point; I don't know what to say."

"Don't worry about it I just wanted an honest answer. I guess I'm a little jacked up right now, but I'll make it."

"Good."

"And thanks for hanging out for a minute. And by the way, I don't think my slippers are all that funny," Kayla said wiggling her toes inside the slippers to make the ears move.

"They're cute and they fit your personality Kayla," he said smiling.

When Bennie finished eating Kayla was ready to set the hook by making it obvious she was keeping distance between them.

It started with him going to use the bathroom. Kayla stood near the entrance then timidly backed away when he went inside. Then she stayed near the door listening and when he came out she bumped into him losing her balance, so he had to hold her steady, then Kayla quickly moved away. Bennie had no idea it was a planned accident but as far as he was concerned it was time to leave. He stood by the couch and picked up the box of slippers.

"Thanks for staying. I wish you didn't have to leave," said Kayla murmuring the last part.

"What did you say Kayla?"

"Nothing," she said closing her robe after purposely opening it during their minor collision. Eyes swelling with helplessness she gave Bennie the face of Bambi sinking in a pit of quicksand then sat down.

"Well I'm gonna leave Kayla, thanks for the wings and the slippers," he said putting his hand on her shoulder.

"I should've asked you to try them on to see if you're gonna like em, but I know you have to go," she said refusing to look at him.

"Yeah next time," he said removing his hand, hopeful she'd look up.

"What is it with you and Lorraine?" Kayla asked abruptly.

"What did she say?"

"What didn't she say? She told me to stay away from you and that no matter what you say you won't be satisfied with me. So if she thought you and I were in a relationship why would she just come out and say something like that? You know what I mean? So naturally I had to take up for you cause if I didn't, she would've kept going. I'm just saying, she don't know how I feel about you. I mean there's nothing going on between us, but she didn't know that!"

"So you took up for me. What did you say to her?"

"I didn't say a lot. I just said you were cute and thoughtful. I didn't want to say too much in case she asked me more questions. Oh and said I wasn't going anywhere because you been good to me." Then she crossed her legs and pulled her robe under her chin.

"That's what you told her?" he said happily.

"Of course I did, and I didn't have to make it up. That's what I know about you, you're classy and intelligent," she said nodding in agreement.

"Thanks Kayla, I appreciate it," he said looking at the door again.

"So would you mind telling me what you did to her?" she asked quickly.

"Nothing really, she blames me for Ronald going to the bars and stuff, but as you can see I don't make him do anything. I really don't know why but it's been like this between me and her for a while. I really don't want to think about that right now, it's just gonna piss me off," he said thinking how Ronald keeps pulling him into more unwanted drama.

"Okay, well can I ask you something else?"

"What?"

"What's wrong with me? I'm not a bad person, I'm a good woman. We both know how I use to make money, but I have a real job now, and my own place. I don't ask anybody for anything Bennie… I mean nothing! So what's wrong with me that I'm not enough?" she asked snatching off her shower cap strictly for effect, then looking away.

"There's nothing wrong with you Kayla. You're a good woman, I always thought so," He responded with compassion.

"Do you really?" she asked still looking into space.

"Yes… I do," he said like a groom standing at the altar.

"Thank you… thank you so much," Kayla said standing to hug him then retreating once again into sorrow. The deception of pulling away was working because he held her a little longer.

"I'm trying to think of something to make you laugh. If I tell you a joke will that help?" he asked dropping the box on the couch.

"No, that won't do it," she said softly, not caring if Ronnie ever came back.

"Then what can I do…tell me?" he asked placing his hands on her shoulders.

An answer came with her expression. She wanted Bennie to pull her closer, so she kept looking at him. A clear invitation was extended, the question was would he accept? Kayla allowed her robe to open a little more, but not enough to see her sensual shape. She so much resembled a darker version of Lisa Lopez from that new group TLC. As he gazed his thoughts were about his friend allowing his wife to harass him for years without doing anything, and he was sick of it.

Within the cavity of decision a passion fire smoldered, kindled from retaliation. Once more Ronald endorsed by his inaction to handle business put Bennie in an awkward situation. So for all the times Ronald was less than a friend he decided to touch her. For every instance he came home disappointed by Ronald's silence, and the times Ronald couldn't keep his mouth shut, Kayla would be thrusted. Last but not least, for Mike Tyson's misfortune, he would have her. Consoling Kayla would be sweeter than ditching Lorraine Halloween night, only this time it was he and Ronald's friendship being lost in the crowd.

He pulled her tiny body closer and ran his fingers through her soft hair. His smile was her answer, and then he opened her robe. Kayla rested her head on his chest and rubbed his shoulder blades. Sweating with expectation she kissed his bottom lip again and again. Her robe fell to the floor as he ran his hands over her body. Tonight Bennie would break sexual records with her for distance, endurance, and depth. They kissed in the living room until their union became widespread. Still Kayla needed to give him a memory other than her body. So instead of calling out his name she said,

"Bennie it's Palmison, my last name is Palmison…Palmison …Pallll…mison, ooh…its Palmison baby say it!"

Chapter 8

Linda continued her memory exercises for several months without perceptible progress. Those crazy dreams all but stopped as she found comfort and confidence reading her Bible and trusting in the Lord. So before Valentine's Day of 1991 with her blackouts nonexistent, Linda stopped going to Dr. Goldstein and began learning to drive. Every other weekend Sonya drove to Jersey and gave her girlfriend lessons, and soon after Linda took the test and got her driver's license.

Not long after, Linda bought a 1985 Crown Victoria from Mr. Soriano the maintenance man who began working at the library three days after Linda first went in. Soriano was a friendly but quiet Middle Eastern looking man with a Hispanic last name. He was solidly built for a man in his late sixties, able to do 50 push-ups and 50 sit-ups every day before he ate lunch, which he brought every day from home. That lunch was always leftovers from last night's dinner, a piece of fruit, and a quart of plain water.

As Linda grew confident driving, she attended service at local churches around New Jersey until she found Messiah Baptist Church in East Orange. On her second visit she joined Messiah, putting her complete faith in God for healing. Ironically, months later in mid-summer while listening to the Pastor's sermon about David and Goliath, Linda associated the memory loss as her Goliath waiting to be slain.

Some weeks later she had an aah-ha, things that make you go hmmm moment. That night Linda dreamt of a huge room with cathedral high ceilings, and polished marble arches over the hallway entrances. She ran happily around the room past a crackling center fireplace. She heard a pop followed by burning pain on her ankle, and she began to cry. The same man she'd felt safe with from previous dreams stood by her, only now he was three times her height. He shook his locks to one side by twisting his neck then whisked her up. Her feet dangling over his muscular brown arm sturdy like the limb of an oak tree. Linda buried her face on his shoulder crying until the older woman she recognized as Yoba Ismeti comforted her. Yoba put a cool cloth on the spot to ease the pain then spoke, but Linda didn't understand. When the woman talked again it was a familiar phrase, "neia abrei Whende."

Suddenly from the hallway the squiggly man walked past the fireplace stopping next to Yoba, who was not afraid. The squiggly man's features looked like his face wasn't finished, and the fingers were clumped like skin mittens. But oddly, squiggly man wore a white tee shirt, dungarees, and sneakers.

A sound interrupted the dream when the squiggly man tried to touch her, and the room began to fade. The phone on her night table stopped ringing as soon as she opened her eyes. She focused on her window and the slight ripple from the curtain. That dream was still so vivid she could still smell smoke from the fireplace, along with pain on her ankle from the burn. Abruptly she threw the covers off and touched the dark blemish on the outside left ankle. Was that how she got this shoe horn shaped scar she wondered?

Tiffany was sleeping when Linda came out of the bathroom, so she went to the kitchen poured some juice, and looked out the window. The past few days she'd been wondering if accepting help to defeat Goliath mattered, or was she supposed to do it alone like David? Last night while Tiffany prayed at bedtime Linda asked God for help regaining her memory. That morning she believed last night's dream confirmed her decision to go back to Dr. Goldstein. So by that afternoon Linda made an appointment for Thursday the 19th of September.

On the day of her appointment she parked in the lot behind Dr. Goldstein's office and went inside the waiting room. Anxiously, she stood in front of each chair without ever sitting down. Finally a patient left and a few minutes later Dr. Goldstein invited Linda into the office. He was glad to see her, wasting no time inquiring as to any improvement. Linda told Dr. Goldstein about joining a church, learning to drive, and Tiffany starting first grade next year. After more small talk Linda told the doctor about her latest dream, and how the squiggly man's shape appeared altered. The doctor made a note of it and when the session was over he said it was time for a different approach to her therapy.

Dr. Goldstein suggested using an exercise in cognitive reenactments. By having Linda close her eyes in dim light he hoped to add more dimension to the memories. Two weeks and two sessions later produced no significant results. At that time Dr. Goldstein discussed another form of therapy so intense Linda would need to be accompanied home when she left. So before making that appointment she called Sonya from the doctor's office, got the okay, then scheduled it.

As Linda left the office on the way to her car something strange happened. She looked down the driveway and thought she saw Mr. Soriano walking by across the street. She walked quickly to the street to say hello, but he'd turned the corner. Linda went back to her car then drove around the corner but didn't see him. So when it was time she picked Tiffany up and they went home. The next time she saw Mr. Soriano at the library she asked him about that day. He told her it wasn't him, so she didn't think any more about it.

The following Thursday Sonya's plan was to leave her job at the Department of Social Services before 4pm to be in Woodbridge, NJ by 5; take Linda to her appointment early Friday, and maybe do a little shopping Saturday. Then on Sunday they'd all go to the 11am worship service at Linda's church, have breakfast at a local diner, then Sonya would go back home. However the day didn't go according to plans.

Sonya had to work until 530pm so when she left she got caught in the evening traffic on the George Washington Bridge, and the New Jersey Turnpike. By the time she got to Linda's apartment it was well past 7pm. After she took off her shoes, got comfortable and ate dinner, it wasn't long before she fell asleep on the couch. Linda tiptoed around until Sonya began to snore. Then she placed a pillow under her head and covered her with a light blanket.

Soon it was time for Linda to settle down herself. She lay in bed with thoughts of facing her Goliath. She tossed and turned for a while watching the television. That didn't help her relax and before long an hour passed by. At 2am she seriously considered canceling her appointment. What if the treatment made her recall a painful memory that made her life worse? What if her blackouts returned, making her an incompetent mother? She flipped onto her stomach fluffing her pillow, and then put her head down. Having the blackouts return was a risk she wasn't willing to take, so she decided not to go.

Then she thought about Sonya cancelling plans with Jeff to take her in the morning. She turned on her side knowing Sonya would understand if the procedure were postponed, and she felt guilt for that. So in the morning she'd take them out for breakfast at the Reo Diner down the block then maybe they'd head to the mall. Linda stretched her arm under the lampshade to turn off the light when her eyes fell on the Bible. She looked at it unmoving for a time, until a small voice inside asked a humble question, "What would David do?" Linda stared at the cover of her Bible with her finger on the knob, and felt confident peace. David never changed his mind. He faced that giant, and so will I, she thought. Then she turned off the light vowing to walk in faith until she finally fell asleep.

The next morning Linda woke to birds chirping outside just before sunrise. She got dressed then set the table for Tiffany's corn flakes, and Sonya's coffee and toast. After breakfast Linda and Sonya dropped Tiffany at kindergarten then headed to the doctor's office. There wasn't a cloud in the sky and the air was crisp. Sonya was glad Linda had become a good driver in a short amount of time.

When they pulled into the driveway of the doctor's office Linda was filled with confidence. She slammed the car door with a smile, and they went inside.

Sonya sat down with a magazine and said, "Your driving is much better. Soon you'll be able to drive to my house and spend the weekend."

Linda looked hesitant but didn't answer so Sonya quickly said, "When you feel up to it, I'm not rushing you. So this year went by fast, didn't it? Seems like it was a little while ago we were watching movies. Girl by the way, you know I brought some with me."

"I hoped you did. So what are we going to watch?" Linda asked looking at her watch to hide the nervousness.

"I'm glad you asked. One is about three sisters that formed a singing group. Honey I think you're gonna like that one, Curtis Mayfield wrote the soundtrack. And let's see, I got two movies from a new guy... Spike Lee."

Before Linda could respond the door opened and a woman wearing a sky-blue nurse's uniform walked in then sat across from them.

"Yeah so um, what else was I gonna say. Oh you said I have to drive when we leave so I'm ready to drive that tank of yours girlfriend. Why you bought a big car like that I'll never know," Sonya said jokingly.

"Well at the time it made sense. Mr. Soriano told me if I got use to driving that car, I'd be able to drive anything."

"You know that kinda makes sense. So where've you been driving to?"

"Girl I been to the Pathmark ... well no, actually I walk to Pathmark most of the time because it's just a few blocks. Otherwise I take it to pick up Tiffany. Oh yeah, I drive to church and that's it. Plus I don't want Tiffany to get use to driving everywhere," Linda said looking at the clock on the wall.

"My best friend is the little old lady that only drives to church on Sunday. I don't believe it," Sonya said laughing with the woman who overheard the remark.

"What are you talking about?"

"You never heard that one before? That's what car salesmen would say when he wants to sell you a car. Never mind it was a joke," Sonya said thinking it wasn't the time to bring up another thing Linda didn't know. They sat quiet for a minute then Linda blurted out,

"Guess what, I've been thinking about finding a stable so I can ride a horse."

"Ride a horse! Girlfriend are you serious?" Sonya asked glancing at the woman across from them again.

"Yes I am."

"You ever rode a horse before?"

"I don't think so, but then again I can't remember. And since I can't remember I probably was doing a lot of things. Maybe I was a pilot or a scientist or better yet a teacher. So I feel like I want to try riding a horse."

"Girl… black people don't ride horses!"

"Oh yes they do. You don't see it, but they got black cowboy groups, riding clubs, and other stuff they do on ranches. As a matter of fact, I know I'm gonna do it cause every time I see a horse on TV, I wish I was sitting on it."

It was then Sonya leaned in close so the other woman couldn't hear then said, "Honey you need a man, you don't need to ride no horse."

Before Linda could reply Dr. Goldstein came in and said, "Ms. Reeves who is this?"

"This is my friend Sonya. Sonya this is my doctor, Dr. Goldstein. Sonya is here to drive me home and she's staying for the weekend," Linda said proudly.

"Sonya, nice to finally meet you. I've heard a lot about you," he said.

"So you all been talking about me huh, what did she say doctor?" Sonya asked surprisingly.

"All good things, trust me nothing bad," he replied.

"You couldn't tell me anyway doc, I know that. Girl I can't believe you were in here talking about me," Sonya said patting her foot.

"Yup I sure did…told him all about you," said Linda smiling back.

Dr. Goldstein looked to the other side of the room and said, "Ms. Reeves I don't know if you met Nurse Aquino, but this is the nurse who will be assisting me today. So give us a minute to set up and we'll get started."

After the nurse greeted the women Sonya said, "Doc, can I come in with her?"

"I'm afraid not, but as soon as we finish I'll come get you," he said motioning for the nurse to follow him.

When the office door closed Sonya took Linda's hand and they prayed together. Before they let go Sonya said, "Are you sure you want to do this? Because you don't have to if you don't want to."

"I know."

"And if that doctor is pushing you it doesn't matter, we can walk out of here right now and he can't stop you! If you want to we can walk out of here right now!" Sonya said squeezing Linda's hand.

"Thank you for saying that because last night I was going to change my mind, but you know what. I'm tired of being frightened of what's ahead of me, and I don't want to teach my child to be scared either. So I'm going to face this, and I love you for being here with me. You are a true friend, and I will never ever forget that!" Linda said sounding as if she were about to cry.

"Okay then in the name of Jesus everything is going to work out!" said Sonya.

They both sat silently until the nurse came back. They stood to hug then Linda said, "I'll be right back girl so don't go anywhere."

"I won't, I'll be right here."

Linda was ushered to a room just left of the office bathroom where the procedure was to take place. She removed everything except her underwear, then the nurse stuck electrodes to her temples and chest. Then she put on a hospital gown with the open end facing frontwards and one over that one facing backwards. Finally Nurse Aquino adjusted the examining table so it would lay flat then clipped a pulse monitor to her pointer finger. Once the nurse made sure everything was working properly, she went for the doctor.

"Ms. Reeves, I just want to go over the procedure again. First, have you eaten this morning or after 6pm last night?" the doctor asked, adjusting his glasses.

"No I haven't doctor."

"Great, then we can proceed. I'm going to administer a mild sedative so you can relax. It won't make you unconscious, just very relaxed; then I'm going to ask you some questions. When we're finished or if for any reason you become distressed, I'll administer this stimulant to get you up again. As you can see Nurse Aquino is monitoring heart rate, pulse, and blood pressure. Now if I ask something that increases your pulse and heart rate, then I'll know how to direct my questions. This should only last for twenty minutes or less. Are you with me so far?"

"Yes I got all that," Linda answered quickly.

"Okay now as you see this session will be videotaped to study your responses. So Ms. Reeves we're going to start. Do you have any other questions?"

"No Doc, I feel good so let's do it. God is with me so I have nothing to fear," Linda said, watching the doctor turn on the camera.

"We're going to start now. I only want you to focus on the sound of my voice and describe everything you see," he said while injecting her.

Linda felt a warm sensation traveling up her arm then her legs. She closed her eyes, searching the darkness behind her eye lids.

"Pressure and pulse normal Doctor," Linda heard the nurse say.

"Thank you Nurse, and from this point, just alert me when her pressure goes up," he whispered.

"Ms. Reeves can you hear me?"

"Yes," Linda answered, feeling as if she were laying on a warm water bed in the dark.

"Each time I tell you to breathe in deeply you will become more relaxed. So I want you to do it now. Take a deep breath and I want you to imagine you're walking in a park towards a small boat tied to a dock."

In Linda's awareness darkness gave way to the light not quite in focus. Her surrounding became clearer until she found herself standing on an embankment with the sun shining overhead. As she walked the grass felt like a cool green carpet under her feet. Further along she heard the faint sound of running water from a small stream. Linda continued until she came to a small wooden boat tied to a dock. The boat floated in a stream about 40 feet across in six feet of water.

"Linda, are you at the boat?"

"Yes."

"Now I want you to get inside and drift away with the calm water… are you there?"

"Yes I'm getting in now," she answered untying the rope then pushing away from the shore with her foot.

"Linda, this stream will take you backwards in time. Look over to the shore and see when you woke this morning. Can you see it?"

The boat slowed and Linda saw the inside her apartment on the left. Sonya was sleep on the couch and Tiffany was in her room, so she said, "Yes I see it."

"Stop at the shore and tell me where you are?"

"I'm in my room."

"What did you do this morning after you woke up?"

"I… I thanked God for waking me," she whispered.

"Good, now we're going to drift away from your room. Keep going back until you see the day your daughter was born, then I want you to stop there and get out.

The small boat listed gently as she drifted slowly pass trees lining the edges.

"Where are you now?" the doctor asked after noticing Linda's eyes dart back and forth behind the lids.

"The hospital room…she is so beautiful," Linda said smiling.

"Are there windows in the room?"

"Yes one window."

"What else do you see?"

"My brother…he's looking at the baby… he's happy for me."

Dr. Goldstein was tempted to ask questions about the relationship with her brother because she rarely discussed him.

"You're doing great Linda. Now go back to the boat and this time you're going to drift far back to that place in your dreams," he said, looking to make sure the camera was on.

"I want you to stop at the place when you ran by the fireplace and got burned. I want you to go there," he said with anticipation.

Pushing away from the bank with her foot Linda drifted once more until the sound of burning logs crackling and the familiar scent of the Nile River wafted through the air.

"Ms. Reeves are you there?" Goldstein asked after she'd been so quiet.

"Yes… I see it," she said, leaving the boat on the right side on the bank.

Linda followed a four-foot-wide path made of cobblestone pass the horse stables into the back of the palace. The inside was familiar from the polished floors to the furniture, the art work, and the painted borders on the ceiling. Dr. Goldstein watched Linda grin while her eyes continued to dart back and forth. She walked next to her father's favorite chair with the curved armrests, touching the plush fabric with her hand. Linda recalled sitting across from him on the matching foot stool listening to bed time stories.

On the mantel over the fireplace was a foot high stone bust of her and the man who wore locks from her dreams. Yoba, her grandmother, and Linda's father walked in from the balcony. Instantly she perceived their love and felt safe, and then she ceased hearing Dr. Goldstein's voice.

"Give me a hug child. Your father and I missed you so much," Yoba said during a group hug. This embrace so real Linda could actually smell the scented oil in Yoba's hair and the softness of skin when their cheeks touched. After hugging Linda said excitedly, "I remember you! You are my Grandma Ismeti! And you...You are my Papa."

"That's right I'm your Papa. Do you know who you are...my daughter?" he asked with his hand on her cheek.

"I'm...I'm Lin."

"No you are not my love! Your name is Whende...say it!" he said interrupting her.

"Whende?"

"Yes...say it again child...what is your name?" her father asked.

"Whende...my name is Whende."

"Yes my love you are Whende! I always said you were going to do great things. Do you remember?"

"Yes I do. You said that many times."

"Whende you can't stay here, you have to go back," Papa said.

"No! I don't want to leave this place, I want to stay here with you," she said painfully.

"I know you don't, but you must. We will see each other again I promise Whende. We will wait for you to come home," Papa said, fading away into darkness.

Meanwhile in the office something unexpected transpired after Linda stopped responding to the doctor's questions. Minutes later the nurse signaled that Linda's blood pressure had risen to 220 over 110. Immediately the doctor gave Linda the injection then she opened her eyes to the nurse pressing a stethoscope on her chest.

"How do you feel?" the doctor asked trying to sound calm.

"Fine... I guess. What... happened?" asked Linda, trying to catch her breath.

"One minute Ms. Reeves, I'll tell you everything but for right now I need you to just breathe deeply and relax. Everything went well," he said as he and the nurse exchanged an odd stare. He watched the nurse take her pressure again. It was still elevated but not like before.

"Doctor why am I breathing so fast, I feel like I've been running?" Linda asked, rubbing her eyes. She could tell something happened because the nurse and the doctor's hearts were going fast like hers.

When Linda's pulse and respiration stabilized she asked again, "What did you find out Doc?"

"We'll get to that, but I need you to answer some questions first. Is your head hurting and do you feel pain anywhere?" he asked while shining the pen light in her eyes to check the pupils.

"No Doc, to be honest I feel like I had a good night sleep. So why was I so…I don't know…eager a minute ago?"

"Well how do you feel right now?" he asked, skipping Linda's question.

"I feel good Doc," answering as she stretched.

"Great! You can put your clothes on and then we'll talk," he said switching off the camera and leaving the nurse to put the equipment away.

When the nurse came back Linda was dressed she went to join Dr. Goldstein in his study. He was at his desk writing and the door was open. When he saw her he walked to the door closed it and took his seat again. He closed the folder, took off his glasses, looked at Linda and said,

"I have to review this tape, make an evaluation, and get back to you. But some interesting concerns have come into play. I don't mean to sound mysterious but it's too early. However I can give you some good news. The treatment did work, and we made some progress."

"You have to tell me more than that. I heard the nurse say my pressure was high and I remember my heart was beating fast. Doc you've got to tell me something!"

"Ms. Reeves it's much too soon, and like results from any test, except for maybe an x-ray, it takes a few days. Please be patient for a few days. I'm cancelling all my appointments for the next two days just so I can have an answer for you as quickly as possible," he said convincingly.

"You are?" she asked feeling somewhat relieved.

"I am. I have to see the patients coming in today, but I've canceled my Saturday and Monday appointments to give you my full attention."

"Fine, I waited this long what's a few more days," she sighed.

"Good…so I have instructions for you to follow for the next couple of days. Just for today I want you to go home and relax. No driving for you, and I don't even want you walking by yourself. Tomorrow if you feel good you can drive, unless you have a headache or feel sluggish. If you feel a little tired it's fine, don't push yourself to do more than you feel like doing. Next I want you to discontinue the memory exercises for the next three days. Don't take any aspirin or consume alcohol, understand?" he said while writing on a note pad.

"I won't," she answered.

"Good, I want you to keep writing down your dreams and memories. And there's something else which I'll explain further on your next visit which will be… ahh one week from today. If you start talking and it sounds like gibberish, write that down phonetically as best you can. The spelling doesn't matter as long as you write what it sounds like," he said stressing the point.

"And why would I start talking gibberish?"

"It's nothing to be concerned about and if it doesn't happen that's fine. Also Ms. Reeves, if you have any severe headaches or blackouts I want you to call me immediately," he said tearing paper from his pad to give to her.

Lethargically Linda walked out to Sonya who took her arm the moment she saw her.

"Can you walk to the car?" Sonya asked.

"Yes," Linda said yawning.

"Girl, on second thought wait here, I'll bring the car closer," said Sonya walking away while Linda stood by the door.

Sonya returned stopping the car yards from the door. She hurried from the driver's side saying,

"Come on sweetie I got you. We'll be home soon then you can rest."

Linda sat down slowly and before Sonya began to drive she said, "I gotta ask…did you remember anything?

"I don't know. I feel the same just hungry and tired. The doctor said he was gonna get back to me after he analyzed the video and did some research, but he said I made progress."

"So it helped, that's great. Now we're gonna get you some food and let you rest, and then we'll go get the baby," Sonya said, starting the car.

"Speaking of horses, I'm so hungry I could eat a horse," Linda said, looking down the street.

"You could what?"

"I heard that on TV. It's funny because that's something I'd never eat, but I understand why people say it. That reminds me, I want to tell you something else. I just wanted to let you know how glad I am you're here. I couldn't have done this without you. Sonya I got nobody. No family, no friends, just you and Tiffany."

"That's what friends are for. I know God put us together so we could be here for each other. And you know what, I'm sure you'll meet more people you can trust in time because you're a wonderful person. Let me tell you something, women can be a trip, and I don't have time for nobody's BS. There's never any drama between us, and you know what else? If you ever needed me to take Tiffany for any reason I would," Sonya said, slowing down for a red light.

"I wouldn't have it any other way," Linda answered with a sigh of relief.

Both women began to tear up as the light turned green.

A few blocks later Sonya turned into the parking lot to pick up Tiffany from daycare. She parked close to the entrance and went inside. In just a few minutes Tiffany ran towards the car in front of Sonya when she saw her mother. Linda opened the door hugging her child from a sitting position. Tiffany stared into her eyes and asked, "Momma, why aren't you driving? Are you feeling okay?"

"I'm fine baby, Auntie wanted to pick you up that's all. Now what about you, tell me how your day was, did you have fun?" she asked while Sonya strapped Tiffany in.

"Yes Momma I had fun all day. First we colored then I made a present for you, but it's not ready yet. Oh! We're gonna have a Halloween party and everyone has to bring some candy. And…and I want to go as a princess, can I be Snow White mommy, can I?" Tiffany asked as Sonya started the car.

"You want to be Snow White, you sure?"

"Yes I want the dress she wore but I want to have my own hair, can I do that?" Tiffany asked sounding adamant.

Intrigued by the youngster's statement Sonya turned around and asked, "Why don't you want the blond hair?"

"You and mommy don't have blond hair and I don't either. I'm gonna be Snow White with my own hair!" said Tiffany proudly.

"Well alright now! Sure you can wear your own beautiful curly hair," Linda said looking at Sonya, then under her breath Linda went on, "Did you just hear what my baby said?"

"Yup, she's gonna be driving this car before you know what hit you."

"That's right she's growing up fast and you know something, I know she's gonna do great things!"

After that comment Linda got quiet and stared ahead at the hood of the car.

"That's all she's been talking about the whole time was going as Snow White. So what else we gotta do Linda, we going home now? Linda you hear me?" Sonya asked as Linda looked straight ahead.

Linda heard Sonya plain as day talking but just then the name Linda sounded foreign. As if it was a fictitious curse word, and she didn't want to acknowledge it.

"Mommy what you doing up there?"

"Nothing baby I just…"

"Girlfriend…you feeling alright, what's going on?"

"I thought I remembered something and I'm not sure how to say it, but I'm fine, let's go home," Linda said forcing a smile then opening the window.

They traveled along Main Street with the air brushing Linda's face. By the time they got home Linda attributed her uneasiness to the drugs and anxiety from the entire day. The queasiness in her stomach subsided with the urge to reject her name when Sonya called it.

"Linda I'm gonna heat up last night's dinner cause you still want to eat, right?

"Yes, and before you go I want you to show me how to make grits. I order them when we have breakfast out and they don't taste the same. So you need to show me how you do it so I can make it for us," Linda said, looking out the window.

"Sorry, no can do my sister, that's a family recipe…sorry," Sonya yelled from the kitchen.

"That's why you can give it to me; you just said it my sister, we're family. We are family, I got all my sisters with me," Linda sang out loud.

That caused Sonya to poke her head out the kitchen with her mouth open.

"No you didn't Linda that's the first time you did that. How do you know that song?"

"I've been listening to the radio when I drive. But don't change the subject. You can show me how to make those grits because we're sisters, you said it yourself," Linda said watching Tiffany enter the living room.

"Girl I'll show you my secret the next time I come over," Sonya said returning to the stove.

When dinner was over the ladies settled down planning to watch a movie later, but Linda fell asleep. That's when Sonya took over. With help from Tiffany they quietly cleaned the kitchen. Afterwards they went to Tiffany's room and put on a fashion show. It was the perfect little girl's room, painted soft pink with sea shells on her bed spread and artwork she'd done in her classroom.

Sonya sat on the floor while Tiffany happily searched her room for models to be in the fashion show. From the bed next to her pillow Tiffany grabbed Sprinkles the tan teddy bear, then Elle the stuffed grey elephant from the chair under her little desk. She put them on the floor in front of Sonya then gathered three Barbie dolls from a small toy chest by the desk. Before she sat on the floor Tiffany went to her dresser for a stuffed bird. Finally Tiffany sat across from Sonya to work on styling the dolls hair while Sonya changed the outfits on the animals. This one-on-one time with Tiffany turned out to be the most fun Sonya had in months. It also nursed her strong desire to have a child she could love and protect.

They wrapped up the fashion show after eight that evening, mainly because there were no more new outfits. So Sonya told Tiffany to take her bath and get ready to go to sleep. Tiffany did as she was told while Sonya put the toys away, making sure she put Sprinkles back next to the pillow. After Tiffany got in bed Sonya sat on the edge to read one of her favorite bedtime stories. By Tiffany's third yawn Sonya closed the book, stood up and kissed her cheek. Her sleepy eyes were so beautiful when she smiled before closing them.

Sonya put the book on the desk then looked at Linda's beautiful child. She longed to experience life moving inside her and the opportunity to become a mother. It was just so frustrating that Jeff wasn't ready to be a father again. As much as she wanted a baby she didn't want to be a single mother if she could help it. She deserved to be Jeff's wife but was he ready to have two baby mamas? Muffling a sigh, Sonya tiptoed to the doorway flipped the switch and a night light came on in the corner.

When she got to the living room Linda was yawning to the tiny rumble of distant thunder. Her eyes blinking as she stretched on the couch anticipating the next break outside. The daughter is going to sleep while momma is waking up, Sonya thought sitting down. Then she began talking about the fashion show, and how much fun they had. Most of the time Sonya talked she thought about Jeff until noticing it was almost 10pm. She abruptly excused herself then went to Linda's bedroom to make a phone call. The idea was to hear his voice, and tell him how much she loved him.

Tonight he was out with some friends from work and that damn J-Rock. J-Rock's real name was Jason but Sonya suspected he gave the name J-Rock to women so they never knew his real name. J-Rock was light skinned with curly hair, in his mid-thirties and arrogant as hell. He was the father of five kids the oldest boy just turned thirteen, and the youngest eighteen months. His children were from three different women and he chose to work off the books to avoid paying the maximum child support. For a woman thinking about becoming a mom it was enough reason not to like him, plus she believed he was a bad influence on her man. Another problem was J-Rock had more history with Jeff than she did. They'd been friends four years before she met Jeff, and it was hard to crack their tight knit boys club.

This time the thunder sounded closer when Sonya began dialing. She hoped Jeff was done with the fellas by now. His answering machine came on so she left a short message. Ten minutes later Sonya left Linda once more, assuming Jeff was out of the bathroom. When the machine came on she told Jeff she'd be awake another hour or so, and he could call. Hesitantly she said, "I love you baby. I miss you…call me."

Sonya slowly moved the phone away hoping to hear him answer. Finally she put the phone down next to the Bible on the nightstand, and went back to the living room.

Linda was in the kitchen fixing something to eat while Sonya stood near the refrigerator thinking about having a glass of wine. She forced a smile after telling Linda Jeff wasn't home. Then they both sat in the dining room table Linda with her food and Sonya without her wine. Inbetween having a conversation she listened for Jeff's call, and tried not to picture him with other women. If he wasn't, he'd be the first man of hers who didn't cheat.

By 11pm Sonya went back to the bedroom to try again. This time a flash of lightning followed when she picked up the phone. Then a gust of wind rustled the leaves outside and the rain began striking the window. As soon as the machine answered she hung up the phone with a slight bit of force, and then went back to the couch. This was turning into the perfect time to get a few things off her chest. So before Sonya sat she went for that glass of wine, then the women began a heart-to-heart discussion. After Sonya took a sip she began telling her everything she'd been through the last few months.

She began telling Linda it didn't bother her when Jeff went to the strip club with his friends. At least he was telling the truth about where he was, and even though it was after four in the morning he was coming back to her house. She said it made her feel good that after looking at those women he wanted to be with her. He'd climb into her bed just before dawn, waking her with a lingering scent of female sweat, perfume and beer on his breath. Honestly the combination turned her on, and they'd end up having really good sex. This time Sonya drank her wine till the glass was half empty then looked down at the coffee table.

Sonya told Linda Jeff was going out twice a month now, and the last two times he never came back to her house. When she spoke to him the next morning, his excuse the first time was he had too much to drink so J-Rock drove him home. When she asked why J-Rock didn't drive him to her apartment he didn't answer. Then he told her when he woke up that's where J-Rock took him. The last time it happened he said he just didn't want to wake her. She watched for Linda's expression, then drank the rest of the wine and went back to the kitchen for more.

When she returned Sonya went on about some other things she'd observed. Sonya said when she was at Jeff's house this past Labor Day, they spent the weekend at his place and she noticed whenever the phone rang and the answering machine came on the volume was turned down. That way you couldn't hear who was leaving a message. When she asked why the volume was down he said it was probably a creditor, and he didn't feel like talking. Why would a bill collector call on a holiday weekend after 10pm? Linda's silence caused Sonya to take a healthy sip then disclose deeper issues.

As soon as she put her glass down and took a deep breath she told Linda she believed her weight and skin color was the reason Jeff wouldn't marry her. Linda tried to tell her it wasn't true but Sonya disagreed. To make her case she reminded Linda that Jeff's son's mother was light skinned, and it seemed he liked women no larger than a size six. Like the girl she caught him smiling at while they were eating at Copeland's Restaurant near off Broadway. All of a sudden her lips blurted out that she thought he was with some light-skinned heifer, and that's why he wasn't answering the damn phone.

This time Linda tried to play devil's advocate and come to Jeff's defense by reminding Sonya with her own words. How he was a good hardworking man and how her eyes sparkled when she talked about him. Sonya interjected affirmatively declaring why she knew Jeff was lying. It was the condoms in his nightstand drawer. He had a different brand plus there were four the last time she was there. When she came back two weeks later he had seven. Her voice cracked a bit before she took a sip then asked Linda why he had seven when they are sold by the dozen. Finally Sonya told Linda she found a phone number with the name Cathy on a crumpled piece of paper in his shirt pocket. Then she had a thought and totally switched to another subject.

Sonya said an older woman from the old neighborhood gave her some good advice, and she wanted to share before she forgot. Sonya pointed her finger at Linda the same way that lady did when she gave the information to her. Make it a habit of doing your man's laundry, she was told. A woman can find out everything just by taking care of his dirty clothes. Linda listened attentively, waiting for the punchline. Sonya explained you can see what's in his pockets because you're doing laundry. You can tell when he gets new clothes, and what kind of stains are in them. And most important, if his underwear and towels are crusty, he's been having sex. That's why she changed her mind about letting Jeff move in with her, and it seemed like that's when he started going out more.

Linda offered no advice because she couldn't relate, and Sonya sensed that. So she swirled the wine around the sides of the glass then stopped. While waiting for the liquid to settle she convinced herself Jeff was with another woman, and she wasn't going to waste her time. In her heart she truly believed all men weren't cheaters. If Jeff wasn't ready for a good wife, she wasn't going to let him stop her from meeting a man who was. The women got up to hug because Sonya desperately felt like crying, but she held the hurt inside for fear of waking the baby. Instead she forced a smile during their embrace then went to the kitchen. Sonya stood at the sink washing her glass and the rest of the dishes while Linda got ready for bed. Sometime later they were back on the couch with the television volume just low enough to cover their voices. This time the conversation shifted to Linda and her love life, or lack thereof.

It began with Sonya stressing that her girl troubles were hers and not Linda's. Taking that moment to mention she knew, without a shadow of a doubt, good decent black men were out there. She went on to name a couple married 27 years, and another in their eighties married 62 years. Linda acknowledged it wasn't her intention be alone, there were just too many challenges facing her right now. The guy Linda was attracted to some months ago that was attending Rutgers turned out to have more than one girlfriend. After that she went on to tell Sonya most of her encounters with men made her uncomfortable. They'd stare at her breasts while she talked, or shout disrespectful insulting remarks when she didn't answer. The only man who didn't act that way was the one she bought the car from, her co-worker Mr. Soriano, and he was way too old.

The lightning flickered outside the living room window causing the women to pause their conversation. After the thunder Linda looked in the direction of Tiffany's room, lowering her voice. She told Sonya it was exasperating having no idea what intercourse felt like, much less to have kissed a man. Sonya acknowledged Linda's frustration then tried to lighten the mood with alternative words for intercourse. Sonya didn't stop until Linda was laughing. When she ran out of synonyms she started with new words for orgasm while Linda listened intently. Before she could stop herself Sonya asked Linda if she ever had an orgasm. Linda covered her mouth looking in the hallway then answered; she'd had two last week. Then she got up still speaking above a whisper to say good night and they would pick up the conversation tomorrow.

As Linda got ready for bed Sonya stretched from the couch switching off the television. She fixed a pillow under her head and pulled the sheet over her body. The sound of rain and wind her companions. Familiar feelings of loneliness swirled in her head while temples aching from thoughts of time wasted, and fruitless emotional investments. Once more she wrestled with the decision to leave a man she loved, like with Eli, eight months before meeting Jeff. Indications of Jeff's infidelity were too difficult to disregard. She was never going to take the last name of Wilson, and that thought solidified like wet cement around her ankles. It was time to pull her feet out before Jeff told her he was breaking it off.

Once the final decision was made Sonya pressed her face in the pillow, opened her mouth and screamed as if she were a mime. With intensity so forceful her throat was actually sore when she stopped. Then she lay still, blending into the decor like the rest of the furniture. No doubt she'd been Jeff's mattress, just something to lie on top of. Could this be how an end table or chair felt when their usefulness was over?

In silence Sonya repeated over and over I will not cry, I will not cry, I will not cry. God has something better for me. God has something better for me. I know The Lord has something better for me. With a fist over her lips she repeated it until she began to believe it, even though the ache was still there.

At the same time Linda prayed on her knees by the bed. She asked God to keep His healing hands on her, and to guide Sonya in the right direction. Then she got in bed turned the light off, and wriggled her toes under the sheet. It had been a long day and by now the storm was over the town of Woodbridge. Facing the window Linda listened to the wind then heard a familiar voice. She turned over so see Tiffany holding Sprinkles to her chest. Tiffany had come to her mother's room when she wasn't feeling well or had a nightmare, but this was the first from weather. Instinctively Linda lifted the covers and Tiffany jumped in with the teddy bear between them.

As the wind and rain rattled the windows Linda talked about how scary the thunder seemed when she was little girl. That made Tiffany ask why she wasn't afraid now. Linda recalled the reason was her brother Bennie. During the storms Linda would run to her brother's room. She'd step around Mister the Rottweiler curled up by the foot of the bed, and wake her brother. He always let her hop in, and then he'd talk until she fell asleep.

So Linda explained the dynamics of thunder and lightning to both Tiffany and Sprinkles. This teaching moment became an educational bedtime story like the ones her brother told. By the time Linda talked about the temperature of a bolt of lightning Tiffany was sleep. She kissed her baby's cheek then touched Sprinkles arm, also yawning herself. Now wasn't the time to start a relationship and chance a man mistreating her baby, she supposed? If she found answers to fill in these blanks and met the right man, maybe she'd consider starting a relationship.

It took less than an hour for the storm to move away, and for Linda to settle down. Faith kept her believing the problems were going to work themselves out, and she'd get to the truth. In the near future Linda would ultimately discover the memories of her brother's comforting stories during the storms were not quite accurate. The fact was she'd been an adult seeing that memory through a child's mind. She was going through stages of healing from the same form of amnesia she fought. The lightning thunder and rain were gone, but the winds remained. Inside the apartment were two women. One desperate to regain her memory, the other wishing she could forget.

Chapter 9

Unlike the night, morning approached with peaceful silence. Linda was about to wake Tiffany when she was interrupted. While staring at the closet door Linda remembered something. When Linda lived with her brother in Harlem there was a brown leather recliner next to his bed facing his dresser. It would have been right there in front of her closet door. Funny she never thought about it before. All those times she'd been afraid during a storm, or had a nightmare about the squiggly man, when she woke her brother was never in bed with her. He was either sleeping in that recliner under a blanket, or downstairs in the kitchen making their breakfast. Linda stared at the closet a bit more, then sat on the edge of the bed with her pad to write the memory down. Then she went to the bathroom and went back to sleep.

Eventually everyone was up well before noon. The women planned on going to Willowbrook Mall but Linda changed her mind. Instead, they ordered breakfast from the Reo Diner and Sonya drove to pick it up. When the evening came they ordered a pizza and chicken wings. In the morning they were all going to church if Linda was up to driving. When the next day came they all got up and dressed to leave by 8am for the 9am service.

After a short conversation outside, Sonya walked to her car and Linda and Tiffany got in theirs. Sonya followed them to the Garden State Parkway and they both got off at the East Orange Exit. Then they drove a few more minutes to arrive at the church parking lot. Sonya took the space next to Linda then they walked around the corner with Tiffany in the middle. The sidewalk and stairs to the church were still wet as they went inside and headed down front to the second row. Sonya went in first, then Tiffany, with Linda taking the end next to the aisle. Sonya figured this was Linda's spot because she liked to sit in front of the teacher when they were in class.

Messiah Baptist Church was an average sizeable to hold more than two hundred people on the main floor, and seventy or so in the balcony. The church had a wide center aisle and one aisle on each side next to the wall. When service began the choir entered from the left, right in front of them assembling under a cross in the middle of the pulpit. Linda leaned over to tell Sonya she was going to join the Usher Board and Tiffany wanted to sing in the Youth Choir next year.

While Sonya browsed through the program, the choir began singing, and shortly after the Pastor, assistant Pastor, and two Deacons took seats in the pulpit. This moment was significant for Linda because it was Sonya who led her to accept Christ, and find a church home. Now the only people Linda cared about were here on this wonderful day. She looked at them clapping with the choir and sighed from mixed emotion. Worshiping counteracted the sting of all recent and future disappointments. This Sunday turned into the best part of the weekend, and Linda brushed a small tear from her cheek and clapped with them.

After service they drove to a nearby diner for breakfast before Sonya went home. Tiffany sat in the booth next to Sonya while Linda sat across facing them. Tiffany saw the picture of blueberry pancakes on the menu and asked if she could have that. Linda told her yes while ordering two teas and an orange juice. Amid the murmuring voices and clanking of silverware, Sonya admitted she was moved by the Pastor's sermon on forgiveness. It made her think as she watched cars passing outside the window. Sonya looked at Tiffany then paused before she reminded Linda of their conversation last night. With care she said the Pastor's words inspired her to forgive a certain person without saying his name. Linda looked up from the menu and nodded in agreement, then went back to reading. Still Sonya made it clear it was still over; she just refused to hold on to the anger.

Suddenly Tiffany mentioned she was going to forgive the boy that pulled her hair last Friday during recess. Sonya hugged Tiffany, praising her decision adding, because God forgives us, we must forgive others. Then she told Tiffany if the boy kept bothering her she had to tell her mom. Linda silently stared at the menu until she placed her order, then she took a full breath and a sip of water. Sonya had a clue who Linda was thinking about but didn't say anything. As soon as Linda put the water down she went to the bathroom to wash her hands. When she got back Linda cracked a smile, then added sugar to her tea. Before she could stir it Sonya held Linda's hand and told her, everything works out for those who love the Lord. The gesture was enough to lighten the mood and by the time the food came, they were all laughing and enjoying one another's company.

At noontime they left the diner with Tiffany in the middle. Now there was little evidence it rained, but the air was muggy. When they got to Sonya's car Tiffany asked when they could put on another fashion show. Sonya set her purse on the seat and told her she wasn't sure, but next time they would have a DJ and spot lights. Tiffany jumped up and down with eagerness while swinging her little purse.

After a few simple directions from Linda to find the George Washington Bridge, they had a group hug. Sonya told Linda as soon as she heard from Dr. Goldstein she wanted to know, and if she needed to baby sit it wasn't a problem. Linda thanked her, saying she would call around 2pm because they both should be home. Sonya started the car, honked the horn, and waved a final goodbye. Tiffany stepped back and they watched Sonya's car until it was out of sight.

For the duration of the drive to Woodbridge Linda was still troubled. God said we must forgive. The Pastor's sermon was clear and his examples made sense. Forgiveness is not for the other person but for our sake. There was only one person she detested in this life and that was her brother. When she got to the Woodbridge exit she took this problem as an issue of faith. Every person is given the same measure of faith; like we all have the same number of muscles in our bodies. To become stronger in faith we must exercise it like our muscles.

Most times after church Linda went home inspired, but today she parked the car, challenged by conflicting views. Tiffany put her dirty clothes in the hamper next to her closet and changed into a tee shirt and shorts. Then she went in the living room and turned on the television, while Linda seasoned chicken legs for dinner in the kitchen. After placing the baking dish of chicken in the fridge Linda sat on the couch. Soon restlessness made her walk to the living room window. She still had her church clothes on except for her heels.

This was a good life she thought, pulling the curtain back to look up the street. Would it be so bad to forgive brother, and by doing it could that speed up her recovery? Linda looked at her car just out front and asked herself if she was going to trust God or not? Just then the wind blew the dirtiest looking plastic bag down the street, then lifted it into a tree branch directly over her car. She watched hoping it would take off again but it was stuck. Somehow this moment touched Linda's heart with peace, and the issue was settled. If for no other reason she decided to forgive her brother because the Lord says she must. When she looked up the bag wasn't there. She searched down the street and in the trees, but it was gone. Linda fixed the curtains, feeling confident about her choice and sat on the couch. She placed her arm around Tiffany's shoulder and began expressing pride about the decision to forgive that boy at school, something Linda couldn't bring herself to do at the diner. While they watched television Linda felt more and more satisfied because of faith. She never had to see Bennie again and he believed she'd died in a fire so no one was looking anymore. That's right, if he thinks she's dead it was going to stay that way.

Suddenly Linda remembered something and went to her room to write it down. The memory was of her and Bennie sitting on this rock in Colonial Park. It was mid-summer because there were people swimming in the pool. That long rock formed the shape of a bench by nature. Bennie told her he and his friends first started going there as teens. Later it became the perfect place to get out of their parent's sight. That rock could seat five, sometimes six, whenever they wanted to smoke a joint, and sip Pink Champale. Linda could see how happy Bennie was spending time and laughing with his friends. It was a special place to him that's why he'd bring her there. She thought of something else but didn't write it down. He was always on guard noticing people before they got close. She remembered he always looked around like a quiet warrior, and she felt safe with him. Before going back to the living room Linda wrote three more words, visit the rock. When the time was right she'd take Sonya to Harlem and sit on that rock if only to prove the memory genuine.

Linda watched the announcement for an upcoming football game then stroked Tiffany's hair. Seemed like a short time ago there was a flutter in her belly and now she was growing out of her shoes before the seasons could change. The thing that wasn't going to change was her determination to be the best example of a woman and mother for Tiffany. If that meant facing uncomfortable issues to have a clear mind, she had no choice but to face it. Next week would be better if she heard from Dr. Goldstein. Then she kissed the top of Tiffany's head. Funny, this Sunday seemed so different from the rest; then she wondered, why is Sunday the first day of the week?

True to his word, Dr. Goldstein worked assiduously to help Linda. All but a few of his appointments were cancelled from Monday to Wednesday. After Linda left his office and the last patient was gone he began reading medical research books at his desk well into the evening. Finally tired strained eyes and blurred letters forced him to stop and go home.

Saturday morning Dr. Goldstein woke early, kissed his wife's cheek before getting out of bed. He went to the kitchen, started the coffee maker, then to his study. Switching on the lamp he emptied his briefcase onto the desk, paying careful attention to the video camera and Linda's file. When he went back to the kitchen, enough coffee brewed to make one cup. He reached in the cabinet for his favorite mug, poured a cup, then replaced the pot to finish brewing. Straight black coffee would give him a quick start this morning, he reasoned, before closing the door to his study.

Sitting at his desk, he watched Linda's session four more times before conferring with a colleague over the phone. Then Dr. Goldstein made two copies of the video tape, and two audio cassettes. Now he sat staring at remarks written in Linda's file and making updates. The next time he tasted his coffee it was cold. For some strange reason after setting the cup down, he believed the tapes should be kept separately. So this morning when he was out he'd stop by the office to leave a copy.

The caffeine was making Dr. Goldstein feel anxious. He put the pen down then spun the swivel chair in the direction of his degree on the wall. There was room for so much more he thought and Linda's case could make it happen. Her results were all negative for abnormalities or tumors of the brain. She'd never been comatose or contracted any viral infections. What could explain why she spoke so oddly under hypnosis, and if he repeated the conditions would the results be the same? Its possible Linda suffered from a subtype of Multiple Personality Disorder, or a form of Asperger's. What if he was on the verge of a new medical discovery? Munchausen's Syndrome by Proxy didn't have a name until diagnosed in the 80's.

He glanced at his desk calendar, waving a pen over the Friday Linda was last in the office. Then he looked back at his degree, then back to that Friday at the bottom of the calendar. Dr. Goldstein began circling Friday the 27th with the pen for no particular reason, then had an idea while looking at the wall. If he diagnosed an unknown condition he'd get to choose its name. There would be lectures at universities, articles in all the latest medical journals, and appearances on talk shows. The name Goldstein would become world renowned in his profession. Then he could hang the plaques by the bookcase and the awards on top of the table. There was another thought that made him smile. He could finally take his wife Julie on that month–long cruise she dreamt about. All he had to do was identify the cause of Linda's affliction.

Dr. Goldstein recognized there were few days left before October so he needed to get moving. He walked around his desk and upstairs to his bedroom. As Julie passed in the hallway he said the coffee was ready and he was getting dressed to leave. When the doctor arrived at his office he left the copies of Linda's session locked in the cabinet with all the patient records. Then he left to meet Professor Stiles, a friend who taught at Rutgers University. Since the Professor spoke French, Latin, and Portuguese he might be able to shed light on what Linda said in her last session. If he couldn't help hopefully he knew someone who could.

Despite some Saturday afternoon traffic Dr. Goldstein arrived an hour early at Rutgers. So he went to the campus cafeteria for breakfast until the Professor's class was almost over. Then he went to room 305 and peered through the glass window in the door. Professor Stiles acknowledged him with a short hand gesture then kept speaking to his students. The doctor stepped aside leaning with his back on the wall and began gently tapping his briefcase against his leg. Suddenly Professor Stiles opened the door inviting the doctor to take a seat in the back.

When class ended and the last student left, Dr. Goldstein went to the front and sat next to Professor Stiles' desk. After exchanging a few pleasantries Dr. Goldstein put his tape player on the desk as if it were a carton of eggs and pressed play. Professor Stiles sat quietly staring at the machine as if it were actually talking. Then he grabbed some paper and asked to hear it again. This time after it started the Professor leaned in closer, intently scribbling every so often. When the tape finished he watched a finger slowly press the stop button then he looked up.

Stiles thought he'd recognized a word so he inquired about the patient's background. What her age was, where her parents were from, and when the recording was made? After answering they stared at each other a few seconds, then the Professor took a small black address book from his inside jacket pocket. He flipped to a page then reached for the phone, resting his hand on top. He told Dr. Goldstein there was a man who might be able to help identify the language. His name was Dr. Shri Azees, a retired Archaeolexicologist with a Ph.D. in ancient civilizations and languages. Professor Stiles thought of Azees because one of the words used may have early origins. He turned the paper around so Dr. Goldstein could see then he said the word "Yoba."

Professor Stiles convinced Dr. Goldstein Azees could be of assistance if he was available. Dr. Goldstein agreed so Professor Stiles made the call, however there was a slight problem. Azees and his wife were leaving for Paris in four days, and wouldn't be back until the end of October. If Goldstein wanted his help he'd have to drive to Pennsylvania about thirty miles from the Poconos tomorrow. Goldstein wasn't going to wait and this was the quickest way to get results, so he agreed.

That Sunday Dr. Goldstein and his wife left a few minutes after 7 to beat morning traffic. Soon after entering the state of Pennsylvania the drive was mostly uphill and after that, more hills with winding roads. Dr. Goldstein stuck to the speed limit as he was warned deer often crossed the road.

It was close to 10am when they turned into the driveway of the Azees home. Before Goldstein shut off the car, the door opened and a couple walked out to the porch. From a distance Dr. Azees favored Archie Bunker and his wife had a contagious smile like Gilda Radner from Saturday Night Live. They were led to the living room to rest from the drive, but Dr. Goldstein couldn't keep still. He sat on the couch across from his wife with his briefcase on his lap. Julie did most of the talking while her husband pretended to listen. After a few minutes Azees smiled at his wife then said, "Honey, I know the doctor wants to get busy so if you don't mind we're going to the study."

"No Dr. Azees, I'm not in a rush. I thank you for your hospitality. It was kind of you and your wife to see us on such short notice," Goldstein said humbly, placing his case on the floor.

"You're not rushing me Dr. Goldstein. I only hope I can be of assistance,"

"You've graciously allowed us to come into your home, please call me Samuel."

"Alright, and you must call me Shri."

Then with a slap on his knee Shri said to his wife, "Bella excuse us, we're going to the office,"

"Go ahead Samuel we'll be fine. Mrs. Azees and I can talk and later she's going to show me the house," Julie said to her husband before he took his briefcase.

Samuel followed Shri near the front door and down the hallway into the office. The room was filled with books in a custom bookcase wrapping around the entire room except for the two front windows and the door. On the left side of the bookcase was a ladder with wheels on the bottom while the top of the ladder was fixed to a rail. With this many books there had to be a clue in here.

"Shri…I've never seen so many books in one room in my life, except in the movies. So I have to ask, have you read all these books?" Samuel questioned jokingly, taking a seat across from the desk.

"Everyone who's ever been in here asks the same question and yes. I've read 99% or so," Shri said, pushing a stack of books across his desk.

Samuel was looking at the books when Shri said, "Let's hear what you have and I'll tell you what I think."

Samuel handed the cassette to Shri who put it in his player and began to listen. When it finished Shri started it over then went to the ladder pushing it to a section of books. He climbed up one step pulled out a book, then stretched out his arm for another. He stepped down and stood next to the ladder. When the tape stopped he said, "Interesting."

"What do you think? Can you tell what she is saying?" Samuel asked.

"Not really, at least not right at this moment. But it's clear she's speaking fluently to someone. What did she do when you played it for her, how did the patient react?"

"I had the session two days ago and she hasn't heard it yet. I'm trying to gather information before I speak with her."

"I see, well what I hear is, each time the patient pauses it's a clear indication of conversation."

"I don't understand. It was just the nurse and me in the room and we weren't talking."

"Let me explain... when people talk on a telephone you don't hear the other person's words. Still you know they're having a conversation, you see. The same applies in this instance; this patient was talking to someone, or possibly herself as a split personality. I can't tell, but she's definitely talking with someone."

"Shri, have you heard of a case like this before?"

"No, I can't say I have."

"Now this makes me believe one aspect of developing treatment is identifying what she's saying, and who she's talking to. Then I have to find out what type of trauma she suffered, and what role her brother played in it."

"I think your hypothesis has merit," Shri said, opening a book on his desk.

This time when Samuel attempted to ask another question Shri stopped him by raising his hand without looking away from the pages. Then he abruptly pushed the book aside to search in another. As Samuel sat patiently waiting, he looked at the books wondering how many were in this room. He counted six rows upward from the floor with different sized sections. The larger sections held 75 books or so across times six levels. As he began the math process in his head Shri said, "What she's saying is older than Latin, and I think it's older than a form of Farsi spoken in Iran. There are similar inflections of Sumerian, or Sanskrit spoken more than 4000 years ago and is still spoken today."

"You don't say."

"Compared to the English language this originated in the fifth century."

"So what we're speaking now started around 400AD?"

"Yes it's changed over the years but it's true, English is one of the younger languages. And you say this woman was born in the United States and her parents too?"

"Yes that's correct, but I never asked if she lived outside the country. So where could she have learned to speak what do you call it, Farsi from Iran?" Samuel asked sounding puzzled.

"Yes your patient could have learned it in Africa or parts of the Middle East, but it's not quite Farsi either. You see here's the thing, she uses the word "Yoba," and she called out to "Yampos." I believe these particular words are Egyptian nouns. There's a similar word "Yanie" used for matriarchal women. It could be the eldest woman in a family like an Aunt or even a Grandmother. In front of "Yoba" she says "Ismeti" which could be a person's name. Then when she used Yoba in context with the word "Yampos," that makes me think it's a root word of "Yampas" which means Father," Shri said turning the book around so Samuel could see. Leaning forward Samuel adjusting his glasses to look then said, "You can read this Egyptian stuff?"

"Sure, I'm able to read Hieroglyphics."

"So I guess my question is, if you can read Highra…what do you call it?" Samuel asked.

"Hiero…glyphics."

"Yes Hiero…glyphics. If you can read Hieroglyphics why can't you understand what's on the tape if the language is Egyptian? And how can people read those Hieroglyphics in the first place?" Samuel asked sounding skeptical.

"The answer to your question, how can we read the inscriptions, is purely by luck. Samuel, have you heard of the Rosetta Stone?" Shri asked interlacing his fingers.

"I've heard the phrase but no, I don't know what it is."

"Well the Rosetta Stone is a tablet found during the 19th Century in the town of Rosetta near the Nile Delta by a French soldier. At that same time Napoleon was shooting cannon balls at the face of the Sphinx and," Shri said pausing. Samuel just raised his hand like a student in a classroom.

"I never knew Napoleon went to Egypt, and what does he have to do with the stone?" asked Samuel hoping to get back to the subject of translation.

"Napoleon has nothing to do with translation of the stone, but whenever I tell the story I mention what Napoleon did. So where was I, when Napoleon saw the unmistakable African features on the face of the Sphinx he attempted to disfigure it with cannon fire. Remember the year was 1799 and slavery was big business in many parts of the world, not just America. He was no different than a lot of powerful men who believed African people were savages and meant to be slaves. So back to the Rosetta Stone, have you ever seen a sign written in more than one language? For instance ah… the word bathroom might be in English and under it the same word in French or Spanish?"

"Yes…yes I have."

"Well the Rosetta Stone is like one of those signs written in Egyptian, Greek, and Demotic script…you see. Before the discovery of the stone no one was able to decipher Egyptian symbols. Now because we can translate the symbols still doesn't tell us how the words were pronounced. You follow me?"

"Not exactly."

Shri put his fist under his chin for a moment then said, "Okay let's use the word "house" for example. In English it's "house," in Spanish it's "Casa." Same meaning, like if they were written together on a sign. We know how to pronounce "house," but there's no way to confirm how to pronounce the word Casa. If no one is available to say the word "Casa" how will you know what it sounds like, you see? That's the mystery of the Egyptian vocabulary. We can translate it, but we can't speak it. I can only make educated guesses based on similar languages from around that era."

Then Shri continued, "there are other factors. For instance, how many words do we presently have for "house" in English? There's "house," "home," "dwelling," "apartment," just to name a few and that's not talking about slang words or cultural separations. In some neighborhoods I heard the word "Crib" used in place of "house," while someone with money would say "mansion." We don't have enough time to discuss the intricacies of human language today, but I'll say this. There's a reason the dictionary is updated frequently to accommodate new words you see."

"Interesting…I never thought about languages that way, but it makes sense. So will you be able to help me?" asked Samuel leaning forward.

"I will try. I can't say for sure but I believe the word "Yoba" is used for "Aunt," "Grandmother," or a mixture of the two. If you leave the tape I can work on it when I get back. Now as I mentioned, my consultations are free, but to research this will be $100 an hour capping at $500," Shri said closing the book on his desk.

"Yes that will be fine, I'll write you a check and I'll leave the tape," Samuel said reaching inside his jacket.

"No Samuel, we'll wait until I get back then you can pay me."

"Okay, I'll speak to you when you get back," Samuel said standing to shake Shri's hand.

Sometime later the men joined their wives in the living room. When Julie finished her tea they said their goodbyes and were escorted to the car. Shri went over the route to the interstate then they all waved goodbye. Samuel drove down the mountain once again, keeping an eye out for deer and wild turkeys crossing the road. When he passed some familiar landmarks he relaxed. In between conversations with Julie he wondered would this trip be a waste of time and 500 dollars.

Shortly after 3pm Samuel crossed into New Jersey with an hour left to get home. As Julie dozed he thought about all that transpired. Shri and his wife were leaving to celebrate 42 years of marriage. Admittedly Samuel was caught off guard by the Azees's hospitality, extending an invitation to spend the night. If the situation were reversed Samuel wouldn't have.

Samuel's father was an old school Jew who taught his son to treat Arabs, Muslims, Blacks and basically anyone non-Jewish with the long handle spoon. Many times he'd heard his father say Arabs couldn't be trusted, and Blacks always wanted something done for them. So when Shri talked about Napoleon and others destroying evidence during the time of slavery, it had the ring of truth. Now time was correcting past mistakes, and the truth was rising. Today history had been taught by an Arab to help a black woman regain her sanity.

Not long after Julie woke up they turned onto their street and pulled into the driveway. Samuel got out and looked at the front door of the house. When he left that morning he never imagined Sunday could feel like a breeze pointing to the next day. All of a sudden he wondered could Shri tell why Sunday was the first day of the week.

The same day in the Bronx Sonya was finally getting home. After finding a space she walked towards her building, spotting Jeff's car across from the dry cleaners. For a minute she was happy that he was upstairs waiting. After taking a couple more steps she stopped to remind herself they were breaking up. Whatever excuse he had wasn't going to work, as she continued walking. Her decision was there would be no yelling or cussing. She wasn't going to get violent, and he damn sure wasn't going to get any pussy.

Sonya exited the elevator holding her door key like a switch blade ready for trouble. When she opened the door Jeff was on the couch in a wife beater and gym shorts. He had a sandwich on a paper plate next to a bottle of beer. He looked away from the football game to meet her while she locked the door. Jeff opened his arms for a hug but she brushed past mumbling on the way towards the bedroom. He figured Sonya needed to use the bathroom, so he sat back down.

Sonya put her purse on the dresser then noted the bed was made, but not the way she'd left it. That meant Jeff had spent the night, then she heard him call out, "Honey I got some cold cuts and hero bread for the game if you want a sandwich. Oh and I went to Johnson's, got you a barbeque rib dinner with mustard sauce. And later I want to take you somewhere."

Now he's going to act like nothing's wrong, she thought, sitting on the bed slipping out of her shoes. Should I have my shoes on when I tell him to get the hell out?

When Jeff didn't hear a response he went to the bedroom. Sonya stared at the wall as he stopped touching her shoulder to say, "I got you candy yams with collard greens, and a side of potato salad."

Sonya took a breath still holding her shoes and said sadly, "Jeff…why are you here? Don't you have some place you'd rather be?"

"What…what are you talking about? I told you I was gonna stay till you got home!" he answered confused. So that's why he never answered his phone. Worrying about Linda, Sonya totally forgot his plan was to sleep here. Then she walked to the closet tossing her shoes inside, not caring where they landed.

"Honey…did you forget?" said Jeff waiting for her answer.

"No I didn't forget! That's still no reason for you not to make sure I got to Jersey. I could've been in a car accident or something," she said reaching for a hanger but deciding to keep her clothes on.

"You're right and I would have called, but I don't have Linda's number. And I figured if something happened Linda would've called here looking for you," and when Sonya didn't answer he continued, "Plus you never told me what was wrong with her so I figured you know…it was something personal. How's she doing, she okay?" he said touching her shoulder with concern. At that moment Sonya was somewhat disgusted with herself for wanting to be held, but this had to be done. With slight force she pushed him out the way and leaned on the dresser. Finally she looked at Jeff and calmly said, "Okay, so how long you been seeing her?"

"Been seeing who?" Jeff asked looking astonished.

"Just tell me the truth Jeff!" she said loudly.

"Baby what are you talkin about? I been right here, come on now you tripping!" he answered defiantly.

What made Sonya angry was he should have replied I'm not seeing anyone, instead of saying who. Before she could control herself she was screaming at the top of her lungs,

"So you not gonna say nothing huh? Then you know what, I want you to get the fuck, outta my house…you lying bastard!!

She'd gone back on her word by yelling and cursing, so Sonya covered her eyes with her hand.

"Baby why you want me to go, what did I do?"

Jabbing her finger in his face she said, "Tell me what you been doing Jeff!"

"What the hell is wrong with you today?" he said holding his head.

"What's wrong with me? Is that what you said, what's wrong with me? I'll tell you exactly what the fuck is wrong with me and don't say a fucking word cause I know…I know!" she yelled in disgust.

"Know what? I didn't do anything."

Sonya stared at him until he stopped talking and said, "You know something Jeff, the truth has a funny way of coming out. People think they've covered all the bases, but it's impossible to think of everything."

"Baby I don't know what you're talking about?"

"Here's what I know. People can get away with shit for a while, sometimes years, but the truth finds a way. Like in those western movies when they portrayed Indians as savages scalping white men's hair."

Jeff interrupted to ask, "What are you talking about westerns and Indians for, and what are you so mad about?"

"Oh I'm gonna tell you. I'm sick of lies, and that was a lie! It was the Indians long braided hair being scalped by the white people. That's what white people do, cut off body parts for souvenirs. They did it to us, it wasn't the other way around, but the truth came out! Then there was the Son of Sam! He was killing all those people and they caught his ass from a parking ticket, which brings me to you! It's a small world Jeff, and people see stuff just by coincidence."

Sonya decided to make up her next example, "I knew a man whose girlfriend was messing around with this other man. They were hooking up way out in Long Island. She figured nobody would see them cause she lived in Brooklyn, but guess what. One of her boyfriend's co-workers was in Long Island that day visiting some people and saw her, just by coincidence."

Sonya gave a slight smile until he worked up the courage to ask, "So what's your point?"

She crinkled her lips, folded her arms across her chest, cocked her head to one side and said, "What's my point? Tell me about Cathy…that's my fucking point!"

Jeff looked down timidly at the floor not knowing what to do. He'd been seen and she knew, he thought. The television announced the two-minute warning before half time from the living room. Jeff took a deep breath, opened his mouth but nothing came out. He was at the threshold of confession, like a criminal sitting in the interrogation room. Only a push was required. That's when Sonya abruptly stepped away from the dresser. Perfume bottles and necklaces clinked when she walked past. Then Sonya spoke as if she didn't care, "So…tell me about Cathy."

Jeff still wouldn't say anything and Sonya refused to mention the name again, instead she baited him.

"You told me you loved me, and I was so stupid!" she said sounding very upset.

"Baby I do love you, I…"

"No you don't! If ya did I wouldn't be going through this. You'd just tell me the truth, so just say it!"

Jeff spoke his confession, "Alright…Sonya I made a mistake, I'm sorry. But if you give me another chance, Sonya, Sonya I swear you won't regret it. It will never happen again. I do love you baby, I really do."

The pain forced her to the bathroom slamming the door behind her. Amidst her sobs she screamed out, "Get your shit, and get the fuck away from me! I don't ever want to see you again!"

"Sonya, can we just talk please. I'm sorry baby, I made a mistake. I wasn't trying to hurt you. That's the last thing I wanted to do!" Jeff said, pleading over the sound of weeping.

Her sobs eventually stopped, then it got quiet. Jeff heard sniffles then water running in the sink. Sonya looked in the mirror then washed her face. Afterwards she sat on the edge of the tub. Jeff leaned close to the door and said, "Sonya…can we finish talking?"

"Yes," she answered with slow deliberation, "You made it very clear you still want to see other women."

"Sonya that's not true baby."

She imagined his face speaking close to the door to hear him so clearly. Somehow she'd felt this day would come so there was a certain amount of peace. He liked those skinny women and it was just a matter of time. With confidence and less need for yelling Sonya said, "Jeff…you're just not a man who wants a good woman, and that's your choice. I understand that. And you know what's funny? I'm not mad at you anymore. But you need to leave me alone so the right kinda man can find me!"

"That's not true; I know you're a good woman. As a matter of fact, remember I said I wanted to go out later? Well…" he was interrupted.

"I don't want to hear it Jeff, we're through you hear me! This is what's going to happen. I'm going to wait until you leave cause I can't stand to look at you right now. And if you don't leave soon, I'm just gonna call the police. Either way you are going to leave!" Sonya said speaking to the door like it was him.

"Okay," he said sadly going to the living room.

When he got to the couch Jeff looked for his gym bag, and began rummaging around inside. He took out a small velvet covered box then went back to Sonya's bedroom. He stood in front of the bathroom and said,

"Sonya I just wanted to say this and when I finish I'll leave, and if you don't want to give me another chance I understand."

Then he got down on his knees inches away from the door and said, "I've been a fool, but I am in love with you. I want to spend the rest of my life with you. I was asking you to go out later because I wanted to go to where we had our first date and do this."

Sonya sat on the tub looking at the door and heard him say, "Hopefully this will be a proposal we can tell our friends about, or at least some part of it. Sonya…I love you and if you marry me I will spend the rest of my life proving it."

Jeff opened the box and pushed it next to the door. Sonya's heart raced as Jeff's voice stuttered, "I…I have this… ring…here and I want… no wait. Sonya I want to ask you to be my wife. Sonya, please will you marry me?"

Jeff stared at the door waiting on both knees not knowing what more to say. Minutes went by without a sound. Then Jeff said, "Honey if you don't love me anymore I'll leave. I don't want to cause any problems I just want to see your face. Can you just open the door please?"

He was on the other side of that door asking to be her husband and she didn't know what to do. Finally Sonya looked in the medicine cabinet mirror. Today's sermon was about forgiveness and she did want to. So she looked in the mirror again, then placed her hand on the knob and opened the door. Jeff was on his knees looking humble. First she saw chest hair at the top of his shirt, and then she saw the ring. It had to be more than a carat with a circular cut, and it was lovely. Jeff took the ring in his hand and asked the question.

"Will you marry me?"

Sonya's fingers covered her lips as she held out her hand. Jeff placed the ring on her finger and stood up. Faint sounds of their lips pressing together were barely heard as the announcer called out the game.

Jeff and Sonya made love and eventually laughed during the course of the day. That afternoon as they spooned, Jeff took a nap. His warm breath on the back of her neck was the perfect combination while admiring her hand. Looking at a ring in the jewelry store is fine; having it on your finger is much better, she thought. She loved how the colors shifted, and the way it sparkled. Who she'd tell first could wait until tomorrow, right now she was engaged to be married. Jeff pulled her body closer then drifted back to sleep. Sonya, satisfied with her decision to keep him, touched his leg with her feet. Earlier that same morning she opened her eyes facing a dreadful existence. Now she was engaged on a Sunday, the first day of the week.

On that same day a dark-skinned man in his fifties sat at a small wooden table flipping through a beige folder in Rahway, NJ. He was in a safe house leased to an organization so secret it had no name. This man was one of 17 men, and a couple of women who used the name West as an alias since the time of Napoleon. Several years ago a different Mr. West working with the same organization met Benjamin Reeves in Africa. That Mr. West was responsible for smuggling Linda out of the hotel in Cairo to the United States. Their organization supplied Bennie with a forged passport for Linda and the private jet. In exchange Bennie let them take charge of the Obeni. Incidentally, the lie Bennie and Linda were siblings started with that forged passport.

The recent Mr. West's title was field Director charged with protecting African culture within an organization. He'd spent Friday night until this Sunday in this three-bedroom home waiting to contact other members. At precisely 11pm Mr. West looked at his watch anticipating a knock at the door. When the knock came he closed the folder and remained seated. Seconds later the door opened and Mr. Soriano entered, then sat down saying nothing. Exactly fifteen minutes later there was another knock followed by someone using a key. This time it was Nurse Aquino who was hired to assist Dr. Goldstein with Linda.

Before sitting down Nurse Aquino went to the kitchen counter, turned the radio to any station with music and sat down. She pulled the blonde wig off her head exposing her short black hair, then she stuffed the wig in her purse. No one spoke for the first five minutes then Mr. West asked a question, leaning in to hear the answer, "What is the report?"

"After the last meeting I sold the client a car. I haven't seen a change in the client's behavior. Her attitude and overall health remains positive. She is actively seeking help to regain her memory from a local therapist. Early this morning I followed the therapist to a home in the Poconos. He visited about two hours and left to return home. I will find out whose home it was and get back with that information.

The client joined a church in East Orange but we do not observe her during worship service. She still maintains the friendship with Sonya who poses no threat. The client still works at the local Library, and picks her child up from daycare. Mrs. West maintains surveillance on the client from the apartment below and that is all," Soriano said, leaning back in his chair.

"Fine, now you," Mr. West said.

Nurse Aquino spoke anxiously and without the Pilipino accent she had at the doctor's office.

"Let's see…um, well first I got inside the doctor's office at 10pm tonight. I was able to get the video and cassette of Friday's procedure. I can tell these are copies," Aquino said, setting a manila envelope on the table.

Mr. West pulled the envelope closer then waited for her to continue.

"I took about twenty patient files from the cabinet then threw them outside in drains at the curb. I used green spray paint on the office walls, and on a few cars outside, then I threw the can in the trash. It should look like a random act of vandalism, or a high school prank. I drove around to make sure I wasn't followed then I came here. And can I just say it's an honor to see the Princess again after so many years! She can walk and talk now; I just can't believe it!" she said with exhilaration.

Awkward silence filled the room then finally Mr. West looked at Soriano and said, "I will be in contact with you."

With those last words Soriano left, locking the door behind him. Mr. West looked out the window then sat back in his seat. He looked disappointed, so Aquino said, "I messed up and I'm sorry, but seeing the Princess walking and talking was unbelievable. I was told years ago when I first saw her at the hotel in Cairo she…I mean the client, would never be able to care for herself. I was so excited and to see how healthy and beautiful she's become!"

Mr. West wasn't sharing her enthusiasm. Instead he opened the folder to a page and said, "I see when you signed on with us you used the name Hansi in Cairo, is that correct?"

"Yes I went by the name Hansi, yes."

"And you were acting as a maid for the hotel?"

"Yes I was. I didn't actually work for the hotel, my badge and uniform were fakes," she answered humbly.

"The man who left this room, did you ever see him in Cairo during the time you worked at the hotel?" asked Mr. West.

"No, only here in this country for this assignment."

"So you assume he knew the client was the Princess?"

"I messed up. That will never happen again," she said immediately.

"We pay you well don't we?" he said looking at the paper from his folder.

"Yes sir."

"We also make sure your family is well cared for?"

"My children and my parents…yes."

"When was the last time you had contact with them, about ten ago months right?"

"I would hate to have you terminated from our employment. You've invested all these years with us and we value your service."

Of course she had no idea termination from their employment fully terminated never to be seen again.

"It will never happen again," she answered apologetically.

"See that is doesn't! And since I believe you, there will be no record of this indiscretion," he said, standing as a signal the meeting was over.

"Thank you Mr. West, I will be more careful," she said closing her purse.

He walked her to the door and locked it, then went to the window to watch her drive away. Afterwards he wrote everything down, including Aquino's outburst and that he told her it would be secret. Then he signed it and wrote the date, the last Sunday of the month and the first day of the week.

Chapter 10

1992 was a challenge to each character in this script. For Lorraine it was keeping eyes on Ronald after crashing Bennie's birthday. She wondered why Ronald hid his wedding ring with gloves the night she busted up their little threesome. When he least expected it Lorraine would drop few questions on her husband like, why couldn't she go since Bennie's girlfriend was coming? Then follow with, why'd you take those gloves off when I came in? So after Lorraine added up her suspicions she was going to force Ronald to make concessions to keep the peace.

For Ronald it was Lorraine's relentless surveillance keeping him from apologizing to Kayla. For Kayla it was the offense of being discarded like a tissue by Ronald. For Bennie it was their drama, plus his own, playing out like an installment of the Twilight Zone. He was an unwilling participant in a dreary urban soap opera. Didn't matter changing the channel, the story was different, the actors were the same, and every episode ended with a bridge collapse. Not to mention Bennie was still looking to dissolve the partnership because the tension between once close friends wasn't going away.

It was the 2nd of February and Ronald hadn't been out for a weekend without Lorraine since he left Kayla with Bennie together. The first day after the incident when Ronald went to the office Lorraine stopped by unannounced. After that she took a new interest in the laundry business by volunteering to oversee deliveries, and inventory stock. In all the years Ronald and Bennie had the stores Lorraine never had a key, but she wanted a set to all the stores. Finally, with Valentine's Day approaching, she surprised Ronald by booking a trip to the Bahamas for six days.

Bennie's first week in February focused on a replacement for Chris, who was getting weaker by the day. Hiring someone to fill his shoes was difficult to say the least. They wanted a person who spoke Spanish, and who wasn't easily intimidated by the occasional rowdy customer. What made it a real challenge was Ronald and Bennie disagreed on all of the applicants. Bennie wanted a person who'd use the job as an opportunity for advancement. Someone interested in going to school, or supporting their family. Ronald fixated on hiring attractive women, or unreliable friends from the neighborhood. In the end, to punish Ronald, Lorraine sided with Bennie to make the choice while they were in the Bahamas.

The person Bennie chose two days after the first interview for the assistant manager position was Jorge Garcia. Jorge was 52 years old, tanned in complexion, with strands of gray throughout his hair. He had a thick mustache and spoke Spanish; a requirement Bennie and Ronald were looking for. The day Jorge completed the application Bennie discussed the code of conduct, and what was expected from employees. They had to be sober during work hours, and punctual. Kleenit employees were not to speak profanity in the workplace, or use customers as their personal dating pool. Afterwards they discussed a temporary work schedule and starting salary. When they were finished Bennie asked Jorge to wait outside by the dryers. While observing Jorge on the monitor Bennie called Mr. Queen, the Private Detective who delivered the sad news about Linda and Tiffany's death in the fire. Mr. Queen kept friends within the New York Police Department that could run criminal background checks, and Bennie wanted one on Jorge.

So while waiting for a call back from Mr. Queen, Bennie watched Jorge sit patiently, pulling his feet from the aisle whenever customers passed by. One time without hesitation Jorge went to help an elderly woman having trouble pulling her cart. If Mr. Garcia's records were clean Bennie saw no reason not to give Jorge the job. So when Mr. Queen hadn't called back after thirty minutes Bennie told Jorge he'd give him a call in a day or two.

There was also that situation between Kayla and Ronald. Since Bennie's birthday Ronald hadn't seen Kayla, or said sorry for leaving that night. Kayla's promotion kept her busy training at another branch near Battery Park so he couldn't call her at work. Whenever Ronald called Kayla at home, if she didn't pick up, he never left a message. So the evenings left Kayla listening to silence from the answering machine. All Ronald had to do was talk and she'd pick up, but if he stayed quiet so would she. As far as Kayla was concerned if Ronnie really wanted to see her, he'd come by her place. Until then, Kayla wasn't going to chase after him.

By Thursday Ronald and Lorraine left for the airport. Friday Kayla went to work and had an awful day. She wasn't able to focus because her stomach was in knots. Kayla wondered if Ronnie knew about Bennie and didn't want to see her. To tell the truth Bennie didn't have to have sex with her, he could have left no matter what she said. So it wasn't her fault, and that's what she'd tell Ronnie. If not that, then it could be Lorraine saw her kiss him before coming over. It did seem like she came out of nowhere. If Lorraine did see, was she the type of woman to stay calm, or wait till she got Ronald home? They could have talked to divorce lawyers and were waiting for the paperwork. Then it could just be everything was fine, and Ronnie had to be cool for a minute. Whatever the case it made her nerves a wreck.

It took almost three weeks before curiosity got the best of Kayla. After another sleepless night she left work early feeling distraught. Kayla told the instructor she wasn't feeling well so he told her to go home. Since she met Ronnie they'd never gone this long without talking. Once again there were no messages on her machine when she got home. Even the cat tried to comfort her, rubbing its head on Kayla's foot, and purring to ease her nerves. It didn't make sense to spend another weekend alone sitting on the couch flicking channels. All of a sudden Kayla saw the clothes overflowing in the hamper and got up. Ronald had a couple of hours before he left work. All she had to do was go to the right store.

Kayla kicked off her heels and looked at the time; it was 12:45. Her heart raced and so did her feet to grab the laundry bag. She went to the closet, took out the metal cart so fast it dropped on her toe. No time to indulge the pain. Instead she opened the cart then hobbled a few steps to the hamper. Kayla continually shoved her hand inside to pull out some clothes. Instantly she changed her mind about the cart, opting to take just enough clothes to carry over her shoulder. Quickly she dumped half the clothes back into the hamper, then with a swinging motion tossed the bag by the front door. Her pinky toe throbbed, and if it were broken that wouldn't have stopped her. Instead Kayla's prescription for pain was to treat it with determination.

Kayla tied her hair in a ponytail on the way to the bathroom. Before she went in she unzipped her dress and threw it on top of the hamper. One look in the mirror reminded her to take out her earrings in case it got nasty. Then she stepped into some baggy jeans, a pullover sweater, and a blue parka. She took a wallet out of her purse, shoved it in the pocket, snatched that laundry bag off the floor, and dashed out the door. When Kayla reached the stoop, Keionte offered to help with her bag. Keionte was an honor student with a crush on Kayla from the time she moved in.

He was also one of the boys Kayla pretended to be scared of so Bennie could walk her upstairs.

Ten minutes later Kayla got out of the cab around the corner of the Eight Avenue Kleenit. Not many people were there so a lot of machines were available. Kayla peaked inside then opened the door, creeping like Old Saint Nicholas to a corner machine. Once the clothes were in the machine she brought a single box of detergent, and got a bunch of quarters. Now and again she watched the office and listened for voices. If Lorraine and Ronald were inside Kayla would just say she came to see Bennie and got her signals crossed. On the other hand, if Lorraine found out the truth and wanted to fight that was okay too. For a small woman Kayla knew how to handle herself from fights with dancers stealing her money in the strip club. Hopefully Lorraine wasn't around so she could find out why Ronnie wasn't talking to her.

As soon as Kayla put the final quarter in the slot Bennie walked through the door. She kept her head down as he went down the main aisle. A woman who must have been a regular customer began flirting with him. She asked when he was going to take her out for dinner. Kayla started the machine then heard Bennie clearly say he had a girlfriend. After that very brief exchange he said goodbye, then went to the office and closed the door. Kayla knew it wouldn't be long before he saw her inside on the monitor so she wasn't going to linger. She added the soap then went to the office and knocked. Several seconds passed before Bennie opened the door. He looked at her with a blank expression. He wasn't happy, annoyed, or startled to see her. Finally he spoke, "What's up Kayla?"

"What's up, how are you doing?" she asked bashfully.

"I'm good," he answered standing in the doorway.

"For a minute I thought you were gonna tell me you didn't know who I was," she answered, looking up at him. He made a small grin then looked past her.

"Bennie were you busy?" she asked timidly.

"Well actually yes, I got some paper work to do and I need to get started on it."

"Okay I won't keep you, but can I talk to you real quick just for a minute…please?" Kayla asked desperately.

"Yeah sure…come in," he said stepping aside then closing the door.

Bennie went to the file cabinet, took out some papers then sat behind the desk. He put a pen and a calculator next to the pile then looked at Kayla. She stood by the chair in front of the desk and just came out with it.

"I never wanted to cause any trouble for either one of you guys. I don't look for drama. Bennie I stay away from drama! So I just wanted to say I'm sorry I wasn't trying to mess anything up for anybody, and that's all I wanted to say."

"Kayla we good…for real."

"For real for real?" she repeated with her familiar chuckle.

"You and me…we good for real. I've just got to add up this stuff, do the inventory, and get something to eat," he answered a bit friendlier.

Kayla uttered a sigh of relief and asked, "And what about Ronnie, you guys okay too?"

Once again Ronald left Bennie in the middle of a mess needing to be cleaned up. It was all making sense now. Lorraine stuck to her husband like glue after that night so Ronald never had a chance to see Kayla, that's why she was here. For some stupid reason Ronald never left messages on Kayla's answering machine in case she got mad and played a message for Lorraine. All this nonsense was beginning to stress Bennie out and Kayla could see it building. "Yeah nothing's changed, we're fine. They went out of town, he'll be back next week and no, he doesn't know about us," he said, not giving any more information.

"Okay that's good, thank you. Like I said I'm not here to cause any problems. So I'm gonna check my machine and let you get to your stuff. I'll talk to you later."

She went to the door turned around and said, "It was nice to see you and take care."

With some reluctance he answered, "it was nice to see you too. take care of yourself."

Kayla sat in a chair across from her machine, watching her clothes go around. She tried to act like hearing Ronnie was out of town didn't matter. Here was that identical ugly feeling again forming a cruel pattern. Kayla looked at the television mounted from the ceiling, wondering if Bennie was watching her from the office. Of course he was but did he view her with pity or amusement, because she was looking for a man that was with his wife?

Before the clothes entered the rinse cycle Kayla stepped outside to get some air. At least she had some answers and began to feel hungry. She walked up the block to the Chinese restaurant for two orders of chicken wings with shrimp fried rice. While waiting she looked through the window at the people walking pass. What was wrong with this picture? When Mercedes came on stage men set their drinks down and yelled out her name. More than once, other dancers complained how some men would leave if she wasn't working that night. Hell, it just took a smile and some clever conversation with a visiting corporate executive to be offered that promotion. Men chased after her, she didn't chase after them. It was time for a man's hands to touch her body, but not just any man. The night she invited Bennie inside she'd had too much to drink. While the sex was good it was strictly for revenge. Her mind was never totally with Bennie and neither was her body.

When the order was ready Kayla returned to the laundry with confidence and a plan. The machine finished so she put her clothes in the dryer then knocked at the office door. This time it took longer but Bennie eventually opened the door. Kayla raised the bag and said, "I got some wings and shrimp fried rice. You said you were hungry and I hadn't eaten all day so I got something for you too. Do you mind if I eat in here? Your girlfriend's been giving me the stink eye since I came out."

"Sure come on in," he said, getting a whiff of the food when she walked by.

There was a small card table in the room when they wanted to eat inside the office. Kayla put the bag on the table, moved a newspaper and a skull cap to the couch then put her coat next to them. Bennie sat back at the desk and started writing. She placed a paper plate and fork on opposite ends of the table then put the food out.

"Bennie how long you gonna be?"

"I'm working on these numbers right now, I'll get to it," he said continuing to write.

Kayla wanted to distract him so she asked, "Bennie do you remember what day was last Wednesday, I mean the date? Was it the 6th or the 7th? I think it was the 7th."

Bennie stopped writing to say, "Wait a minute, let me write this down."

"Never mind, forget about that, just tell me does February have 27 or 28 days this year?" she asked, placing a fork and napkin on his side.

"February can't end with 27 days. It has to have 28 or 29 depending on the year," he said, trying to regain his thoughts.

"Oh that's right. So let me see…there are four weeks, no wait, how many days this month?" she chuckled, watching him think about what she asked.

"It's um…ahh man I messed up. I wrote a four down. This doesn't go here," he said, sounding irritated.

"That gets em every time. It's hard to add up numbers when somebody's talking about numbers. Like when you're trying to remember a song and somebody keeps singing something else. You got to concentrate; you've got to focus Mookie!" Kayla said, making him laugh a little.

He shook the pen at her then put it down and came to the table. The ice was broken by her infectious laugh then she said, "Alright now Bennie that's more like it. I don't want to eat by myself, and when my clothes are finished I'm outta here. I got to go home and feed my dog."

"A cat named Dog, I still can't believe it," he said laughing a little.

"See it works. You can't help but laugh, that's why I did it. Now come on and eat while it's hot, then I'm gonna get out of here."

She opened his container and they sat down together. Then Bennie said, "Thanks Kayla this was nice."

Now Kayla began to select her words carefully. "No problem and you're welcome. You told me you didn't eat, and I was starving. We have Coke and grape soda, which do you want?" she asked placing a straw in front of him.

"Let me have the Coke."

Once he had a bite Kayla tasted the chicken and said, "This is okay, but mine tasted better. What do you think? Do you like this, or do you like what I gave you at my house?"

Bennie stopped chewing to raise one eyebrow.

"The wings man, you know I'm talking about the wings," said Kayla, trying to look serious.

"Yours were good no doubt," he said watching her perk up.

Kayla let those words marinate and when she was ready for another wing she said, "I didn't know you had a girlfriend, how long you been with her?"

"Who told you I had a girlfriend?" he asked sounding aggravated.

"Wait a minute," she said gesturing for him to relax, "I just asked cause I heard you tell that lady you had a girlfriend, that's why."

"Oh…you were out there then?"

"Yes," Kayla said wiping her face.

"Well I don't have one. I always say that because I don't date the customers. It's bad for business."

"You telling me you never dated any of the customers?"

"That's right."

"Well I'm glad I wasn't washing clothes before you knew me. And by the way, I didn't date customers either," she said hoping that would sink in.

As they ate Bennie remained quiet. Where was the guy who got familiar in the middle of her living room? When he wiped his mouth Kayla asked, "Are you wearing the slippers you got for your birthday, tell the truth?"

"No I haven't. I put them in my room and when my dog saw them he thought they were a toy and ripped them up…I'm sorry. I didn't think he'd do that."

"Okay," she answered with regret.

Kayla was about to offer to buy another pair, then changed her mind. This was a chess game, and the board had to be played with caution so she continued eating. That's when Bennie broke the silence and said, "I really was going to wear them Kayla."

"I believe you," she answered with some delight.

There had to be something Bennie was passionate about, but she couldn't think what it was. Kayla noticed a newspaper on the couch and reached for it.

"Is this your Amsterdam News?" she asked.

"Yup."

"This paper's been around a long time."

"Yup, I've been reading it and the City Sun since before the Tawana Brawley incident."

"I remember Tawana Brawley and no matter what the news said, I believed her. It's not like they're gonna come out and admit they did it!" Kayla said, sounding a bit annoyed.

"I always believed her…always," he said with compassionate eyes.

That was it Kayla thought. He was into black issues, justice, culture, and history. So Kayla asked, "Do you remember that picture of Malcolm X at my house?"

"Yeah those black and white photos are special. They make me think of the old days," He answered wondering what that had to do with anything.

"I was thinking about Malcolm X the other day. Did you know Spike Lee is coming out with a movie about him at the end of the year?

"Yeah I knew, I'm gonna go see it when it comes out."

"Me too, but I was gonna say I thought about how Malcolm changed when he realized he was wrong about Elijah, and race relations," she said finally having his attention. "That's what I'm trying to do. I've made some mistakes that I'm not going to repeat. You know I don't dance anymore and I feel good about that. Didn't I tell you I gave all my outfits to Diamond?"

"Yeah you told me. How is she doing?"

Kayla held the soda can close to her face and with a stern tone said, "No you didn't just ask me about Diamond again did you?"

"No I wasn't asking."

"Bennie I get you with that every time. I'm playing with you man. I talked to Diamond a couple of weeks ago and she's fine," Kayla said taking a drink and continuing, "Did I tell you I gave her all my outfits cause I ain't never going back there again. If I dance again it will be for an audience of one. And I been hoping no one comes in the bank that knew me as Mercedes. But if it happens, that's the price I have to pay for what I did. So I decided to get a certification for public accounting since I like working with numbers, that way I won't be in the public as much."

"So how's the promotion coming?"

"It's going good, thanks for asking. I've done a lot of reading to learn the correct procedures for stuff," she said, giving him a reason to ask more questions.

"Procedures like what?"

"Well like what to do if God forbid the bank gets robbed, which I can't talk about. Then there's the different identifying codes for transactions and order forms, stuff like that. Now all I have is two more weeks and I'm finished. After that they'll send me to another branch for more training and then hopefully I can find one close to my school."

"Well I'm happy for you, and I know you're gonna do it," he said, this time with a full-blown smile.

She could tell Bennie was pleased so while he was tuned in to her wavelength Kayla said,

"I know you don't like being in the middle of this mess..."

Bennie tried to interrupt her. "Kayla...I don't want to talk about..." then she stopped him and said, "Wait...I'm trying to say I came over here to tell Ronnie I can't see him anymore. I made a mistake and it's not going to happen again. The man has a wife and I know better now. Bennie you know me; I'm as loyal as a damn puppy dog. When his wife came in that night I played along for his sake. Another woman would've let Lorraine know who she was really with, but I didn't want to see him get hurt. So I took one for the team as they say," said Kayla briefly laughing, "But it really felt like falling on a grenade. And if I had to make the same choice I'd do it again. That way Ronald didn't get in trouble, and she didn't blame you for being with us."

"And she definitely would've blamed me, she always does."

"What did you do to her?"

"Nothing!" he answered sadly.

Bennie refused to give Kayla ammunition to use against Ronald even if it shed light on their personal problems.

"Well she don't like you one bit. So anyhow like I said, I took one for the team, and kept you out of it." She said wiping her mouth with a napkin.

"Thanks Kayla."

"No, I should be thanking you for helping me get over that night, cause I'd never hurt you either Bennie or say anything about us. I went along but don't think for a minute it was easy for me!" said Kayla closing her container.

"I feel you."

Little did Kayla know Bennie didn't give a damn if Ronald found out they had sex. He'd come close to telling Ronald one day after coming back from an errand in the Bronx. On the way to Third Avenue Bennie crossed the bridge into the Bronx and read a sign for a carwash coming soon. It was on the exact spot he'd proposed to Ronald near the Bronx Terminal Market. That pissed him off and when Bennie returned to the store Lorraine got on his case about water on the bathroom floor. All that needed to be done since she'd hung around so much was get a mop, and clean it up. Instead she waited for her husband to step out then told Bennie to do it. The only thing that kept Bennie from telling Ronald right then was Lorraine being there.

"So I got that off my chest and now I'm going home," Kayla said standing to clean the table. When she finished Kayla put her container in the garbage then stood within arm's reach to say, "Bennie the last time I saw you I was a bit tipsy. Don't get me wrong, I knew what I was doing and I wanted you to be with me that night."

"We had a nice time Kayla," he said, eyes glancing from her head down to her knees.

"Tell me something. Did you do it because of the liquor, or did you just want me? I need to know so please tell me the truth," she asked submissively.

"I didn't drink that much."

It was a strange way to answer her question but she accepted it. Tearing up Kayla said,

"Bennie that's good to know. You have no idea what it means to hear you say that. Feeling worthless was…was hard to accept. That's one of the reasons I think I laugh so much, it's work being mad with people all the time. Men can do some vicious things when they don't respect you. You dated a dancer before. She must have told you stories, or maybe not. On the other hand I'd be lying if I said it didn't feel good when those bills were thrown at me. Then to be shoved to the side like a dirty old rag was my wakeup call. I'm glad to know you don't think I'm a piece of trash."

Kayla's words would have melted the coldest heart. Bennie pushed his chair out and opened his arms to hug her. Then as she looked at the floor he said, "Don't let anyone make you feel like trash because it's not true."

Kayla held her face on his chest wrapping her arms around his waist letting out a sigh of relief. She wasn't pulling away this time, instead she held him until he let go.

That's when she took a step back, looked up at him and said, "I won't…and by the way when you left my house that night what did you say to those kids, cause they haven't bothered me?"

"Nothing, they weren't there when I left."

"Alright, well thanks again," she said stepping away.

Kayla waited for him to speak and when he did he said, "You take care of yourself and thanks for the wings."

She smiled then walked to the door, put her hand on the knob and said softly, "Why you make it so hard for a sister?"

"What?"

"Will you come by and see me tonight? I want a real friend and I need to know you came over because you wanted to."

"Kayla I don't know…I might," he said with a blank expression.

"Alright well I'm going home to finish cleaning up, then I'm gonna take a nice bath. You remember the address?"

"Yes I remember."

"Alright then, about ten I'll be relaxing in the tub…all wet…just thinking about you," she said after one of her giggles.

Bennie shook his head saying nothing, so Kayla asked one last thing, "Bennie…you remember my last name?"

"Yeah it's Palmison."

"What did you say?"

"Palmison," he repeated.

"Just one more time baby, what's my name?" Kayla said happily.

Finally he laughed and said, "It's Palmison…Palmison."

"Well all righty then," she said closing the door behind her.

Bennie went back to the desk and tried working, but was frequently distracted. He couldn't stop watching Kayla on the monitor. There was a new conception beyond what ordinary eyes could appreciate. A man seeing Kayla wouldn't consider under those baggy clothes was one of the sexiest strippers in five boroughs. They'd never accept that a stripper became a bank manager and could prepare and file your income taxes. Or that behind her sometimes-goofy demeanor stood a kind, honest, vulnerable, and resilient woman who liked Malcolm X.

Once again Bennie tried to write but his eyes focused on Kayla folding clothes then filling her bag. He wondered if she'd find an excuse to come back, but that didn't happen. When she finished she threw the bag over her shoulder and walked out the door. Bennie watched, hoping she would return, but that didn't happen either. Eventually he went back to work starting at the beginning because Kayla's stunt might have compromised his addition. Bennie finished around 8pm then went out to walk the aisles preparing to close the store. One woman folded the last of her clothes near the front door while another lady waited for the dryer to stop. He flipped the closed sign to face the outside then locked the front door. He stood there looking through the glass at the people walking past. When the women were done he dimmed the lights then put the money in the safe and headed home.

The dog waited on the other side of the alcove and began wagging his stubby tail. This was one of those nights Bennie wasn't in the mood to walk Mister. Instead he went to the basement with Mister following and stood by the backyard door. Then he turned on the flood light and went outside. As Mister went back and forth sniffing, Bennie gave thought to Kayla's proposal. It was amusing the way she got him to say her last name before leaving. It unquestionably stirred a memory that excited him. On the other hand, going to her house was just asking for trouble he thought, with his hands in his pockets. How open would she be sexually if he came over this time? Then there was the way Kayla said she'd be all wet just thinking about him. He should go and wear her little tail out just for saying that.

Finally Mister picked a spot, that's when Bennie took a plastic bag from his back pocket. In the evening light he visualized Kayla in the tub with the water making that swishing sound. Maybe she had suds to make her look like that woman from the movie Superfly. Bennie picked up after Mister and he threw the contents in a container he kept outside. She said the drinks had nothing to do with what happened, and she and Ronald were over so why not go? He was comfortable around her and since Kayla took one for the team, he could have sex with her again.

Once Mister finished they went back in the house. Bennie gave the dog fresh water and food then sat on the living room couch. He envisioned taking Kayla for a ride that very moment. Before getting too aroused he grabbed the remote but didn't turn the television on right away. He sat still until Mister appeared licking his lips after the meal. Bennie rubbed the dog's head while that stubby tail wagged and his tongue draped to one side. Lightheartedly he asked the dog a question, "Mister what do you think? It's been a long time since I had some. Should I go over there? That means I gotta call Jorge to open the store on his day off."

Mister watched intently as if asked to do perform a command. With his finger paused he got a bit more comfortable then abruptly spoke out,

"I'm gonna stay home with you buddy…alright? Don't think I forgot about the last time you tried to stop me from going out. I wished I'd listened to you. So I'm staying right here."

Mister seemed to understand and lay his head on Bennie's foot. That finger was still over the button but his mind was on Kayla. She admitted being with Ronald was her mistake, and that she never meant to cause any harm, and he believed it. Plus Kayla told the truth when she said she took one for the team. Bennie hated to think what would've gone down if Lorraine found Ronald was cheating with Kayla and he was there. Maybe it was time Kayla played on a winning team Bennie thought, while touching his crotch. That night they had sex he was better than Ronald. Kayla might have tried to fake an orgasm to make him feel better, but the second one was real. On the other hand it doesn't matter, he's not going anywhere. So he pressed the button for the television and took off his sneakers. But before he settled on a channel he asked himself the question that haunted him for the past few hours. Why'd Kayla have to say she'd be all wet just thinking about him?

For the past week the only chore done diligently at Kayla's place was keeping the litter box free of clumps, and feeding the cat. Everything except for work was placed on the back burner. So when she came back from the laundry she saw the apartment with fresh eyes. It seemed as if a miniature tornado passed through the living room leaving a trail of opened and unopened mail, magazines, clothes and shoes. Instantly she put the laundry bag down, cracked the living and bedroom windows and started cleaning. Bennie couldn't see this mess she thought as her heart began to race.

Kayla threw everything that didn't belong in a black garbage bag, and then shoved it in the back corner of the closet. After vacuuming she changed the sheets, made the bed while keeping an eye on the time. Suddenly, after fluffing the pillows, she saw the picture of Ronnie on the dresser. Everything belonging to him had to disappear. Kayla threw the picture on the bed then went for another garbage bag. She opened

Ronnie's drawer and took out his underwear, tee shirts and socks then put them in the bag. Then she went to the bathroom and removed his cologne, deodorant, toothbrush and bar of soap. Afterwards Kayla went back scanning the bedroom for any trace of Ronnie's stuff. Wait a minute she thought, Ronnie has a robe and slippers in the closet. So she snatched the robe from its hanger, stuffed it and the slippers in the bag and put it in the corner of the closet. There was some regret over their ending relationship but it was Ronnie's loss, not hers. If there was ever a time to move on, it was right now.

By 9pm sweat ran from her forehead down between her breasts, but the house was acceptable. Then she shut the windows, lit a scented candle and wondered what they could have for dinner. They'd had Chinese food earlier so maybe she'd have a pizza delivered. Now Kayla headed for the bathroom to start the shower. She thought about the conversation at the office, and the hug Bennie gave her. Wait a minute she thought, turning the water off and pushing the stopper in the drain. She told Bennie she'd take a bath and that's what she was going to do.

So Kayla dropped two bath oil beads in the water then set a bottle of scented lotion on the sink. Tonight his hands could feel the silkiness of her skin combined with the slight trace of peaches. As she felt the water over her skin Kayla became tremendously excited. Last time Bennie showed stamina and the ability to wreak pleasurable havoc upon her body; no doubt brought on by the abrasive relationship he and Ronnie shared. A blind man could see Bennie was a private person so why did Ronnie tell his business all the time. The first night Ronnie volunteered information about his best friend dating a dancer. After that Ronnie said Bennie seemed moody after discovering he'd been in a yearlong relationship with Terri, who turned out to be a serial killer. But for some reason she was told never to mention a woman named Linda, who stayed with Bennie and suddenly left. Or a trip Bennie took to Egypt where they found him tied and gagged in his hotel suite. Whatever that energy was, Kayla hoped Bennie brought it back tonight. Which made her wonder, how far she should go on their second encounter? Bennie deserved to experience more pleasure than before, just so he'd come back.

Realizing she'd lost track of time, she ended the bath and concentrated on what to do with her hair. Kayla pulled the hair into a ponytail then used her bathrobe to cover a light blue nightie. After that it took a few minutes to decide if she should wear panties or not. Out of desperation Kayla put them on so not to appear eager.

Finally she sat on the couch a little after 10pm. At 10:30 she walked around the apartment with fleeting hope then sat back down. The cat noticed the change and kept staring at her as she waited. By 10:45 there was still no knock or buzz from the intercom. By 11 Kayla accepted that Bennie wasn't coming. She sighed then blew out the candle, turned off the television and the lights and went to her room with a glass of wine. The cat curled up on the floor near the bathroom then his ears perked up towards the living room. Seconds later Kayla heard three rapid knocks at the door and went to investigate. It was Bennie in the hall when she looked through the peep hole. He heard a noise from inside and simply said, "It's me."

"Okay just a minute," she said trying not to sound too pleased.

Kayla quickly put her robe on then went back to unlock the door. She turned the light on then invited Bennie inside. His presence made her feel powerful and confident again like Popeye busting open that can of spinach. One hand locked the door while the other decisively guided him backwards against the wall. He was here so the time for small talk was over. Kayla took the lead but kept him in suspense with her silence. She allowed the force of gravity to carry her hand from his chest past his stomach and take hold of his belt. Then tilting her head to one side and with an erotic smile said, "Wait a minute, just stand right there…I'm gonna give you what you came for. I just want to ask you a something?"

"Hey, I had to walk my dog and get cleaned up, plus I never had your number. Then when I got here I didn't know which bell was yours," he said sounding uneasy. His eyes told the story. He wanted her to do more with her hand but she enjoyed tugging on his belt. It was delicate acts like holding the door or pulling out her chair that got Kayla's attention. He saw the light blue nightie under her robe and became aroused. Teasingly Bennie said,

"You want me to leave?"

"Bennie…can you stop talking for a minute? I just said you're gonna get everything you came for. I told you back at the office…we're good! But that's not what I want to know," she said with her familiar giggle.

"Well what is it?"

"All I want to know is do you want breakfast in the morning, that's all?" she asked moving closer.

He noticed her chest heaving with each deep breath, then touched him a bit lower.

"Yes…yes I want it."

"You want it?" she asked slipping one arm out touching him with the other hand.

"Yeah."

"Good, then I'm gonna keep being real honest with you. I was taking a bath and I got all wet just thinking about you," she said leading him to the bedroom by his belt.

Hours later just before dawn, Kayla was awake watching Bennie while he slept. Was he the last man on the conveyor belt of her life she could have a child with and celebrate anniversaries? Only time would have the answer. Quietly she got out of bed, took a shower, and put on a long yellow tee shirt that stopped at the knees. Then she went to the kitchen to make scrambled eggs with sausage, grits with cheese and toast. If the aroma and clanking of pans didn't wake Bennie, she'd bring the breakfast to him.

Bennie finally woke to noise and the smell of food from the kitchen. There was initial confusion being in a strange bed waking up naked. The last thing he remembered was Kayla kissing his chest then resting her head there in the early hours of the morning. His time last night was better spent with her than home alone. Hell he might even come back before Ronald returned; he thought stretching loudly. Bennie sat up on the edge of the bed with his feet on the floor. It was after 7 in the morning. Mister needed to go out and he had to check in with Jorge so it was time to get moving.

Before Kayla cracked the eggs she heard the toilet flush and went to investigate. Bennie was standing next to the bed stepping into his boxers when she asked,

"How did you sleep?"

"Good," he answered slowly.

"There's a fresh bar of soap, a face cloth and towel in the bathroom. When you get out the shower I'll start making the eggs. Oh and there's a new toothbrush next to the towel," Kayla said kissing him on the cheek.

She walked briskly towards the kitchen to turn off the sausage. She listened for the shower and when he finished in the bathroom. Minutes later he went to the kitchen, took a seat, and said, "I left the towel on the edge of the tub."

"That's fine," said Kayla setting plates on the table.

"Thanks for breakfast," he said tasting the meat first.

"I don't mind at all, but you're welcome."

"I like this sausage, what kind is it?" he asked enjoying the flavor.

"It's turkey sausage, you like it?"

"It tastes good and so do these eggs."

"Thank you. So you liked the wings, you like the food. Is there anything else you like?" Kayla asked keeping her eyes on her plate.

An awkward amount of seconds passed before Bennie spoke. Finally he said the only truthful thing he could think of.

"Everything's been great so far."

She smiled, letting his comment linger, then looked at him. With the fork suspended over the plate Kayla said, "So I gotta ask you something,"

Bennie stopped chewing like he was expecting a brick to fall on his head, then he heard that familiar chuckle.

"Why do you always think I'm trying to give you a hard time? You should see your face," she said laughing.

"I've got a lot on my mind. I gotta take the dog out, check on the store, but you're right, I need to chill out," he said taking a breath.

At that moment he took a really good look at Kayla's face. He never noticed she had a tiny black mole on the right side of her bottom lip. Even in the morning she was an attractive woman.

"I understand, we all go through stuff. What I wanted to ask you was...did I break something last night? You walked in here kinda slow there sweetie," she said with a smirk on her face.

Then Bennie began to laugh aloud for the first time in months. He wiped his face with the paper towel and said, "You thought you broke me! I'm the one that took it easy on you."

"Oh really...You took it easy on me! Baby you were making all kinda noise last night! I thought the cops were gonna knock on the door!" said Kayla rocking in her seat.

"I heard you too now, come on."

"Yeah but you...you was loud! Next thing I knew I came out the bathroom you was sleep...out for the count. Am I lying?" she said emphasizing the last few words slowly.

"That's not what happened. I remember when you got back in bed," he answered flippantly.

Kayla bit a piece of toast then said, "It was nice, I ain't complaining."

Minutes later Bennie finished eating, wiped his mouth then sat back. He turned his wrist somewhat to glance at his watch. Kayla looked at the kitchen clock while he drank some juice. She smiled, interlocking her fingers with elbows on the table. Bennie was about to get up when Kayla said, "I know you gotta go just give a few more minutes Bennie. I want to put all my cards on the table so there are no surprises, and we can still be friends okay?"

"Sure," he answered raising one eyebrow then taking another sip of juice.

"First off, I'm not asking you to be my man. I'm not ready for that right now, but I want you to know how I feel. I...do like you. I trust you. You listen to me, and I can be myself around you. You know what I use to do and you know I'm not that person anymore. So...I decided I'm not gonna come to the laundry anymore, I'll find somewhere else to do my clothes. If I ever run into Lorraine I'll act like we're together until you tell me not to," said Kayla waiting for a response.

"Okay Kayla," Bennie said nodding his head in agreement.

Taking a pause Kayla watched the cat walk under the table then continued, "Now as for you and me, I still want to see you but that brings up something I've never asked you, but now I need to know. Do you have a girlfriend?"

"No I'm not with anybody."

"Because I don't want a man who has a wife, or girlfriend. I'm not going to put myself through that again!" she said with a very serious tone.

"I hear you," he said listening intently.

So far she hadn't said anything Bennie was opposed to. Then Kayla smiled as if a weight had been lifted, then she said, "Do you want to see me again?"

"Sure," answering as if he really didn't care.

"Good, so this thing we're doing is just between us, for as long as it lasts. If you find someone and it's serious, or I meet somebody we'll go our separate ways right?"

"I feel you," he answered agreeing to that bargain.

"Okay so I have to get my key from Ronnie. What day is he coming back? I'm not allowed to change my locks."

"He'll be back this Thursday," he answered reluctantly.

"Well maybe when you see him you can tell him I came by and asked for my key."

"Why don't I tell Ronald you came by and to call you, then you can tell him!"

"That reminds me, wait just one minute," Kayla said heading to the bedroom.

She returned with two pieces of paper and a pen, sat down, and copied from one paper to the other. She gave Bennie one of the papers then said,

"This top number is mine, and the bottom one will be the new one. They told me the new one will be working Tuesday so Ronnie won't be able to call here. Plus the new number is unlisted, but when I think about it, I'll take care of this myself. I'm not going to make it your problem."

Bennie relaxed as Kayla put the pen and paper on the table. He was impressed with her wanting to keep him out of the drama.

"Now that sounds like a plan."

"That sound good to you?" asked Kayla looking contented.

"Yes it does. The less I'm involved with this the better," he answered glancing at the paper.

"That's why I said it, to keep you out of it. And now that that's out of the way, what is it you expect from me?" she asked getting up to lean against his arm.

"Kayla I can tell you right now, I don't want any drama from you," he said vehemently.

"I understand and you won't," she answered placing her arm around on his shoulder.

"Cause you know stuff starts off good in the beginning, then after a while things get stupid! I'm not going through any bullshit with anybody anymore! And if this is how you say we're gonna be for a while, then just do it, that's all!" said Bennie sounding slightly hostile.

"Well damn…where did all that come from?" she said leaning away.

"You asked me what I want…well that's what I want," he said looking at the numbers again.

"Fine baby…I hear you. Look, don't mess around and get me turned on again, cause I'll have to jack you up," she answered with a suggestive laugh.

Kayla put her arms around him pulling his head to her chest then caressed his face.

"I'm not gonna hurt you baby, I'll look out for you…I promise?" she added turning his head towards her.

He answered by caressing her body through her clothes like he were entitled.

"Bennie you're about to start me up again," she said relishing his erotic touch.

"So what if I do," he responded touching the inside of her thigh with the back of his finger.

"Didn't you say you had to go?" she asked looking tenderly at him.

"I do."

"Well why don't you come back later tonight, we'll do something different," Kayla said touching his cheek with her thumb.

"Yeah like what?" he asked sounding excited.

"I don't know, maybe I'll give you a relaxing massage with some hot oil so you don't be so damn grumpy."

Bennie put the paper in his pocket then stood up before answering. He wanted to see Kayla again but kept her in suspense so not to appear desperate. With a last squeeze he said,

"Thanks for breakfast…I'll be back a little earlier tonight. if I can. Let's put it this way, if you don't hear from me by five that means I'm coming."

"Fine…so just in case what do you want to eat?"

"I don't know. I tell you what, this time I'll bring something," he replied walking to the door.

"What you gonna bring me?" she asked eagerly.

Bennie thought he could go to Johnson's in the Bronx for ribs, or some fish and fries from Saint Nicholas. Finally he said, "Kayla…you ever had a calzone?"

"A calzone, what's a calzone?" she asked looking at him like he said something crazy.

"You never had a calzone?"

"No, I never even heard of a calzone. What is it?" she asked with excitement.

"You'll see Kayla, I'm gonna bring you a calzone from Three Boys in the Bronx. I've been going there since I was a kid. Now they'll be cold, but we'll heat them in the oven. You do eat pork?"

"Do I look like I'm Muslim? Yeah I eat pork man," she said giggling out loud.

"Okay so I'll bring some of each," he said with his hand on the doorknob.

Bennie wasn't letting on, but inside he really wanted to come back. Kayla took his dinner suggestion as a positive sign she'd see him later. It caused her to hover those few seconds awaiting a last passionate gesture that never came. He simply opened the door without affectionate expression, or semblance of gratitude. What she did receive was a see you later, added to a crooked smile. Then just like that he turned and walked away.

Kayla remained in the apartment except for her head. From that position she watched like a spy in a movie. Bennie never looked back and once he got close to the elevator, after some people got off, he stepped on. Slightly offended Kayla shut the door then leaned against it to think. Why didn't he look back at her? What had she done wrong this time? He finished his breakfast so it wasn't the food. There's not a man alive that doesn't like a woman serving him, so that can't be it. Her performance last night was good, so he damn sure couldn't complain about the sex. Unlike the first time when it was for revenge, this was pure mutual attraction. And when their night ended Bennie was put to sleep by the caress of her hand, and intermittent kisses on his bare chest. After that he slept like a baby tucked in by his momma. On that note Kayla contemplated further while cleaning the kitchen.

It was difficult but she confessed Ronnie was a bad choice. No matter what that sweet talker said, he was never going to leave his wife. After clearing the table Kayla stood in front of the sink and made a promise. Ronnie was the last married man she'd ever get involved with. The next issue was what really stood in the way of a future with Bennie? Well the first thing she had to admit was being Ronnie's leftovers. Most men don't care about leftovers when it comes to cooche. Given the chance they'll stick it to their girlfriend's sister, her momma, any of her cousins, her best friend, and her daughter.

Rarely do they commit to a long-term relationship afterwards. Then she remembered one exception the new mayor, Rudy Giuliani, who married his cousin.

Feeling optimistic Kayla turned the water on and squirted soap on the sponge. She wouldn't get her hopes up, but one thing was true. Bennie was coming back tonight to be with her, and he was bringing calzones. If he continued coming over there was a possibility. Nonetheless she had until Thursday when Ronnie came back to figure out what to do.

Bennie left the building then walked around the corner to his car. It was a brisk partly cloudy morning in February with the possibility of rain. His first stop was to check in with Jorge at the laundry, then take care of Mister. Before Bennie went inside the Laundry he drove by twice before parking. Bennie walked in to business as usual and was pleased. Jorge sang while cleaning trash from under one of the tables when they saw each other. They shook hands then headed to the back office to talk. Jorge agreed to open the store again tomorrow in exchange for Monday off. After that Bennie told Jorge he'd be back in a few hours then headed home.

Now that the store's schedule was settled, next on the list was walking the dog. Bennie decided to take Mister to the park instead of letting him go in the backyard. As soon as he got home Mister greeted Bennie at the door with stubby tail wagging. The dog got more excited standing on his hind legs when Bennie got the leash. Minutes later they headed up 145th Street to Riverside Avenue, then down into the park. Bennie looked for a spot in Riverside Park where he could see the Hudson River, New Jersey and maybe a passing boat.

They went down the strip past several benches stopping at one near the handball courts. Bennie rested his arm on the back of the bench while Mister sat next to him. Finally he took a deep relaxing breath and earnestly thought about what he was going to do about Kayla. She'd become a pardon from anguish. A very pleasant distraction, and if anyone needed a distraction it was Bennie. He should've been in therapy, or talking to a grief counselor about the loss of his child. His reason for resisting psychological help wasn't a black thing. It was admitting the truth about Linda, the baby, and the illegal way they got into the country. Odds were after providing that information he'd get locked up, or sent to Belleview hospital. So despair became his rock and hard place, and without recourse the depression got worse. At least once a week Bennie had nightmares about Linda and Tiffany dying in that Bronx building. He'd see Linda choking from the smoke, then she'd fall down with Tiffany tucked under her arm and lose unconsciousness.

His other dream was a true nightmare leaving him uncomfortable days afterwards. . In that one Bennie was next to Linda when the fire broke out. As soon as he reached for her arm to get her out, he'd be in the hallway on the other side of a door. Linda screaming his name for help was heart wrenching. The knob didn't turn so he'd step back to kick at the door. When that didn't work he charged at that metal door with his shoulder. Each attempt made the door glow like iron in a fire. The heat was real and when the screams stopped he'd awaken drenched in sweat. After this many years it was too late to ask God to spare their lives and take his.

Each day pain and related stress was his to bear alone. It was particularly difficult a few days after Bennie's birthday when a woman came in the laundry with her daughter. Watching from the monitor saddened him because Tiffany would've been that age if she'd lived. That little girl was so excited just to draw in her coloring book. Something Tiffany would never get to do, and that thought brought him to tears. If there was a time he was glad to be in the office alone it was then. Bennie wept until his eyes were dry and bloodshot. Since therapy wasn't an option, his prescription for pain was meaningless sex and hard liquor. That's about the time Kayla placed a fence of cheerfulness around him. Plus she came with the tight lips of a priest during confession, a trait of hers he respected most.

Loud voices turned Mister's attention toward the handball court. Two men trash talked as a third pointed at the line where the ball went out of bounds. Once three agreed, the last man threw his arms up in disgust then took his position to finish the game. Bennie faced the river to review mental notes. Kayla had her own place, a promising career and was upwardly mobile. In the bedroom she was confidently uninhibited, and attractive. Her body was flexible like a ballet dancer, or a gymnast. Last night she arched her back then looked at him when she placed her head on the pillow. That's when he noticed a two inch vertical scar below the hair line at the base of her neck. If Kayla was standing or had her hair pinned up you'd never see it.

Then there was the sound when she reaches her moment, something he'd confirm tonight. When Kayla's arrives at the blissful place, she closes her eyes, bites the side of her lip, then makes a slow haaaaaa, haaaaaa, haaaaaa, haaaaaaa sound. It was quite appropriate for a woman that giggled after almost every sentence. Anticipation had him smiling as he looked across the water. Tonight Bennie would take Kayla to a Def Comedy Jam show in her apartment. Foreplay would be old-school Redd Foxx followed by Richard Pryor, with Sinbad hammering the closing.

Bennie rubbed the dog's head as the sun shined over the George Washington Bridge. A wind gust lifted Mister's ear to one side. Past the bridge far north the sky was very dark. They'd been there almost an hour not noticing the clouds closing in. When Bennie stood the muffled sound of thunder echoed in the distance. By the time they got out of the park he'd come to a decision about Kayla. She was still Ronald's leftovers. The girl you pass to your buddies for the next lap dance. Sooner or later something was going to go wrong. Yeah Kayla was loyal but for how long? She was bound to get attached or feel she was being used so why prolong it? So on the way home Bennie decided to tell Kayla their time had come to an end.

Twenty minutes after they got home the rain and thunder started outside. Bennie fed Mister then drove to Three Boys to get the calzones. After the pizza shop he went back to the laundry to give Jorge a sausage calzone. Then he went home to shower and change clothes. By 6pm Bennie was outside Kayla's building searching for her buzzer. He went early to tell her how he felt. If she wanted him to leave he'd be back before it got too late. Before he could push the button Kayla was coming out. She wore an oversized yellow rain coat with a scarf on her head. Confused yet happy to see him she said, "Bennie I'm glad you caught me, I thought you were coming after eight."

"I know…you want me to come back?"

"Boy stop playing and get in here. I was on my way to the store," Kayla said holding the door for him.

"I'll take you," said Bennie wiping water from his brow.

Switching the calzones to the other hand he waited for an answer, then Kayla said quickly,

"You so sweet but that's not necessary, you already got a parking space. I'm just going down the block."

"Are you sure?" he asked staying still in the hall.

"I'm sure sweetie, it's alright I'll be right back."

Before reaching the elevator to take him upstairs Bennie presented a bouquet of pink roses hidden behind his back. Kayla's face lit up then she said, "Are those for me?"

"Of course they are for you. You like em? I didn't know what color to get but these had your name on em so I got them," he said while the doors closed.

Kayla took the flowers raising them to her nose. She swelled with emotion and said, "I love them Bennie, I really love these flowers. They're so beautiful, thank you," she said kissing him on the cheek.

"And so are you," he answered, realizing even dressed in an oversized raincoat with no makeup she was still eye-catching.

Kayla quickly reached her door then went to the kitchen. She took a plastic pitcher from the cabinet filled it with water and set it in the sink. Then she put the flowers inside the pitcher, giggled at the sight then said, "My flowers will be fine in this water until I get back."

"Kayla you got to put this other bag in the fridge," Bennie said once as she walked past.

"Could you do it? I was on my way to the store, and I still got to get dressed when I get back," she said looking for the remote in the living room.

"Do you want to see what a calzone looks like?"

"Not right now baby, I'll see them when I get back," she said, tying up a small bag of garbage to take with her.

"I told you I'd take you, I don't mind," he said, closing the refrigerator door.

"Thank you baby but no, I got this. Just chill out and relax. I'm going to the supermarket and pick up a few things. There's some beer in the fridge, so take your shoes off and get comfortable, it won't take long," she said handing him the TV remote.

"Well that's what I'll do," Bennie said taking off his coat.

Kayla was messing up his plan which was to hand her the food when he arrived. Then while she looked inside the bag he'd say what was going to happen between them. That way if she said no it would be early when he left. Now he had to sit here until she came back.

"That reminds me I have something for you," said Kayla stopping at the door.

She darted to the bedroom then came back placing a Modell's bag at his feet.

"What's this."

"It's a pair of shorts, some lounge pants, and two tee shirts. That way if you want you can get out of your wet clothes. Oh…I remember you like vodka right?" Kayla asked walking to the front door.

"Yes," he smiled.

"What do you chase it with, juice or soda?"

"I drink it straight, but you can get some Pepsi."

"Since we don't have to be drunk to take our clothes off, I'm gonna have some wine and have a good time…uh huh. You know that song?"

"Yeah I do."

"We don't have to take our clothes off, but I plan to…eventually," she said giggling.

After Bennie turned on the television Kayla asked one more question, "Are you staying for breakfast?"

"I don't know, we'll talk when you come back."

She was going to ask what that meant, instead she chuckled saying, "Talk about what? Boy you staying, stop playing."

Then she went to the couch, kissed him on the lips and left.

Bennie scratched his head then pulled the bag between his legs. That sound brought the cat from her bedroom to rub against his leg and walk away. First thing he took out was a pair of pajama pants with the Giants logo. Next were two tee shirts like she said, and a pair of grey sweat shorts. Kayla's thoughtful gesture was making his words more difficult to say. No sense in changing into these clothes until she got back so he put the bag under the table.

As Kayla shopped for a vase to put her roses in she'd come to a conclusion about Bennie's odd behavior. He was going to ask her if she was ready for a relationship. Why else does a man give a woman flowers, unless it's serious. To make sure, Kayla hatched a plan on the way home to find out Bennie's intentions.

Less than a block away from her door the rain came down like she'd walked past an open fire hydrant in the summer. Kayla was drenched so there was no use running and risk dropping her bags. When she opened the door to her place Bennie was sitting on the couch. Soaking wet Kayla gently put the bags on the floor and announced before she closed the door, "Bennie I gotta pee so bad! Can you get the door?"

She headed to the bathroom taking off the raincoat and closing the door behind her. Bennie shut the front door then took the bags to the kitchen to start unpacking. Kayla came to the kitchen, found the new vase, and put the flowers inside. Then she searched for the perfect place to put them, finally settling on the table in front of the couch.

While she did that Bennie put the eggs, sausage, and soda in the fridge. Kayla then went to take a shower. Sometime later she opened the bathroom door naked, covering her breasts with her arm and called to Bennie.

"Can you pour me a glass of wine with a couple of ice cubes and bring it here please?" she asked, teasing him then giggling.

There wasn't an inch of Kayla's body he hadn't already seen, but covering up just then excited him. Soon as Bennie got up Kayla went back in the bathroom. He went to the kitchen fixed her a glass of wine and brought it to the bathroom. The door was ajar so he tapped on it and Kayla said, "Just put it here on the sink please."

This time she was wrapped in a light blue towel sitting on the edge of the tub putting lotion on her legs. She never bothered to look up when he set the glass down. After he left suddenly she blurted, "Did you open the Stolich…naya? I think that's how you say it. I asked the guy at the liquor store for a good vodka and he said this was it."

"Yeah it is, we call it Stoli for short…no I didn't open it yet," he answered stopping just outside the door.

"Well I got it for you, what you waiting for?" she asked rubbing her arms.

"I'm gonna have a beer first."

"Okay I'll just be a few more minutes," she answered merrily.

Bennie went to the fridge, opened a beer then sat back on the couch. Whatever happens it's gonna be fine, he thought taking a sip.

Not long after Kayla came out in a pink Terri cloth short set. She put her glass on the coffee table near the flowers and sat in the opposite corner of the couch.

"Okay I'm ready," she said sighing slightly.

"You're ready?" he said strangely.

"Yes…You've got something on your mind today so just tell me what it is. Did something happen at work? Cause you seemed happier this morning when you left," she said looking directly at him.

"There is something on my mind Kayla and I don't want to hurt your feelings, I really don't," he said staring down at the beer.

For a second she had the same face at the bar when Ronald pushed her away. Then Kayla said, "Bennie, on stage I've heard every insult any man could think of to say to me. That's why I put everything on the table this morning, so just tell me. You got a girlfriend now, is that it?"

"It's not that! I got to thinking about what we're doing. This whole thing with you, me and Ronald is a house of cards. It's like a match about to ignite gasoline. This thing is gonna blow up in our faces, sooner or later. Kayla you know it's true."

Abruptly Kayla went to the kitchen with her glass. It was quiet until the fridge opened and ice cubes fell into the glass. He was right to keep his clothes on because there would be no sounds of her slow laughter tonight.

"Kayla, I never messed with a woman Ronald liked. Maybe when we were kids but that's different," he said walking closer to the kitchen.

Kayla leaned with her back against the sink looking into her glass. Bennie stood by the table and continued, "This is not easy for me! And it's not your fault, it's mine. I started this."

"I…I was looking forward to seeing you all day, and now you're not staying? Why'd you bother bringing me flowers? Was it just to make me feel worse?" she asked breaking the silence.

"Because I wanted you to have them and…I didn't say I was leaving, it all depends."

"Depends…depends on what?" she said sounding annoyed looking at him.

"I was going to say we got till Ronald comes back Thursday, it's up to you," he said straightforwardly.

"You know what I was thinking after you left this morning? I was wondering if you thought it was easy for me to be with you and Ronnie? You know like…like I was some kinda hoochie freak or something, cause

I'm not somebody's whore! I mean that's the elephant in the room, that's what men laugh and high five each other about. You got some pussy… well guess what, she gave me some too," she said looking serious.

"You want the truth?" Bennie asked, not fazed by her outburst.

"Yeah, tell me what you really think please," she asked with the black woman's neck nod.

Bennie paused and said, "Look…I know you're a good woman and your past has nothing to do with anything. The truth is I don't have those deep feelings for anybody right now. That's why I said it's not you or anything you did. I'd be saying this to any woman I met right now."

A tiny part of his broken heart wanted to tell Kayla he didn't give a shit one way or the other, but he wasn't that far gone so he said, "Besides, if I didn't want to be here I wouldn't have come. But I know this thing between us can't go on for long so…"

"So…what?"

"So…I thought if you wanted…I thought we could… you know."

"Could what?" she asked sounding frustrated.

"Maybe we could do this and let it go before it turns into a mess, that's what I was thinking."

Kayla watched him the entire time then took a sip from her glass. Her truth was she wanted him to stay but gave it some thought. After one more sip and a breath she said, "I knew this couldn't last but I thought we had more than a week."

"And that's another reason I'm here Kayla because you're straight up. That's why I'm saying something right now instead of breaking it off later."

She sat at the table pushing her glass aside then interlocked her fingers like praying hands. Waiting for a hint this was a test, or he'd change his mind, Kayla said, "Thanks for being upfront with me. Shit, I can't even be mad at you if I wanted to. So let me get this straight. We got till Ronnie comes back to town is that what you're saying?"

"Yes."

Kayla watched Bennie from her peripheral vision with elbows on the table, her chin rested on interlocked fingers. Her earlier thoughts that morning of she and Bennie having a life were unavoidably coming to fruition. Finally she said, "I gotta say it, that's what I like about you Bennie."

"Now you see why I didn't get too comfortable. We had to talk before…before you know, things happened."

"No, no I get it," she answered moving the salt and pepper shakers apart.

"Kayla I'm going through a lot of shit! My mind is fucked up and I got some stuff to work out. I know you deserve better than I can give right now."

"I hate to hear it, but you did the right thing having this conversation with me now. So…if I want you to stay…you'll stay?" she asked looking a little uncertain.

"If you still want me around then, yeah I'll stay."

"I feel some kinda way about this but I get it, and I understand your point. Now the end doesn't have to come as a surprise for either one of us," she said forcing a slight grin.

"Right, that's the way I was looking at it," he smiled back.

She put her fist over her lips blowing air through her fingers and said, "Well if…and I'm saying if, we do this, I got to have something I want! And if you can do it then put those pajamas on, and I can see what the hell a calzone looks like.

The gentle tone was gone when he answered, "So what is it?"

"What is it? Why do you come back at me so hard?"

Immediately Kayla recognized an opportunity to have the upper hand. Sometimes when she danced drunken men would become abusive and rowdy. That's when she'd find a compassionate person of the group. He'd get the tearful eyes intended to melt hearts, and open wallets. It was Kayla that got Bennie to the apartment, but could Mercedes make him want to stay? Once Bennie looked at Kayla's sad face the tone softened when he asked again,

"What is it Kayla?"

"I need you to lighten up on me for one! You can be real mean and cold. I want you to…to be yourself, and I want you to…to laugh, if you feel like it. I…I want to know I'm important to you at least for these last few days we're together. And I want us to still be friends when it's over."

Bennie interrupted saying, "Alright."

"No I'm not finished! If there comes a time when we bump into each other I want you to remember we were good for a little while. That's what I want from you," she said finally looking into his eyes.

This raw emotion was more sensual than any costume or rump shaker move she could ever use, and it made him want her more. So he replied, "I understand Kayla."

"Bennie…I want to sit on the couch and watch a movie with my head on your shoulder. So can you give me that? Can you please let your guard down and have some fun with me?" Kayla asked reaching for his hand.

"Yeah…I can do that," he said stepping closer.

"Can you really?" she asked wiping the corner of her eye.

"Yes," he said with a bigger grin.

"Okay…now let's see what calzones look like," Kayla said followed by her usual laugh.

Bennie took two calzones from the bag and said, "These will take about twenty minutes in the oven, and you can freeze the rest after today."

The calzone was shaped like a half-moon with a small hole on top. Kayla held it judging the weight, smelling it before setting it down.

"What kind is this one?" she asked cheerfully.

"That's chicken parmigiana, and this is sausage."

"I can't eat a whole one of those. That thing is too big," Kayla said brushing his fingers with her hand.

"I was going to heat both so you could taste them."

Kayla got up, slipped her arms around his waist and rested her head on Bennie's chest. He was glad to hug her and she felt it. Asking him to be affectionate wasn't unreasonable at all. In fact he was glad to pretend knowing it would be for a short time.

"When I get hungry, you gonna make them for us?" she asked still holding on to him.

"Sure I'll hook it up for you tonight," he said confidently.

Kayla stepped back, put her hand on his chest as forcefully as yesterday evening when he got there.

"Bennie…after Thursday all this is off limits for you. I believe what you're telling me. So I'm just saying…as much as I'd want to let you back inside, you can't come back!" said Kayla very serious.

Shit Bennie thought let's see if she says that crap after tonight. Instead he replied, "I know."

"Oh you know huh? As long as you know, that I know, that you know, that no means no…and I mean it. When this door closes, it's closed for good!"

Bennie smiled and Kayla kept a firm hand on him tilting her head to the side as if to say, I'm for real about this. "And I don't want you stalking me and acting all crazy either," she said chuckling.

"Kayla I'm not gonna stalk you," he said laughing with her.

"No…you laughing but I'm serious. Don't be calling me or showing up over here…for real."

"I won't," he answered sliding his hand down the side if her hip.

"Oh and one more thing, Diamond is off limits and that's all I'm gonna say," she said taking hold of his belt buckle.

"I don't think about Diamond Kayla," Bennie said finding humor in her jealousy.

"Yeah, well she thinks about you. Every time I talk to her she asks about you. I know I ain't got no right to ask, but I am!"

"I'm not gonna mess with her Kayla. If I wanted Diamond I would have done it a long time ago," he answered honestly.

"I know that's right. So I'm gonna fix some drinks, and you can change in the bedroom." she said standing on her toes to kiss his cheek.

Willingly he followed directions and went to the bed room. The scent of Kayla's perfume lingered in the air. He removed his clothes then sat on the bed to put on pajamas and tee shirt. This was a nice gesture he thought after touching the soft material, and all Kayla asked in return was for him to relax and unwind. Was that too much to ask?

Bennie sat still listening for movement from the other room. To the left he saw his reflection in a full-length mirror atop the dresser. Bitterness and worries were noticeably taking toll on his features. New wrinkles between his brow and jawline exposed a weakened individual forced to surrender. Gone was the guy with aspirations of making a difference in his community. Why had a man who longed for true love and a family given up?

A hand covered his lips to stop the answer, but the truth came out through thought. It was time to finally admit even though Terri was a brutal killer, he missed her. Bennie remembered those island vacations, their jogs around Central Park and just holding her murderous hand. He even longed for the way Terri would pull him out of bed by the feet until he wound up on the floor. If he wasn't thinking about Terri his thoughts were of Linda when they met in Africa. How her name was actually Whende and they'd spent an unforgettable passionate night together. Turned out it was forgettable for Whende who happened to really lose her memory.

Upon further self-reflection loneliness was getting to him and random sex couldn't replace the small gestures that added to passion. Like spooning and waking up to morning breath and crusty eyelids. Or Terri farting and pretending not to know why he was leaving the room. Two relationships ripped away by unbelievable circumstances. Which brought about another question, because Terri and Linda are dead, were his emotions dead as well? There were times Bennie felt like King Midas ruining everything he touched. Maybe that was the problem, holding on to contentment.

Silence ended when Kayla called from the living room, "How's it going in there?

Bennie faced the man in the mirror recognizing he got lost in his thoughts. She was on the other side but didn't open the door, so he answered, "It's good…I'll be there in a minute."

"Okay I'm not rushing you, I just wanted to make sure you didn't get lost," she said cheerfully.

Upon further reflection he decided tonight could be different. After all, Kayla accepted the limitation of this short relationship, so why not show some genuine affection? Right then he committed to enjoy the last precious moments in this brief liaison, like a convict on death row having that last meal.

Once Bennie and his reflection were in agreement he went to the living room as Kayla came from the kitchen. She put their drinks on the coffee table and asked, "Do you like them? Are your jammies comfortable?"

"Yeah baby they feel good," he said sincerely.

Then he put his arm around her waist and kissed her passionately.

"That was nice. Do it again," she said eagerly.

They kissed in the living room then hugged and let go. Nothing exploded; there wasn't a fire or stray bullets injuring either of them so he sat on the couch and said, "You told me to be me, so that's what I'm doing,"

"Well I like it and I really like my flowers," she said sitting close by.

They got cozy on the couch in front of the TV while Kayla talked. She was an only child born in Philadelphia. Her mother worked for Kayla's school in the cafeteria, while her father was a bus mechanic for the city. Kayla said the family would walk to the local diner for ice cream sometimes when Dad got off work. It was the happiest time of her life until a month after her thirteenth birthday. That's when her father was accidently killed by a piece of metal during a small explosion at work. Kayla believed Bennie would sympathize with the loss of a loved one, so she kept talking.

Less than a year after her father's death Kayla's mother met a smooth-talking drug dealer who introduced her to heroin. It wasn't long after mom became an addict, and lost her job at the school. The next four years her mom spent in and out of rehab, until Kayla found her dead at home next to the tub. Apparently mom fell face first from the toilet with the empty needle still in her arm. She told Bennie she didn't cry for a couple of days because oddly, there was comfort knowing momma wasn't suffering any more.

After the funeral Kayla moved to Brooklyn with her mom's younger sister Monique. It was a stable environment for a while. Kayla's love for mathematics made her valedictorian, and then she enrolled in Brooklyn College. Suddenly she took a sip of wine then changed the subject to being allergic to bananas. There was some uneasiness, and she abruptly went to the kitchen with their glasses. Minutes later Kayla came back smiling with refreshed drinks and sat back down. Bennie coaxed her foot onto his lap and held it. Attentively he massaged as the first step in foreplay. After a while he stopped, reached for his glass then asked for her other foot. Kayla sounded excited, like when you open a present at Christmas. She quickly shoved a throw pillow under her head and lay back eagerly to enjoy the pampering. His fingers were long and slender while the skin was a beautiful shade of silky dark chocolate. As she watched, Kayla uttered arousing moans while her toes were touched. The shape of Bennie's mouth and firm body was turning her on. Each time sex was better than the last, and tonight would be no exception.

Slowly he lifted her foot singling out the middle toe, kissing it several times. His intention was to stimulate Kayla incrementally until she bubbled over. The sensation of lips across her foot was the most erotic feeling she'd ever experienced. His eyes took a northern route from ankle to the calf then thighs, finally settling within her crotch. She rocked her hips in a circular motion ever so slowly. The question now, was he willing to really put those lips to use? Instead he merely rested his hand on the inside of her thigh, his pinky a hair's breadth away from contact. She held on with excited anticipation until as if by accident, that pinky grazed her private place idly reaching for his glass. It was the precision of the touch that made her want more. Bennie smiled at her, took a drink then went to the kitchen to prepare calzones.

From the couch Kayla told him where to find the foil and how to turn on the oven. Bennie removed two calzones from the fridge so they'd be room temperature when they went into the oven. As Kayla began to relax after that short ride she couldn't help but think about the feeling of emptiness soon to come. Was there anything left to change Bennie's mind about their final agreement? Most men wonder how women wind up stripping assuming it's about abuse, but Kayla's reason came merely from a dare.

When Bennie came back Kayla was in the same spot on the couch. When a commercial for McDonald's came on Kayla said it was her first job as a teenager. Her mood changed but she continued talking about the first semester of college. It was around that time Aunt Monique met Teddy in the middle of October. Bennie asked what Teddy was like and Kayla never answered. Instead she talked about her aunt being just six years older with no children. Eventually Monique let Teddy move in after two months. Kayla continued sleeping in the living room on the sofa bed, and Teddy slept in her aunt's bedroom.

The living situation was fine until Kayla's second semester in April, and then it got worse. Teddy lost his job three weeks later for absenteeism and never bothered looking for another one. His days consisted of smoking weed, watching TV, and eating cornflakes. Soon Teddy started walking around Kayla in his boxer shorts when Monique wasn't home. Then he came into the bathroom while Kayla was taking shower to ask if she needed anything from the store. Kayla kept saying no until he left. Good thing the shower curtain had a garden print so he couldn't see anything. Then he'd act normal for a while, but Kayla knew he was testing to see how far he could go. One night Kayla heard her aunt's bed post thumping against the wall. Teddy purposely spoke loudly so Kayla could hear even after Monique shushed him. The next morning Teddy leered at Kayla making sure she saw his morning hard on before going to the bathroom. Kayla took her glass, waited, and they drank together. Bennie put his arm around her shoulder and she continued.

Monique was a 911 dispatcher with rotating weekends who firmly believed Teddy was in love with her. Her aunt said Teddy talked about getting married one day and starting a family. It was the main reason Kayla refused to upset the one family member that came to her rescue. So Kayla stayed quiet since Teddy wasn't using forceful intimidation. His strategy with women was to keep pushing, wearing them down until they said yes. As far as Kayla was concerned if Teddy was the last man on earth, he still didn't have a chance. However as weeks passed without Monique confronting him about his behavior, Kayla's silence only fueled his ambition.

The next night Monique worked late Teddy tried to get slick. He went to the kitchen then sat on the edge of the sofa opening a beer while Kayla was doing her homework assignment. Before he could say anything she threw off the covers, got dressed in the bathroom and left. By then it was almost midnight. Outside the air was cold enough to see the frost from her breath. With nowhere to go she went into the subway to get warm. When the A train came Kayla rode the first car with the engineer to feel safe. She took that train to the last stop, Far Rockaway in Queens, then got on the next A train to 207th Street in Manhattan. When she got to the last stop in Manhattan Kayla got off to wait for the next train back to Brooklyn. She told Bennie it was after 3am and she was tired, but she knew what had to be done. It was time for her to finally be on her own, even if it was a tiny furnished room. Actually she might have saved enough money now depending on the rent. When she got back the next morning Aunt Monique was asleep, and Teddy was gone. That day she missed class, and forty dollars from her stash inside the couch cushion. Still she was grateful; Teddy could've taken the whole $280.00. So while Auntie slept Kayla changed clothes then went to the newsstand for the paper. Afterwards she took a Gypsy cab to Junior's on Flatbush for breakfast. Before the food came she'd circled four listings to check out. Now all she had to do was change some dollars into quarters and call from the phone at the corner.

The waitress was pleasant so Kayla told her she worked at McDonalds, was going to college, and why she had to move. Suddenly the lady looked over Kayla's shoulder then advised her not to bother with two of the locations. After that something amazing happened. The woman told Kayla the restaurant was looking for a waitress, and the job paid a little more. Kayla thought about it during breakfast and decided to make a change. That day she found a better job, and a furnished room in a Brownstone off Atlantic Avenue. It was on the second floor with one window facing the backyard. She had a single bed with a metal frame and one small dresser next to a closet. The building was very clean, and the rent was affordable at eighty dollars a week. Another thing was Kayla had to share the kitchen and bathroom with two female tenants on the same floor. All things considered it was her first place, and it was perfect.

The landlord was an old woman named Mrs. Grier who resembled Rosa Parks. Her grey hair was parted in the middle with two braids ending in a ponytail. Mrs. Grier wore those old-fashioned glasses with a cord that hung around her neck, and she moved around well for a woman in her seventies. Her husband was a police officer killed in the line of duty almost ten years ago. Kayla happened to mention her Aunt Monique was a dispatcher who clenched the deal for the room.

Bennie stopped Kayla to ask what reason she gave her aunt for moving. Kayla took a sip of wine then rested the glass on her leg. Exposing Teddy's lascivious behavior and thievery would've only caused auntie grief. That's when her philosophy of taking one for the team was born. Kayla offered a half truth about a boy in her class she wanted to date, which meant they could both use the privacy. Monique asked if that was the only reason and Kayla said it was, sticking to the story to this day. Two months later Teddy got caught cheating when Monique came home unexpectedly, and she put him out. Just then the cat brushed against Bennie's feet then disappeared under the table. It was obvious he wanted to hear more so Kayla talked about moving and working at Junior's.

The calzones were placed in the oven and Bennie returned, casually putting his arm around her when he sat. She looked into his eyes, touched his knee and snuggled on his shoulder. Finally he asked what happened with school, and why she started dancing. Kayla chuckled and told him it all started with a dare one night before Valentine's Day.

At the time she'd been dating Malik from her school for over a year. They weren't in the same class anymore because last semester he changed his major. While working at Junior's Kayla became familiar with the repeat customers, and a few became her regulars. Two were older men from the Kings County Criminal Court that flirted and tipped her well. One was old enough to be her father, and the other ten years her senior. She also met three women who came on the weekends in the evening. They were always polite and nicely dressed, so Kayla had no idea Diamond, Cinnamon and Colorado were stripping. Cinnamon was a busty woman in her late forties while the other two were three or four years older than Kayla. After a while the ladies started sharing funny stories about customers, and stupid stuff other girls did in the clubs. One particular night Kayla's shift was almost over when Cinnamon and Diamond came in without Colorado. Diamond was visibly upset because Colorado accidently fell down the stairs trying to catch a train. Her leg was broken and would be in a cast for at least five months. That's when Cinnamon had a proposal when Kayla came back with their order.

Cinnamon told Kayla about an invitation only event in Queens, and they wanted her to come. All she had to do was learn a choreographed routine the men went crazy for. As Kayla was about to say no Cinnamon counted six one-hundred-dollar bills and laid them on the table. Cinnamon told Kayla the money was hers, and she'd make another six hundred by the end of the night. The men were expecting to feel on her, but there was no sex involved. Kayla stared at the money until Diamond dared her to come with them. Actually there was something thrilling about having men fantasize about her. If she were home with her parents the answer would've been no. Kayla told Bennie because of her age she enjoyed the mounting attention of men which made their offer thrilling. So when Diamond told Cinnamon Kayla was scared, Kayla put the money in her pocket and told them she'd be ready when they finished eating.

They all went to Diamond's apartment so Kayla could try on some outfits. After that they worked together on the routine then left for Queens. At first Kayla was nervous then the money started raining on the floor. That night, with the six hundred she got from Cinnamon, Kayla made another thousand. That was more than she made in three weeks waiting tables so she kept doing it.

Towards the end of March while Kayla was giving a dance in a Bronx club Malik walked in with some friends. A man cupped Kayla's bare breasts as her hips slowly grinded on his lap. Suddenly the person grabbing her arm and calling her name was Malik. Embarrassment caused her to snicker, then she walked past him and his friends. Malik followed and was stopped by security from entering the ladies dressing room. Horrified, Kayla stayed in the dressing room the rest of the night, then went to Tasha's place instead of going home. The angry look on Malik's face bothered her so much she skipped school the next week. When Kayla returned to class she ran into Malik in the hall and he ended their relationship. The whole day she felt as if all the students knew and were talking about her so she left before the class was over. After that Kayla sadly told Bennie she quit school and waitressing too.

Kayla lifted her head and smiled briefly, telling Bennie that was more than four years ago. Realizing she used the name Tasha instead of Diamond, she told Bennie to only call her Diamond. Then she looked him sternly in the eye as a reminder that he wasn't supposed to have any contact. But the best part of her story was she didn't need to lie to her aunt about where she worked.

This was the longest Bennie ever heard Kayla talk without snickering. He pulled her close until she put her head on his shoulder. Kayla took a deep breath as if she'd put down a heavy bag. Silently she caressed his leg, snuggling in the comfort of his touch. Bennie asked why she quit dancing and her explanation was relatable. She asked if he'd ever seen his parents in his face. One night an hour before she was leaving to meet Diamond she looked in the same mirror Bennie had earlier in the bedroom. She said when she looked up, staring back were her mom's forehead, eyebrows and the shape of her nose. Kayla said she knew she couldn't dance anymore and it was time to quit. Three weeks later she applied for the teller job and was hired.

Sharing her past was a last-ditch effort to impress Bennie so he'd have second thoughts and return after Thursday. While her last words lingered, Kayla confessed her laugh was her way of dealing with uneasiness and shame. He stared into her eyes and told her she had nothing to be ashamed about. They kissed passionately until Kayla couldn't wait any longer. She straddled him, pulling off his shirt and kissing his neck. There wasn't going to be an intermission or pauses of any kind right now. He'd pressed her play button one time too many. His touch had attentive tenderness and intensity unlike the first time, he barely looked at her. Tonight Kayla was convinced they were making love. Their lips locked the entire time until the moment was reached. Instead of declaring love she uttered the slowest "haaaaaa" in his ear. Later they ate then stayed in the bedroom intertwined, falling asleep in each other's arms.

In the morning, with groggily blinking eyes, Kayla was slightly awake as Bennie dressed to walk the dog. He leaned over kissing her on the cheek and said he'd bring back breakfast. Before rolling on her stomach she told him to take the keys off the counter to let himself back in.

When Bennie returned Kayla was still sleep. He walked to the edge of the bed and touched her shoulder. When she looked up he told her to come eat while the food was hot. Minutes later she came to the table dragging her feet like a character in a zombie movie. There was a spot of toothpaste in the corner of her mouth, and her hair was a wreck. She tried for a few seconds to fix her hair then gave up when Bennie placed containers on the table. Kayla watched with delight, happy to be pampered for a change. He placed the first container in front of her and removed the lid. The aroma of buttery grits, scrambled eggs and beef sausage was heavenly. Then he placed a plastic knife, fork, and plenty of napkins within her reach while shoving a corner of the toast in her grits. Straightaway Bennie opened another container with a pool of butter melting in the center of a stack of pancakes. Lastly, she got orange juice with packets of jelly, then he sat down to eat. After breakfast Bennie cleared the table then they got dressed and walked to Blockbuster for videos. Kayla picked "Backdraft" and Bennie got "Silence of the Lambs." Later that evening Bennie left to take care of Mister and they watched the last movie. When it was over Kayla got her clothes ready for the next morning, they made love again and went to sleep.

Once the alarm rang at 6 am Kayla wasted no time getting out of bed. Her first stop was the bathroom, then the living room to turn on the radio. Bennie watched as she sped by like a movie on fast forward. One second she was there, and then she wasn't. Of all the days spent with Kayla, this morning had rudiments of a real relationship. The somewhat insignificant cyphers couples take for granted, like jockeying for space in the bathroom, or minimal eye contact when getting dressed.

Bennie was in his underwear at the sink squeezing the toothpaste on the brush when Kayla squeezed past to turn the shower on. He watched her from the mirror checking the temperature of the water. Before he could rinse she'd taken off the nightgown confirming relationship nakedness; the point when couples recognize they've seen each other undressed enough times that it's normal. Totally naked she touched his shoulder reminding him not to flush the toilet and got behind the curtain. Those were the exact words Bennie would say to Terri when she stayed at his place. Then sometimes just for laughs Terri would flush anyway then get in the shower with him.

When they got outside it was cold and the sidewalk was bustling. Kayla shivered tucking her free hand under Bennie's arm as they walked. Embracing this gesture she wished he had the courage to see this relationship could work despite the unusual start. It had the makings of a show-stopping story for their tenth wedding anniversary dinner.

Bennie continued down the steps of the train station to say goodbye, feet away from the turnstile. She kissed him lightly on the lips then asked was he coming back tonight. Above the clanking noise from people using the turnstile the answer was no, but he'd see her Tuesday evening after work. Kayla looked at her watch then went through the turnstile, never looking back.

The following day when she got home Bennie came over still pretending to be her man, right up until Wednesday night before Ronald came back. And true to her word Kayla let him go, but remained optimistic. When she didn't call by Friday night she believed it was truly over.

Chapter 11

Ronald drove from his home in Long Island early Friday arriving at the store thirty minutes before opening time. It was still dark when he removed the lock then pushed the metal gate up until it slammed still at the top. Ronald locked the front door behind him then went to the office and sat behind the desk. When Bennie walked in the joy they once had greeting each other had faded to an ordinary cordial hand shake. Bennie sat on the opposite side of the desk then asked about their trip. Ronald said aside from being on the beach and having dinner it was fine. He described it like going to the store for a pair of shoes. Then Ronald added the weather was nice and Lorraine had a good time. After moving the phone a few inches closer Ronald told Bennie Lorraine was leaving for Atlantic City with Sharon and Veronica in a few hours. They'd planned this girl's trip two weeks ago because Veronica finally broke up with Devin. His drunken behavior was getting worse, and she had to let go. Lorraine would be back Sunday evening and back at the office Monday.

Apparently Ronald's mind was elsewhere since he kept eyeing the telephone. Bennie thought about just coming out and saying he'd been fucking Kayla, that way Ronald would have motivation to finally dissolve their partnership. The upside was freedom from this twisted love rectangle consisting of himself, Ronald, Lorraine, and Kayla. The down side was Kayla was putting past mistakes behind and moving on, and he'd promised not to say anything. So Bennie began to fill Ronald in on other matters.

Bennie sat in the chair crossed his legs and told Ronald he'd caught some kind of stomach virus to account for Jorge's sudden overtime. After that Bennie gave updates on finances, maintenance, and inventory. At fifteen minutes to six Ronald put the phone to his ear and dialed. Seconds later he seemed baffled then quickly hung up, and dialed again. Kayla wasn't answering and neither was the machine. Ronald now realized her number was disconnected as Bennie fiddled with his finger nails. Looking worried, Ronald put the phone in the cradle and stared at the wall. Ronald's in for a big surprise when he finds out Kayla's finished with him, Bennie thought.

Ronald rubbed his chin a second then asked had Bennie heard from Kayla? Bennie responded simply repeating the question. Ronald admitted a problem with her phone then asked again. Bennie told him Kayla had stopped by the day after he and Lorraine left for vacation. Bennie knew Ronald checked the surveillance system periodically so he might as well tell the truth. Instead of volunteering information Bennie made Ronald keep asking questions which was even more annoying. So he gave the facts in brief controlled sentences. Bennie said, "Kayla knocked on the door looking for you I told her you weren't here. She washed some clothes and went to the Chinese restaurant. I asked her to pick up something for me. I let her eat here at the table and she left."

After that Bennie told Ronald he was going home and he would turn the lights on, and unlock the front door on his way out.

That same day Kayla came home from work to her cat and empty living room. She went to the answering machine in the bedroom hoping Bennie called. It reminded her of the ache waiting for Ronnie's call and she walked back to the living room to take off her shoes. Tonight she and her cat named Dog would sit on the couch and not think about being alone.

Shortly after nine that evening a chain across the door stopped it from opening fully. Kayla got up from the couch and stood behind the door. She knew who it was but she asked in a very bored voice, "Who is it?"

"Come on baby open up. Why you got the chain on the door?" Ronald asked trying to look inside.

Kayla took a deep breath ready to face the inevitable and slid the chain off.

"Hey baby nice to see you," said Ronald closing the door behind him. He moved to hug Kayla but she stepped back, raising her hand up like a stop sign.

"I know it's been a minute, but I got here as soon as I could. Baby you…you don't seem glad to see me."

Kayla looked without saying a word at first. She was pissed at Ronald, hurt and angry. Now it was Kayla's turn to toss him away and see how he likes it. "Kayla I'm sorry," he said reaching for her hand.

Kayla moved away, folding her arms across her chest, and said, "I want my keys Ronnie."

"What?" he asked stepping back.

"You heard me!" she said louder.

"Come on Kayla I just want to talk about what happened."

"Ronnie I don't care! All I want is my damn keys, and I want them right now! I'm not playing with you. We're done!" Kayla demanded, laying her palm flat with the other hand on her hip.

Before he could turn them over Kayla snatched them from his hand and said angrily, "Now I want you to leave me alone!"

This was a side of Kayla Ronald never experienced but he knew the secret was to keep talking.

"Kayla, why you acting like this? Come on now, I just want to tell you what happened. After that night at the bar she came to work with me every single day! I never had a chance to call to say I'm sorry. So I'm sorry for what went down," he said humbly.

Kayla looked in the corner, then at the television, then Ronald explained, "Baby I couldn't call right away, then the first chance I got you changed your number so I had to come right over."

This man hasn't spent time with me in months Kayla thought. If he had tried to call he'd know my number was changed less than a week ago. Now he's playing me for a fool again.

"That's right I changed my number," she answered boldly holding the keys tight.

"You didn't have to get a new number Kayla, that's wrong," Ronald said softly.

"Oh hell yes I did!" said Kayla raising her voice.

"Why…how was I going to call you when I wanted to come over?" he asked desperately.

"Cause you not gonna call me anymore! Look…never mind all that, just…just go back home to your wife Ronnie, okay! I mean that's really where you want to be so…so go, I ain't mad at you."

"Well you sound like you are."

"I don't even know why I'm still talking to you… it is over, that's all! You've hurt me for the last time," said Kayla with a cracking voice.

"Kayla I missed you so much and I'm here now. I been thinking about you every day and I'm sorry about what happened at the bar. I know we had plans but when I saw Lorraine and…and I…I panicked. I didn't know what else to do! But there wasn't a day, not one day I wished I could've told you I was sorry. After that, Lorraine's been going to work with me every day, and I couldn't get away. Honestly this was the first chance I got to come over," he said earnestly.

"Ronnie you stopped spending time with me long before Bennie's birthday, so don't even try it! You talking some bullshit now and I don't want to hear it, I'm telling you I'm not in the mood!" she yelled.

"You're right…you're right, and it won't happen again baby," he said softly holding his arms out as if ready to catch her.

"I know it won't you son of a bitch! It's time for you to leave Ronnie. You gotta get out right now!" Kayla said opening the door.

Ronald's mouth hung open in skepticism and he said, "For real Kayla?"

"Yeah for real!" she said with her words echoing in the hall.

Knowing Kayla's voice carried he stepped out and she slammed the door loud enough for the entire floor to hear.

Ronald headed toward the elevator then turned around. He stopped at the door poised to knock again, choosing instead to tap gently with two fingers. Was the lady in the apartment across from Kayla looking out the peephole? Still he tapped until a voice from the other side said, "Will you please leave me alone?"

"Kayla…Kayla can you hear me? I'm not gonna bother you anymore I promise, but I want to tell you one more thing," he said with his face inches from the door.

"Kayla, come on now. Kayla…Kayla just let me say this and I will leave and never come back. I don't want to talk about this in the hall," he said slightly above a whisper.

During a very long moment of silence Ronald waited unsure. On the other side Kayla stared at her once lovely roses now wilted and sagging. She heard his tap again and unlocked the door. Right away Kayla went to the far side of the room crossing her arms.

"Thank you," said Ronald staying close to the door after closing it.

Saturday, shortly after 6 the next day the phone rang waking Bennie from a good night's sleep. With one eye open he reached for the phone wondering who'd be calling this early. Maybe it was Kayla?

"Hello," Bennie answered groggily.

"What's up Ben…how you doing?" asked Ronald nicely.

"What's going on Ron, something wrong at the store?"

"Nah we're good, I'm in the office but I had to tell you something that's why I'm calling," said Ronald.

When Ronald wouldn't go on talking Bennie wanted to say what the fuck is it? Instead he waited taking time to yawn. Finally Ronald said, "You know Lorraine is in Atlantic City. If Lorraine asks you tell her we was out last night cause you wanted to talk. So we had a talk you know like one of our how long we known each other conversations."

"Alright no problem," Bennie answered in suspicion.

With one ear on the pillow and the other to the phone he couldn't believe Ronald had the nerve to ask for an alibi. He constantly pushed their brotherly bond to the limit. Still Bennie said, "Sure so we talked last night um, what time did I leave last night so I know?"

"Shit man you right! Say um…say we talked till it was almost time to open up this morning, don't give no special time."

"Alright I got it, so I'll holla at you later," Bennie said thinking if they stopped now he could go back to sleep.

That's when yesterday's events came back forcing the remaining eye open. Ronald called Kayla but couldn't reach her. If he showed up there he had to give her keys back. So where was he all night? If Kayla told the truth Bennie would consider the possibility of a relationship with her. It was the confirmation he was looking for when he fell asleep thinking about her. So he must have been with some other woman and was looking for a reason to say so.

"Is everything okay with you?" asked Bennie giving Ronald the chance to say more.

"Yeah I'm good, nothing to worry about," then after a brief pause he blurted, "I was really over at Kayla's house. Let me tell you, Ben she was mad as a motherfucker but we good now. Shit you know the deal."

"Yeah I hear you Ron. Alright then so you're good, I'm going back to sleep."

"Hey dude one more thing. Kayla told me you told her where to get the calzones," Ronald commented.

"Yeah I mentioned it, so did she get them?"

"Yeah she had some in the freezer. I had half a chicken cutlet parm for breakfast."

First I'm his alibi and now I'm feeding this mutherfucker too. Before he completely snapped Bennie said, "I'm going back to sleep; I'll call you later."

"One more thing!" Ronald said quickly, "I need you to open up for me cause I'm going back over there tonight. Can you do it?"

"Alright!" he answered reluctantly then hanging up while Ronald was still talking.

Bennie rolled on his back closed his eyes knowing he wasn't going back to sleep. He wondered if Ronald suspected something went down when he was gone, and that was the reason for this early phone call. Just last Saturday Bennie was on a bench looking across the Hudson River happy, actually considering a relationship with Kayla because she was so down to earth. Now the day felt rough like sandpaper. Those two bitches deserve each other he thought, throwing the covers back and standing to his feet. He was mad with himself for wasting time last night wondering what Kayla was doing and if she missed him, now he knew.

This day had to start off differently and end differently. Bennie walked around the house from the kitchen to and back to the living room then back to the kitchen. Bennie opened the door to the fridge and stared inside. Then he closed it and went to the living room to sit finally deciding to ride his bicycle. He went to the basement to check the tires, and changed into a navy blue sweat suit. Afterwards Bennie carried his Panasonic Grand Tourer on his shoulder to the sidewalk. It was the perfect day for a ride 48 degrees with hardly any wind. This was a great idea he thought, putting the headphones over his ears. He looked up the street in the direction of Yankee Stadium but chose downtown towards Central Park. All that was left to do now was put the head phones on, press play, and ride away.

Minutes later Bennie passed the newsstand on 125th Street and Eighth Avenue where a blind man sold papers and magazines back in the day. That man was famous in Harlem because he could hear the difference between a quarter, a dime, or a nickel when it dropped in his dish. As Bennie peddled away he turned for one last look, not seeing the light turn to red. It was car tires screeching that alerted him to the mistake. Now was the time to focus, Kayla and Ronald weren't worth getting run down for.

Soon Bennie entered the park from 110th Street. People of all ages were out walking, riding, running and now the new thing was skating with roller blades. When he reached 59th Street and Columbus Circle he got off his bike in front of a bench near the entrance. Without unzipping the pocket Bennie felt the Walkman button and pressed stop. Then he removed the headphones and sat down pushing the bike by his side. His idea worked, he hadn't thought about Kayla or Ronald the entire time.

It's funny how familiar places bring back memories long forgotten. Just a hundred feet away Bennie saw the spot he'd once sold straw hats for Sonny in the summer of 75. A few months that summer on Fridays and Saturdays Sonny gave Bennie a green duffle bag filled with different styles of straw hats. On those weekends Bennie sold straw hats from a blanket on the sidewalk until evening for $5 apiece. After Sonny's cut Bennie made between $70 and $100 in two days, which wasn't bad for a sixteen-year-old kid. At that time Ronald and he were best buddies so Ronald joined him sometimes. During the day they'd get chili dogs and grape sodas from Tony the frank man's wagon. Tony was very nice, nothing like the Italians that chased Bennie from Little Italy years later.

That same summer a black man in his twenties presented Bennie with another opportunity to make a few dollars. For reasons unknown Bennie was given a hundred joints in a plastic sandwich bag to sell for a 60-40 split. In two weeks all Bennie had to give the man was $60 dollars. Back then if you were caught with some marijuana the cop confiscated it, or made you throw it away. To sell the joints Bennie brought packs of incense with him the next weekend to sell alongside the hats. When someone inquired about the incense Bennie would whisper he had something to go along with the incense. The black people that got incense knew what that meant. Bennie sold enough at Columbus Circle to pay the man that weekend. For three weeks Bennie held the $60 and the guy never came back. With the summer coming to a close he and Ronald went inside a movie on 42nd Street to sell the rest.

It was Enter the Dragon; "Fists of Fury" and "The Chinese Connection" were playing all for a dollar. Back then you could smoke cigarettes and weed in theaters. So if you lit up a joint it wasn't long before someone followed the smell then asked to buy a joint. Ronald and he were so high from the weed they had to watch all three movies twice. Now you go to jail for a dime bag. It just proves time changes situations, appearances, and affections. Back then Ronald was his best friend, now that too had changed. Around 3 o'clock the chilly air was a signal to head back. Bennie had reminisced to the point it was no longer pleasant. He looked around one more time then threw his leg over the bike placing one foot on the pedal. Kayla didn't even wait one fucking week before being with Ronald.

When Bennie got uptown past 116th Street the red light forced him to stop near the crosswalk. He was wondering what to eat later as this couple walked in front of him. Suddenly the man stepped onto the curb turned around and said, "Isn't that your nephew…that's your nephew?"

When he turned to look the man was speaking to Thomasina.

In 1985 before Tiffany was born Bennie met Thomasina one evening. While Linda recovered from her accident Bennie wanted unencumbered companionship, and Thomasina filled that need. She waited at the counter of a small store on the East side of 125th Street to buy beer. After the shopkeeper put the can of Old English inside a paper bag Thomasina lingered until Bennie finished. He was instantly attracted to this younger version of Cicely Tyson and her smile sealed the deal. Thomasina was missing a tooth and she'd lick her tongue over the space as friendly enticement. After a brief conversation Bennie drove across 125th and parked near the entrance to the Henry Hudson Parkway. They drank beer and talked about an hour, then had sex in the back of his car. Afterwards he took Thomasina home and was introduced to her husband Derrick as one of her older sister's sons. Thomasina was only six years older than Bennie but her sister was much older than her. So for the next few months when Bennie called Thomasina house he'd ask to speak to his Auntie.

It made no sense that he could come over, speak to Derrick, leave with his wife, and bring her back hours later. Derrick never questioned where Thomasina went with her nephew or talked about her side of the family. Either Derrick was extremely stupid, or he knew and didn't care. Eventually Bennie stopped seeing Thomasina almost seven years ago, now here she stood.

"Boy you better get off that bike and give me a hug," she said guardedly.

Bennie got off pushing the bike on the sidewalk, never taking eyes off Derrick. Thomasina put her arm around Bennie's neck kissing his cheek, holding on until she felt the hug returned.

"See I told you that was your nephew!" said Derrick, taking his opportunity to greet.

Thomasina stepped back, looking at Bennie from head to toe then asked, "How you been boy? I ain't seen you in a long time."

"Yeah I know…I know," Bennie answered, not knowing how much to say.

Shaking Derrick's hand Bennie couldn't think of Thomasina's sister's name if in case Derrick happened to mention her.

"You don't care nothing bout your Auntie no more," she said holding Bennie's hand.

"Na, that's not true. It's good to see ya'll," Bennie said, keeping the bike between him and Derrick if things went wrong.

"So what are you doing around here?" Thomasina asked, throwing her neck to one side then crimping her lip.

"I went for a ride, so I rode around Central Park now I'm going home."

"On your way home…um hum," she answered mockingly.

"What're you doing over here?"

"We've been living here for three years. That Eastside apartment we had before was too small so we moved right at that second building over there," she said pointing down the street.

"Where, that building right there?" he asked looking down the block.

"You see where those guys are going up the steps…that one," said Derrick.

"I see it," Bennie answered taking a longer look at Thomasina.

"I'm on the second-floor apartment 210," she said.

Before anyone had a chance to speak Thomasina said, "Honey, get me some cigarettes and a six pack please."

"You just bought a pack when we left remember?" Derrick answered looking confused.

"I know! I want another one, plus I want to know why he ain't come to see me, ask about me or nothing," Thomasina said sounding playful.

Before Derrick left he said, "You see how your aunt treats me Bennie…You want something?"

"No thanks," Bennie said, as he watched Thomasina unzip her bomber jacket.

"So how you been?"

"I've been good Thomasina. Haven't been on the bike for a while so like I said, I just went for a ride."

"And you got tired of riding me too?" she asked, moving her tongue over the empty space.

Thomasina was still cute, and that gesture with her tongue brought back memories. It caused Bennie to relax and smile a little. Then she said, "Bennie you changed your number, and you stopped calling. I got really worried…I did!"

"I'm sorry I…"

Before he could finish Thomasina slapped his arm, followed up with a sad face, then continued, "You know I even went to your place to see if you were okay. And by the way Bennie, I always knew that wasn't where you lived but I never said anything."

"Thomasina it was just getting…complicated."

"Complicated…how?"

"Look…I just didn't want to have to hurt nobody that's all," he said looking in the direction of the store.

"Baby I told you; he don't know about us…and he still don't. You heard him call you my nephew, right? He don't know…I swear!" she said emphatically.

"What if he asks me something about your family? I don't even remember your sister's name."

"My sister's name is Angie, but he ain't never gonna ask you that," she said opening her purse.

"You sure about that?"

"Yes…I'm sure. So you gonna call me?" she asked, giving Bennie her phone number.

"Yeah I will," he said hesitantly.

"Good, now I want you to come not next weekend, but the next weekend that way he'll be home to watch the girls," she said smiling.

"Fine I'm gonna call you Thomasina."

"I just want to know; did I ever leave you unsatisfied?" she asked moving her tongue again.

"No, you didn't," Bennie answered seeing Derrick walk towards them.

"My nephew told me he was sorry and he's gonna keep in touch with his Auntie," Thomasina said happily.

"That's good," said Derrick.

"So he's gonna pick me up Saturday after next in two weeks…right?"

"Yes," Bennie answered, rolling the bike into the street.

Thomasina watched him ride away. When he was half way down the block she yelled, "It was good to see you!"

Instead of looking back he waved, then pedaled faster until the wind whistled in his ears.

Running into Thomasina after all these years was some coincidence he thought. If he called on her there was still the awkward situation of pretending to be her nephew. On the other hand the sexual farce they played made it interesting. Actually Thomasina had an upbeat personality if his memory was correct. Riding past 125th Street Bennie remembered she liked the song Insatiable by Prince. One night Thomasina asked him to play that song over and over, while she sang naked holding her forty ounce. That same night she told Bennie to pick any page from Players or Black Tail Magazine and she'd copy it. Then she let him take Polaroid pictures so he'd never forget. Sadly he had to destroy them when Linda came to live there.

The worst thing about not riding the bicycle for a while is that your ass hurts. A pain he felt as soon as he walked to the front door. Inside Bennie held the paper with Thomasina's number contemplating whether to throw it away or call. Then he remembered something else Thomasina would do. She was the only woman who called him Daddy during sex. It sounded strange at first then he got accustomed to it, and it actually turned him on. He looked at her number wondering was this chance meeting the way to permanently put his feelings for Kayla away. Bennie called Thomasina that Thursday agreeing to pick her up at her building Saturday after next.

That day the temperature was below freezing and the wind made it feel like 10 degrees above zero. Thomasina stood by the stoop in a short purple jacket and tight fitting jeans talking to a neighbor. Bennie pulled into a nearby space making eye contact then waved to her. Instantly Thomasina came turning her back to Bennie to say, "Cheryl this is my nephew Bennie…one of Angie's boys,"

"Bennie nice to meet you. Yeah I see the resemblance right around the cheeks."

Thomasina flashed a huge smile. As Cheryl turned to walk away she said, "Your Auntie is a real sweetheart, she really is. That's my girl."

Grinning Thomasina unzipped her jacket, placing a hand on her hip and said, "Bennie…I want seafood. I want to go to City Island."

After all these years Thomasina was still eye-catching, and Bennie began a silent conversation with that region between her thighs. Seconds later her hips answered with a delicate message of consent. With eyes set firmly on a goal, nothing was about to keep him from this moist opportunity.

"City Island…sure why not," he said happily.

At that point Thomasina rested a hand on his door and mischievously said, "I wasn't sure you were coming, but you're gonna be coming tonight…that's for sure."

Then she did that thing with her tongue and walked around to get in. Before opening the door Thomasina leaned in and quickly said, "Baby, please say hi to Derrick so we can get out of here."

"Where's he at?" Bennie asked looking around.

"He's right over there in the window," she answered, pointing to the second floor.

Bennie tilted his head out the car spotting Derrick in the window next to the fire escape. That familiar regret flared up because of his role in this pitiful threesome. Once more Bennie asked himself, "How could Derrick not know what was about to happen? Didn't he see his wife flash that body to her so-called nephew?"

"What's up man?" Bennie yelled, looking questionably at Derrick.

Unable to understand Derrick's reply Bennie waved, leaned back in the car, and drove away. This situation wasn't ideal and the awkwardness between he and Derrick never stopped. Bennie was still going to take Thomasina to eat, then straight to bed.

When they got to City Island Thomasina held Bennie's hand from the car to the restaurant. Inside they were seated at a booth by the window facing the lot. After the waiter took their order Thomasina asked a question.

"Bennie you still got those pictures I let you take of us?" she said before taking a sip of water.

"No Thomasina I don't, I had to get rid of them."

"Why…what happened?"

Bennie made up a story about a non-existent girlfriend and sadly said, "Well my girlfriend was poking around in my closet and I thought she might find em, so I had to cut them up when she left."

"I know that's right!" Thomasina laughed then said, "I understand, you did the right thing baby. So… ya'll live together?"

"No she's got her own place, but she's out of town for a few days."

"That's perfect…So tell me something about her, what's her name?"

"Thomasina don't ask me her name. Shit…what do you need to know her name for?" he asked sounding annoyed.

"I was just talking that's all," and before she could speak Bennie said,

"You know something Thomasina…I'm starting to think this was a mistake. I'm serious, I really do!"

Thomasina felt embarrassed, looking over his shoulder at the booth behind them then lowered her head. Somebody had to hear Bennie and now he was ticked off. She watched him examine the silverware then look around like he wanted to leave. For a few seconds every word, laugh, cough and clinking of utensils was amplified. Bennie's thoughts turned to Thomasina's husband. He began to wonder did Derrick ever ask why her nephew stopped coming around during those years, and what reason did she give?

Gingerly Thomasina reached for Bennie's hand since he refused to look at her.

"I just wanna to be with you Daddy," she said softly.

That was the only time she'd called him Daddy and they weren't having sex. It was a phrase to bring remembrances of Thomasina's submission and pliability. Bennie began to relax after hearing her sadness, "I missed you. I've missed you a lot. All these years and you didn't come and see me. I don't know what I did but I would never hurt you. You hurt my feelings; you really did. So after all these years do you miss me even a little bit?"

Her words were taking effect and he finally answered, "Yeah I missed you to…Auntie."

Thomasina exhaled with relief. While her hand was on top of his she massaged his pointer finger from the nail to the base of his knuckle. That sexy gap in her mouth began to stir him up and Bennie said, "So anyway, I don't have the instant camera that spits the pictures out anymore. As a matter of fact nobody uses them anymore now that the digital cameras are coming out."

"They got digital cameras?" she asked just to keep him talking.

"Yup and I don't think they even make film for instamatics anymore."

"That's too bad…So after this are we going back to your place? Cause you know what I want to do," she asked letting go of his hand.

"Oh, yes we're gonna get together," he answered nodding in approval.

"But I gotta be back home by two," she said quickly.

"Sure no problem."

There was something about Thomasina's resilience that made all the drama worth it. She never let anything bother or upset her for very long. After a brief silence she said,

"Bennie…you remember the time I was on my way to your house and those guys kidnapped me?"

He frowned for a second or two then said, "Yeah…yeah that's right, I remember! And we went back a few days later to the spot and found your wallet and some of your clothes. I'm glad they didn't hurt you."

"It wasn't a few days. We went back the next day, that Sunday," she abruptly said.

One Saturday night Thomasina caught a gypsy cab to meet Bennie. Along the way the car slowed down after turning, so a man could jump in the back seat. Both the driver and guy were black, and up to no good. The man in the back held a knife to Thomasina's throat daring her to make a sound. The driver went to the Tri-Borough Bridge toll plaza, then down to Randall's Island. They stopped in a dark isolated area and turned off the engine. At knife point she was forced to undress while the driver watched from the front seat. Seeing Thomasina topless the driver remarked,

"We gonna do this bitch!"

Suddenly car headlights approached. Once the man focused on the car Thomasina took that opportunity to kick him in the chest. She grabbed the door handle, got out and started running. Wearing only panties she headed back towards the ramp to the toll booth. Halfway up the ramp a car appeared in the distance behind her. Assuming it was the men who abducted her, Thomasina instinctively hopped over the cement guardrail gripping the edge with both hands. Good thing she held on to the side because she ended up dangling thirty feet above the ground. After the car passed she pulled herself up like a character from an action movie. With breasts scraped from the cement Thomasina got on solid ground then sprinted for dear life, dodging oncoming cars until reaching the nearest toll booth. Topless and crying hysterically she got help from the Tri-borough Bridge Police.

The NYPD took an incident report then drove Thomasina home wrapped in a thin brown blanket. On the way home she found out from the police how lucky she was. Last week the body of a young black woman was found dead under an overpass not far from the Tri-Borough Bridge raped, and stabbed to death.

Bennie hadn't thought about that incident in years, and the assumptions he made caused his head to lower in shame. That night when Thomasina didn't show up he was furious. He remembered thinking how she was going to have to do something extra special the next time. Then early the next morning she called, told him what happened, then asked would he take her back to Randall's Island. That Sunday afternoon she led the way until they found the exact spot the cab took her. They looked around in the grass until Thomasina found her purse, wallet, the blouse she wore, and one shoe by the edge of the road. Before they left Bennie found the other shoe next to her bra a few more feet away.

Thomasina's hand covered her mouth and Bennie again said empathetically, "I'm just really glad they didn't hurt you that night Thomasina."

"Shit I'm glad too! That thing happened so fast all I knew was I had to get out, because them niggers was gonna kill me like they did to that other woman. Yup…so I had to get away, and I just kept kicking that muther fucker and got out. Thank you Jesus!"

"Did the cops ever catch those guys?" asked Bennie remembering the scrape marks on her breasts days after the incident.

"No!…Well I don't really know for sure. Shit I told the police I was scared cause the cab picked me up on Park Avenue around the corner from my house. That night when they dropped me off I said those men could have my address, but they didn't seem to care and neither did Derrick. Do you know that nigger wouldn't even walk with me to the corner store!"

"No shit for real?

"Yeah I kid you not. He didn't go with me to wash the clothes or go shopping…nothing. So remember I told you that white detective from Homicide came to the house. I forgot his name, but I told him what happened. Did I ever tell you he didn't write my statement down? Nope he never wrote down any of that shit! All Detective What's His Face did was give me his card and when I called, he never called me back. So after a week I threw that fucking card away and that was it," she said making a throwing motion with her hand. For a minute Thomasina rocked tensely in her seat then abruptly went to the ladies room. Obviously almost losing her life was still hard to talk about.

Her brief absence brought into focus her good qualities. Thomasina was perky and fun to be with, and her behavior consistent. It had never been an issue Thomasina liked cheating on her husband, and Bennie wasn't about to abandon this moist opportunity. Bennie was as comfortable being in control of Derrick's wife as taking his bike out for a ride. No doubt Thomasina would be doing some riding tonight.

Minutes later Thomasina returned to the table happy and ready to continue with dinner as if their discussion never happened. After dinner Bennie stopped at the local store for a 40 ounce of her favorite drink Olde English. Instead of the studio Bennie used in the past, tonight he took her to his house. After introducing Mister to Thomasina she was free to roam around the brownstone while Mister was in the backyard. Afterwards they got cozy on the living room couch. Thomasina took one drink and refreshed Bennie's memory. Recent and past events were taking a toll, so there was no reaction.

For years after losing Whende Bennie floated in orbit between just fine and despair, giving only minimum affection with each encounter. Afraid of losing ability to show love he took a chance. Kayla convinced Bennie to come back to earth and enjoy a few days of pure passion. Added to that prescription, deep conversation for Bennie's injured soul that Thomasina couldn't refill. He and Thomasina never kissed much less watched a movie together. It was straight to business then home to Derrick until the next time.

Eventually tedious ceremonial sex ensued, only pleasurable for Bennie until the last few seconds. Afterwards Thomasina returned from the bathroom happy to drink more beer and dance around naked. She was still desirable like that first cup of coffee in the morning before work. Sometime later they had sex again then he took her home. Thomasina served her purpose and Bennie was back in his bed before 2am. Ten minutes later he was thinking about Kayla and was she asleep or not.

Five days late for Kayla wasn't a problem. Sometimes during stress it happened, but a week later she began to worry. In the month of March she was more than three weeks late, and there was a strange taste in her mouth when she woke up in the morning.

The first time Kayla got pregnant Malik was the father. Despite being careful she found out shortly after they broke up. Despite the way he humiliated her at school days before Kayla felt he had a right to know. Because his telephone number changed she waited outside the main entrance at 10 in the morning. Around lunch time she saw Malik walking out with a friend. When they got to the bottom of the stairs Kayla politely asked to speak with him. When his friend attempted to leave Malik told the guy to stay. Kayla mustered up the words to tell Malik in front of a stranger he was going to be a father. Instantly he laughed in her face while backhanding his buddy on the shoulder. Then Malik told Kayla to go tell one of those many Tricks she'd been messing with. He was loud enough that everyone heard. After that Kayla had an abortion, dropped out of college, and found her way to Manhattan.

Determined not to get pregnant until she was ready Kayla started birth control, never missing a day despite the absence of a steady boyfriend. However the very beginning of this New Year started off with struggle. Ronald wasn't spending any time with her. Training for the new position was demanding so she missed taking her pill a few days here and there. As much as Kayla wished, there was no rewind button for life. She'd given her body to two men in the same week, and becoming a mother wasn't the plan. Kayla had countless opportunities ahead, and it wasn't the right time to have a baby.

Sitting on her bed Kayla picked up the cat, holding it close to her bosom. If a man loved her as much as this cat, that would be enough she thought. After a moment of clarity she put the cat down. Ronnie made excuse after excuse not to be around or call to say check on her. Kayla decided if her friend wasn't back in two more days she'd take a pregnancy test, and if it was positive she'd tell Bennie. If she was pregnant nothing was going to make her get rid of another child.

Several days later Kayla came from work, kicked off her shoes, and then tossed her jacket on the floor. She left the bathroom in a mental state of disarray. The test coupled with a slight soreness in her breasts was confirmation. Her friend wasn't just out of town; she'd left the country and wouldn't be back for months.

Feeling light headed, Kayla stumbled into the living room. Emotionally void, she collapsed in front of the couch and cried. After a time Kayla rolled on her knees but didn't get up. Kayla crawled like a baby to the couch cushion resting her head in her hands. Her father taught her to pray but she stopped after he died. If ever there was a time to talk with God it was right now. With head in hand, an honest dialogue long overdue was spoken aloud.

"God…I haven't prayed since I was a little girl when my Daddy taught me. You know the one, now I lay me down to sleep. I stopped saying it before I went to bed after he died."

Kayla's hands squeezed around her head as she continued, "I don't know if you will listen to me. I know I haven't been living right like I should…I'm sorry, I'm sorry God. I was hurt and mad, not at you God. Maybe I was mad after my Daddy died and You didn't save my mother. That's the reason I stopped praying but You know that. But God I'm trying God, I'm really trying to do better and I am. I…I don't strip anymore, and I never ever will! I…I have a real job now and…and I won't ever go back to dancing for money, I won't! But God, I want to keep this child. I mean I am keeping this child! And um…so…so I'm asking you to…to… to help me. I'm asking for you to…to let the baby's father um…do the right thing, that's all. He don't have to love me. I can deal with that, but I need him to…to just help me, that's all I ask please God please."

With nothing left to say Kayla sat on the couch for an hour making a plan. The training classes were over, and since she'd never taken so much as a day off, the next two and the weekend belonged to her. Before she told Bennie she had to be sure she was pregnant. So early Thursday morning Kayla went to her doctor and that test confirmed everything. When asked the last time she had sex Kayla used the day she was with Bennie, which made the due date November 14th, give or take a day.

From the doctor's office Kayla went to the nearest ATM, withdrew $500, then took the train downtown to Bamberger's. There she found a charcoal grey dress and jacket with silver buttons on the cuffs. It was just the type of outfit a corporate woman would wear at the office to look sexy and professional. When Kayla left the store she decided to take a cab home. On the way uptown she told the driver to let her out at the Coach store where she found the perfect dark grey leather purse.

Friday morning Kayla was the first one at the hair dresser. She chose a shorter hair style like Halie Berry wore in a magazine. By twelve o'clock, with hair and nails done, Kayla went home to get ready. Outfitted and standing in front of the bedroom mirror she draped that new purse over her arm. This dress fit perfectly, Kayla thought, as she traced the material with her hands. The jacket showed just enough of her hips to make it the sexiest outfit she'd ever worn outside of any club. She practiced standing and what position to place her feet to create the perfect tension on the seam of the dress. Armed with this new look and French manicure Kayla was determined to look as pleasing as possible. Bennie was about to bear witness to a classy successful sister worthy of his love and affection. When he laid eyes on her he'd melt like butter then take her and keep her for the rest of his life.

Not long after, Kayla opened the door of her cab down the block from the laundry. Stylishly she placed her foot down in those high heels and got out. Years of stage work prepared her to walk with ease and confidence. Every man took a double take as she passed. When she saw Bennie's car near the entrance her palms began to sweat. Her stomach felt queasy but she took a deep breath and went inside. Bennie's back was to her with an elbow propped atop the washer talking with one of the customers. He wore a simple dark blue work shirt with the laundry logo over the breast pocket tucked in his jeans. Kayla stayed in the distance until the conversation ended then she went closer. Bennie spontaneously smiled until he saw who it was then his demeanor changed to indifference, nonetheless Kayla smiled brightly then asked, "How are you sir? I see you're working hard as usual."

His expression begged the question, why was she there? Quickly Kayla did a half turn towards the window just enough to give him a side glimpse, then faced him again.

"Can I talk to you for a minute in the office?...Its important." she asked shyly.

When Bennie didn't move she walked ahead to the door and waited. Now he'd gotten the front, side and the back view of his new life.

Kayla stayed in the doorway so their shoulders touched and Bennie would catch the scent of perfume on her neck. After unlocking the door and pushing it open she went in assuming her first practiced pose. Bennie made no eye contact until he got behind the desk. Tensely she pressed on to say, "So how you been?"

"Good," he answered reluctantly.

He didn't seem impressed with her new look, so she moved two paces closer like a Sheriff about to have a gunfight in a western movie. Bennie countered by shoving both hands in his pants pockets and waited. Kayla let her bag rest on the edge of the desk and said, "Now you see…there you go…acting all mean to me again. You said you weren't gonna do that to me anymore."

Kayla removed her hand from the strap to step towards the corner of the desk. Bennie watched her slowly stroke her hair then the last button on the bottom of her jacket. Kayla had no idea she was about to meet the Bennie Thomasina knew so well.

"Alright so you said you wanted to say something, so what's up?" he responded, like there was a foul odor in the room.

Suddenly her left temple began to hurt and the jacket collar felt rough to her skin, then Bennie said, "Well what is it."

"I know you weren't expecting to see me so soon but I had to see you," she said sounding unsure.

Kayla hoped he'd remove his hands from the pockets, hold her, and ask what the matter was. His silence made it excruciatingly challenging but she continued, "I…I couldn't tell you this over the phone but I wanted you to know to… to know I'm pregnant."

Bennie clasped his hands together, smiling, awkwardly relieved. This was gonna turn out like she wanted because he seemed strangely happy. Then he asked, "You're pregnant? Kayla did you say you were pregnant?"

"Yes Bennie I'm pregnant," she answered feeling relieved.

"That's good I'm happy for you," without hesitation Bennie asked, "So what did Ronald say?" he replied looking at her as if she were dirty.

"What…I don't understand!" replied Kayla with her mouth wide open.

"You heard me! Did…you…tell…Ronald he was going to be a father? Did you tell him? What did he say about it?" Bennie asked with some intensity.

"What do you mean? Why would you say that Bennie? Ronnie and me that's over I told you!" she responded sounding shocked.

Barely raising his voice but with anger and intensity he said, "Why would I say that? Are you serious right now Kayla? You know how Ronald likes to run his mouth right? Shit if he's telling you my business, he must be talking about you too right…right! Of course that's right Kayla…shit. Ronald told me all about ya'll right after he got back! How you was all mad. Yeah you was mad alright, but you made up didn't you, didn't you?! Come in here telling me you're pregnant. You forgave him for two whole nights so get the fuck outta here with that bullshit! You hear me?"

Bennie's behavior put Kayla in such fear it knocked the wind from her. She stepped back clutching her purse without answering.

"I…can't…fucking…believe you! I guess you don't know, he told me everything Kayla…everything. He even said how good the damn chicken calzone was. Yeah he let me know that too! So I'm gonna say it like this. You better go tell Ronald you're having a baby cause that's between you and him! I'm not trying to hear your bullshit Kayla… you got that!" Bennie said moving close in such a way that actually frightened her.

This was far worse than what happened with Malik outside the school. The air felt thick like trying to breathe through a straw. Shaken up Kayla turned quickly to leave and as the door closed Bennie watched on the monitor. Midway down the aisle she stumbled hitting her knee on a lady's laundry cart. Believing customers overheard Kayla focused on the front door like a deep-sea diver scrambling to reach the surface to stay alive. When Kayla got outside she still couldn't breathe so she walked around the corner near the Chinese restaurant and stopped. In the midst of passersby she felt like crying, but didn't. In the back of the cab on the way home she wanted to cry, but didn't. A woman needs to keep eyes on every driver and where they're taking her.

Within the safety of her apartment Kayla let the purse fall on the floor by the door. The first shoe kicked off went under the couch. She almost fell taking off the other shoe on the way to the bedroom. Not until Kayla sat on the bed and faced the mirror did she break down and cry. Why did bad things always happen to her, she asked her reflection? Why couldn't she just go back to the days of eating ice cream with her parents, or finish school like she'd planned. What had she done to make her life so awful? That's when her cat began rubbing her leg until she picked him up.

"At least you love me don't you Dog, yes you do," then she chuckled and said, "I'm so glad I called you Dog. And you know what? Everything is going to be fine. It didn't go the way I wanted so I'll just go to plan B."

Sleepless nights were the norm and tonight wasn't any different so Bennie took Mister for a walk well after midnight. He went up St. Nicholas past the very bench where he'd hired Mr. Queen to find Linda years ago. As Bennie looked at the bench from the sidewalk it seemed like everything he touched went wrong, from family to friends and girlfriends. Kayla said she was on the pill back in January so how could he get her pregnant? Unless it was one of the last times he let true passion get the best of him. There was also the possibility she was lying. If it weren't for that call from Ronald he might have fallen for her story. So the only thing left to do was wait to see what she does. If a blood test proved he was the father he'd deal with it then. That's when Mister nudged Bennie's hand with his head and looked up as if to say, "I got you, let's go home."

That same Saturday evening Bennie brought Thomasina home for some much needed distraction, but it wasn't enough. Before Thomasina came back to bed Bennie stared at the ceiling trying to understand Kayla. Why she bothered to snuggle, or to press her lips under his ear and breathe hope into his mind. Why signal he was the one then do the same with Ronald. At least he knew Thomasina wanted some beer, some laughs, some sex, a few dollars now and then, and to go back to her husband. You couldn't ask for more truth than that.

Just about 11:30 the doorbell rang. Bennie put a robe over his pajama bottoms then told Thomasina to be quiet. He went down downstairs, looked through the side glass to see Ronald blowing into his hands. When Bennie opened the door Ronald went straight to the living room and waited.

"Ron what are you doing here?" Bennie followed trying to gauge Ronald's disposition.

"Man I need a drink," Ronald said pouring one then sitting down.

"Dude I got a girl upstairs. I can't do this now, this ain't a good time," said Bennie pointing at the ceiling.

"I'm sorry Bro but I gotta talk to you for real," Ronald said taking a drink then letting his head fall between his shoulders.

"Ron…serious I can't do this right now," Bennie said pointing out he was standing in his robe.

"Ben…how long we known each other?" Ronald asked knowing it would change the dynamic.

"All right let me take care of this," Bennie said, cautiously watching Ronald.

When he went back Thomasina had been listening while cowering behind the door. She waited in her panties holding her bra, with the other arm across breasts.

"Shit baby I got scared! I thought that was your girlfriend so I started putting my stuff on. Who's that downstairs?" she asked with a sigh of relief.

"That's a friend of mine so listen…we gotta cut it short. I gotta handle some stuff," said Bennie ready to change into his clothes.

"I don't understand since that's not your girlfriend why do I have to go? Can't I stay up here till you finish what you gotta do?"

"Not this time Thomasina," he answered pulling up his socks.

Thomasina put on a sad face but got dressed anyway. On the edge of the bed about to slide on her last shoe she jokingly asked, "Bennie I was just thinking…if that was your girlfriend, what would've happened if she caught us."

"Well first of all she got a key so she wouldn't be ringing the bell. Plus I always touch base to make sure she got to her destination before I come and get you," Bennie said, quickly thinking up something for his nonexistent girlfriend.

From the first invitation Thomasina noticed no hint of a woman's touch at Bennie's place. It seemed unusual that this woman wouldn't mark her territory. At the very least there should be toiletries in the bathroom, clothes in the closet or space in the dresser.

"Okay I figured you had it covered baby but something ain't right," she said facing him like his answer wasn't enough. So with hands on her hips she asked again, "Yeah I hear you baby but, what do ya think would really happen if she caught us?"

Her persistence pissed Bennie off and he responded, "Well it wouldn't be good for you. It wouldn't be good for you at all Thomasina. It would be like…like if Derrick got in my face about us. I told you before what would happen! It would be real fucked up for the both of you. But you say he believes I'm your nephew right?

"Yeah I told you he does," she answered quickly.

"So trust me you don't want her to catch us! So you ready to go?" he asked politely.

"Yeah I got everything," she said looking in the mirror one more time.

Thomasina followed Bennie downstairs and into the living room where Ronald sat. Without calling her name Bennie said, "Hey man I'm gonna walk her to the corner to catch a cab and I'll be right back," Ronald glanced at Thomasina then back at the floor to say,

"You want me to go with you?"

"Nah this won't take long," Bennie said coaxing her to come.

Thomasina waved bye when Ronald looked up then followed Bennie out the door.

They walked up the block to the corner waiting for an empty cab. As Bennie watched he wondered about when he got back home. He had talked until he opened the door for Thomasina then he said, "Call me when you get home Auntie."

"I will, I'll see you soon right?" she asked smiling back.

"Yeah I'll let you know," Bennie answered while taking a long look at the driver.

Before the light turned green Bennie checked the car's license plate then waved bye to her.

As the cab drove away Bennie stepped back from the curb and watched. He dreaded going home but he had to. Too bad he couldn't go back to happier days of carefree laughter with Ronald. Back when they'd walk to Little Willie's Candy Store, or played cards on the stoop. The abuse of their friendship kept happening with no end in sight. Now as adults their paths veered apart. If Bennie didn't break this friendship habit now he'd be stuck like an alcoholic or dope fiend. Kayla finally forced their alliance to a halt. One thing was going to change after tonight, The Phrase. If Ronald asked Bennie had he been with Kayla he was going to hear the truth. Yes…yes I was with her, that's how long we've known each other.

Before Bennie went to the living room he put Mister in the backyard. If there was an altercation Bennie didn't want Mister to attack.

"Alright Ron what's going on," Bennie asked standing a few feet away.

"Kayla…Kayla's fucking pregnant man!"

Bennie waited just looking silently.

"I asked if it was mine then she tried to slap me, but I caught her hand. Ben she said she's not gonna get rid of it. She said I used her and she was done with me. Then she started talking some shit about being tired of taking one for the team. What the fuck that was about I still don't know. She said it a couple of times, I'm not taking one for the team anymore! Yo Ben…I don't know what's gonna happen if Lorraine finds out," Ronald said finally looking for advice.

"Wow…I don't know what to say," said Bennie pouring his own drink.

Bennie wasn't sure what Kayla was going to do, but now her decision was made.

"She said I gotta pay for childcare off the books and that's it. She said she don't want nothing else from me, and if I don't she's gonna tell Lorraine.

"Really, she said that?"

"Yup, so she wants me to pay for it and I don't have to do anything but stay the hell away from her. She said she don't want me to have nothing to do with the kid. I mean I don't want to anyway, and I know it sounds messed up but hey it's the truth!" Ronald said pouring another shot.

"You weren't using a rubber?"

"At first all the time then she showed me her birth control pills and well…that was it," Ronald answered reluctantly.

"So what happened?" Bennie asked for his own curiosity.

"Kayla said she got thrown off around your birthday when Lorraine walked in on us at the bar. Pushing her on you that night was my mistake and it messed her up so she missed a few days and then didn't get her refill when she should have," Ronald said hesitantly.

"That's what she told you?"

"Yup and I believe her so it is what it is. She could make me pay a lot more and tell Lorraine so I gotta do what I gotta do. I gotta give her what she wants, you know what I mean?" said Ronald looking for confirmation.

Bennie didn't know how to respond so he simply said, "I hear you Ron and you're right, we all got to do what we gotta do."

Chapter 12

(The Return)

On the 26th in two days it will be Thanksgiving. The turkey was defrosting in the fridge; the collards were cooked and frozen last week. All that was left was to get ingredients for macaroni and cheese. Jeff was bringing sweet potato pie, apple pie, and vanilla ice cream. Sonya's mom was making stuffing and candied yams. Linda was bringing egg nog and apple cider and Sonya was excited. Linda had been to her apartment once since running from her Bennie. Now because no one was hunting for her she could travel freely. Then in a few weeks Sonya and Jeff would go to Woodbridge on the weekend to celebrate Tiffany's birthday on December 12th.

From the kitchen Sonya was considering the best month to get married. May wasn't too hot for an outside wedding at the Botanical Gardens. Plus, the travel deals start in the month of May. She thought how nice it would be relaxing on the beach and making love on their honeymoon. The farthest Jeff had been from N.Y. was to Maryland for a crab fest weekend. On the other hand, if their wedding was in mid-June the kids would be out of school and Jeff's son Calvin could be in the wedding.

Calvin was the spitting image of his father, and he was a good kid. Calvin could talk fresh, and Jeff never let him get away with it. As time went by, the boy warmed up to Sonya and they got along. No doubt Calvin's mother had something to do with that. Regardless, Sonya intended to put those bitter feelings for Jeff's ex Joslyn aside. She planned to meet with her next year to bury the hatchet. They'd sit like mature adults and find common ground which should be a shared love for the boy.

When Sonya wanted to rest she'd think of something else to check. Was there enough butter, sausage, bread crumbs and seasoning for the stuffing? Did she have a can of cranberry sauce for Jeff? Sonya went back to the kitchen, opened the cabinet, caught a glimpse of sparkle from her ring and froze. Extending her hand, she tilted it, admiring the ring for the umpteenth time. Jeff picked a clear flawless center cut diamond just over a carat and she loved it.

It also seemed Jeff was sticking to his word after proposing and changed his ways. That's why after three months of being engaged Sonya suggested he move in. She called it a trial run for marriage, a way to weed out any issues. Jeff had stopped going to the strip club with Jay, but still had a beer with him occasionally after work. He also attended Sunday service, pulled out her chair, and opened her door.

As the days went on, Sonya believed Jeff was in love and her size 12 didn't matter. One day while they walked he said he wanted another child after they got married. Later that night while they made love, he looked at her in a way she'd never seen. He was not just inside of her, he was with her, embracing her body in the present and their future. Some days later when Jeff told her the guys were throwing him a bachelor party, she didn't protest. Sonya's only warning was, "I trust you! So don't do anything stupid!"

Sonya walked through the obstacle course of his things in the living room. When Jeff moved in compromises were made and there wasn't enough space for a family. He brought his 55-inch TV, a wall unit, a VCR and tapes in the living room. After Jeff put some clothes in the closet there wasn't much room left. Everything that overflowed between them went into a storage unit.

Sonya didn't want to spring a lot on Jeff at one time, but they had to move. She watched the neighborhood change and didn't want to raise a child in this part of the Bronx. They could find something better, like one of those newly built two-family townhouses near Yankee Stadium, or somewhere in Yonkers. She noticed people were moving back south to the Carolinas and Georgia. A working family could buy a nice home with a garage for less money than in New York.

After a deep breath Sonya was in the kitchen opening a strawberry yogurt, and fishing in the drawer for a spoon. She was going to lose at least fifteen pounds before trying on her first wedding gown. Linda, Tiffany, and Sonya's mom were accompanying her, and they'd make a day out of it, ending with manicures and pedicures.

Then she had to find a place for the wedding. Sonya wanted the ceremony to be in the same venue as the reception. That seemed less of a hassle to leave the church and go elsewhere for the reception and Jeff agreed. Before the reception they had to pick invitations for about 50 people. Then she had to decide on a color for bridesmaids' dresses and find a good DJ. And there was the caterer, and decorations, and what all that was going to cost. She never expected Jeff to pay for everything so she might have to take a loan from the credit union. How was all this going to work? she thought, eating yogurt while her heart raced? Then there was the baby. Sonya wanted to have Jeff's baby, but only when they were married. He said he didn't mind waiting, but was he buying time just to change his mind? Sonya ate more while reflecting on the day she saw Jeff and Cathy together.

The last week in July Jeff gave up his apartment to move in with Sonya. It was over 90 degrees that afternoon. Sonya left Jeff's building with a box and saw him talking to a woman by the U-Haul. He looked like a deer in headlights after spotting her. Jeff moved size six's hand from his arm, keeping focused on Sonya. The woman had a sleeveless purple cotton dress that flapped with the slight breeze. When Sonya walked up, "Size Six" had the nerve to say hello, then tell Jeff she missed him. Before Sonya could put the box down the woman crossed the street against the traffic and went into a corner building. Jeff avoided eye contact trying to take the box, but Sonya wouldn't release it until she knew where the woman was going. Afterwards Sonya let Jeff carry the rest and waited by the truck. When they were done Sonya didn't get in the car until he answered all her questions.

Upon further investigation Size Six's name was Cathy, the name on the number she found in his pocket. That skinny bitch lived across the street all this time. On that hot day in the sun with people passing by Jeff had to explain. He said Cathy was saying goodbye and that he stopped seeing her before he proposed. She could tell he was scared and while he talked Sonya dared him to look in the direction of Cathy's building.

With half the container finished Sonya wondered what would happen if she found out later Jeff never stopped fucking her? She hated the thought of fighting over a man but if that bitch slept with Jeff after today, she might get her ass kicked. Would he like that she stood up and fought for his affection? What would happen if the fight made him change his mind and he left her standing at the altar? What would she do then? Maybe he's going to always want someone fitter? Maybe Sonya should postpone the wedding until she was sure? Just one more doubt added to the troubles plaguing her today.

Later that same evening in Woodbridge, NJ, Tiffany worked on second grade math given by her mother after her first grade homework was finished. It was the only thing Linda credited her brother with, encouraging her to learn when she was growing up. She remembered Bennie making anything she was interested in accessible, from science to math and engineering. Linda had books about ancient civilizations, poetry, and questions on morality. Because of him she'd encouraged her daughter the same way. Tiffany's school allowed her to start first grade at five years old knowing she'd turn six in December.

Around Tiffany's last birthday Sonya and Linda went to Dr. Goldstein's office for another hypnosis treatment. The same nurse was present and this time the procedure revealed nothing new. No unintelligible language spoken by Linda or new memories revealed while under hypnosis. This time Linda suffered from a severe headache and Sonya had to take her to the emergency room. When the pain was gone Linda went to Goldstein's office alone. He showed the video from her first session and the last. She didn't understand the language, and the doctor had no answers. Goldstein said he thought the language was very old but could not prove it. Then he said it might be a rare case of reincarnation, but he couldn't prove that either.

The entire time Linda followed his instructions to the letter. She did the memory exercises incessantly which only proved she had normal recall. The only change after her last appointment had to do with her dreams. The visions of unknown people and seemingly familiar places stopped. Not even a nightmare about the squiggly man chasing after her. So after the worst headache of her life and no apparent progress she discontinued sessions with the doctor.

Linda accepted the gap in her life and focused on herself and Tiffany. She picked up the broken pieces like black women have always done and moved on. Linda joined the Usher Board at church and put Tiffany in the youth choir. Later she quit working at the library to work part time at Tiffany's school. She stopped reading in favor of movies on the VCR. For some reason Linda needed a break from reality and movies helped her to relax. She opened an account at Blockbuster taking suggestions from Sonya The Five Heartbeats, Sparkle, The Blues Brothers, and The Godfather 1 and 2. Linda cried at the end of The Color Purple and cheered for Richard Roundtree in Shaft. During Shaft and Black Caesar Linda saw the Apollo Theater on 125th Street, Harlem Hospital, streets around 8th Avenue, and the car chase on Riverside Drive. She recalled

Bennie taking her to Riverside Park as a little girl to see the Hudson River, and the New Jersey shoreline.

Eventually Linda got curious about sci-fi and horror movies too. Sonya explained that just like fake blood the special effects make it look real. With that warning she rented the movie Alien, and they watched it when Tiffany slept. She and Sonya sat on the couch with a bowl of buttered popcorn between them and the lights off. Linda's legs were crossed with her fist over her mouth. Sonya grabbed Linda's leg when the alien burst through the man's chest, then again when the alien was full grown. The next day Linda said she was going to watch it again. The thrill of being safe in her living room and scared at the same time was unique. Most of all Linda was happy a woman was the hero and killed the Alien at the end.

Sonya felt the time was right for a movie based on a true story and it was playing now. While Tiffany was in school the ladies went to the matinee for Spike Lee's Malcolm X. For more than a week Linda called Sonya to discuss the film. Malcolm was a highly intelligent and courageous man. It saddened her more that his own people turned against him. Sonya, on the other hand, blamed the coordination from the United States Government for Malcolm's death. Conflicting ideas of racism, leadership and betrayal were hard for Linda to comprehend. Before Thanksgiving they had another discussion about Malcolm X, and the condition of black people in America. That conversation led to their first heated argument.

After dinner while Tiffany washed dishes, Linda got the cordless phone and sat on the couch to make an overdue call. Linda hadn't talked to her best friend in more than a week and now the phone was ringing. Sonya picked up on the second ring with a flustered voice,

"Yeah who is it?"

"Hey girlfriend, what's going on…how you doing?" asked Linda pushing the phone tightly against her ear.

"Oh hey…I'm not doing anything, what's up?" Sonya asked with a frowny face.

After an awkward silence Sonya couldn't help but ask, "Is the baby okay?"

"Yeah girl Tiffany's fine, she's doing the dishes right now, but she's good. I called to see how you were," said Linda feeling the tension.

"Well I'm fine. Just getting stuff ready that's all," Sonya answered trying not to sound too pissed off.

Neither woman recognized the unique dynamics of their circumstances. At times Sonya treated Linda like her younger sister and a child. Like most children a time comes when they rebel, and Sonya couldn't handle it. Linda's theories and observations about social issues often differed. Sonya found it hard to listen when she had to explain everything to Linda including who Oprah was for God sakes. Their last conversation left Sonya hurting like a mother being insulted.

For Linda, memory lapse never dulled her influential nature of royalty or aristocracy. Without realizing she'd speak to Sonya with a commanding voice as if speaking to a servant. While Tiffany and Sonya were the most important people in Linda's life, she managed a lot of stress. Linda carried the pain of betrayal from the person who raised her after their parents died. Her trust was broken, and she wasn't going to let it happen again. So Linda questioned Sonya so feverishly about anything and everything. It was like the kid that asks what makes the sky blue and why is water wet? Then another question followed by another and if Sonya didn't have an answer, then why didn't she have an answer?

Consequently, like most mothers would do, Sonya forgave and moved on. Linda quietly twisted her hair then said, "Sonya I miss you."

"Girl I miss you too."

"I'm sorry for yelling at you. It was so silly. I didn't mean what I said. All this stuff is new to me and sometimes I feel…I feel like I'm lost. It seems like I don't belong here or something. When I'm outside the air…"

Linda paused to lower her voice and listen for Tiffany that's when Sonya asked, "What's wrong with the air?"

"Sonya the air doesn't smell sweet anymore. It smells bad all the time like it's dirty," Linda said trying not to get upset.

"Honey that's probably Bayonne you smelling. Sweetie, you can smell the stink from those chemicals for miles if the wind's blowing the wrong way.

"You think that's what it is?" asked Linda finally cheering up.

"Hell yeah that's what it is! don't worry about it honey," Sonya said reassuringly.

"Okay so…so are you still mad at me?" Linda asked sounding like an anxious child.

"No not anymore," Sonya said exhaling.

"Good…so enough about me what are you over there doing?"

"I'm just having wedding bell jitters, there's so much to do. Jeff's is getting on my damn nerves. He's probably having a beer with that fool J-Rock. Right now I'm in here making sure everything is ready for Thanksgiving. You still coming?"

"You know we're coming. Tiffany can't wait to see her Auntie," said Linda happily.

"Great I'm ready to see her too and wait till you see what I've done with the place," Sonya said looking at her ring again.

"Okay so guess what I did last Friday girl, just guess?" Linda asked excitedly.

"Linda I don't know just tell me. I'm dealing with a lot right now so what did you do?"

"I…watched…Aliens. Aliens the second movie and let me tell you, it was scary but it was good! That reminds me, do they have a phone that you don't have to hold to your ear? You know like say I could put it down, but we could hear each other and keep talking. That way I could fix my hair, if I had to use both hands."

"I don't think so and if they make one it's probably expensive."

"How could I find out?"

"Girl I don't know! But what were you saying about the movie?" said Sonya trying not to get aggravated.

"Well it was the same lady that got away the first time, and there were more aliens, and there was a little girl, and it was real good! You said you didn't see the second one?"

"No I didn't and I don't think I'm gonna watch it," Sonya said thinking about when Jeff would be home.

"Well girl it was better than the first one. I watched it three times," Linda said.

"Okay girl I see you like scary movies. I'm gonna find something else like a ghost story, or a Dracula movie."

"What's a Dracula?"

"Linda I'll…we'll talk about it when you get here and that reminds me, you've got the directions I gave you?" Sonya asked feeling the onset of aggravation.

"I got it sticking on the refrigerator."

"Good, so I'm gonna finish what I was doing and if we don't talk before then call me when you're leaving the house," Sonya said gently rubbing her temples.

"Okay but there was something else I have to tell you. When I leave your house Thursday I'm gonna drive by my brother's house."

"Wait a minute…what?" Sonya abruptly asked.

"I thought about it when I left Church last Sunday. All of a sudden I felt I need to go back and see where I grew up and…" Sonya interrupted.

"And what take a chance he might see you! Girl let me tell you something! You can't go over there; it's not a good idea!"

"Sorry you think it isn't but I can't help it, I have to," Linda said as Tiffany walked in.

"Momma I finished the dishes, and I left the knives for you. Is that Aunt Sonya? Can I talk to her?" Tiffany asked reaching for the phone.

Linda took the phone from her ear holding it to her chest and said, "Not right now but you're gonna see her in a few days."

Tiffany sat down then Linda quickly said, "Baby go to your room, we talking, I'll be finished in a minute."

"Alright," said Tiffany.

Linda waited until Tiffany was in her room then said, "Sonya…Sonya I'm back."

"Linda, listen to me. Don't go over there… please?" Sonya begged.

"You don't understand. There's a chance I could find who Tiffany's father is, so I need to go! I'll be fine trust me," said Linda stressing her point.

"Linda…I'll go with you another day and we'll take my car."

"No I can't do that Sonya! You didn't see Tiffany's face when she asked me about her father. I need to be able to tell her something and you'd understand if you were a mother," said Linda rebelliously.

The last comment sent Sonya's headache over the top. It was the most hurtful thing one woman could say to another. Now the urge to curse Linda out was overwhelming because she knew how much Sonya wanted children. Without a second thought Sonya hung up the phone and went to the bedroom. Seconds later, realizing she was talking on an empty line, Linda put her phone down too.

Sonya went to her nightstand for aspirin then to the bathroom. Two pills lodged at the back of her throat, then she let enough water run in her hand to swallow them. These were the times Linda really got on her nerves. Why would she risk being discovered, especially with Tiffany? Not to mention it could be a neighbor that sees her and tells her brother.

Five minutes later Sonya got a phone call. She started to let the answering machine get it then changed her mind.

"Hello," said Sonya.

"Sonya…that was the dumbest thing I've ever said in my life. I didn't mean it. I'm worried and it's catching up with me. You were just looking out like a good friend should," said Linda pausing for Sonya to speak.

"Sure," Sonya answered rubbing her temples for some relief.

"You're absolutely right…going alone or with Tiffany is a mistake," Linda said trying to get the words out before bursting into tears.

"It's alright, I still love you," said Sonya feeling a bit better.

"Sonya it's just that Tiffany…" Linda stopped fearing Tiffany was listening.

"What happened Linda, tell me?" asked Sonya sitting at attention.

"Wait…okay she's in the bathroom. So a few weeks ago we were on the way home from school and she asked me about her father," Linda said whispering into the receiver.

"Girl we knew this day was coming, so what did you tell her?" Sonya asked waiting in suspense.

"Well first I told her to wait till we got home because I was driving. Actually I forgot what I was gonna tell her cause she caught me off guard and just… soon as we got in the door she put her book bag down and asked me again and…and I told her he was dead, and went to heaven. Then she wanted to know how long ago and if I had any pictures. The only thing I could do after that was tell her when she got a little older, we'd talk about it again," said Linda talking softly.

"Linda why didn't you tell me before."

"Because I was upset, and we weren't speaking and I thought I could handle it so I didn't say anything. That's when I got to thinking, if I went back to the old neighborhood just to look around it might help me remember something," Linda said in quiet desperation.

"I get it," Sonya said moving the phone away from her ear. Then her head fell back until she saw tiny cracks in the ceiling. She heard Linda voice and held the phone closer.

"Sonya, would you come with me…please? I don't want to go by myself. We'll make it any day you say, just the two of us. How about a week day when Tiffany has school that way we can leave early and be back before she gets out," asked Linda respectfully.

"Sure… I'll go with you. I was trying to look out for a friend. I didn't mean to boss you around," said Sonya feeling less stressed.

"Thank you, thank you, and girlfriend you were right, it's a bad idea going alone. And like you said, we'll take your car and I'll hop in the back before we get there," Linda said apologetically.

"I hope this helps you girl, I really do. We'll pick a day before New Year but after Tiffany's birthday. Get you some sunglasses and a wig and go while Tiffany is in school."

"Yeah and we'll get a wig for you too." Linda said jokingly.

"I might go as a blonde."

"So we'll see you around eleven so I can learn how you make your mac and cheese," said Linda, walking to the kitchen.

"Linda?"

"Yes?"

"Linda promise me you won't go over there without me. I know how head strong you are!" said Sonya urgently.

"I won't," Linda answered quickly.

"Because if you tell me you're not gonna go, I'll take you at your word," said Sonya firmly.

"I will not go. I will not go! I promise."

"Then I'm gonna get back to work. If you need me for anything I'm here. Listen…I don't care what happened before, you are my sister and I love you. So that's that and we'll see you on Thanksgiving."

Linda went to the kitchen to wash large knives and went to bed. She searched her memory for what was on the street, or how the Brownstone looked. The house was brown with four levels midway down a hill on the right side of a one-way street. There was a tree in front, and a two-story home on the opposite side. But what if that was a false memory and when she got there it wasn't true. A desire to scoop up her sleeping child and go under the cover of darkness crossed her mind. It was only because of a promise to her best friend that Linda dismissed the thought and went to sleep.

On Thanksgiving Day, the same urgency returned while driving to the Bronx. She was crossing the George Washington Bridge when the impulse to take the FDR Drive came. If not for the promise she would've gone with Tiffany in the car. Before Linda went home that night, she told Sonya the urge to see her old neighborhood felt like an addiction mounting each day. Because of that before Linda left on Thanksgiving, Sonya agreed to take her on Tuesday.

On December 1st, they dropped Tiffany at daycare and headed to Harlem. At 155th Street they turned onto Edgecombe Avenue overlooking Yankee Stadium in the distance. Continuing down the one-way street Linda remained quiet then suddenly she blurted out,

"Stop Sonya, stop right here!"

"What is it Linda?" Sonya asked stopping alongside a parked car.

"The rock, that rock I told you about, it should be right down there," Linda said grabbing for the door handle.

"Girl wait I'm coming with you and put those sun glasses on before you get out!" Sonya said.

They crossed the street and peered through a tall chain link fence. Desperately Linda moved her head around searching below. As her fingers grasped the fence she saw a foot path below between the trees.

"Sonya look! See there down on the left…that funny looking rock. That's the place right there… that's the bench. That's where my brother would bring me and we'd sit and talk."

"Your brother took you down there? It looks like a place to get high. I wouldn't want to go down there," Sonya said in disbelief.

"We use to sit down there on that rock facing the diving board of Colonial Pool," Linda said holding on to the fence.

Linda calmed herself and went back to the car. Her chest heaved with excitement over solid confirmation of a true memory. Sonya looked down the hill to the corner, started the car and said, "Here's what I think we should do. We're gonna drive down the block slowly but we're not going to stop. We're just going through and I'm gonna turn at the corner, circle back around and then we'll stop…okay?" Sonya said awaiting agreement.

Linda confirmed only with a nod because her focus was on the street. Sonya drove to the corner waiting for the light to change while Linda looked around.

"Here we go girl. Don't forget to put that hat on," Sonya said driving into the block.

"I remember that building use to be empty, now it's a store," Linda said confidently.

Midway down the block Sonya slowed as they got close to the house. Linda looked until her neck could twist no longer and faced forward. At the end of the block Sonya turned right to circle back around. Soon they passed the fried fish place and her favorite bodega on the corner. This time when they returned Sonya parked four houses up for a better view. Not long after, a tall slender man emerged from a white two-story house across the street from her brother's. Linda remembered Larry was his name, and the last time she saw him was the day she ran away. His glasses were different, but his walk was the same. Linda kept her head forward holding her breath as he walked just yards away. Once parallel to the driver's door, Larry looked at Sonya and kept going. That's when she shut the car off and settled down for surveillance.

Linda's disguise kept her at ease when people passed. Sonya leaned forward to see more of the house. Ten minutes later Larry came back with a newspaper and coffee then sat on his small three-step stoop.

"What do you think about going over there telling him you were a friend of mine from school and see what he says?" asked Linda.

"If I do that he might see the car and come over and see you. If we drive around the block and I walk back, that could work," Sonya said willingly.

"Yeah that sounds good. Let's do that."

Before Sonya touched the key Larry was walking across the street to a man with a dog. He stopped in front of her brother's house and started talking. The dog sniffed Larry's hand after getting a rub on the head. Suddenly Linda grabbed Sonya's leg and said quietly," that's…my…brother."

"Where?" Sonya asked looking around quickly.

"Right there in front of the house talking to Larry," answered Linda still gripping Sonya's leg.

"Damn that's a big ass dog," remarked Sonya.

"His name is Mister. I can't believe it, that's Mister," said Linda eagerly.

They watched like a hiker discovering a deep crevasse feet away. Mister smelled the ground as the men talked then abruptly stared up the street. He sniffed again then started to bark. Linda's brother told Mister to sit but the dog continued to focus in Sonya and Linda's direction.

"Sonya…start the car!" said Linda slapping Sonya's leg.

"I am!" Sonya said turning the key.

Mister became overly excited and tried to get away from Bennie. The car was on when Bennie decided to let Mister walk up the street.

"Sonya they're coming this way why are you sitting here? We gotta go!" said Linda holding her hand over her mouth as the dog led her brother.

"I gotta wait for this car to pass," Sonya answered looking in the side view mirror.

Linda tilted her head covering the right side of her face with her hand. They were one house away but close enough to hear her brother ask Mister where he was going. Finally, a gap in the oncoming traffic allowed Sonya to pull away. The women's hearts raced like a scene from an action movie with two seconds left before the bomb goes off.

"Holy shit girl!…damn that was close!" Sonya said looking in the rearview mirror.

"I think Mister caught my scent," said Linda still crouching.

"You think that dog remembered you after all these years?" Sonya said slowing down.

"I think he did. He was making his way over here that's for sure," Linda said keeping her head low.

Three blocks away Sonya stopped at the red light, looked in the rearview mirror then said, "um…you can let go of my leg now."

Linda sat up like a rabbit peeking from a hole in the ground and let out a sigh of relief. Ignoring what could've happened they laughed at the narrow escape.

Soon they passed Harlem Hospital and the Schomburg Library. "Tiffany was born there," Linda said looking back quickly.

"I know honey, I remember. So…you think this is enough for today?"

"Yes," Linda said softly.

Sonya made a left then another until they were headed back uptown. Suddenly Linda said,

"Don't go up 145th Street, one of the laundries is on Eighth Avenue."

North of 155th Street close to the entrance of the FDR Drive, Sonya stopped. She wanted to gauge how Linda was doing. With the engine running she pressed Linda a little more about what she was thinking. Linda quietly insisted she needed more time to process. After crossing the George Washington Bridge to the New Jersey Turnpike Linda said, "I can remember the guy across the street. His name his face and the dog too, but I can't recall anything about my parents."

After that she didn't talk the rest of the drive. When Sonya tried to get more, Linda would repeat the phrase, "I feel okay Sonya, I'm still processing."

The women were back in Jersey a little after 1pm. After Linda got in she took three Tylenol tablets with a glass of water. The pain was from hunger she told Sonya and went to the fridge. Linda made two sandwiches from leftover meatloaf, and fell asleep on the couch. When it was time to get Tiffany, Sonya picked her up and bought her a slice of pizza.

In the evening when Sonya was leaving, Linda and Tiffany walked her to the car. Sonya motioned for Linda to come to the driver's door while Tiffany stayed on the sidewalk. While the car was running with the window down Sonya leaned out and said,

"promise you won't go back without me."

"I won't."

Satisfied Sonya left with them watching until her car turned the corner.

It was after 10pm when Sonya called to say she was at home with Jeff. Before hanging up Linda swore they'd be friends forever by quoting from The Color Purple. The scene when Celie and Nettie were separated. Linda said only death would keep her from her friend, and while Sonya took it lightly, Linda was dead serious. Unpredictably today's brief visit down memory lane would be the catalyst to Linda's recovery. Like the three-day fast Bennie and Linda underwent to be together, healing would come in that length of time.

Tonight Linda's pain was noticeable but not as intense. Tilting her head toward the ceiling then down to the floor brought relief to the area where her neck joined the base of the skull. That persistent pressure wouldn't stop the prayer she had in mind. Linda raised her nightgown and kneeled, resting clenched hands atop the mattress. She took the deepest of breaths and placed her forehead on her hands. Fully exhaled Linda asked God to heal her and give her courage to face her fears. Not only did she pray for guidance and power to forgive her brother, she asked the Lord to keep Sonya and Jeff safe and give her the wisdom to do right by Tiffany. For a few minutes Linda remained reflecting on her request. Then she got under the covers to relax until the sheets got warm. Tonight she'd sleep with all the lights on except in Tiffany's room.

It was curious she couldn't see her brother's face but knew him from 30 yards away.

After five years she knew it was Bennie and not because Mister was with him. There was a connection, not anger or the feeling of betrayal like when she fled. All these years he'd been a menace, now Linda wondered was he happy. She recalled walking the dog with him feeling like nothing could ever harm her. Except for the last time they were together she had no reason to distrust him. She started to wonder how Bennie mourned their deaths. Did he sob with uncontrollable regret and blame himself for driving her away? Perhaps she'd never know but once she settled down and went to sleep, she had a dream.

Mister patrolled the halls of a recognizable palace. His paws made a tapping sound on the hard floor when he walked. Linda stood barefoot in her light blue nightgown. When she focused towards the balcony the sun was the color of a blood orange. The breeze touched her like warm silky water on her skin. She was so glad to be home. At the end of a long corridor the Squiggly Man came out of her bedroom. He was not like waves of jelly, but solid now. Mister went to him as if waiting for a command. Linda had been frightened of the Squiggly Man all her life but not now. Nobody moved. Then suddenly Linda woke up. It was after 4am and the lights were still on. She peeked in on Tiffany and checked the doors and windows. She went to the kitchen for a glass of water then went back to her room. An hour later she had another dream.

This time she was walking in her brother's Brownstone barefoot again, wearing the same blue nightgown. There was thunder and lightning but no rain. Linda followed Mister from the second-floor kitchen upstairs towards her brother's bedroom. The outline of his body was beneath the covers with the back of his head on the pillow. She feared the thunder but wasn't afraid to get in bed with him. The covers were over her shoulder and he told her she was safe. The thunder and lightning ceased, followed by warm air over her body. She laid still and thought how good it was to be home.

The next morning it was Tiffany waking her mother. She was going to take Tiffany to school, but they'd be a little late. Before getting out of bed Linda wrote those dreams in her journal and put it back in the nightstand. When she got Tiffany to school, instead of driving away she sat with both hands on the steering wheel. Thinking of yesterday she mustered the courage to revisit her painful memories. Somehow Linda sensed Bennie wasn't happy and wondered how he reacted to the news of their deaths. Did he scream in anguish and cry for days without eating? Of course he did. That assumption would be the first time she felt even a speck of sympathy for him.

Before Linda knew it the children were coming out to play for recess. She remained in the car watching Tiffany with the other girls jumping rope. She was having fun being a kid just like the other girls. Not long after, the children lined up to go back inside. It was a unique experience seeing her child from a distance and got Linda thinking about last night.

Sometime ago at the library Linda read a book on the nature of dreams, and their possible significance. One theory suggested dreams organized thoughts for later review. Dreams were said to be effective in discarding random useless clutter from your mind too. That's why it's believed during REM sleep when people wake they forget a large percentage of their dreams. One chapter claimed dreaming was a path for people to connect problematic thoughts and emotions in a safe environment. Whatever reason God allowed people to dream, Linda was tired of running away. What she was going to do was be like Ripley from the movie Alien. Next time she'd confront the squiggly man in her dreams she wasn't running away.

The bell sounded and happy children with their book bags exited. Hours before, Linda thought about leaving but had nowhere to be, so she stayed. When Tiffany came out they went right home. After dinner

Linda's head started to hurt in the same odd place. She took two pills for the pain and exercised her neck like last night. After assuring Sonya over the phone she was fine, Linda started Tiffany's bath. Kneeling to check the temperature she scooped water with a cupped hand. Something about the water passing between her fingers was uniquely calming. She scooped more and watched it run down her hand like a newborn seeing it for the first time. For some reason this act intrigued her until she thought of taking a bath after Tiffany went to bed. Ultimately when Tiffany finished, Linda took advantage of a pain-free head and went to bed.

Like the night before, Linda left lights on throughout the apartment. At bedside her single request of the Lord was for strength to forgive her brother. In bed unanswered questions circled the room like a drunk settling down after a night out. What were the circumstances surrounding her accident and memory loss? When did it happen and who was the witness? Yesterday she was in shouting distance of her past and remained quiet. If Linda had a question for Bennie it would have been any of those. She would have asked why he would encourage pride in her and take it away?

That night the room faded, giving way to a trail of dust in her wake with the sun overhead. The heat of the day was real and so was the noise. She was on a dirt road standing in a golden chariot pulled by a team of black horses. Their manes are adorned with turquoise beads braided with gold strands. Holding the reins of power belonged to her by entitlement. Reaching the bottom of the hill she was back at the stables. A little boy of dark completion held the horses when she stepped down from the chariot. He smiled, bowed his head, and called her Osique Sakatet. The words Osique Sakatet echoed then faded away as if yelled in the mountains. The urge to respond was halted by her dry throat. Suddenly Linda swung her legs out of bed to head for the kitchen. There was a pint-sized golden goblet on the counter filled to the brim with water. The cheeks of her mouth were dry like sandpaper. Hastily she drank, not bothered by water running down her neck. She left the goblet on the counter then wiped her face with a purple silk scarf then headed to Tiffany's room. There was nothing in the hallway, just a long smooth marble wall. She looked hard but Tiffany's door was missing. Anxiety set in. She took a deep breath to yell for Tiffany and woke up in her bed.

Without hesitation Linda ran to Tiffany's room to find her sleeping. It was quiet and the lights were still on. She wasn't dreaming this time her thirst was real and she went to the kitchen. There was no purple scarf or gold cup, and the floor was dry. She thought about calling Sonya after the second glass of water, but it was after midnight. It took two additional glasses to finally quench the thirst. Facing the sink it occurred to Linda there was more going on than dreams and dehydration.

Sitting on her bed with journal in hand Linda tried to think. What did that boy holding the reigns call her? It sounded like Osike Sakit, or Osique Sakatet. She scribbled it down phonetically and thought about those horses. She had driven them before. Those horses had names, but she couldn't think what they were. Later Linda looked in on Tiffany and checked all the doors and windows.

With a belly full of water Linda sat up against the headboard. Compelled, she revisited the day she ran away. It happened in front of the mirror on the second floor just outside the living room. In a daydream she embraced a passionate kiss. When the haziness cleared it was her on the couch with Bennie, a true thought long forgotten. If her eyes were closed there was pleasure. When she opened them it was a sense of disgrace and a reason to run. That thought got her out of bed and pacing until she sat by the window and looked outside. Before she knew what happened dawn was coming, and she had to get Tiffany ready to leave in two hours.

Linda took Tiffany to school, went back home and had a glass of orange juice with two slices of toast. She was tired and afraid to go to sleep and dream. Since she didn't sleep the day dragged on until it was time to get Tiffany. When they returned to the apartment something was wrong. The furnishings were in the same, but the decor just didn't belong. That evening Linda tucked Tiffany in telling her good night. Her child's smile was the same as her brother's even down to the shape of her chin.

She went to the couch, watched some television and thought about Dr. Goldstein. Linda never saw the video of the sessions. Then his office gets vandalized, and her paperwork is gone. Now she'll never be able to see what happened or hear the words she spoke. Was the language the same as her dreams or something else?

Her head jerked back from a nod, so Linda walked around and sat back down. The headache started in the same spot, so she took three pills this time for the pain. If she called Sonya she'd come, but Linda couldn't bring herself to bother her. Instead she encouraged herself, massaging her neck. Linda vowed to stand up like David facing the giant and Ripley from the Alien movies. In between rounds it couldn't hurt to put her feet up, lay her head on this pillow and relax.

Before long the sound of water rippling over rocks gave way to an overhead view of a stream. There was no boat, just her body floating in the direction of the flowing water. She had an aerial view of her Woodbridge apartment in the distance. Further downstream, hidden amidst the trees, was the blue and white Harlem Hospital building, the Schomburg Library across the street, and her brother's Brownstone. Hovering she watched the stable boy brushing one of the horses. He couldn't see her so she went in the direction of an enormous pool near the palace. Linda was cognizant of the dream and confidently went inside.

In front of the fireplace sat a golden goblet on a table carved from the darkest ebony. This was where she saw the squiggly man. Suddenly he was at the end of the hall, instantly they were feet apart. Without opening her mouth Linda asked who was he, and what did he want? Like ripples slowing down in a pond the face became clear, and it was Bennie. He was in a purple robe and his arms beckoned her to come closer. She feels the cushion on the couch and tries to wake up, but she can't breathe. The only air left was back inside the dream.

Linda floated back to the dream to confront Bennie, the Squiggly Man and took his hand. His lips never moved but she heard Neia abei Whende, Neia abei. Immediately she broke the grip and ran out the door. Without looking back, she could hear him following. She ran too close to the edge of the pool and tumbled in. The entire time Linda knew she was dreaming while going under. She gasped for air unable to wake herself. It was a struggle so violent Linda was back in the apartment. With a bird's eye view Linda watched her body wriggle as if drowning on the couch. She had to go back if she wanted to live. Suddenly hands took firm hold, pulled her from the pool, and she did not run. It was Bennie's hand. Once again she heard his voice, but his lips didn't move. Like an echo filling a canyon she heard, "Whende… do you remember now? Do you remember now? Do you remember?"

Linda woke up holding a pillow and one couch cushion on the floor. Exhausted as if she'd run for miles, Linda wondered if she was truly awake. It was as if she could fall asleep again if she just gave in. Scared, she reached out for the pillow, and then forced herself up. Driven by severe thirst, she accepted this as reality. Before going to the kitchen she checked on her sleeping child. Linda stood over the sink drinking from a cupped hand a few times, then got a glass. Once she'd had her fill, she went back to her room and wrote in the journal.

Everything about the next morning was unusual. Linda's skin was ashy, and her mouth remained dry. When the time came to take Tiffany to school, Linda shook the steering wheel with both hands. She waited as if the car should move without starting it. After a few seconds Linda turned the key, and they were on their way. When she returned home she had a bite to eat then called Sonya at work. As she hung up the phone and looked at the coffee table it felt odd. There wasn't enough extravagance or elegance, so she started cleaning. There wasn't enough work in the complex to keep her mind off last night. Why did the squiggly man who'd tormented her since childhood look like her brother? What was making her skin flake like dandruff? And why was she so damn thirsty? By 2pm Linda finished three more quarts of water and had to make her way back to school. The rest of the cleaning would have to wait till she got back.

Later that evening after Linda did Tiffany's hair they planned to stay up a little later because it was Friday night. Linda ran a bath, adding some oil Sonya suggested to help her dry skin. She put one foot in then the other and the temperature was perfect. The water was like bathing between silk sheets. She laid back relaxed, rubbing water over her forehead. Linda held the side, closed her eyes, took a deep breath and submerged her head. Had this entire day been one long dream she thought? A mesmerizing pinhole of light twirled in the darkness growing each second. Engrossed by the light she knew this wasn't a dream. Linda tried lifting her head and couldn't. She pulled on the side of the tub while pressing her legs on the bottom for lift. The problem was her head felt weighted down like an anchor. Large volumes of water splashed out as she kicked. Linda was about to drown, and the idea of Tiffany finding her dead the next morning was unacceptable. With all her might she thrust her head above from the water. Gripping the side, Linda choked up water and coughed violently. Tiffany came to investigate, saw her mother's condition and started to cry. Linda calmly sent her for towels from the linen closet while she pulled the stopper to let the water out. Tiffany ran back, spread towels on the wet floor, and held her mother's hand. At that moment Linda saw Bennie's compassionate eyes and cheeks bones in Tiffany's features. Linda stared at her child until the drain burped the last gulp of water. While Tiffany changed into dry pajamas, Linda stepped out the tub. A few minutes before midnight on the 4th of December Linda called Sonya and said, "I know who Tiffany's father is."

"Who...who is he? Wait...wait" Not wanting to wake Jeff she went to another room.

"It's hard to explain. There's so much more to it." Something wasn't right. Linda's voice was too calm and before she could say another word Sonya said, "Don't say anything else, I'll be right there!"

Sonya hung up then told Jeff she had to leave. She didn't panic but her actions were precision. Sonya took money, house keys, her purse, and Jeff got dressed and walked her to the car. By ten minutes after one in the morning Sonya was parking in front of Linda's apartment. They sat on the couch. Linda took a breath and shook her head. Sonya held Linda's hand, never saying a word. Linda began to rock back and forth holding her hand over her mouth. Taking one more very deep breath Linda let the hand go and said, "I remember everything…everything." Sonya thought it wise not to ask but couldn't resist.

"Linda…who is Tiffany's father?"

"Well first I need to say this, Bennie and I are not brother and sister. We aren't related in any way…but he is Tiffany's father," said Linda with a slight smile.

"What…I don't understand…how?" Sonya asked with her mouth wide open.

"It's a lot so you just got to let me take my time. First…I know who I am. I know where I was. I know how I got to this time. Things still aren't clear. So first…Bennie is Tiffany's father. He was the man who tore my veil," said Linda speaking as if an enormous pressure was lifting.

"Okay he's not ya brotha but what ya you mean tearing your veil? I don't get it," Sonya asked looking stunned.

"That's how we say it. He parted my veil or tore it. You know the veil only women have," said Linda placing her hand between her legs.

"Oh… I get it now girl! You're saying he was your first."

"He was."

"You remember where ya'll met?"

Linda answered happily, "yes I do. The first time he was outside my Dega, and on a clear day you can see the Pyramids."

"I'm sorry…a Dega, what's that?"

"A Dega, that's my house. I wonder if it's still there. Anyway, so he was…" suddenly Linda stopped speaking.

A raised finger in mid-air halted the conversation. Linda wondered for a second if Sonya would believe the truth. That she and Bennie met many thousands of years ago before there was a hint of an America, or any of the known Pharaohs of Egypt? That he was a wiggly image in the bottom of her pool. His image as a squiggly man would haunt her but eventually come to her rescue. Maybe she'd talk about the Obeni, the ancient device that created the portal through time every 76 years. Within a few short moments Linda knew she couldn't say any of it. Like Bennie withheld information from Mr. Queen, she had to avoid the truth at least for now.

Linda got up from the couch and said, "He was visiting Egypt where I was born. We talked for several days. After I got to understand the warrior inside the man I chose him to be my first."

"Then he needs to know you and his child are alive."

"Right now I'm still not clear on how I got to this country but I remember this…he saved my life. I need time to sort this out and I will make myself known to him."

"Honey that story is…is incredible I almost can't believe it! Linda that is just…just wow! You know I'm here for you Linda," said Sonya watching Linda stand.

"I know who I am. Linda is not my name! I am Osique Sakatet! Osique means Princess…but my family calls me Whende. You…may call me Whende." she said boldly.

"So you're royal blood, ah…ah real Princess like Eddie Murphy in Coming to America?" Sonya asked enthusiastically.

"I don't know what that is but yes…I am. I will have to tell Bennie we're not dead. First I will learn what I can on my own then I will go to him with my questions," said Linda in a commanding tone.

Not only had Linda's voice changed but so had her body language. She moved with pride in her stride as if walking a balance beam. Suddenly Linda began to speak a tongue not heard in centuries. At times her voice inflected a question then she'd continue. When Linda quieted down she sat back down and said, "I remember my language Sonya. That's how I used to talk."

Sonya had no idea how to comfort Linda who was beginning to look tired. Linda held her chest like she was having a heart attack. Between gasps she said. "Sonya I can't fall asleep. What if I wake up and forget who I am again? What happens if I wake up and I don't know my child?"

"Honey you have to calm down you're hyperventilating," Sonya said running to the kitchen for a paper bag. She told Linda to cover her face and breathe into it. When she calmed down Sonya said, "you're gonna get through this girl. Everything is gonna be alright. I'll be right here with you. When you fall asleep, if you have a nightmare or something I'll just wake you. I'll ask your name… so what is it?"

"My name is Whende. I want you to call me Whende." said Linda fondly placing the bag on the end table.

Like a true friend Sonya stayed so Linda could rest. Every so often Linda would wake, and Sonya would ask her name. She'd say it was Whende then lay her head down. This went on until Saturday morning. During breakfast Tiffany gleefully rambled while the women stayed mostly silent. Later Linda told Sonya to take Tiffany out so she could think. When they returned late that afternoon Linda knew what she wanted to do. Her mind was set on reuniting with Tiffany's father when it felt right.

Chapter 13

With each passing day Linda healed until her memory was completely restored; even the conversations with her grandma Laneie and father Afermose, and where they took place. Their faces were clear in her mind as if they'd spoken yesterday. While researching the word Obeni on the library's computer she stumbled upon an underground book her brother wrote. He'd used the pseudonym Leon Allen Bryan, with the title Tales of the Obeni. He used an ordinary black couple on the cover and a picture of his brownstone on the back.

The book was read as fiction to everyone but her. It explained how she got the name Linda. What he did to save her life in Egypt, and why he brought her to America. She found out Bennie had a girlfriend Terry but ended the relationship. The last chapter of the book was read with a pile of soaked tissues through Linda's teary eyes. It wasn't her fault she'd held contempt for him nor was it his. Bennie had been a hero like Shaft coming to her rescue.

Shortly after reading Tales of the Obeni, the organization made contact. Ali Soriano, who worked with Linda at the library, followed her after leaving Tiffany in school. He made his introduction in the parking lot of the ShopRite near her apartment. He spoke in her native tongue then bowed with one knee on the ground. She understood Soriano to say welcome back my Queen. People began to stare so Linda asked him to stand but he wouldn't. Not until she spoke her true language did he rise. After that he'd spend the next few hours updating her.

Speaking in ancient Egyptian, Soriano said it was his honor to serve Queen Sakatet. He went on to tell her the organization remained faithful for thousands of years in anticipation of her return. Soriano had the same pleasant smile when they'd eat in the lunch room.

Soriano went on to say their members got charges dropped for Bennie when he was arrested in Cairo. He went on explaining how the organization assisted Bennie in saving her life. Once they returned to Bennie's time, her physical functions were like a newborn baby and all knowledge erased. A doctor gave her the first of many vaccinations for present day sicknesses. Not long after, she had a passport created and a new identity. The day after that she and Bennie were on a private jet headed to America. Not only did Soriano give validity to Bennie's book about The Obeni, but he also removed her remaining feelings of regret.

On that cold February day standing in a ShopRite parking lot a Princess was now the Queen. Subtly Soriano acknowledged several persons in the vicinity as part of a security detail like the President of the United States. Like a newly elected president there were adjustments. Queen Sakatet was informed the organization had levels of clearance. Anyone who could speak in her native language was at the highest level. Those unable to speak it were lower level hired to follow instructions. Once that was understood they went to the next step.

Everything from her apartment was moved to a house near Montclair NJ the next day. As a queen she was driven everywhere and if she choose to walk, her detail was nearby. The nurse from Dr. Goldstein's office became Tiffany's chaperone. Ms. Aquino was introduced to Tiffany as a family friend, like Aunt Sonya. In addition to security there was a chef, an advisor and concierge. It was exactly the treatment she was accustomed to.

The last significant piece of information given to the Queen was her fortune. All that was left to do was pick up where she and Bennie left off. In this future they'd rekindle their love and be a family. Four days after a February snow storm, a Queen returned to Harlem for her King only to suffer enormous disappointment.

The 26th was the last Saturday in the month. Queen Sakatet fixed her hair and found some African attire and beaded earrings. She tried to recreate her look the day Bennie fell in love with her. Before noon she left Jersey in a black Toyota Land Cruiser with limousine tint accompanied by two of her security. All they knew was they were taking her where she wanted to go and not much more. Blessed with a fully restored mind, some explicit memories surfaced. It was the night Linda told Sonya she had no recollection of having sex. Today Queen Sakatet remembered every second, every sound, and rhythm of intimacy like it was yesterday.

It happened in the evening amidst the sounds of wind and rain. There was yearning and determination in Bennie's embrace. She could see herself caressing his shoulder blades, and the eagerness once their lips touched. Oh yes the memories were all there, and it was good. This time they'd have to wait till after a royal ceremony to consummate. Then his new name would be King Kiefeus, and they could pick up where they left off.

An unsettling feeling replaced steamy thoughts once they crossed the George Washington Bridge into Manhattan. Before long the cruiser parked behind a dirty snow mound in front of Bennie's house. She'd imagined him doing everything from crying to fainting to asking question after question. In a moment there'd be no more guessing. Before she could open the door, a woman walked down the stoop from his house. She turned to head up the street when Bennie called out the name Lizzy. Ironically the woman stopped a few yards from the back door. He reached for a hand she refused to let him touch. Something he said made her face him. With one press of a button on the armrest a Queen could put an end to this foolishness. Instead of showing her face she lowered the window an inch to listen. She heard her king tell that woman he wanted to spend the rest of his life with her. Hearing that the woman rushed into his arms. As Bennie cradled her he noticed the car running and the back window cracked. In case someone was listening he took Lizzy back inside the house.

If she kept her composure the men in front would have no idea what just happened. Sakatet was familiar with his expression of love because she'd witnessed his expression years ago. Bennie was moving on and he believed she and Tiffany were dead. It was clear her King had picked another woman, so why force him to choose again when he was happy. There was nothing left to do but leave him in peace. The Queen went back to NJ and decided that night to go back and live in Africa.

The following Monday Sakatet called Sonya to invite her and Jeff to see the new house. After Sonya got the copy of Bennie's book they didn't talk as much as before. Conversations became difficult because Sonya was overly concerned her best friend was losing her mind. The events described in the Obeni book were hard to believe. When Sonya asked questions Linda had plausible explanations. For instance, the book said the Obeni allowed Bennie and Linda to travel through time, but it could only happen with the arrival of Halley's Comet. The next chance to use the Obeni would be in 2061. That meant they'd be over 100 years old if they lived. If that wasn't enough, Linda said a man named Yemot discovered the comet thousands of years before Halley. Lastly, Sonya couldn't ask anyone to help prove it was true. Linda feared if certain agencies knew, they would take Tiffany away. Hopefully seeing Linda at her new home would ease Sonya's concerns.

The following Saturday Sonya and Jeff waited outside of their apartment. A black man wearing a charcoal grey suit got out of a black stretch limo and approached them. He said he was there to take them to Jersey. He opened the back door inviting them inside. Before leaving he went over the controls for the heat and how they could lower the partition if they had more questions. They were greeted by another man dressed the same way at the house who opened the car door. He escorted them through the door into the grand entrance hall. Sonya and Jeff were astounded by the space and elegance of this home. But it didn't compare to their first sight of her coming down the hall.

The woman they knew as Linda walked with deliberate assurance as if the very foundation belonged to her. She gave the impression if she'd walked into a brick wall it would've fallen. With no idea what her friend had become, Sonya was speechless. Linda wore a full-length tan gown with yellow sleeves made of silk. It took Jeff to break the silence by saying happily, "Linda…You hit the lotto didn't you?"

She stared squinting at Jeff then smiled and said, "Something like that."

"You see Sonya I told you, I told you!" Jeff said clapping his hands.

"Jeff I want to thank you for taking exceptional care of my friend. I know Sonya loves you, and you love her. Make yourself at home; Sonya and I need time to catch up. This gentleman is Ray. Just let Ray know what you want. If you decide to eat or go out he'll arrange a car to take you," she said leading Sonya away.

"Okay thanks…bye baby see you later, have fun."

Sonya heard Jeff but never said anything. The ladies walked through a living room larger than Sonya's apartment into a sun room facing a backyard in-ground pool. They sat next to each other at a glass round table with six chairs. Still speechless, Sonya observed an extreme improvement in Linda's appearance. Not only was she walking differently, the very tone of her skin gleamed. Silver strands adorned her locks, and the earrings looked handmade. Even her body looked healthier as if she'd joined a gym. Linda took two glasses from a tray, filled them with water and said, "Tiffany will be glad to see her auntie. She's missed you, we both have."

"Linda I feel helpless because I don't know what to do or how to help."

Suddenly Tiffany came running full speed into Sonya's arms followed by Ms. Aquino. After the hug Sonya looked at the woman and said, "You look familiar, do I know you?"

Linda intervened saying, "Remember when we were in the doctor's office last year?"

"Yeah and…oh shit you were the nurse in the waiting room that day," Sonya said shaking a finger at Aquino.

"That's right, they've been looking out for me," replied Linda.

"Girl who is they?" Sonya asked instantly.

"We'll talk about that later, right now, it's so good to see you. Ms. Aquino when you come back for Tiffany have Bella bring refreshments."

"Yes Queen Sakatet," Aquino said before leaving.

"Auntie did you know my momma is a real Queen?" Tiffany asked looking up at Sonya.

"Ahh…I just found out," answered Sonya hesitantly.

To ease the tension Linda said, "Yes it's true like Murphy Coming To America."

Sonya and Tiffany talked until Ms. Aquino returned for her.

"Neia abei Auntie," said Tiffany taking one more hug.

"Huh?" replied Sonya.

"It means I love you," Linda answered as the child left.

At the same time Chef Bella pushed a cart to the end of their table. Metal lids covered the food like room service in a hotel. Once they were alone the Queen went on to tell her story. With her hands on the table interlocked she said, "I want to say nothing has changed between us Sonya. I will always trust and care for you as my sister, and I promise to be honest with you. In return you must accept me. I'm accustomed to telling people what to do except my Yampos and my Yoba. That's my father and grandma on my mother's side."

"Alright well…you said you were going to see your brother I mean, not your brother, your, ahh, Tiffany's father, what happened? What did Bennie say when he saw you?" Sonya asked scooting closer.

"I was there and…and he's in love with another woman. He made his choice so that's that," she said trying to act like it wasn't hurting.

"Girl what you mean he made his choice. You gotta say more than that! What the hell happened?" Sonya asked scooting even closer.

"He's given himself to another that's all! No Queen begs a man to be with her. I think that day God was trying to tell me something because, I showed up the very moment he said he wanted her. Five minutes earlier, or five minutes later, and it would have been different. He would've seen me and known I was alive," said the Queen.

"Are you sure this is what you want to do?"

"Yes…yes my mind is made up and that's all I have to say about it!"

"Fine," Sonya said sounding like she disagreed.

"Will you and Jeff stay for dinner and spend the night? Please say yes I have more to tell you."

"Yes…I think we can" said Sonya taking her first relaxing breath.

"Thank you. So now you must listen. The Obeni story, while unbelievable did happen. I was born thousands of years ago, and I don't belong here…let me finish. That's why…I'm leaving. We're going back to where I was born. When I prepare a place I want you and Jeff to come visit as much as you want. You could get married there if you want. But from this moment…don't call me Linda anymore. It's not my name. My name is Sakatet, but my family calls me Whende. You and my child are my family, you can call me Whende. Will you do that?" said the queen taking Sonya's hand.

"Yes," Sonya answered hesitantly.

"If something happens to me…I want Tiffany to be with her auntie. Will you do this last thing for me?"

"Linda…I'm sorry…Whende, Whende what's wrong, are you sick?" Sonya asked squeezing her hand tightly.

"I'm fine but she doesn't know these people like she knows you. They work for me. You love us, there's a difference. That woman you recognize was from Dr. Goldstein's office. She was also the maid at the hotel in Cairo. That organization has secretly guarded me the entire time. So will you be her Godmother?" said Whende.

"Yes of course, I love that child. You know I will," Sonya answered tearing up.

"Thank you Sonya. Now there's one more thing. Because you are my family I have a small gift for you. My father had a warning about money. He said you rule riches, riches don't rule you. Your value cannot be measured in money. Be happy with it and without. Do good for the less fortunate, but never beg someone to take it. Even The Bible says the love of money is the root of all evil, that is true even in this time. So this is what I have for you," Whende said, giving her a white card with a name and phone number.

"What's this for?" Sonya asked turning the card over.

Holding the other hand Whende said simply, "This…is…because I love you. Crystal Epps will help you get settled. This house… is yours, I'm giving you a hundred million dollars. I'm leaving at the end of the week. You're welcome to stay here with me until then."

Sonya reacted like anyone receiving such news. Her gaping mouth remained open. Sonya stared at the card then at Whende, and back at the card. Finally Sonya asked,

"Whende do you know what I'm thinking?"

"No, I don't."

"No one has ever given me anything like this. Thank you, thank you so much. This is hard to accept because I feel guilty," Sonya said.

"Why?" questioned Whende caringly.

After pausing Sonya said, "It's cause I know this is real, but your story is…it's hard to accept. I wanna believe you, I really do!" said Sonya holding back tears.

"That's alright, one day you will. Neia abei Sonya neia abei, I love you," said Whende.

"When will I see you again?" asked Sonya sadly.

"Sonya I'm not going to disappear. Anytime you want to talk or visit that's fine. Actually, you should call Ms. Epps in the morning or right now if you like. She's available for you around the clock," said Whende. Following Whende's explanations of Crystal's duties Sonya decided to call later.

When dinner was served Jeff and Tiffany joined the ladies in the dining room for a specular feast. Later Jeff got comfortable in one of the guest rooms to watch a movie while Whende, Sonya and Tiffany stayed together. For Sonya it was like getting to know her best friend again. Other times she felt it was another weekend sleep over.

Sunday morning after breakfast Sonya told Jeff the good news and called Ms. Epps. Monday morning she and Jeff quit their jobs and by Wednesday they'd moved to New Jersey. Sonya spent every minute with Whende until her departure from Teterboro Airport Friday evening. Executive treatment allowed Sonya to say goodbye at the steps of the Whende's private jet. They hugged till their arms were tired then hugged some more. In six weeks she and Jeff would attend a Royal ceremony near the Queen's birthplace. Sonya watched the plane climb then vanish into the blackness of the night sky. Then she took a chauffeured limo back to a huge home that now belonged to her

The next morning Whende called to say she'd arrived, and they would talk in a few days. During that time Sonya and Jeff settled into a life of leisure and responsibility. They spent two days in the home alone planning how to use their money to uplift their family and friends. Ultimately riches didn't inflate Jeff's ego at all. He warned of letting money come between them and falling prey to addictive spending.

Ms. Epps proved extremely useful making sure all their needs were met and making suggestions when necessary. They'd agreed to keep the chef, the chauffeur, and the cleaning service on weekdays. Still Sonya's heart carried a heavy burden of confidence. This morning was like waking from a dream except she wasn't in the Bronx. While Jeff slept she went to the window and thanked the Lord for this day. She had the man she wanted and so much more.

The hedges were immaculately trimmed and in spring when the flowers bloomed it would be perfect. Sonya saw the grounds outside along with furniture reflected in the window pane like a double exposure. It reminded her of the last conversation she had with Whende. They'd had wine, talked more about the book and questions Sonya had. It was easy to believe Bennie; a business man went to Egypt. Or that he inadvertently found an old relic called an Obeni in an antique shop. She could even accept his story of being arrested for breaking into a museum. It was hard to believe Bennie went back in time not once but twice and managed to bring Whende back too. If time travel caused Whende's memory loss, why didn't the same happen to him? Whende's response was a simple one. Bennie had foreknowledge of the future so he couldn't lose his memory.

Later that night Sonya wondered did Whende still believe in the Bible since Egyptians believed in more than one god? Her response was profound and again perfectly logical. Whende told her because she was living in this time, she accepted her Bible as truth. The reason being, The Creator always was and always will be unchanging. It's only our perception of The Almighty that changes with time.

Sonya looked at Jeff lying in bed, sighed and thought, people are not able to travel back and forth in time. It's just not possible, except Sonya had a hundred million reasons to believe Whende told the truth.

Chapter 14

Kayla sat legs folded on the floor with her back against the couch. On the coffee table next to her was a stack of 1991 tax returns. April 15th was tomorrow and there were two left to finish. This year she'd done 29 tax returns in less than a month. Every year by word of mouth she found more clients and the bonus money always came in handy. At $100 for state, and federal, it was a nice amount to squirrel away.

Empty expectation is a bitter pill to swallow; so last night she had a serious heart to heart with God. Kayla put prayers in place of wishes and suddenly her thoughts became clear. She was getting her degree and giving this baby an opportunity for a better life. If other women can raise a child and go to school so can she. Looking at her picture of Malcolm, she thought about what he'd become instead of how he started. From a drug addict, con man, and thief, he developed into one of the most well-known leaders of our time. That meant Kayla wasn't going to feel guilty for stripping anymore. One day she'd meet a good man, but not if she kept sleeping with Ronald. Last week he tried working his way back with flattering comments but she didn't give in. When he came back last night she made her expectations perfectly clear.

Just before 10 pm Ronald stopped by, thinking time alone would change Kayla's mind. When he got close she boldly removed her robe and tossed it on the couch. With nothing but a long tee shirt she let him get a good look. Her nervous subservient chuckle and feeling of obligation to take one for the team was now nonexistent. Having no desire for Ronald made an ultimatum easy. Being with her tonight meant he agreed to leave Lorraine tomorrow. Kayla wasn't asking for a marriage proposal; Ronald just had to divorce his wife. She followed up by telling him if he thought about staying over and changing his mind she'd tell Lorraine everything. It took a few seconds before Ronald chose to swallow his lust then leave.

Paradoxically while Kayla longed for a meaningful relationship, Bennie retreated to the safety of an affiliation destined to go nowhere. Thomasina's limited approachability offered a measure of security. One constant remained; Thomasina had to be home before sunrise. While she portrayed Derrick as verbally abusive it was clear she wasn't leaving him. So Bennie continued with her until they moved from Harlem to Far Rockaway Queens on the first of August.

The Saturday before Labor Day weekend Thomasina said Derrick was in rehab and wanted Bennie to see their new place. Not once had Bennie set foot in their home in Harlem. He knew the risk of sleeping with a man's wife but in the man's house was asking for trouble. If he killed Bennie that's a crime of passion and Derrick might get away with it. But Thomasina said it was safe so Bennie went.

It was after 10pm when he got to her place, and she was excited to see him. They had a two-bedroom apartment on the third floor a hundred yards from the boardwalk. No matter what conflict he had before, she was just what he desired. So badly that he didn't think it odd she locked the door and put the chain on. After a short tour the night turned into lots of laughter. Thomasina made fried chicken with white rice. They listened to music, had drinks, and had sex in the kitchen and the living room.

Bennie fell asleep after 3am on the couch only to be awakened by voices arguing. In just boxers covered with a blanket he lay still. Ironically being there wasn't a bad idea last night, but daybreak shed new light on his stupidity. His clothes were in arms reach folded on a chair with his gun hidden under the shirt. He remembered opening three condoms and tossing one of the wrappers by the couch. Thomasina must have taken care of it when he was sleep.

Soon as he was fully dressed his mood changed. If a confrontation was going to happen he wanted to get it over with. Fuck her man, what's he gonna do, he thought, walking towards their room? When they saw Bennie Thomasina said, "See you done woke up my nephew!"

Bennie watched Derrick for signs of aggression but there was none. Seconds later he told them goodbye then turned to leave. Thomasina could see Bennie was upset when she opened the door for him. Cheerfully she said, "Thanks for stopping by, and let me know you got home. I'll call you later."

She did her sexy missing tooth smile then kissed him on the cheek. Bennie walked away without saying a word. Why did he have a thing for these crazy women? It wasn't until he drove about a block that he relaxed, vowing not to see Thomasina again. They spoke the next day, and Thomasina never acknowledged the mix up. The only thing she said was,

"It's a good thing you were on the couch when Derrick came home."

After that Bennie ignored Thomasina's messages for an entire month. Finally he took her call in late October. Bennie told Thomasina he wasn't ever coming to her house again, but she could come to his. Then he hung up before she could say more.

The following Thursday Ronald called desperately needing to talk. He told Bennie yesterday October 28th at 3:33 am, Kayla had a boy. Ronald went on to say he'd worked up the courage to tell Lorraine. She didn't take the news well at all. Instead of crying, Lorraine started breaking his stuff, beginning with albums in the living room. She took Honey, Fire and Skintight broke them in half. After that Lorraine threw vinyl records like Frisbees into the walls. When he tried to protect the records, she pushed a rack of CDs over and stomped on the cases. Ronald's only recourse was to repeatedly apologize. Eventually she tired after ripping half the clothes in his closet. Exhausted, Lorraine slammed the bedroom door and cried herself to sleep.

Bennie held the phone listening with indifference. Ronald said he spent the night sitting on the couch. When morning came Lorraine had a demand. Since Kayla was Bennie's girlfriend, Bennie could be the father of her baby. Bennie thought Ronald would tell Lorraine about that night in January, but he didn't. Lorraine said Kayla needed to take a paternity test and Ronald agreed. Ronald said he knew the baby was his but it would satisfy Lorraine. After the call Bennie sat in the kitchen unable to concentrate. The ticking of the clock seemed unusually loud right now. The truth was coming and nothing could stop it.

Restlessness encompassed Bennie's next few days, but his nights were worse. If the test showed Ronald was the father it was all good. On the other hand, if Bennie was the father their partnership and friendship were unquestionably over. On the plus side Bennie would have a second chance to be a parent. A third scenario, though unlikely, was neither of them were the father. If that turned out to be the case then Kayla could go fuck herself.

During this time Thomasina left messages on Bennie's answering machine. He'd listen to her voice and wonder how she was doing. One night he gave in and took her call. She kept apologizing for the mix up last time until Bennie said he wasn't upset anymore. It was hard to stay mad when she dulled his pain. Truth be told Thomasina was no more than a hobby like building model cars or planes, but you could get hooked on the glue. Now she wanted Bennie to come over the first Saturday of November. She said Derrick was visiting his sister in Philadelphia and wouldn't be back till Monday, Sunday evening at the earliest. When Bennie hesitated Thomasina said she'd make up for last time so he agreed.

Bennie got to Thomasina's late that afternoon with her favorite beer, some vodka and soda chaser. She made him comfortable like before never happened. Thomasina was kidnapped, almost raped and murdered, but managed to find light in dark times. This night had a new level of intimacy. They watched the sunset from her balcony. They took a shower together and went to her bedroom. Later that night after Bennie adjusted the pillow Thomasina pressed her back against him and went to sleep.

Sunday morning Bennie woke up naked under the sheets to loud voices. It can't be Derrick again he thought dressing like the house was on fire. With intimidating posture, he went to the living room. Thomasina saw him and said the same thing as before, "Look what you did! You woke my nephew up!"

Standing by the couch Derrick said, "Sorry man I'm trying to get something straight with your aunt."

Pissed more with himself, Bennie snatched his things, and without uttering a word, headed to the door. Whatever Thomasina said afterwards he never heard. There's something wrong with those two he thought. Every time Derrick is not supposed to be there he shows up? If he walked in while Bennie was on the down stroke, then what would happen?

When Bennie got outside Thomasina was yelling goodbye from the balcony. Without looking he started the car and went home with the intention never to go back. Someone in this triangle was going to get hurt when it wasn't necessary. The next day when Thomasina called, Bennie made it very clear he wasn't going to see her anymore.

The following Tuesday the truth came about the baby. When Bennie didn't hear from Ronald about the results he called the office. Ronald answered sluggishly, "the boy is mine dude, I'm gonna be a father."

"Really…okay dude. I don't know what to say um," Bennie said releasing an inaudible sigh of relief.

"Yeah I meant to tell you last week but a lot going on but yeah, it's mine. I mean shit I didn't need no test, but Lorraine wanted to make sure. She ain't happy about the situation at all, not one bit. We're still working stuff out. So far I'm gonna pay for day care and child support. Kayla said she wasn't going to stop me if I want to see the child, so we'll see. Anyway,

I gotta go. I'll catch up with you later," said Ronald like a guy with a heavy load on his shoulders.

Now if Ronald discovered Bennie slept with Kayla, it couldn't change who the father was. Bennie just dodged a bullet, yet was still unsatisfied with the outcome. Deep down a second chance at fatherhood slipped away. The plan was to watch a little television; instead he went on a tirade blaming women for his mistakes. Like Adam in The Garden Of Eden, Bennie blamed God too. After all, that desire for the pleasure those curves offered came from God. Previously that rationale was all it took to ease his conscious, but tonight would be the last time he'd blame The Lord for his own faults.

Waves of light and sound can't be seen with human eyes, but they're real. The same is true with prayers. Prayers travel from a source through a spiritual realm of time. Bennie's mother sat in the kitchen rubbing her stomach trying not to worry. It was four years after the murder of Emmett Till and his picture in Jet magazine was still a haunting reminder of the times. She prayed after movement inside her belly before the baby had a name, or knew it was even a boy. One of her prayers reached Bennie on this night, and with it conviction.

The Holy Spirit began to speak with truth and love to him.

"You are not blameless. They are confused and so are you... do better!"

Bennie continued watching television struggling to justify past conduct. Finally asking himself why he had to be the one to do better? He'd opened doors, pulled out chairs for ladies at restaurants. Nobody he knew did that. It's not like he was physically abusive or ever called women bitches. If a woman said no, he knew it meant no; and he never said he was in love when he wasn't. He told them what he'd do and what he wouldn't. If they stayed they accepted his terms, so how was he supposed to do better?

The noise from the television was irritating so he turned it off. Now the silence forced Bennie to consider what really happened. He realized all the years of excuses and held the weight of not caring. He thought about meeting Paula at a club called the Goats in The Bronx. The place featured naked women, good music, and alcohol. No one could've convinced Bennie he wasn't having a good time. Paula's love ran deeper than any he'd ever experienced. Affection so strong she allowed her girlfriend to sleep with him. The least Bennie could have done was encourage her to stop stripping. Maybe Paula could've been a bank manager like Kayla. Admitting his error the burden of guilt lightened, but not for long.

Bennie went downstairs for a drink then changed his mind. No amount of Liquor would change his experience tonight. Like Scrooge visited by ghosts, he thought about the past. Years before Terri, the trip to Egypt or the start of R& B Kleenit. The Sista he met at Sherman's Barbeque on 7th Avenue. She was in her mid-twenties, about 5'5 and average like the girl next door. Bennie watched her scribble on a small pad then show the man behind the counter. Her attraction was being a deaf mute, and he had to have her. Bennie went to her apartment twice and never went back. One day Bennie said to Ronald,

"Hey…at least she can't cuss me out." They laughed so hard Ronald stepped away to compose himself.

In the loneliness of Bennie's room there wasn't a damn thing funny about it now. The woman was attentive and done nothing wrong. The least he could have done was learn a little sign language. Attempts to recall her name caused more despair. She was one of many names forgotten and tossed away like discarded tissues. He sought escape from this conscious nightmare, but the worst was yet to come. Before the mute woman, Bennie left another in worse condition.

One night Ronald was in Bennie's car on 158th Street close to Riverside Dr. They were talking about opening a laundry while having a beer and smoking weed. Bennie heard a noise and looked around. He saw movement in the rear-view mirror. 100 yards down the street a woman ran in their direction. She was naked screaming for help when he started the car and drove away.

This mind-blowing recollection dragged Bennie into truth. He couldn't blame Ronald because it wasn't him behind the wheel. What kind of man turns away like a coward from a woman in distress? The fact was he hadn't been the good man he believed he was, and it hurt. It was a sick feeling not being able to take it back. Seems Lorraine was correct not wanting Ronald corrupted by his friend.

While he'd felt sorry for himself he never thought about how tough black women have it. All the shit they go through before they're even grown up. More than ever, Bennie regretted writing a book suggesting a brother was in love with his own sister. Didn't matter they weren't actually related; it was just stupid. When he couldn't think any less of himself, something happened. Bennie swore not to let that happen again and made another admission. He vowed to stay away from women with husbands and boyfriends. For the rest of the night until he fell asleep he said, "I will do better. I will do better. I will do better."

Chapter 15

Morning opened a floodgate of memories changing Bennie's perception of women. At age 15 he worked in a summer youth program in the neighborhood. One day he and a girl the same age went to the store. On the way back a group of black men were standing on the corner. One man yelled out, "Hey…your sister's got a nice ass!" Bennie knew men shouldn't speak to a young girl like that. He should've told some older men in the neighborhood, but once again he did nothing. Time came to recognize the mistreatment black women often endure alone. Some are targeted early by those closest to them. Meanwhile their intelligence and courage downplayed, while the capacity to forgive and carry on are considered weak. If repentance were dues he felt he'd be paying forever.

Bennie was about to let Mister in the backyard when the conclusion came. The feeling was akin to learning to walk through the pain after an injury. But with his new outlook came an appreciation for life, and the changes he'd make as a man. Bennie could never change what he had done, but he could do better. It became his mantra for the rest of the day. He could do better. He must do better. He will do better. He will treat women better, especially black women. Finally expressing that sentiment to God, he was going to do better.

Days of reflection were uncomfortable, so he planned a getaway for Saturday. Last time he felt like this, Kayla had slept with both Ronald and him in the same week. For whatever reason, saxophonist Sonny Rollins would go to the pedestrian walkway of the Brooklyn Bridge. If a bridge brought peace and inspiration, Bennie was going there too. He wanted to ride his bike but the forecast for Saturday the 14th called for rain. Instead he went to the Metropolitan Museum of Art. He'd taken Linda in 1987 shortly before Tiffany was born hoping to jog her memory, but nothing happened.

To be as different, Bennie traded jeans and sneakers for slacks, a button-down shirt and dress shoes. Then he took a taxi downtown to the museum. He wasn't there fifteen minutes before he spotted her entering the lobby. From down the hall a trained eye evaluated her gait, age and stature. She packed shotguns on her hips under a small frame. Becoming conscious of falling back to objectifying behavior, he went in the opposite direction towards the Egyptian area.

The exhibit began with a row of glass-covered display cases. Inside were gold bracelets, beaded necklaces, and fashionable ear pieces. Not far from those was an amusing item Bennie had known well, a wooden afro pick. Except for a few broken teeth and the fist on the handle, it was just like the plastic one he stuck in the back of his Afro in high school. More inescapable evidence Egyptians were black people from Africa with wooly hair.

The next case had a baked clay wash bowl and water pitcher with a broken handle. After the last case Bennie stopped at the bust of Queen Hatshepsut who ruled Egypt several years with a king. As he studied her facial features someone commented, "Isn't it strange the noses are broken off a lot of their faces."

The voice was melodic, as if each word were a musical note. Unexpectedly it was the woman from the lobby. From a peripheral view and short glance Bennie saw her entirety.

The woman's naturally curly brown hair was shoulder length pulled into a ponytail. The eyebrows arched, and her complexion was how he liked coffee. A thin line

of skin accentuated the lips as if The Creator signed her like an artist finishing a masterpiece. She was small breasted and proud by her posture, and she had braces on her teeth. Bennie noted all that in two seconds.

Ultimately agreeing, he responded, "I think a lot of them were knocked off on purpose to hide their features."

"Me too…It reminds me of that guy who made a bust using his wife's face. I forget his name, but he was excavating a tomb. He commissioned a clay bust using his wife's face. Then he took it to the site, pretended to dig it up and said it was the face of Nefertiti," she said firmly.

"Really…I didn't know that."

"Yeah you've seen the one that looks like Iman the model, that one!"

"I'm not surprised," said Bennie then she continued.

"And I'm not prejudice but the history books at school didn't tell the whole truth. So many men…and women, made sacrifices and contributions. Every good thing doesn't need to be white, that's all I'm saying. Take Indians for instance…American Indians were dark, that's why they called them Red Men. If you don't believe it look at original photos of Indians between 1800 and 1900. They're as dark as the face on the Washington Red Skins uniform. I just think everybody's beautiful in their own way, right?" she asked, showing off the braces.

"You're right," answered Bennie, seeing her hazel eyes for the first time. They had a magnetic calming property like clear waters on a tropical beach. He felt something then looked away, took a breath and asked a simple question, "What are you doing here?"

"I had to get away for a while to clear my head. Art helps me do that. Why are you here?" she asked attentively.

"I'm here for the same reason…to relax and do something different, that's all," he answered as she walked ahead to the next exhibit. While her back was to him he said, "I'm Benjamin, it's nice to meet you um?"

"Elizabeth…I'm Elizabeth, nice to meet you Benjamin," she said, looking him over closely.

"You mean like the Queen in England?"

"Yeah…but call me Lizzy," she said showing more of the braces.

He tried to get away from her before, but here she stood. The answer to his next question could solve everything. Like police at a traffic stop Bennie said, "Lizzy I want to ask you a question."

"I know…you're looking at my braces; they come off Monday and trust me I can't wait."

"That's good but that wasn't it. I was going to ask were you married?" he said suspiciously.

Befuddled her head moved back and she said, "No I'm not married."

"No boyfriend?"

"Hold on a second…why you asking me?" she asked feeling insulted.

"Because if you gotta man I don't want any problems that's all."

"Wow, you get right to the point don't you? I like that. Yes I'm single, now are you? You're not wearing a ring but that doesn't mean anything," said Lizzy losing her grin.

"I've never been married."

"What about your girlfriend? You didn't say anything about her."

Bennie noticed the tempo of her words and responded, "I'm not seeing anyone."

"And why is that?" said Lizzy with one raised eyebrow.

"Lizzy can we talk over there for a minute?" he asked pointing to a long hardwood bench. Amidst human traffic they had a conversation.

Elizabeth learned Bennie co-owned four laundries in Harlem, and he found out she was a doctor. Lizzy started her dentistry practice in Jamaica, Queens a year ago. Until that day he never thought of a woman dentist much less a black woman. Impressed he asked question after question until the melody returned to her voice. Once that happened his question came out abruptly, "can I see you again?"

"You want to see me, in what capacity Bennie?" she asked with a raised eyebrow.

Believing he sounded desperate he replied, "Well how about as one of your patients?"

"You want to be one of my patients? Smile…now open your mouth," she asked tilting his chin from side to side.

"What do you see Lizzy?" he said looking at her eyes.

"When was the last time you saw your dentist?"

"Let's see, I think it was three years ago, I had a root canal," he said touching one side of his jaw.

"Bennie you're supposed to see the dentist once a year," she said scolding him.

"I know I know you're right."

"So that's how you want to…see me?"

Her emphasis on "see me" seemed playful so he answered, "Well we could go for a drink or something, whatever you want to do."

"I don't allow patients to call me Lizzy, it's inappropriate. They call me Doctor Winters. You'd have to call me Doctor Winters but it's too late, you asked me out."

"Can we do both?" Bennie asked charmingly.

"Honey you don't want both…trust me. Let's say we're seeing each other and had an argument. Now you come to my office. You want me to give you that needle in your mouth, and don't forget the drill. You want that?" she said pretending to hold one.

"I see your point," he said with a frown.

"Here's what we can do. Give me your number and I'm gonna think on it. So far you've been upfront…I like that, so I'm gonna call you so we can talk more. Are you okay with that Bennie?" Lizzy asked, standing to put on her jacket. It was the perfect opportunity to touch her again, so he took the jacket. After slipping it on, his hands rested momentarily on her shoulders. With any luck Lizzy would recall the feel of his hands later. He extended his card slowly between two fingers like in classy black and white movies. Impressed with the gesture, Lizzy put the card in her purse as they left.

Outside at the bottom of the stairs they faced each other for last words. Light rain cancelled any prolonged goodbyes. Bennie hoped for a memorable hug. Instead Lizzy offered a brief hand-held goodbye, went to the crosswalk, and waited for the light to change. Turning back to see him was a good sign she'd call, so he stood still and waited. Once the light changed Lizzy hurried across and down the block, never looking back. Disappointed, Bennie went home, walked Mister, and thought about her eyes.

Sunday afternoon Bennie's ears were on high alert for the phone to ring. It was like sitting in fifth grade waiting for that note to come back. Was Cheryl going to check no or the yes box and be his girlfriend? Four classmates passed a folded piece of paper until he opened it. Cheryl marked the no box with a check then followed up with an unsolicited explanation. It was because at times he wore orange or green socks with brown pants, and by late evening Lizzy still hadn't called.

When Bennie came home Monday evening there was a message from Lizzy saying she'd call back. Around 9pm when she called they had an interesting talk. Lizzy's braces were finally off and she was getting used to the feeling. She was still giving thought to dating him and wanted to know more. Bennie found out the reason for her caution was the emotional roller-coaster from the last two relationships. One guy was a mechanic at a car dealership who was intimidated by her success. The last man constantly found fault with her and became verbally abusive. Lizzy said she did not get that impression from Bennie and that is why she called.

As the conversation went on Bennie reciprocated with details of a prior relationship. He wasn't about to mention Thomasina or Kayla, and certainly not Linda. He talked briefly about Terri. Where they met, how long they were together, and finally that she was murdered after they broke up. Lastly, Bennie told Lizzy Terri was a suspect in the murders of a few men. He told Lizzy it was not easy to talk about but if she wanted to know more, they were news articles.

Pleased her questions were answered without hesitation, the melody in her voice returned. Lizzy's sentences mimicked wind chimes in a light breeze, so he kept talking. Not long after, Lizzy suddenly asked what he was doing Wednesday evening? Bennie said he'd be home doing paperwork. She asked if it was okay to stop by his house and he said yes. After he gave her his address, she gave him her phone number and said she'd see him around six.

First thing in the morning Bennie made sure there were no dirty clothes in the hamper, and he changed the sheets. He put stuff in order, dusted and vacuumed the entire house. After walking Mister for the evening, he gave the dog a bath then mopped the kitchen floor. Early Wednesday morning he scooped up the dog shit from the backyard and sprayed each room with air freshener. For the rest of that day Bennie was as nervous as a schoolboy anticipating the fight at the end of the day. Lizzy was coming and he could stare into her eyes again. In the living room he imagined how he'd please her.

When it was near time for Lizzy to arrive it was almost dark, so Bennie stood just outside his door at the top of the stoop. He'd already showered, rubbed shea butter on his skin, and dabbed cologne on his neck. It would soon be time to turn the heat on for the winter but right now the temperature was perfect for a pullover sweater and jeans.

Bennie anxiously watched every car coming down the street and any woman walking by herself. Suddenly he realized his plan for Lizzy hadn't changed. How could he act better if he thought the same? Years thinking of women as possessions or seeing them as you would shopping for a car. Were the features appealing and how does it ride? This time he'd focus on what kind of person Lizzy was. It was obvious she has what it takes to finish school and start her own practice. On the other hand, if she was coming for it, she was going to get it.

With new intent his tension was gone and soon a woman approached looking at each Brownstone until she saw him. Bennie came down the stairs to meet Lizzy at street level. She had a plastic shopping bag and a purse over her shoulder. Lizzy appeared slightly apprehensive then said, "Hey Bennie I'm here. So this is where you live…nice?" She backed up for a better view of the building and he followed. Lizzy pointed at the roofs and said, "in this row of Brownstones yours and those two buildings' top facades are triangle shaped…that's interesting."

"It's funny you noticed but yes I'm the last triangle," said Bennie smiling.

"These old buildings have so much character…they're beautiful," she said facing him.

"Yes…yes they are," he answered looking at her and when she smiled Bennie said, "It's good to see you again Lizzy. I'm glad you're here, come inside."

She raised a plastic bag and said, "I brought Chinese food from my favorite place. I didn't know what you liked so I got some of everything."

"I was going to ask if you were hungry but this smells good, thank you."

"Well then, let's go," she said walking with him up the stairs.

When they got to the hallway mirror Bennie called Mister and said, "Don't be scared I'm going to introduce you." Before Mister got too close he told him to sit. Then he told Lizzy to call him, and the dog came. While he sniffed her ankles Bennie told her to tell Mister to go. When she did he backed away. Now Bennie told her to call him back and the dog returned. "Now he understands I want him to listen to you," Bennie said.

"Are you sure?" said Lizzy hesitantly.

"Lizzy…I promise he's never so much as growled at anybody after what we just did," Bennie said, using that instance to rest a hand on her shoulder.

"Okay cause that's a big damn dog! Why'd you name him Mister?" Lizzy said relaxing.

"He got the name from a Sidney Poitier movie."

"Oh yeah, Mister Tibbs, I've seen it…it's one of my father's favorites. For a second I thought you named him after Billie Holiday's dog. His name was Mister too," she said, calling the dog over again.

"Really I didn't know," he said gesturing to her to follow.

Bennie took Lizzy through the living room to the kitchen where she set the bag on the table. Bennie put her coat on the back of a chair and went to wash his hands when Lizzy said, "Bennie aren't you gonna show me the house?"

"You want to see the house first?"

"If you don't mind."

"Sure…well this is the kitchen, and we can start downstairs," he said leading the way.

Downstairs Bennie opened the door to the basement where the furnace and oil tank were. The earthy smell of those wooden stairs was enough for Lizzy, and she backed away. They continued to the backyard door and went outside. Lizzy saw the yard was fenced in half concrete and half dirt. Bennie told her this was where he let Mister go when he didn't feel like walking him outside.

From there they walked up three flights to the top floor. Minutes later they came one flight down to Linda's old room and Bennie's bedroom. Lizzy thought his room was nice and went to the window.

"I can see my car," she said peeking through the blinds. Bennie looked out then stepped back. He wanted to kiss her, that's when Lizzy said, "I need to use the bathroom."

Bennie pointed and said, "I'll wait for you downstairs in the kitchen, and use any towel to dry your hands."

"Thank you," she said closing the door.

While Bennie was in the kitchen, Lizzy had a look around. The tile and tub were clean, but he could use a new shower curtain. Then she wrapped a few sheets of toilet paper around her hand and flushed it. One toothbrush on the sink was a good sign, so she opened the medicine cabinet while water filled the tank. A can of aftershave, some mouth wash, Band-aids and razor blades were also a good sign. Other than a random sock behind the door his place was neat.

Lizzy went to the window again, listened, and slowly opened the top drawer of the nightstand. Bennie had toenail clippers, a box of toothpicks, receipts, a couple of watches, and a bunch of condoms. Then she opened the door to his closet. A woman marks her territory so if he's got a girlfriend the evidence will be here. Seeing nothing fishy she went down to the kitchen.

The food containers were in the center of the table. When he reached for plates Lizzy said, "Bennie I can't stay too long. Do you mind if we talk outside?"

"What happened," he asked still holding the plates.

"Nothing happened… I'm not leaving right now. I still want to talk but I have an idea," she said spontaneously.

It was the first of many spur of the moment suggestions she'd make. Lizzy put an eggroll on a napkin and said, "I want to eat outside in the fresh air if you don't mind?"

"Nah I don't mind at all," he said taking an eggroll and a few more napkins.

Lizzy put on her coat left her purse on the chair and stood at the top of the stoop near the front door. Once she sat Bennie hurried inside returning with two cushions under his arm. Halfway into his eggroll they exchanged glances as people walked by.

"This was a good idea," Bennie said.

"Yeah I like the fresh air so I get some whenever I can, and I see you keep cushions. When was the last time you sat out here?" asked Lizzy wiping her mouth.

"It's been a while," he answered looking up at the night sky. Of all the things he pictured them doing tonight this never crossed his mind, and it was perfect. Lizzy went inside and returned with more food and a plastic fork for him. Then she moved the cushion closer so they could eat shrimp and broccoli from the same container.

"How does it feel to chew without the braces?"

"It feels like…like having my mouth normal again," she answered bumping her shoulder against his.

While they sat Bennie found out Lizzy had an older brother named Bruce. Her parents were still married in the home they grew up in Rosedale, Queens. Her father was a doctor and so was her brother. In a few years the family planned to open a clinic down south, possibly Charlotte or Raleigh N.C. She also owned a newly built townhouse not far from Yankee Stadium, with a rental apartment on the top floor.

When it was Bennie's time to share he talked about the rocky relationship with his partner Ronald and his wife Lorraine. There was no mention of Thomasina, or the book he'd written using the name Leon Allen Bryan. Tonight was extraordinary and he wasn't about to ruin it with too much truth. As if he didn't know the words were gonna come out Bennie said, "I'm glad you came over Lizzy."

"So am I," she said closing the container.

"What should we do for our second date Lizzy?"

"Second date? You're calling this a first *date*?"

"Why not? We met, had dinner, and got to know each other," Bennie said waiting for agreement.

"Okay I can see it."

"And I want to see you again if you let me," he said firmly.

Lizzy looked up the street then back at Bennie. She had a habit of being analytical and methodical, but relationships aren't equations. "I'm gonna be honest with you. I came here to see your living situation," she said shamefully.

"Lizzy…I told you I was single, and I am," Bennie said placing his hand on her knee.

"You did, I know. So let's be honest with each other."

"Sure," he said removing his hand.

"Bennie my problem was, and I say was…I was never clear about what I wanted, and that's my fault so here's what I need. A monogamous relationship eventually leading to marriage. I'm woman enough to be every woman so there's no need to be out there searching. I'm not gonna play house. If a wife isn't in your plans I understand. I want to love my man and have children. My gift is my heart Bennie. I need to trust you with it. So can I…can I trust you?" said Lizzy slightly crumping her lip.

"Yes…you can," he answered taking her hand. Embracing his fingers, she used her other hand to massage the top of his knuckles.

"Now what do you expect from a relationship? What is it that you want from me?" she asked still holding his hand.

"Well let's see…I don't wanna argue over stuff that don't really matter. I feel like we brought over on a slave ship together. Your enemy is my enemy, your success is my success, know what I mean?" he asked fervently.

"I get that."

"I can tell you I won't make it harder for you Lizzy. You've accomplished a lot. I can't imagine what it took to finish Dental School, and I want to hear all about it. I like you Lizzy and…and you don't have to wonder about me. I want us to spend time together. If it's you and me, I am where I say I am. I don't know how else to say it," he said modestly.

"Okay we shall see," she said letting go of his hand.

They took the food inside and Lizzy got her purse. She waited at the bottom of the stairs while Bennie got Mister's leash. He locked the door and Lizzy took his arm and walked to her car. She put her purse on the seat then turned to say goodbye. As she petted Mister, Bennie asked her to let him know she got home. He wanted desperately to kiss her but kept some distance. Instead of a hand shake Lizzy's embrace was an intimate hug. So tight he caught a delicate scent of coconut from her hair. He wasn't letting go until she did. The lips from the Egyptian Exhibit were inches away. Bennie strategically placed a kiss lasting only a second on the corner of mouth. A move meant to be more personal than passionate. Lizzy said she'd call later and left. He watched her turn right at the corner then he took the dog for a walk. Afterwards he sat on the stoop for a bit wondering, what could go wrong this time?

Lizzy contacted Bennie just before 9 and they spoke till midnight in two separate calls. They agreed that was their first date and talked about the places they'd like to go next. She also mentioned she wasn't seeing patients until the Monday after Thanksgiving. An hour later Lizzy said she needed to do a few things and said goodnight.

Bennie put the leftovers away then headed to his bedroom. He noticed a sock behind the door while brushing his teeth and laughed. Lizzy had to have seen this, he thought, tossing it in the dirty clothes. Standing beside his empty bed he couldn't recall a woman putting all her cards on the table. Lizzy said what she expected at the risk of that being their last date and he admired her for it.

As he was about to get in bed Lizzy called to say goodnight again. Inside he felt excitement like a teenager's first kiss. They ended up discussing current events, her days at school, politics, and God. The longer Bennie listened; her melodic voice became comfortingly hypnotic like the sound of ocean waves. The high and low inflections on specific words put thoughts in his head. He wished Lizzy were there and wanted to tell her but didn't. Instead, he held fast waiting for a hint of permission that did not come.

Inspired by a morning stretch Bennie called Lizzy immediately. It was the first time he'd dialed and the first opportunity to hear her answering machine. All he said was good morning and have a great day. While he was in the bathroom the phone rang. It took restraint not to run out and pick up with a mouth full of toothpaste. Eventually, Thursday morning they connected and twice more by day's end. The next day Lizzy made her decision.

After walking Mister for the evening, he received a simple invitation. With a sensuous whisper.

"Bennie…I want you…to come over…I have something to show you."

"What you wanna show me…Lizzy?" he asked trying to match her cadence.

"You really want me to say it?"

"Yes baby…say it," said Bennie listening intently.

After a curious pause Lizzy said, "well it was gonna be a surprise… but if you must ask…it's my statue of Imhotep. I want to show it to you… tonight."

"I look at everything you want me to see. Just let me wrap up a few things and I'll be right there," said Bennie looking for paper to take down her address.

"Good…I'll be waiting."

"Is there something you want me to bring?"

"No just you, that's all."

After that Bennie moved with all deliberate speed. He showered, dabbed cologne on his neck and navel, then got dressed. There came a hit the pause button moment, so he poured a shot of Vodka then sat on the couch. The dog came in and sat feet away staring at the glass. If Bennie perceived a signal from Mister to stay home would he ignore it like the last time? If he went what was the priority? At this point the only thing he could offer Lizzy was erogenous. He knew nothing about listening and responding to a woman's emotional needs. If he did, he'd have noticed how psychologically broken Terri was. This was a fresh start if he took advantage of it. A second chance to be a father and one day husband. Without taking a drink Bennie put the glass on the counter and left.

It was cold when he reached the car, but he refused to go back for a jacket. Not long after driving he felt the heat, twenty minutes later he passed Yankee Stadium. Now that Bennie found Lizzy's townhouse the nearest space was over three blocks away, so he parked and started walking.

Lizzy unlocked the door to a man pretending not to be cold. Minus conversation she led his frigid hand to her room to warm him. Except for jazz music in the background, their silence became the sound of love. Lizzy's kiss carried a hint of warm apple cider, and soon her wings spread like an angel. Only the scent of coconut from her hair and Bennie's compliance to hold on until she let go remained. Following her lead he never spoke and neither did she for the first round.

While Minnie Riperton played, they laid as naked as the truth they told each other. Lizzy admitted there may come a time when either one acknowledged they weren't compatible. But as they spooned, both committed to giving love the chance to flourish. Later that night Lizzy peacefully slept while Bennie wrestled with his thoughts. Priority one was keeping her away from Ronald and certainly Lorraine. He wasn't concerned about cheating because he always held a take it or leave it approach. Any women before Lizzy went in the history section. If this relationship didn't work, it would be something she did. With that conclusion he was able to relax confidently and go to sleep.

In the morning Lizzy came from the bathroom and slipped back in bed to snuggle. She had an idea to make their first encounter distinctive. Men could ruin a moment by saying some dumb stuff like, "Damn baby… it's sooo good baby. I know you like this baby. Come on baby just do it for me…please?" Last night Bennie took the hint and never said a word and made it idyllic.

While he slept Lizzy hugged him in hopes he'd be the one. The last man that laid in that spot was good in bed too; the problem was he'd rather tell a lie when the truth would do. Time would tell if Bennie would respect her body as well as her mind. She kissed the back of his neck repeatedly to wake him. He turned over, stretched and without opening his eyes said, "morning Lizzy."

"Good morning…how ya doing?"

"Fine," he said opening his eyes. Even in the morning her words had melody.

"And how'd ya sleep?"

"I slept good baby…really good," he said with hand over mouth to spare her from morning breath.

"That's because it's a new mattress delivered yesterday. And those are new sheets and pillows," she said resting her head on his chest.

"Oh okay," he answered rubbing the crust from his eyes.

"It's a thing I have to do. A new relationship must have a new mattress, and just so you know I'm not running to the mattress store all the time," she said looking serious.

Lizzy removed her arm from under the covers proudly pointing to the dresser. "Did you notice Imhotep the first doctor? He's right there," she said as if completing a promise.

"Is that who that is?" he asked going to the dresser. Comically he struck the same pose as the statue before going to the bathroom. After closing the door Lizzy yelled, "there's a new toothbrush next to the sink."

"I see it," he answered cheerfully.

"And there's a clean towel and face cloth on the back of the door."

"Oh I see it, thank you baby."

Angling the brush at those back teeth he glanced at the cabinet mirror then spit in the sink. When Bennie saw the reflection again, he had serious thoughts. Every time he tried it never ended well. Terri was a murderer, Linda was killed, Kayla tried to put a baby on him, and Thomasina was a cheater. How brief would this chapter of contentment be with Lizzy he wondered? Suddenly there came the urge to flee before something bad happened.

Bennie finished brushing then quickly washed his face. Back in the bedroom he said,

"I'm sorry I gotta go and walk Mister."

"I thought we were gonna have some fun this morning, but I understand," Lizzy said pouting her lip.

"Lizzy you can come with me but we gotta go now," said Bennie reaching for his pants.

"No you go, it takes longer for me to get ready," she said getting out of bed and putting on a robe.

After Bennie was dressed Lizzy walked him to the door. Her eyes were so enticing he didn't want to leave. Passionately they kissed until she broke away. Lizzy opened the door and said, "you better go now before you get yourself in trouble."

"I'll call you later," he said walking down the stairs. Lizzy hurried to the front window and watched until he was out of sight.

Naturally Bennie came for Thanksgiving and met Lizzy's parents, her brother Bruce, his wife and their two children. Lizzy and Bruce got their eye color from mom, who looked like she and Lizzy could've been sisters. Her family made Bennie feel welcome without pretending the entire time. After dinner while the women cleaned up the guys departed to the living room for football.

The Giants were playing the Cowboys, and Bruce and his dad were Dallas fans. At halftime it was Giants 3 the Cowboys 6. Teresa, Bruce's wife, came in followed by the rest of the family. Lizzy sat on the arm rest next to Bennie with her arm on his shoulder. After a few minutes her father said, "So Bennie…what are your plans for Elizabeth?"

"Daddy!" Lizzy said sounding like a small child. The room was quiet, even the children were waiting to see what happened next.

"No Lizzy, he has to ask…I would if it were my daughter," said Bennie confidently, then gave her father an answer. "Mr. Winters we're still getting to know each other but, I want to be with Elizabeth. I don't know how else to say it. One day when you and Bruce have time we can meet up? I know a place that makes twenty different flavors of wings. On the other hand, I don't know if Mr. Winters will want me around after the Cowboys lose."

It was the perfect response to a slightly tense situation. Like a tennis match all eyes turned for the response from her dad. Mr. Winters replied sternly, "well, it's like this…if my Cowboys lose today, we'll get you next time. And if the spot you're talking about has Jerk wings, you got a deal."

"Yes sir…they do," Bennie answered sipping his beer.

Suddenly Teresa said, "I think it's time for momma's peach cobbler. You like peach cobbler Bennie?"

"Sure do," he said smiling at Lizzy.

"I'll get you some cobbler baby," said Lizzy touching the back of his neck. For an instant the possibility he and Lizzy could be the grandparents on Thanksgiving was possible. The final score had the Giants losing to the Cowboys 30-3, but it was Bennie who had the win with her family.

After Thanksgiving Lizzy was busy preparing for Monday's return to work. Her high level of dedication to the patients was admirable, however it didn't stop them from talking during the day and before she went to sleep. It was official, they were a couple. On Tuesday the 1st of December, while walking Mister, Bennie decided to give Lizzy a house key.

On the way home Bennie's neighbor Larry crossed the street to talk. Mister smelled Larry's hand, got a rub on the head then sniffed the ground. Before they could start a conversation the dog suddenly barked at something a few houses up the street. Bennie told Mister to sit but he began to whine pulling the leash to go forward. Except for a car starting there was nothing out of the ordinary, but Bennie allowed the dog to take him past their house. Mister barked at a car that had just left a parking space. It looked like two women drove down the block, but he never got a good look. Mister never acted strange before as if his feelings were hurt. If Bennie hadn't held the leash tight the dog might have run away. Larry asked what was wrong but there wasn't an answer. Once inside Mister went to Linda's old room and sat with his head on top of his paws.

There wasn't an explanation for Mister's actions but after some soul-searching the truth was clear. Previous women were fruitless pursuits. To have a future with Lizzy the past had to be buried deep the way trauma victims forget. From this moment Bennie would insist The Tales of the Obeni story is just fiction. After talking with Lizzy, he collected every picture of Linda and Tiffany and placed them in a shoe box. Thinking a moment of weakness would overcome him Bennie cut them into tiny pieces. Then dumped that in the kitchen trash can and poured syrup over them. After that he went to a storage room in the basement with garbage bags. He collected all of Linda's clothes, school books, artwork, and copies of the Obeni book he wrote. There was another copy in the living room bookcase. Before Bennie could remove it Lizzy called. They talked until she was ready to hang up and he went to sleep.

First thing in the morning Bennie got rid of those bags in different cans blocks away.

With no evidence of an agonizing past, he had every reason to move on. Part of moving forward meant recognizing his ignorance and discarding macho habits. Except for Linda, Bennie's relationships were literally hands on. Since high school he was a private butt squeezer. Could Lizzy eventually get tired of his hand on her ass ten times a day? It wasn't worth the risk, and neither was going to the strip clubs anymore. A new circle of friends was needed. Men who are married with long-term relationships who had children for a start.

Every weekend they were together and sometimes Lizzy spent the night during the week. Mister got accustomed to her coming into the house without Bennie and she would let him out to the backyard. Mr. Winters and Bruce met at Bennie's then went to a sports bar on the Eastside for wings. Lizzy and Bennie sat outside on the stoop again before it got too cold. Laughing aloud she talked about Bruce nicknaming her Lizard when they were kids but when it happened it hurt deeply.

As Bennie learned, Lizzy was always coming up with ideas. One day she sat with her arms extended like she was playing an invisible instrument.

When he asked what she was doing she said it was practice eliminating discomfort to patients. It was her idea they see Diane Reeves sing at the Blue Note. After the show they walked around The Village, had dinner then took the train to his house.

At times Lizzy spoke metaphorically. For instance, one day she called on her lunch break to say her tank was empty and needed to be filled. When she arrived, it was more about spending the time and having her feet rubbed while they watched Martin on television. One day she said he was in park when he should be in drive. When he didn't understand he was told to catch up mustard. That was around the time Bennie decided to stop cutting his hair and grow locks.

For Christmas they celebrated the eve at Lizzy's and the day at Bennie's. Bennie got her a twelve-speed bike so they could ride together, and she got him a nice bottle of cologne. The thought of falling in love again felt like walking on a highwire over a lake of hot lava. Most mornings Bennie needed encouragement to get to the other side.

Lizzy was ready to say the L word, but unlike their nonverbal conjoining, she wanted Bennie to say it before she did. He would call her his sweetheart, honey, and babe all the time. He could tell her how much he missed and desired her effortlessly. Cautiously, Lizzy waited but things changed after meeting Lorraine and Ronald.

After Bennie's birthday in January, Chris their manager died from AIDS. Witnessing Bennie's anguish, Lizzy shifted two appointments to meet him at the funeral. Raymond, Chris's brother and Chris's wife Danielle sat in front of a closed casket. One glance and it was obvious Danielle was sick too. Shortly before the service Ronald and Lorraine came and Bennie introduced them to Lizzy. Before the service Ronald and Bennie spoke to the family while Lorraine asked Lizzy questions. While he comforted Danielle at the front row he saw Lorraine's lips flapping the entire time. After returning to his seat Lizzy said she had to leave. Clearly displeased, she remained silent until reaching her car and said, "I'll call you later." When they finally talked that evening Lizzy said, "Bennie that woman doesn't like you, and you know what, I don't want to be around her again. If she talks about you again it's not gonna be pretty...trust me!"

"What did she say?"

"You know what...It's not important now, everyone has a past. I want you to know I trust and I believe you. You are where you say you are... right?" said Lizzy with some anxiety.

"That's right I am, and I want this to work, I really do."

"I do too, you know I do. So now's the time to tell me is there anything I need to know?" she asked somberly.

"Like what…just ask me Lizzy…what?"

"Do you have children? That would be something I'd want to know," she insisted.

"I don't. I would've told you," he said firmly. That was the moment he knew he was falling in love. And when this tense moment passed he'd find the courage to say it.

The next weekend Lizzy stayed at her house. Despite the friction they spoke regularly and just before Valentine's Day Bennie sent a bouquet of flowers to her office. The next time they got together Lizzy came Friday right after work. Every romantic gesture Bennie could think of she got. Scented bath beads in the water, tiny candles, chocolate covered strawberries and Luther in the background. When Lizzy got out of the tub, he covered her with a towel and lay her on the bed. Then she got a full massage with warm oil until she couldn't move. He left her to relax in her thoughts and when she was ready, he brought on the waves.

It was a great weekend until Thomasina left a message Sunday morning on Bennie's answering machine. He forgot to turn the volume down and while they were in bed Lizzy heard this sexy sounding message. **Hi Daddy…it's Thomasina…I wanna say happy Valentine's Day. Your auntie misses you…call me, I need to see you.**

His eyes stayed glued to the ceiling until the message ended. When Bennie turned Lizzy was staring at the ceiling too. She was immediately told he'd ended it months before they met. Lizzy took a breath as if inhaling a cigarette then exhaled. She went to the bathroom, came back, and smuggled beside him. The rest of the day went without questions until Monday morning.

Bennie was at the corner bodega by 7am getting Lizzy coffee for her drive to work. Upon his return Lizzy was standing in the kitchen holding a copy of Tales of The Obeni. She explained she was looking out the window glanced through the bookcase and found it. Looking extremely puzzled she told Bennie she wanted to know why his picture was on a book by Leon Allen Bryan. Bennie explained how the first chapter makes the reader believe a brother and sister were in a sexual relationship when it wasn't true. In actuality they aren't related at all he told her. Despite his plausible explanation she insisted on reading it, and put the book in her purse.

After work Lizzy called to say she'd just finished chapter eight. What a wild imagination for the character to go back in time and find love.

Then she wanted to know why he used his name and took the pen name Leon Bryan? Then he used the real names of Ronald, Lorraine, and his ex-girlfriend Terri. Her critique continued, stating his story was confusing because he wrote it like it really happened. We know time travel is impossible, but it gives a reader something to think about. What would Lizzy say when she read the part about Thomasina who left a message. Turned out Lizzy finished the book and praised his effort without asking any questions.

The weather report predicted a winter storm with 24 to 33 inches of snow starting Wednesday afternoon. Lizzy cancelled appointments from Wednesday through Friday and planned to stay at Bennie's until Sunday. Monday before the storm, he went to the market and the Bronx for calzones. On the way back he rented four movies from Blockbuster. The first snowflakes came Wednesday afternoon, and by midnight everything was covered by snow. Thursday morning everyone on the block including Larry began shoveling. Lizzy helped sprinkle salt on the stoop. Before going inside, they threw snowballs until it got cold. Little did he know on Saturday they'd have their first argument, and possibly the end of this brief relationship.

Lizzy's concerns turned into doubt and headaches. The problem was Bennie sounded genuine when he said I miss you, and I can't wait to see you again. The other thing was her family liked him. Lizzy's dad was fine knowing she was there in the storm, and she had a key to his place. For those reasons she made an extra effort to give him the benefit of the doubt. After the brief conversation with Lorraine, things just didn't add up.

These were his friends and the first thing Lorraine said was, "so you're the new one huh?" followed by, "just be careful girlfriend you can't trust him." No matter how hard Lizzy tried, she couldn't forget those words any more than she could forget the characters in Bennie's damn book. Hell, she'd met two of the people face to face. It made her wonder were the rest of the characters real people too. In his book Thomasina is married, calls Bennie her nephew, and is still calling him. The only part Lizzy knew couldn't be true was traveling back in time to meet an Egyptian Princess, change her name to Linda, and bring her back to Harlem.

The 26th was the last Saturday in February and except for piles of snow in the street, traffic moved cautiously. That morning Lizzy woke from a dream about a woman she'd never seen. A lady with a missing tooth busted into her office looking for Bennie. In the dream Lizzy thought about pulling out her teeth when she woke up. The thought of hurting a patient over a man was the last straw.

Bennie came upstairs already dressed to ask if Lizzy wanted coffee. She passed without speaking and turned around suddenly. The question was met with an awkward stare and Lizzy asked, "You know how much I care about you…right?"

"Yes, and I care about you too baby," he said looking puzzled.

"We gotta talk," said Lizzy somberly.

"What's up baby?"

Hoping his answer made sense Lizzy asked with sincerity, "Bennie tell me…what's so special about me, cause I don't know what's going on? Something isn't right. Our relationship isn't reciprocal."

"I don't know what you want to hear."

"Now you don't know what I wanna hear…wow," she responded quickly.

"That's not what I meant. Is this about that call? Baby… I told you that's over. I'm not doing anything," said Bennie compellingly.

Lizzy took another breath, pointed to the phone and said, "Is that why ya turn ya volume down on the machine when I'm here? Cause if you didn't want her to call, you'd change the damn number, that's what I don't understand!"

"I didn't change it because of business, but I will. I'll get a new number Monday no problem," he said like that was the end. Then he put his hands on her shoulders while she stared at the wall.

"Your friend Lorraine called me the New One! That's what she said…I'm the New One and…not to trust you. She said you're always dragging her husband to strip clubs. These are your people, why would she say that to me?" Lizzy asked in a raised voice.

"Lizzy I never had to force Ronald to go to the club and I don't go anymore, that's the truth."

"You know something? I thought you were in drive, but you've been in park with me the whole time. See I'm right in front of you but you keep me in your peripheral, that's why you can't see me!" she said shaking her head satirically.

"I don't know what that means Lizzy," he said appearing confused.

"I know!" she said walking to the bathroom. She closed the door, turned on the water and watched it flow down the drain. She heard him say he was going to make coffee and to come downstairs.

Lizzy wondered was this how it felt after a regrettable one-night stand? At this point the flowers delivered to her office, the date nights, and foot rubs felt insulting. Those times he'd say I miss you Lizzy, I can't wait to see you Lizzy sounded profane. Just last week That's The Way Of The World played on the car radio and he said he loved that song. So he could use the word love for Earth Wind and Fire, but not when it came to her. Thank God she refilled her prescription for birth control.

Shortly after Lizzy was in the kitchen with her coat on. She handed Bennie his keys and said, "I don't think I can do this anymore. I can't do two out of three, and I won't. You and I want different things."

"You can't do two out of three. Lizzy, I don't get what ya mean?"

"It's a Meat Loaf song, figure it out," she quickly answered.

"Baby I thought today we were gonna…" she interrupted, "I thought so too. And just so you know I'm not angry with you so don't think that." Lizzy walked toward the hall to the front door and Bennie followed. "Lizzy what is going on, what did I do?"

With nothing left to say Lizzy forced a slight smile then turned to leave. She was outside past the house when Bennie called out her name in desperation. Lizzy stopped a few yards from a black Toyota Land Cruiser parked in front of a snow mound. She refused his hand but faced him for the last time. Bennie said he wanted to spend the rest of his life with her and softly said I love you. When Lizzy said she loved him too he noticed the car close to them was running and the back window down a bit. In case someone was listening, he persuaded her to come back inside. Just before going up the steps Bennie saw the front plate was from New Jersey.

Once inside Lizzy sat on the couch to listen. Bennie admitted he'd been overly cautious while working up courage to trust again. He told Lizzy his declaration of love meant sacrifice, fidelity, and protection from the smallest creepy crawly or anyone trying to harm her. In the end Lizzy was a melody he couldn't risk losing. Later that night conjoined, their affirmation of devotion became a new sensation. Through the night Bennie would say I love you over, and over, and over again.

Chapter 16

Queen Sakatet settled in Egypt at a palatial estate fifty miles from her birth place with a new passport bearing her original name, Osique Sakatet. At age 33 she'd lived about 5 of those years as Linda Reeves, an American. She was also the richest person alive with a fortune in the trillions. All that money couldn't relieve the headaches, stop nightmares, or lower her 170/94 blood pressure. Accepting Linda's memories as part of her own made it somewhat manageable. Because there were blanks of history, she did what any normal person would do, tried to get caught up.

It was tough controlling an empire when facts made Sakatet furious. When she was born much of the east coast was under a mile-thick ice sheet. The Greeks got credit for learning in Egyptian universities, while some suggested aliens from space built the Pyramids. After that Sakatet gained a new perspective on the unimaginable brutality and kidnaping of her people for the slave trade. Greed and pollution in the future almost drove her favorite animals the whales, to extinction. Modern people lost love for Mother Earth and that frightened her because Mother could shake people off like fleas.

After arriving in Egypt, the Queen found the spot her father Pharaoh Afermose's Palace once stood. Buildings now occupied the land including a street covering where the pool use to be. While the past pissed her off, the present made her furious. The air was dustier then before, and it seldom rained here. When she watched television and movies, that annoyed her too. Most of the heroes were white men, and there weren't enough people of color in the past or the future. Sakatet was from a time when most of the world's people weren't white. Now there's an endless assault on people of color. Of all these changes the worst was her King, her first, her man, pledged love for another woman. On the other hand, June was a few months off. That had Sakatet excited like a child looking at presents on Christmas eve. Sonya, a true friend and sister would be with her soon. Together they would plan a wedding like nothing seen in a hundred years.

Back in the United States, Jeff and Sonya were getting acclimated to a millionaire life. With support from their coordinator Crystal Epps, life was virtually worry free. Sonya gave Jeff twenty million dollars to see how he'd behave. After several weeks she was pleasantly surprised to see money made him more responsible. Even before the money, after Sonya forgave Jeff for his indiscretion with Cathy, he spent each moment showing he could be trusted. Jeff joined Sonya's church and attended on a regular basis. He also made a substantial anonymous offering after receiving the money. Ms. Epps took care of child support for Jeff's son Calvin, got him in a better school, and a nicer place for he and his mother to live. Then he brought a Mercedes Benz and upgraded Sonya's engagement ring several carats. Jeff stopped hanging out with J-rock, but they stayed in touch over the phone. The rest of his time he spent with her and Calvin.

Sonya set her mom up financially at the same time making anonymous daycare subsidies to working parents. She bought a couple of designer hand bags, some new outfits, and hired a personal trainer to lose weight.

One month after Sakatet left New Jersey, Sonya and Jeff chartered a private jet to an exclusive island in the Caribbean. They stayed a week relaxing, laughing, and making love to the sounds of the ocean on the beach. When they returned from the trip Sonya was tired and suddenly had no energy. They hoped she was pregnant, but her period came a few days later. Truth was a storm was coming. It was the kind that devastates and takes lives, and no amount of money could stop it.

Not long after Sonya began to feel better Jeff brought cellular phones. It was like carrying a small lunch box, but you could call from anywhere outside. When he called J-rock to give him the new number J-rock insisted on talking in person. As one of Jeff's friends J-rock got a new car and some money too. Jeff figured J wanted to ask for more money but that wasn't it.

At J-rock's place Jeff got an unexpected look of concern while taking a seat on the couch. His friend stood anxious as the conversation instantly focused on Cathy, someone they had in common. About two years ago Cathy and Jeff had a brief fling, and he broke it off. When Sonya found out it almost ended their relationship, but she gave him another chance. After that Jeff didn't care whether J-rock slept with Cathy. Frantically J-rock asked had Jeff always used a condom with her. The reason was he'd received a call from the Bronx Health Department. When J-rock went there a woman told him Cathy was HIV positive and urged him to get tested at once. He took a test that day and found out he was negative. Now Jeff realized why his friend was getting so personal. Jeff shrugged it off saying he'd always used a condom, but that was a lie.

J-rock stomped one foot on the floor relieved, while Jeff's left temple began to throb.

J-rock came back from the kitchen with two beers and handed one off. It was hard for Jeff to swallow or look his friend in the face and pretend. If he stayed to finish the beer the truth might come out, so he made an excuse to leave.

During the drive home Jeff's concentration wandered across the lanes. If he took the test and it was negative, he didn't need to tell Sonya anything. But if it was positive his fiancée had it because of him. Now the sun was setting when he backed into the garage. Jeff grew nauseous heading inside. Walking like someone with cinder block boots, he knew what had to be done. Lord my life was going so well, why did you let this happen to me?

Bill Withers played over the radio as Sonya danced around. She saw Jeff pointed at him and sang, "my brother...set me right down and he talked to me." Sonya made way toward him bouncing her head to the beat. "I yah yah said brother you just keep on using me...until you use me up!" she said playfully trying to make him dance. When Jeff wouldn't she hugged his waist and sang, "Baby...baby...baby when you love me I can't get enough!"

As the song ended Jeff held Sonya like it was the last time then she broke away. Taking his cheeks in her hands she said, "honey, don't ever forget how much I love you."

"I know," he answered with a heavy heart.

"And because money can't change the way I feel about you, I made dinner. Yup...I wasn't gonna have Bella make my man's favorite meal. I made smothered pork chops with gravy, real mashed potatoes, collards, and cornbread. You just sit baby I'm gonna tell you what's happening while I get your plate," said Sonya walking to the kitchen.

Unable to concentrate, Jeff mixed some of Sonya's words with his. After hearing a plane was coming for them in June, he wondered if Sonya would hate him for the rest of his life. A suggestion was they could get married at the Queen's palace, or anywhere. Her muffled words mixed with the aroma of smothered chops was punishing.

"Now if we wait till Calvin's out of school for the summer, we could take him...what do you think?" Sonya asked setting the plate and silverware down, "Jeff did you hear what I said?"

"Sorry what were you saying?" he asked watching gravy stream from a pool in the center of the mashed potatoes.

"Never mind, eat. I'll tell you all that stuff later," said Sonya sitting on the other side. It was a perfect plate at the wrong time, and he couldn't bring himself to lift the fork. "What's wrong, is it too hot?"

"Nah I was just thinking how happy I've been and about the day I asked you to marry me. Sweetheart thanks for giving us a second chance. You are the only woman for me. I…I love you Sonya and I always will," he said unable to look at her.

"I love you too Jeff baby," Sonya said. When he wouldn't face her she asked, "What's going on?"

Once he spoke it all came out. "Sonya I…I mean we have to get a test. There was a woman a long time ago and she might have that HIV," he said finally looking her in the face.

Sonya's heart raced with an old familiar discomfort. The feeling she'd get when Jeff wasn't picking up the phone. Then she said, "What you mean she might have HIV? Who is she Jeff? Don't let it be that skinny bitch from across the street."

"Yes…her,"

"Did she tell you?" asked Sonya angrily.

"No! I had a talk with J-rock and," then Sonya interrupted, "he knows about this too? What da fuck does he have to do with it?"

"J-rock got a call from the Health Department cause he was with her, but he's negative."

"You see Jeff…you just said he's negative. That means she's gotta have it or they wouldn't need to give him a test…right. So what you're saying is you might have the Monster, and if you do you gave it to me. Oh my God help me!! How could you do this to me? Jeff…last year I told you about Billy from my job. He was sleeping with Maxine on the third floor, and Shelia who works next to me. Maxine got it, then gave it to Billy. Billy turned around and gave that shit to his wife and Sheila, then Sheila gave it to her husband. The next time I saw Maxine she looked like an old woman, and she's dead now! Just what the fuck have you done to me Jeff!" Sonya asked screaming out.

"I didn't mean for this to happen, but it's gonna be alright," he said with composure.

"You think it's gonna be alright huh?"

"Sonya I'm sorry, but I had to say something so we can get checked out," he said expecting points for honesty. She stared back with a blank expression and said, "I don't have shit to say to you. I'm done! I'm just fuckin done!!"

Jeff watched Sonya walk away not knowing what to say. After a while he covered the plate with foil and heard sobbing from upstairs. Years before Sonya cried from her apartment, but this was different. Acoustics within this larger space amplified sound like an opera stage. No matter what room Jeff went to he heard her pain.

On a Monday in mid- June a plane left after 9pm from Newark Airport landing in Africa eleven hours later. An announcement to set all watches ahead seven hours to 3pm. Instead of the main terminal the plane taxied to the cargo area stopping in front of a hangar. The engines shut down, stairs were brought out, and three black cars waited at the bottom. Two men stood outside the first and third car while a woman waited by the second. Sonya stood at the top holding the rail inhaling fresh air. At the car she remembered meeting Ms. Aquino the day Whende said she was leaving the US. The women shook hands then introduced herself to Jeff and Calvin.

The motorcade drove through a dusty valley with sparce vegetation, then up a winding mountainside road. Miles later they took the left fork into the circular driveway of the Afermose Estate, named after the Whende's father. Four drummers began playing while several dozen people stood in line. Sonya couldn't believe the structure was about the size of a football field. In the distance on the north and south side of the main building were smaller houses. Sonya would later discover all buildings were connected by tunnels. Like an iceberg most of the square footage was underground.

Inside Sonya, Jeff and Calvin were offered cool white moistened towels with glasses of strawberry and cucumber infused water. The ceiling was high like in a church or movie theater. There was marble, polished stone walls, and wooden floors. It was like the set of the Ten Commandments except they forgot to remove clocks, wall sockets and light fixtures. Before entering one of the Queen's chambers Aquino had them place their towels and glasses on a table just outside.

Queen Sakatet sat atop a magnificent throne inlaid with gold. Sakatet's dress was the length of a bride's gown colored with orange and blue linear patterns. The crown was her natural hair skillfully braided and intertwined with beads to accentuate the rose-colored jewels in her necklace. Even young Calvin was in awe of this moment. With a gesture of the Queen's hand everyone except Ms. Aquino left the room. Once they were alone the Queen stepped down walking faster until she and Sonya hugged. Swaying side to side they cried, then Sakatet opened up making room for a group hug with Jeff and Calvin.

"So have you been behaving yourself young man?" Sakatet asked.

"Yes Ma'am," Calvin replied nervously.

"And you have such nice manners. You are my family so you may call me Aunt Whende. I have a surprise for you Calvin, do you like horses?"

"I think so."

"In the morning you can go to the stables and look at the horses," she said resting a hand on his shoulder.

"I know you all want to relax, and Tiffany can't wait to see her Auntie Sonya. Ms. Aquino will show you where you're staying and after that Jeff, I want to catch up with my girl," Whende said, looking as if Jeff had a choice.

"Sure, I know ya'll gotta talk," he said compliantly resting a hand on his son's shoulder.

Ms. Aquino took them back to the car for a short ride further down the road. This house was like their home in Jersey and by the time they explored and unpacked it was time for dinner. Sakatet sat at the head with Tiffany to her left then Sonya. Young Calvin was placed to the right of the Queen and next to his father. So pleased to see Sonya Tiffany barely contained herself. After dinner Sonya was exhausted and needed to rest. It was agreed the ladies would have breakfast in the Queen's chambers to make plans.

Early the next morning Calvin ran through the adjoining door waking his father and Sonya. Calvin wanted to start an adventurous day at the stables, so he and his dad skipped breakfast. At the stable, father and son had riding lessons then ate in the afternoon. A better surprise she had for Calvin was something he knew. Inside one of the larger rooms is a mockup of 3rd Avenue at 149th Street in the Bronx reaching to 180th Street. Calvin could operate more than one model subway train in different directions. There were tiny cars parked on the streets and replicas of every building. It would be well into the evening before they turned off the trains. Secretly Whende hoped to make this visit so remarkable Sonya and Jeff would stay on this side of the ocean. If it meant bringing every member of their families and friends, Whende would make it so.

As planned, the ladies ate breakfast in Whende's chambers. Afterwards they went to a lower floor for manicures and pedicures. In the massage chair the conversation turned to racism, relaxers, and Jheri curls. From there Whende complained about traveling with security and traditional customs of royalty. Unknowingly she angered Sonya suggesting Black people had become weak for not taking freedom by force. Most of that morning Sonya was quiet but that statement caused her to give an alternate perspective. Sonya suggested those kidnapped who survived the Middle Passage and other atrocities became the strongest of all. It got so quiet the women manicuring stopped and looked up at the Queen. None except Sonya dared address Whende in that tone. One more thing she missed being basically alone all these months.

When their nails were dry the Queen's assistant wheeled in four racks of clothes and other fashion accessories. For the next few hours, the ladies picked fabrics, and designed outfits with help from the royal seamstress. It was like being in the department store without ever leaving home.

By dinnertime their hair had been styled to match new outfits and Sonya still seemed distant. Calvin and Jeff on the other hand had the most exciting day of their lives and couldn't stop telling it. Once dinner was over, like the night before, Sonya turned in early. Whende thought like best friends they'd share a bottle of wine and have a few laughs like old times. As Sonya, Jeff and his son departed there was an obvious change, and it had nothing to do with time zones. More likely it was coming to terms with when Whende was born, and how she got there. Tomorrow if Sonya was still acting distant, she had to explain why.

The next morning Whende had an idea. Impulsively she arranged a tour to the Valley of the Kings for Calvin and Jeff to keep them busy. Then she had breakfast sent to her chambers with instructions for Sonya to attend. Once Sonya got there Whende said, "Come with me. I need to show you something." She slipped her arm around Sonya's waist leading her within the Palace where few could go. Side by side they went three flights down a stairwell, opening a door to a long hallway. The only sound was the echo of their footsteps until they came to one of those doors used in bank vaults. On the other side they entered an unbelievably large warehouse.

As they walked, Sonya learned the first section held papyruses and scrolls hermetically sealed like in fine museums. The contents had been copied and transcribed then placed on floppy discs. They continued past rows and rows of crates, finally stopping inside a large room off the main floor. That room was called the Queen's room, which held so much jewelry and gold, its walls reflected an odd light like that of a sunrise. Whende announced this was the Royal Vault, then directed attention to a table with two stone busts.

"Sonya…these are my parents. My father the Pharaoh Afermose, and my mother Queen Kymeka," she said proudly.

"Girl...you look like your mama Whende! Your eyes, even your cheeks are the same. Honey, I thought this was you! It's like when old folks say your momma spit you out, you could be twins!" Sonya said.

Whende opened a drawer below the table, took out a wooden box, opened it then handed her a softball sized sculpted piece of onyx. "That sat on my table near the window, that's me. Now come this way, I need to show you this," Whende said enthusiastically. Still holding the onyx Sonya followed to the other side of the room. Whende stood on the tips of her toes uncovering something, then stood back.

"Is this...this is the Obeni isn't it?" asked Sonya with astonishment.

"Yes, and the word is O-ben-eye. That's how you say it," answered Whende.

"It's just like your brother...I mean I don't know what to call him now, but it's just the way he described it, even down to the grains within the glass. Oh shit! There's a slot for the missing piece at the top. Hey... can I touch it?"

"Go ahead."

"Whende how old is this thing?" Sonya asked, never taking her eyes off it.

"15,000 years old give or take a 100." Whende responded, recognizing whatever was wrong, Sonya wasn't thinking about it.

"But how can it be that old? It's not falling apart; this feels like ordinary wood," said Sonya skeptically. That's when Whende removed a straw from the paper, took the lid off a clay pot, dipped the straw inside and gave it to Sonya to taste.

"It tastes like...like honey."

"You're right, that's pure honey. This honey was put inside this pot thousands of years ago. Pure honey will not spoil, like the Obeni it defies age. The next time it opens a gateway to the past will be in the year 2061. Hopefully our children can put this to good use," Whende said looking at the Obeni proudly.

Then Sonya was given a history lesson. Whende talked about the different ages like the Beetle, the Ram, and the age of the Fish which they were living in. Sometime within thirty years the age of Kefieous, the Black King, was coming, and nothing could stop it. One of the signs would be more than a million black men assembling from all over the world to a single place. Later an African leader will be chosen to lead a major world empire.

After that Whende spoke about the generations who waited faithfully for her return. How they kept the secret organization intact and were honorable stewards of the dynasty's fortune. And with an army of thousands at her command the least she could do as Queen was comply with a few archaic regulations. Then Whende shared some sad news of her own. A thorough examination by her doctor revealed she can never get pregnant again.

Before gloom had a chance, Whende gave Sonya a small felt covered box to open. Inside was a gold bracelet imbedded with blue sapphires. "Those are the original gemstones; the jeweler just copied the bracelet because it's so old. This is my gift to you and any of the other pieces you see you can borrow for the wedding. Here hold your arm up so I can put it on. Something borrowed something blue right?" said Whende locking the clasp.

"Whende it's the most beautiful thing I've ever seen," Sonya said with tears welling in her eyes.

"Something's wrong Sonya and I want to know what's happened? If I spoke harshly to you in the past months, I didn't mean it. That assertive personality came back with my memories. You know when a Pharaoh or Queen gives commands people do it without a lot of questions. Girl…talk to me like we use to when I lived in New Jersey, cause you are my family now and I'm yours. I know this year was hard to accept, but it's true about how I got here," Whende said urgently.

"I'm not gonna lie Whende, it was hard girl, but it makes sense now," Sonya said looking around while touching the bracelet.

"And I see you went down a size, you look good," then Whende asked, "are you going to talk to me? We said we were sisters like in the Color Purple remember. Only death will keep me from it. You said I could count on you to take care of Tiffany."

Those words broke Sonya, and she began to cry confessing Jeff had given her the AIDS virus. She'd been to several doctors and the diagnoses were the same. Her immune system wasn't strong like Jeff's, so she was declining quicker. When anger came over Whende, Sonya was clear she wasn't mad at Jeff, and they still planned to marry. Suddenly in a domineering tone Whende said, "Sonya he's not worthy to be your husband!"

"Whende…I love Jeff, you know that!"

"I don't care it's not right. These Black men are weak, so damn weak! There's not a fucking warrior among them!" Whende shouted.

"Whende, Jeff made a mistake; men make mistakes…we all do," said Sonya expecting empathy.

"Men are all the same I tell you. They are all jackals, all of them!" Whende said pacing in place.

"I see some things don't change with time. You call them jackals; now a days women call them dogs. But they're not all the same girl, not all of them!"

Sonya asked, "Was your father a jackal?"

"Don't you talk about my father…you hear me!" Whende said aggressively.

"Bitch what you gonna do, have me killed? Shit I'm already dying damn it! What the hell can you do to me? You wanted it to be like old times, well here it is!" yelled Sonya tauntingly.

After a tense staring match Whende said, "Don't say you're dying; I won't allow it! What I'll do is…is make a call and…and send for the best physicians and, let me see…where's a damn phone!" said Whende shaken by the news.

Grabbing her wrist Sonya said, "Sweetie we've done that, and I didn't want to tell you over the phone. I'm sorry, but right now what I need you to do is be my sister."

The women held each other, cried, settled down briefly, only to look at each other and cry more. Once they gained composure it was time for one more difficult conversation.

There was an important issue that had to be addressed. Like her HIV diagnosis, Sonya waited for the right time to bring it up. By now they'd sat on a couch holding hands, each with their own pile of balled up tissues. Sonya took a deep breath and said, "Whende do you trust me?"

"Of course, what are you talking about?" she answered holding Sonya's hand tighter.

"I tell you as my girlfriend, my sister and now your faithful subject. Whende, my Queen, you've made a mistake," Sonya said bowing her head slightly.

"Whatever it is I'll fix, it tell me," Whende answered earnestly.

"Just listen. Bennie deserves to know you aren't dead. I never spoke about it because you're wise. In time you'd do what's right, but you can't afford to wait. I agree with you, a Queen doesn't beg. I get it, but honey you're proof some things don't change with time," Sonya said letting the words sink in.

"I must be an example. I can't do what other women do, I can't," Whende said sadly.

"Then I'm gonna ask this. Before you met Bennie, did you ever wear something cause it looked cute but felt uncomfortable? Come on now, you know I'll take off some heels first chance I get. You gonna tell me you never did that?" said Sonya flippantly. Taking silence for confirmation Sonya continued, "Girl because I love you I gotta say you're not the first woman to hide the truth about a baby. And you're not the only one hurt by seeing another woman in her man's face. And you won't be the first woman to fight for the man she loves. Now tell me you haven't thought about going back to see him?"

"I have," Whende answered reluctantly.

"I know! And you know something else, you were upset with him for something he really didn't do. The book says he came to your rescue and cared for you when you couldn't. It sounds like you picked a decent man. Is that why you fell in love?"

Whende searched like the answer floated above and said, "He wasn't resentful because I was knowledgeable. I liked the way he spoke, and how he stood up to me. In case you didn't know I'm accustomed to having my way."

"I know that's right! so here's my question, do you still love him?"

"Yes…yes I do."

"Will you go back to him?"

"Yes," said Whende relieved.

"So how you gonna get miss thang away from him?" Sonya asked happily.

"That's no problem…I'll just kill her," answered Whende vehemently.

"No…no girl you can't do that!" said Sonya quickly.

"You're right, that's not a good idea, I'll just have it done this time."

"Woah slow down, wait a minute! You don't do that!" Sonya said standing up. Whende remained silent then said, followed by a laugh, "I'm fucking with you."

"Girl stop playing! You had me going," said Sonya feeling her heart race.

"Sonya you should've seen your face," said Whende making the same look. They laughed a bit more and Whende asked, "Okay so…so how should I do it?"

"Use your gifts baby. You keep acting like things are different when nothing has changed. Do what women have done for centuries, like Cleopatra, Foxy Brown and the lady who got Samson to give up the secret to his strength," Sonya said looking for understanding.

"What are you talking about?" asked Whende frantically.

"Entice him…seduce him. Wear something nice, get your hair done, use that smile and those hips. Push up the girls, show that man the Queen's stride," Sonya said adjusting her bra.

"Ohh you mean these girls," said Whende giggling while imitating Sonya's gesture.

"There you go, you got it. Then walk up to him like this," Sonya said walking past as Whende watched.

For the next few minutes they took turns walking, exaggerating the sway each time.

"This what you gonna do. You're gonna walk up to him like this. Then you gonna say…what are you gonna say?"

"I don't know, but I'm not going anywhere right now, I'm gonna stay here with you," said Whende taking Sonya's hand.

"Bullshit! You're gonna take care of this as soon as possible. I'll be fine I promise. Whende you can't put this off. How long would it take to arrange the trip?"

"A couple of days but," said Whende before being interrupted.

"You and I will plan everything, wardrobe, makeup and what you want to say. We got time before the month is over so let's say after the fourth of July, no later than a week after," said Sonya still holding Whende's hand.

"Should I take Tiffany?" Whende asked.

"We'll figure everything out," Sonya said reassuringly.

"Fine," said Whende sighing in relief.

"One more thing. I want you to know I accept you as my Queen," Sonya said bowing kissing Whende's hand.

Chapter 17

In the beginning of spring Kayla handled the duties of a new mother well. Her son brought more joy than imagined. Ronald Louis Jefferson Jr. was almost six months. She'd considered Malcolm Xavier but named him after his father, and Louis after her father. Kayla's son had his father's last name because no one was going to deny his legacy.

Before the baby was born Kayla got another promotion and salary increase for exemplary service. Ronald tried a couple more times for sex, but she wasn't having it. In the meantime, Ronald paid for daycare and medical insurance. After three months maternity leave Kayla went back to work. She woke at 6am, dropped the baby off in a cab, then caught the train to be downtown at 8:30.

The first Friday evening in April Kayla got out of a cab as usual. She carried the baby sleeping in his rocker, a baby bag, her purse, and groceries. Keionte had a crush on Kayla the day she moved in and took the opportunity to help. This Friday would be the first time he'd been inside her apartment. She had him close the door so the cat couldn't get out and he stayed watching her get settled. When she stopped walking around there was something about his face she'd never noticed. Keionte had sideburns and hair growing under his chin. Kayla told him he was handsome and asked his age. Apparently his 18th birthday was two days ago.

Keionte was beaming at the opportunity to just stand on the other side of her door. In a few weeks he and mom will be relocating to Charlotte, NC, because she got a transfer and bought a house. At this moment Keionte's mom was in Charlotte signing all the papers. Kayla smiled and for whatever reason hugged him like a boyfriend. It could've been the months of wearing maternity clothes and not feeling sexy anymore. It might've been because the young man was always respectful. He'd never know she pretended to be afraid so Bennie would escort her upstairs the night they came from the bar. Kayla was still holding on tight when he abruptly moved his hips back and she felt why. He wasn't too young for the departing birthday gift she had in mind, so it didn't seem wrong to kiss him on the mouth.

Keionte was invited to come back once the baby was asleep with two conditions. Don't tell anyone they both knew, and their little fling was over when he moved. Naturally he agreed and came back shortly after nine. He began awkwardly fumbling as if it were his first time. Kayla was patient and what Keionte lacked in experience he made up for with stamina and enthusiasm. It was the ego boost she needed to feel like a Mercedes instead of a beat hooptee. In May Keionte called a few times after he and his mother settled in. Those conversations lasted until shortly before he enrolled in the University of North Carolina. Right about then Kayla met a most unusual man, one she never thought of dating.

That May, Aaron Baker was making a deposit when a racist white man harassed Kayla. He was upset because the bank wouldn't reverse an overdraft fee. Kayla explained the bank complied previously, but this was the fourth incident. Hearing his request rejected the customer slapped a cup holder of pens from her desk onto the floor. Calling her a black bitch he started around to her side raising his fist. Suddenly Aaron grabbed the man's arm pulling him from her office. When the incident was over Kayla thanked Aaron who shook her hand and left.

The next time Aaron came to the bank he visited Kayla's office to say hello. She invited him to sit and get a better look at the man who came to her rescue. Aaron was slim, early thirties, not quite six feet, he worked out, his hair was dark, he had an infectious smile, and he was White. Minutes into their conversation he asked Kayla to dinner, and she said no. Her reason was dating customers is not allowed. The next time Kayla heard from Aaron was in a letter mailed to the branch. Inside was his card with a note saying he no longer had an account. Let's have a conversation when you're available. The reason Kayla even considered calling Aaron was they had a common interest; he was a Certified Public Account and she liked working numbers.

After soul-searching Kayla's rationale for not calling was based simply on fear. When she danced for White men in the past it was more uncomfortable than if it were the brothers. With more time and liquor, came specific insults. First they'd call her a chocolate baby, or jungle bunny. Later when all caution was gone, it was sweet Black bitch, and finally that nigger. Interracial couples can find love but was Kayla willing to find out?

Lacking any high expectations, she made the call. Not long after an uneasy start Kayla asked Aaron one question, why her? He said the first time seeing her was in April and she was behind the counter. First he thought she was a teller until she went back to her office. It was after throwing out that customer did he find the nerve to ask her out. Believing his story, Kayla agreed to dinner the next weekend.

They met in the Village outside the West 4th Street train station across from the basketball court. Kayla's main objective of the night was to observe. Sometimes good looks transcend race; Aaron was an attractive man by any standard. How would Aaron publicly acknowledge they were out together? Amazingly it never became an issue. Aaron pulled out Kayla's chair for everyone in the restaurant to see, something Ronnie never did. At dinner Aaron's attention stayed on Kayla, something else Ronnie never did.

Afterwards they walked aimlessly in Washington Square Park taking a listen to street musicians, then past the NYU campus. Since Aaron was an accountant they discussed changes in the past tax season, tax law, interest rates and what the Fed might do. Aaron was impressed when Kayla spoke of abatements and accelerated depreciation. He asked had she thought about taking an actuary position within her company. It was probably a bump in salary with less work. Not only was that something to think about, but the entire night was also wonderful. Finally back at West 4th Street Aaron hailed Kayla a cab. Kayla refused his offer to pay the driver while holding the car door. Before she got in he said, "Kayla…you're the most interesting woman I've ever met. Can we do this again?"

"Because I'm interesting, is that all?" she asked tempting him to say more.

"Interesting and very beautiful."

"I'll call you when I get home and yes, I'd like that," she said confidently as the door shut.

The next morning Kayla had to see where Aaron lived before it went further. If he didn't allow her to come it would be a major sign. Turned out Aaron didn't mind a morning visit and met her downstairs. He had a two-bedroom on the Westside below 85th Street, and there she'd find out if he was single.

As if she came with a search warrant Kayla noticed everything in plain sight. Aaron's place was not very neat, which was a good sign. There were sneakers, socks, and tee shirts in a pile behind the couch like he rushed to tidy up. On one side the bed sheet touched the floor, and the top cover was crooked. So far this was a single man's abode, but the bathroom would tell the truth.

Aaron wasn't nervous when Kayla went to the bathroom and closed the door. There was toothpaste slime on the edge of the sink but one toothbrush in the holder. Nothing suspicious in the garbage so she looked behind the shower curtain. One half used bar of soap and one towel. She flushed the toilet while gently opening the cabinet under the sink. Except for shaving cream and razors no feminine products or cosmetics.

Her curiosity satisfied; she told Aaron she was heading to her Aunt Monique's in Brooklyn to get her son Ronald. Aaron asked to go with her but Kayla hesitated before saying yes. Then Aaron asked was it because she didn't want her aunt to meet him? Malik from college was the only man Kayla introduced to her aunt. Maybe this was a blessing because after this Aaron had no reason to keep her away from his family. Kayla told Aaron he could come, then she used his phone to let Auntie know she was bringing a male visitor.

Monique opened the door and after the initial surprise she hugged Aaron and welcomed him. While Kayla got the baby ready Aaron and Monique seemed to hit it off nicely. When they were leaving Aaron carried the baby's bag downstairs. The idea was the taxi would drop Aaron off then Kayla and the baby as the last stop. It all worked out perfectly and Kayla was home before 3pm.

Two weeks later Kayla met Aaron's mother Helen at her home in Poughkeepsie. Aaron didn't tell his mom anything other than he was bringing a friend. After hugging her son she saw Kayla. Helen's reaction was the same as Monique's, amazement then total acceptance.

The next day Kayla invited Aaron over for a home cooked meal. After an early dinner they had an honest conversation about their future as a couple. They talked about some issues they agreed on and some they didn't, but it went well. He asked Kayla to give him the same chance for a lasting relationship as anyone else. She promised she would, and he left.

That night before Kayla went to bed she prayed. It was more than a year ago she asked God to make Bennie the father of her baby. Because her wish was ignored, she stopped praying. Ronnie saw Ronald just twice and never wanted to hold him. Now she had a man who played with the baby every chance he got. So on her knees she talked to the Lord again. This time instead of praying for wishes Kayla prayed for guidance. If Aaron was the man for her let their love flourish; if he wasn't, that would be okay too.

During the night Kayla made the decision not to tell Aaron about her past as a dancer or her abortion. The next day Aaron called her at work and Kayla told him he was her boyfriend. After that phone call most days they were inseparable. Kayla had keys to his place, and he had them to hers. Over time it was clear Aaron showed more love to Ronald Jr. than his own father. The baby stopped crying soon as Aaron held him. He never thought twice about watching the baby or taking him on little errands. They had a blended family dinner at his place with Kayla's aunt, and Aaron's mom, which went well. There came a time Aaron said those three little words and she said them back. By the first week in June he proposed and Kayla said yes.

Meanwhile by the first week of April Bennie's locks had grown another inch. Managing this style involved more than having a haircut every other week, but each month it got easier. On Saturday four college teams were left when Bennie met Bruce and Mr. Winters for hot wings at a bar in Queens. During halftime Bennie anxiously admitted his love for Lizzy. With utmost respect he asked Mr. Winters' permission to marry his daughter. The answer was a handshake and hug followed by an approving yes. Bruce made it a group hug then they took their seats. After a round of shots and congratulations Bennie shared some of his plan. He'd ask Lizzy this month after her birthday and Mr. Winters and Bruce swore to keep it a secret. Three days later Bennie purchased a clear cushion cut two and a half carat engagement ring.

Thursday April 15th was Lizzy's 29th birthday. She had patients but none the next day giving her a three-day weekend. Friday Lizzy's family met Bennie's sister Demetrice at City Island for dinner. In a private room filled with laughter they ate then Lizzy opened her cards and gifts. Later when the cake came some guests joined in to sing happy birthday. Standing up Lizzy blew out all the candles except one. Bennie had the ring inside his jacket pocket in case Bruce or Lizzy's father let the cat out of the bag. By the end of the night he knew they'd evidently kept their word.

After the celebration Lizzy went to Bennie's to spend the rest of the weekend. When Bennie got to the bedroom after tending to the dog, Lizzy was asleep. He watched her for a minute then used the opportunity to put the ring in the second drawer of his nightstand. First thing in the morning, before the morning cuddle, he'd ask her.

It wasn't sorrow and regret keeping him awake tonight; it was joy and expectancy. Maybe proposing first thing in the morning wasn't the best idea. What if he tied the ring to Mister's collar and asked Lizzy to call him?

When she sees the velvet box Bennie could get on one knee remove it and ask her.

By the time Bennie went to sleep it was after three. When he woke up Lizzy was in the shower. He jumped up moved the ring from the second drawer to a shoe in the bottom of the closet. That way while they were taking Mister for a walk, he'd take it with him. Before he could turn around Lizzy asked, "what ya doing in there?"

Bennie answered awkwardly, "seeing what I was gonna wear, and by the way, I'm so glad I'm not one of your patients."

"Come again!" she answered placing a hand on her hip.

"Yeah…because if I was your patient, you wouldn't be here," he said trying to get a kiss.

"That's right, and you know what else? I'm glad I'm not your doctor," said Lizzy as they embraced.

Later they took Mister to Riverside Park. Ironically sitting on the same bench the day he went to Kayla's apartment more than a year ago. They watched the occasional ship pass under the George Washington Bridge. Lizzy talked about the fun she had the night before and how her family really liked him. As his arm rested on the box in his pocket he couldn't ask her. After further reflection, this bench and this place was emotionally contaminated so he would do it later.

That evening when Bennie was ready, he couldn't find the damn ring. It wasn't in the jacket pockets or the nightstand. In a slight panic, he looked in all the shoes on the closet floor. Lizzy watched him walk around like he'd lost something. Before she could ask Bennie remembered the box was between the couch cushions. It was now or never he thought, settling himself. He took a deep breath and said, "Lizzy…there's something um…I…I know what you were telling me that day and I understand. It's a Meat Loaf song, Two Out Of Three Ain't Bad. I listened to it, and you have all three from me baby," Bennie reached between the cushion nervously holding up the box. He couldn't look in her eyes. There was a gasp while he got down on bended knee. Bennie opened the box and said, "Lizzy I want you! I need you! I love you! Elizabeth Winters…will you marry me?"

"I love you too, and yes…yes I'll marry you," she answered while he put the ring on. Later both agreed on a year's engagement with a wedding in the summer of 94.

On another day Lizzy rode her bike from her house in the Bronx to Bennie's, and from there they both rode to Central Park. The sky was a gorgeous blue with cotton balls for clouds and joy on every breeze. The park was full of people rollerblading, running, walking, and holding hands. They stopped to watch the Central Park Skaters at an outdoor rink and makeshift DJ. They sat on the grass talking and kissing now and then. Nothing mattered so long as the melody of her words flowed. What Lizzy said next was unexpected but that was her way.

She leaned close to tell Bennie she was staying on the pill at least until their first wedding anniversary. It was then she shared her desire to relocate south. The family would pool their resources and open a family practice in Raleigh NC, or another southern city. For a long time Bennie hand been weary of the partnership, and Lorraine's vindictive nature. If Ronald couldn't buy Bennie's half for the friend price he'd get more from an outsider. Honestly Lizzy and her family were a lifeline desperately needed. The longer Bennie stayed, gave Ronald, Lorraine, or something unexpected to ruin a fresh start.

At the same time after the Queen's decision to make herself known to Bennie she sent three men and women posing as couples the next day. They sat in different sections on a commercial flight arriving at JFK International Airport on the 25th of June. The group never acknowledged each other on the plane or at baggage claim. One couple took a taxi then checked into a hotel near Lincoln Center. Another rented a car and drove to a hotel near Newark Airport and checked in. The last couple had an apartment in Harlem to coordinate with the others.

The Queen's private plane touched down at Newark Airport the evening of July 6th. Less than an hour later she was in her suite reading a report on Lizzy and her family. The file had recent photos, dates of birth, addresses, bank accounts and their routines. There was a separate file on Ronald and Lorraine because they knew some details about her.

Oblivious to the Queen's motive, security proposed two plans for first contact, and she opted for the second. Bennie would be at the 8th Avenue office Thursday between noon and 2pm. There were cameras on the north and south walls and one facing the entrance. There was a blind spot by machine 34# and 35 and those were the machines to use. The Harlem team would secure the machines that morning until it was time.

Thursday morning the Queen had two bites of an apple, some water and that was it. She hadn't been this nervous since her father left to battle a neighboring province. Even the reflection in the mirror made her uneasy. To blend in she wore a white blouse, form fitting jeans with open toed shoes. Linda dressed like this, but the Queen never wore pants after regaining her memory. When Leah, her female guard, came in the room wearing a similar outfit the Queen felt better. That lasted until her car parked around the corner from the laundromat.

Leah carried a laundry bag slung over her shoulder to block the Queen's face from the front camera. The team stationed in Harlem was there early that morning securing the right machines. After that a chair was strategically placed so the Queen's face wasn't seen. Not long after Bennie came and went right to the office. Being a few yards away had her heart racing. He'd begun growing the traditional locks of a king while keeping a slightly graying goatee. It was then she knew she still loved him.

As planned Leah knocked on the door to tell Bennie the washing machine wasn't working. He followed rolling a basket out of the way until he got to the machine. A black woman rose from a chair and said, "Bennie."

He recognized that face, grimaced and said, "Linda?"

"Yes…it's me…I missed you…I had to let you…" Before she could finish Bennie fainted, falling like a tree in the forest. His back hit a basket and his head narrowly missed the edge of a cement corner that could possibly have broken his neck. Customers rushed over while one lady yelled "it's a heart attack!" In the commotion Leah convinced the Queen to leave while the Harlem team watched.

Walking quickly Leah reached the car first and held the door open. Soon as they were inside the driver was about to leave when the Queen said, "What are you doing?"

"It's not safe we must go!" said the driver loudly.

The Queen leaned closer so as not to yell in his ear to say. "If you move I will have your head in a basket by evening!"

"Yes my Queen," he answered, swallowing a lump in his throat. She sat back twisting her neck to see what was happening. The sound from the siren got louder then Leah touched the Queens hand and said, "I'll let you know what's going on." Leah left, disappearing around the corner, returning with good news. Except for a lump on the back of Bennie's head he was fine and walking around. Hearing that news the Queen made some personal changes while deciding to remain in Harlem.

Inside Bennie wondered how he wound up on the floor with people standing over him. A man took his pulse while a woman told the customers it wasn't a heart attack. Paramedics found Bennie's vitals normal and against their advice he refused to be transported to the hospital. After the commotion Bennie sat in the office touching a tender spot in his head. He recounted following a customer to a machine and thinking he spoke to

Linda. But that couldn't be because even though the woman looked like her, Linda's been dead for years. Now was the time to watch the footage to see what really happened.

Bennie rewound to the moment he came to relieve Jorge for lunch. After the women came in he paid close attention. The face of the first woman was clear but not her friend. He saw himself following the lady after she came to the office. Now her friend stands with her back to the camera then he passed out. It looked like a man felt for a pulse and slapped his face till he woke up. After the medics came, that customer walked out. Bennie watched the same fifteen minutes noticing nothing different. Finally, he convinced himself it was a daydream instead of a nightmare and went about his day.

Friday morning in the alcove Bennie found a letter under the front door mail slot. It was sealed with his name and no stamp. Inside a hand written note said, "**SORRY ABOUT YESTERDAY. TIFFANY AND I ARE VERY MUCH ALIVE. WHAT HAPPENED BETWEEN US WASN'T YOUR FAULT. MEET ME AT NOON ON ST. NICHOLAS AVENUE AND 140TH OUTSIDE THE PARK AND I WILL EXPLAIN EVERYTHING, LINDA.**"

The second time reading it he forgot to breathe. Was it possible Linda was alive after more than six years, or was this Lorraine's doing? But what if it were true?

Forecast for today was hazy hot and humid. Bennie left for the park before noon with Mister strictly for moral support. His feelings were an emotional tennis match played between rage and hope. Didn't matter who was winning when each point was agonizing. Luckily there was a breeze at the park created from the passing traffic. As he walked outside the park a gentleman left so Bennie took that bench and looked around. Towards uptown a couple held hands. In the opposite direction two guys sat talking. What caught his attention was two black men in Harlem wearing black slacks with long sleeve white dress shirts. So as not to stare, he looked away to find another man and woman wearing the same outfit, and all four had on sunglasses.

Simultaneously two men dressed alike caught Bennie's attention. One stood at the corner of 140th Street. The second stood further away from the men on the bench. A black SUV double parked then a woman came from behind stopping at the back door. She opened it for someone to step out. Mister's stubby tail wagged excitedly, and he whined pulling the leash forcing Bennie to stand. It was her. It was inconceivable but it was her.

She called Mister and Bennie let go. The dog jumped up licking her face like an overjoyed puppy. He tried not to hyperventilate as she came closer. His mouth hung open as she wrapped her arms around him. Incapable of moving he felt her hair on his cheek, a fragrance on her skin, and the breath filling her lungs. Accepting this as reality Bennie hugged back and their tears flowed. "I'm so sorry I made you run away," he said struggling to get out the words.

"It wasn't your fault. I know that now," she said holding his hand.

"I blamed myself when I thought you all were dead…what happened? Where've you been all this time?" he asked unable to look away.

"Please sit I have a lot to tell you."

Tightly holding her hand Bennie waited and Linda said, "There's something you need to know…I remember everything. You taught me to read. You let me sleep in your bed when I was scared of thunder. You took care of me, and I will always love you for that," she said petting Mister's head. It was difficult to look at him when she said, "I know who I really am, and you're not my brother. I was born Osique Sakatet but you called me Whende," she said waiting for a reaction. Now Bennie held her hand tighter and she continued, "last year after Thanksgiving I saw you and Mister outside the house. He caught my scent and ran towards the car. I wasn't ready to talk so we drove away. The next time was after it snowed in February. I came to tell you I remembered when I heard you talking to her outside. You sounded happy so I didn't say anything."

"You were there?"

Her response was a simple nod.

"I knew somebody was in that car…wow!" said Bennie taking a gulp of air.

"I'm sure you have questions and I'll tell you everything, but not right now. I'll send a car to the house Tuesday evening, and I'll bring a picture of your daughter," she said letting go of his hand. With royal stature she stood in front of him looking around as if it all belonged to her. "Neia abeir Bennie…neia abeir," said Whende heading to the car. Leah held the door and once they were inside the car left, and so did the people on the benches. Bennie wiped the sweat from his brow then touched Mister. It was too hot now so they left, but the mission was far from over. A small detail discreetly kept pace making sure Bennie made it home.

The sound of the door opening along with hastened footsteps found Bennie staring at the floor. "Baby, are you okay?" Lizzy asked dropping her purse on the table.

"Yes," he answered slowly.

"I didn't hear from you at lunch so I called the office. I gotta find out from Jorge you had an accident yesterday and the ambulance came. We talked, why didn't you tell me, I would've come over last night?" she asked desperately.

"I slipped…hit my head…that's all…it's nothing," he answered dismissively. Lizzy felt the lump on the back of his head then looked into Bennie's eyes. She had him follow her finger from left to right then said, "Why didn't they take you to the hospital? They should have taken you!" she asked, holding his cheeks.

"I…I… didn't want to go," he answered slowly.

"Honey you don't sound like yourself so we're going to the hospital," she said grabbing her purse.

"No…I'm good," he said unable to look at her.

"Honey trust me, you could have a concussion and not know! We're going to get you checked out!" Lizzy said forcefully.

The ride to the hospital and wait in emergency was all a blur for Bennie. As they held hands waiting to be seen he wondered why his life was a minefield, triggering one explosion after another. After a thorough examination Bennie's blood pressure was high and that was all so they were able to leave. There are people that know a storm is coming when a particular part of their body aches. Others notice the wind, the sky, and the smell of rain in the air. For Lizzy the first sign was Bennie putting the seat back and staring out the window. When they got back she let Mister in the backyard and Bennie quietly went upstairs. While minor, the next thing had Lizzy feeling snubbed when it didn't occur.

After Mister was done she went upstairs to the bedroom. He'd stripped down to his underwear and got under the covers. As Lizzy undressed there was no grimace from him, not even the typical raised eyebrow. Hell Bennie caught the flu in February and still managed to smirk seeing her walk in her underwear. He thanked her for taking care of the dog then turned on his stomach. Resting an arm on his shoulder she cozied next to him and said, "Goodnight sweetheart I love you and everything's gonna be alright."

Like a man taking a last breath his chest heaved to say, "I…love you too." Her man was tense, and it wasn't from a fall. Tomorrow Lizzy had to find out what was going on.

Bennie laid still listening to sounds on the street but never sleeping. By the light of early dawn he tiptoed to the bathroom and sat on the edge of the tub. In the middle of his shower Lizzy came in to say good morning. Not only was this a new beginning, but it had also been weeks. She needed that special touch so she joined him. After squeezing shower gel on the loofah Lizzy gave it to Bennie. Soon they'd make love amidst the suds and life would return to normal. Except this morning he did only what was asked. Her neck, shoulders, lower back then gave her the loofah. As he stepped out she said, "how do you feel?"

"I little tired but I feel okay," he answered drying off quickly.

"Okay baby…I love you," she said feeling confused.

"I…I love you too Lizzy," he responded meagerly and closed the door.

Tilting her head until water ran down her face Lizzy exhaled. Her decision was made months ago, if they broke up again it was for good. The problem was her feelings were deeper than before. Looking in the mirror nothing about her changed physically so the problem wasn't her. She spun the ring on her finger searching for an excuse. The thought of breaking off the engagement was unbearable. Suddenly Lizzy recalled the first year of high school when her dad spent two nights on the couch. She never knew why and it didn't matter because her parents were still together. Then she remembered her mother saying,

"love has to be tested every now and then." This time twisting the ring meant assurance of mutual commitment.

So what if Bennie was acting unusual, he wasn't intimidated by her accomplishments like the last two boyfriends. This man respected her mind and her body. Lizzy conceded to acting like a turned-out teenager with a crush. She developed an addiction to Bennie's attentiveness, and this weekend when it ran out she started tripping. Okay so he wasn't in the mood; that was his right. Laughing aloud Lizzy dried her hair and relaxed. Bennie was the man she was going to marry and have children with. There was no major storm on the horizon, just a rainy weekend. What mattered was their love, and trusting he was where he says he was.

Since absence is thought to make hearts grow fonder, Lizzy decided to go home. Her excuse was she'd allowed paperwork to back up which had to be done for the coming week. Her real reason was she needed time alone to separate facts from fiction. It also gave Bennie a chance and space to clear up whatever troubled him. Most likely it was something to do with Ronald and he wasn't ready to talk about it. Before leaving Lizzy made it clear they had no issues and promised to call later.

It took several trips to the closet Tuesday before finally settling on his attire. Bennie chose a light grey suit, sky blue dress shirt, no tie, and black shoes. He'd made up a story but couldn't put it into effect until Lizzy was on the way home. Precisely at ten after six Bennie left a message on her answering machine. He told her there was a water problem at the Amsterdam location and he would call her when he was finished. Staring at the phone the taste of his lie like vomit lingered in his throat. Lizzy didn't deserve this treatment, but he didn't know what else to do.

At 7pm a black Mercedes double parked in front of the house. As many times as Bennie replayed the incident in the laundry he was sure the driver was the woman taking his pulse after his fall. Dressed in a woman's dark tuxedo she closed the door behind him. Thirty minutes later he was at the Parker Meridian Hotel in Midtown. From the lobby he was escorted by another lady to a deluxe suite. Bennie was invited inside by Leah whom he recognized as the woman who knocked at the office door. They remained silent, glancing at each other periodically until the Queen entered looking nothing like the first two times.

In the distance she stood like a proud Olympian, her appearance more from the period she was from. A silk sandy colored sleeveless one-piece ankle-length robe cinched at the waist replaced the tight jeans and top. Her locks were weaved into a zig zag pattern accentuated with tan beads. Finally, she spoke, "Leah, that will be all."

"Yes my Queen," said Leah exiting to an adjoining room. Bennie was spellbound unable to look away. Here was every woman he'd ever fantasized from Chaka to Pam Grier, with a little Clair Huxtable rolled into one.

Now he bore witness to the poised stride of a Queen coming closer. Her sway integrated ballerina grace with objective pursuit. She stopped at arm's length and said, "I see men's desires haven't changed. I said that when we met, remember?" Bennie could only admire her skin and how it shimmered like bronze. Open arms embraced personal space nonexistent as they held each other. Her scented oil took him back to their first night they lay together. Seconds dragged on until she kissed him, and he kissed her back.

"I know what you're thinking, I'm still me...see," she said guiding him to the couch, attempting to condense six years of absence from him in a fraction of time.

Starting from leaving his house to living with a baby at Sonya's in the Bronx. How she got robbed and moved to NJ. Finding her necklace with two corpses. She talked about therapy to restore her memory. Seeing him from a distance twice and meeting the people sworn to protect her. Reminding

Bennie of Mr. West who got him out of jail in Egypt. Leaving out any talk of her fortune, she brought up the nightmares with the Squiggly Man.

"I didn't know you were the Squiggly Man in my dreams Bennie," said Whende placing her hand on his for emotional support.

As if something slipped her mind Whende went for pictures of Tiffany. Bennie emptied the large envelope looking at each of the photos. Pausing at one he asked,

"is this how she looks now?"

"Yes, that was taken a few weeks ago," said Whende.

"She looks…like my mom," Bennie said choking up a bit.

"I haven't told her about her father but I will, when the time is right… and you can see her if you want."

"If I want! Of course I want to see her!" he proclaimed.

"And you will but we need to discuss a few things," she said grimly.

Whende had questions like the Queen of Sheba after meeting Solomon and the first was, "What would've happened to us if I never lost my memory?"

"I believe we'd still be together," he said without hesitation.

"And if someone harmed our child…would you defend her?"

"You know I would!" Bennie answered confused.

"I believe you. When I talked about desire I also meant as a protector, my mate for life. It's taken months to catch up on centuries of world history and the more I learned…the angrier I got."

In her attempt to explain Bennie experienced an empathetic side of royalty. Whende reminded Bennie of their ride through the city in her horse drawn chariot and the Black people living their lives. Then she talked about Greeks in Egypt. How they learned everything from architecture, science, math, and taught it to Romans.

As Whende continued she'd jump ahead centuries then go backwards to make a point. Now she spoke of the slave trade, systematic brainwashing, and torture of African people. How they had less rights than the animals on the farm. If a mule stopped working it wasn't whipped or killed for running away. She talked about Mary Turner lynched on May 19,1918, seven years before Malcolm's birthday. Because Mary turned attention to her husband's lynching she met the same fate. After a white mob lynched Mary they cut the baby from her stomach and stomped it to death. This was the first Bennie heard of Mary Turner, but he would never forget.

After that Whende talked about movies, television, and media's influence on the human psyche. Filmmakers, directors, and writers organized the removal of people of color from the future and past. Another premise is always the same, only White men have courage. When are Black men the heroes who save their families or the world from threats instead of being cast as the brainless cowardly clown? "When I thought like Linda my mind was controlled like the rest. As queen I must destroy discrimination and injustice as if they were an attack from alien monsters!"

Now she spoke of the slave revolt in Haiti, the massacre of Native Indians, and the extermination of Jews in Germany. When that war was over she said America welcomed those same Nazis. Years later Jewish survivors tracked down some Nazis making them pay with their lives. Jumping to reconstruction she cited instances when former slaves thrived, only to have property confiscated and livelihoods destroyed. Whende got so frustrated she stopped speaking English without knowing.

In her day warriors in combat saw faces requesting mercy and awarded it. Now weapons kill from miles away with the press of a button. "Why is it when confronted with truth the powerful smile and dismiss?" she asked rhetorically and resumed. "My people are so easily misdirected and won't fight oppression to its end!"

After sipping some water Whende said, "I only had my memory back a few months and I'm already sick of this shit aren't you?"

"I deal with it every day!" Bennie answered fiercely.

"Good! Because at this point it doesn't matter why the powerful are jealous and brutal; mistreatment of my people must end! It will take at least a generation, but we will end it!" Whende said clenching her fist.

"What's your plan?" he asked wide eyed.

Like Tubman, Malcolm, King, and others few are willing to pay the price for standing against injustice. At last Bennie understood Whende's spirit wasn't corrupted by generations of oppression. No doubt she would have fought or jumped overboard rather than be exploited. So he asked again, "what's your plan Whende?"

"There comes a time when freedom and justice are paid with blood. Black people fight for everybody's liberation except theirs. You tell me, should a King rest or fill his stomach while his family starves? No...it's our right to fight anyone for freedom my King! Leaders have sent men to war for centuries, the question is do they go for greed or liberation?" she asked grasping his hand.

After a moment of silence Whende said, "I choose you as my King and the chances for success are better with you ruling beside me."

"What do you wanna do?" he asked urgently.

"I've studied the Constitution and the laws aren't applied equally so we will put a stop to it. There's no statute of limitations on murder so…anyone who participated in lynching will be brought to justice!" she declared.

"How? Are you saying you're gonna kill all the White people?" Bennie asked in a low voice.

"Of course not! They'll have a chance to turn themselves in. If they don't then they'll just…disappear," responded Whende nonchalantly.

"Disappear! Whatta ya mean disappear?" Bennie asked after swallowing hard.

"Umm…I'll tell you everything when you choose what…" said Whende stopping to answer the phone. She went to the dresser and said, "yes…she's where? Don't do anything just bring the car in ten minutes, we're coming down."

The call was from the detail following Lizzy. They told The Queen Lizzy was on the way to Bennie's house and her decision was to say nothing.

She stood near the couch and said, "I'm sorry to rush you off, something came up. Before you leave I don't blame you for going on with your life, but now you have a decision to make. Know this…you are my king…my king! If you choose her I won't stand in your way, and you can still see Tiffany. Three months from now a ceremony will take place. At that time her father chooses her new name. Afterwards if you're staying with us I'll tell you everything."

"Alright," was all he could say.

"For your safety don't discuss me or anything that happened tonight even if you think they work for me. A small group know about our relationship and how I got here. Don't assume who knows…remember that!" said Whende taking his hand.

As they left the room Leah was in the hallway by the elevator. The next floor down two additional female security got on. When they reached the lobby four more security were spread about. Leah led the way opening the car door while the two ladies took positions by the front and back of the car. Whende touched one of Bennie's locks twisting it between her fingers. "I want to kiss you but not in front of them…not yet," Whende said hugging him tightly. Her cheek pressed against his and she sang a few lines from That's the Way of the World and said, "I remember you singing that to me, but do you remember these words? Neia abeir Bennie."

"I do," he said unable to let go or say he loved her too.

Before Bennie got in Whende said, "in a few days the money I took from you will be returned, it's a bit more than you gave me."

"Where do you live Whende?"

"Not far from where we met my King," she answered then went back inside the hotel.

As night approached Bennie considered Whende's other suggestions after hearing she'd make people disappear. She talked of anonymously paying debts, legal aid for the falsely accused, scholarships for students who attended HBCUs. The idea he believed most promising was new video technology. Using visual evidence to expose injustice and corruption in high places.

The car stopped at 81st across from The Museum of Natural History. In the dim light Bennie took out one picture. He imagined Tiffany's voice and the touch of her skin. For now the scale measuring joy and heartache tilted in his favor. His child was alive, and he had the chance to be a father again.

Just so happened it was a day Lizzy couldn't wait to leave the office. Her regular receptionist had a week vacation and the woman from the temp agency had a problem following instructions. Plus Lizzy had to straighten her out for addressing her as Elizabeth instead of Dr. Winters. If that wasn't enough after lunch the odor from a patient's infection upset Lizzy's stomach. By the end of the day she didn't want to be alone at home. So when Lizzy heard the message she decided to help herself and Bennie too. She'd make sure Mister got outside and have her collar loosened in the process. After months of regular sex it had been a minute. So Lizzy left Bennie a message saying she was coming over to help and left minutes later.

The last thing Lizzy wanted was to appear desperate, but specific relief was required. Her man could caress with passion equivalent to a thousand quivering butterflies. Other times he pounded Lizzy like a chicken cutlet exploring how deep the rabbit hole goes. Tonight she chose tenderizing to erase the abnormality of the past few days.

When Mister met Lizzy at the front door she let him into the backyard. Then she scooped the mess into the outdoor container. Inside she wiped him down and put fresh water in the bowl. Mister followed Lizzy upstairs where she saw his machine blinking with two messages. Another woman would've listened but Lizzy wasn't going to spy this time. Instead she showered then went through his dresser, the excuse being she wanted something of his to wear. Finding nothing suspicious Lizzy took a black tee shirt and some gym shorts and went back downstairs.

Shortly before 8pm Lizzy sat in the living room with the dog. The way Mister looked with his head between his front paws made her wonder if he knew something. Lorraine's warning not to trust Bennie played over more than once these past days. To drive the thoughts away she'd repeat what he'd told her as she rubbed the ring. I am where I say I am.

After looking out the window Lizzy fixed some cold ginger ale, took a cushion, and sat outside on the stoop. It was a fairly busy Tuesday evening in Harlem with people just out and about. Just down the block there was apparent drug activity she never noticed. A few minutes later two men stopped at the bottom of the stoop. The one drinking from a can inside a paper bag asked for a cigarette, and Lizzy said she didn't smoke. When the man came to the second step Mister stood next to Lizzy staring at the stranger like Tyson before a fight. Immediately they left continuing up the street. Now face to face Lizzy put her arm around Mister's neck held him close then told him to sit back down.

As it got darker Lizzy was convinced there were better places to settle down. For the first year or two they would enjoy each other before having children. Her dream house had a balcony outside their bedroom. They could have their coffee and watch the sunrise. A patio for outdoor parties and enough space for an inground pool. Suddenly Lizzy turned and said, "and you're coming too Mister."

Not long after Lizzy finished the soda a car stopped in front of the house. A woman got out from behind the wheel and opened the back door. A man got out, thanked the driver and stepped on the sidewalk. After Mister stood, Lizzy realized it was Bennie dressed more like he'd been on a date than an emergency. His expression was like the previous days, a man not happy to see his fiancée. The dread was more apparent because of lingering at the bottom of the stoop. When Bennie wouldn't speak, Lizzy said warily, "you look nice. You want to tell me what's going on?"

Chapter 18

It was the discomfort of a hangover without drinking alcohol. Temples throbbed as if his head were squeezed in a vise. Bennie couldn't remember going to sleep but there he was in bed still dressed. Whoever said joy and sorrow can't cohabitate was wrong because Bennie swung in between both emotions like a pendulum. On the one hand his daughter was alive, on the other Lizzy was no longer in his life.

Last night two hearts were damaged in a way that transforms an idea of love into a cruel fantasy. After the limo left, Lizzy waited for an answer to her question. Like someone seeing life flash during trauma Bennie decided in a split second to tell Lizzy the believable truth. If they were together afterwards it would be her decision. She waited in front of the hallway mirror and followed him to the living room. Difficult as it was, Lizzy sat close to him on the couch trusting his explanation made sense. When the night was over they would never look at each other the same way.

Hesitantly Bennie handed Lizzy a picture explaining he knew nothing of the child. His bizarre behavior made sense if he'd been afraid to tell. Lizzy offered Bennie a reassuring hand until hearing the little girl's name was Tiffany. Recognizing the name, Lizzy let go focusing on Mister, from there it only got worse. He admitted fainting seeing her mother in the laundry last Thursday. "Is the mother's name…Whende?" she asked looking distant.

"Ahh yes," he answered grudgingly.

"All those names in your book are real people. I don't know why I didn't see it?" said Lizzy like a simmering volcano, "Ya ex-girlfriend Terri…the killer, Ronald, Lorraine, Larry from across the street, your sister. Shit!…Thomasina called here so of course there's a Whende!" Everything after was a blur with only thoughts of Tiffany, a pleasant alternative.

The question wasn't if he wanted to be her father but how soon. Bennie got up, enthused to imagine their first meeting and what he'd say. While it was several years away, for some reason he thought about her first date. Practicing a Father's Warning with a stone-cold face in the mirror for the man who picked her up. Reminding her never to leave her drink unattended was another thing he had to do.

Tiffany wasn't old enough for double digits so there was plenty of time. Instead he thought of things his father did with him. Bennie would teach her to catch June bugs with watermelon rinds. Next they'd carefully tie a long piece of tread to its legs and fly it like a kite. He could teach her how to fish or take her skating with the Central Park Dance Skaters. All that and more was the future, and it was good.

Bennie removed his shirt and pitched it into a hamper like a basketball. A sleeve hanging over the side didn't matter; it was still two points. That's when a flashing red light caught his attention. Last night the stress was so intense he refused to listen. In the blink of an eye, elation vanished hearing Lizzy's message, "hey sweetie… sorry you still have to be at work but help is on the way. I'm gonna take care of Mister and I'll see you soon. I miss you so much umm…I love you."

Ironically, "I love you" would be the last melodic phrase he'd hear from Lizzy. With the final click of the machine his thoughts were back to the conversation and Lizzy's question,

"Bennie…where were you tonight?" Her head cocked to one side hoping his answer made sense. Bennie's choice was either bite through his lip or talk, so he told the truth.

He began with seeing Linda and waking up on the floor. Bennie told Lizzy he got a message to meet at the park around the corner last Friday. As he continued previous lies were about to unravel like knots after Lizzy said, "sooo…I remember you…telling me Linda's character was made up, but now she's a real person like everybody else…right?"

"Yes," he sighed watching her heel tap the floor.

"I don't even know why I'm asking. Sooo tonight's emergency was a lie and you were with her?" asked Lizzy with labored breath.

"It's how I got this picture of my daughter!"

"Sooo…where'd ya meet ya baby's momma this time?"

Bennie quickly said, "she had a suite downtown…but nothing happened Lizzy. We just talked…that's all. We talked then I left and…and that's it, nothing happened." He noticed Lizzy sat quite still while Mister watched intently. She watched her hand slowly leave the ring on the coffee table and said, "I was good to you. I know I was."

"Elizabeth…nothing happened with her, I didn't do anything!" he said grabbing her arm.

"Man…you better take your fuckin hands offa me!" she said snatching away, "There is something seriously wrong with your ass, trust me!"

"Lizzy," said Bennie calmly, "you're not wearing any shoes."

"Now you care! Fuckkk…you!" she yelled pulling the door so hard it banged against the wall.

"Let me walk you to the car."

"Don't do shit for me!…I can't believe I fell for that bullshit! I am where I say I am. You're a fuckin bastard!" she said pointing at him before leaving.

Her anguish coupled with his guilt were still fresh this morning. Bennie called Lizzy's office to see if she made it in. Not recognizing the voice he asked to speak to Dr. Winters. After a brief hold he was told she was with a patient. Without leaving a message or his name Bennie hung up. Thursday FedEx delivered his keys along with a note that said, "I hope you find what you're looking for."

The last time Lizzy spoke to her mother was when she called from Bennie's Tuesday. Thursday Lizzy spoke briefly with her father that night. Friday her mother grew concerned when she didn't call during lunch to catch up. When Lizzy told her mother she was going to bed early with no mention of Bennie, what Mrs. Winters heard was discomfort in her daughter's silence so Saturday afternoon she and Teresa were at Lizzy's door. Both tried the key without success, so they rang the doorbell repeatedly. Lizzy opened the door, turned around shuffling her feet like an elderly person. While Teresa followed, Mrs. Winters looked for clues. A single shoe on the kitchen floor. A half-bottle of wine on the counter, one glass with residue and two corks. Not until Mom saw boxes of oatmeal cookies did she know this was serious.

Lizzy sat in between the ladies with her head hung low. Teresa rubbed her shoulder while mom took a hand. Touching that finger absent of the ring released a flow of emotion. Tears held at bay for the sake of patients was part of it. The rest came from a pathetic feeling about herself. When Lizzy was able to speak she said the wedding was off and why.

She told them Lorraine's warning and Thomasina's message on Bennie's machine. The book he never mentioned writing she found accidentally. How he used real names except when it came to author credit. Without pausing Lizzy told them about a nonexistent emergency Tuesday night, and Bennie having a daughter. In his book Linda was a character he traveled through time to meet. Lizzy never believed it since time travel is impossible, but it was metaphoric. Truth is he's got a 6-year-old and her momma is Linda. He said he knew nothing about a child, but he wrote about a baby in his book. Based on this info Mrs. Winters wished she'd asked more questions about Bennie but Lizzy was so content.

Lizzy's mom made coffee, leaving the sister-in-law to console her. Teresa's first question was did Lizzy still have the ring? Hearing the answer she said it should've been tossed in the backyard. Another woman might have except Lizzy blamed herself for everything. The family knew where Lizzy met Bennie but not the whole story.

The second floor was where Lizzy was headed but she elected to follow an attractive piece of chocolate. When she caught up Bennie's lack of interest merely fueled her sweet tooth. Of course the nigger was too good to be true. A straight man over thirty with his own business and no kids, an anomaly for sure. Exposing his sensitive side, taking delight in her metaphors made Lizzy feel more than adequate. It was her fault, forcing him to profess love when he wasn't ready. Even now with the locks changed if that sweet tongue made a lie plausible, she'd consider letting him back inside again. Lizzy was like the rest, ridiculed for a choice of addiction. One more pitied link in a chain of damn fools because she still loved him.

Mrs. Winters set the coffee down waiting for her daughter to lift her head. They weren't letting Lizzy self-medicate with wine and oatmeal cookies any longer. The vote was two to one to get out of the house, and resistance wasn't an option. So while Lizzy got ready Mrs. Winters called home to tell her husband she'd be back Sunday. Under her breath she told him not to worry. Lizzy wasn't hurt physically, but the engagement was off.

Later they caught a gypsy cab to the Dallas BBQ on Fordham Road to eat. Teresa loved their tempura while mom and Lizzy ordered ribs. The waiter suggested Blue Hawaiians from the frozen drink menu, and they agreed. The drinks arrived in 20 oz frosted mugs garnished with tiny umbrellas and tall straws. Sour at first, this drink tasted better with every sip.

Before the food came a young couple was escorted to an adjacent table. The man pulled her chair out before he sat down. Bennie did that for her too Lizzy thought, chewing on the straw. Wedged between conversations from her table and a happy ass couple, Lizzy plotted. She needed closure and an excuse to see Bennie one more time. If he didn't reach out she'd retrieve the needed belongings next weekend. Five pairs of shoes, sneakers, a drawer full of underwear, clothes from the closet, earrings, and that medical journal. The journal was old, but she wanted it, and her feminine products. Lizzy wasn't leaving the coconut oil for her scalp or a new tub of shea butter. By the time they left the restaurant Lizzy convinced herself to see Bennie one more time.

At Blockbuster they agreed a comedy was in order. A lady returned Boomerang with Eddie Murphy and Teresa wanted it. The soundtrack was all over the radio, and it featured a lot of black talent. So they made popcorn and split the last open bottle of wine. Turned out it was very funny, but the plot was a poor choice at this particular time. Afterwards there was quiet tension. Teresa apologized for her choice although Lizzy insisted she was fine when they turned in for the night. Mom went with Lizzy and Teresa took the guest bedroom. After saying goodnight Lizzy wanted to share her thoughts but mom wouldn't understand. So she turned on her side, let out a sigh and laid still. About twenty minutes later mom sat up against the headboard with a pillow behind her back. Bedtime stories were for little girls with teddy bears, but this tale was strictly woman to woman.

Softly mom spoke not to be heard beyond their room, "sometimes you meet a man and never forget him. Before marrying your father his name was Jerome." When Lizzy turned over mom continued, "the year Kennedy was elected President I was nineteen and Jerome was…28 I think. Jerome talked about civil and voting rights, and tension in Vietnam. I wasn't ready for seduction from the kinda man they call Dr. Feel So Good. Well…I'd slept with him twice before finding out he had a family. By then I didn't care…I was in love with him."

"What happened mom?" Lizzy asked, when she got quiet.

"One night he said it was over…moved on like I was nothing," said mom with one short laugh.

"I'm sorry," said Lizzy considering mom in a new light.

"Elizabeth don't be sorry for a dead-end when you can turn around, you hear me? It was a long time ago and guess what? I met a wonderful man…your father, and I have no regrets…none!" mom said watching Lizzy's demeanor change.

"I just feel like I never gave him time to explain, I just left." Lizzy said hoping for a sympathetic ear.

"Has Bennie tried to explain?"

"Not yet," she answered softly.

"So he says he didn't know there was a child. Well that's happened before but it doesn't stop him from convincing you he still loves you! Elizabeth you graduated at the top of your class. You want Bennie back; I know you do but he's not a cavity baby…you can't fix him. Believe me, if he sees no value it's easy to let go…I'm sorry," said mom looking tearfully at Lizzy. With tonight's message unenthusiastically accepted, Lizzy cried loud enough to wake Teresa. Individually and collectively, they wept for another broken heart.

As the night progressed lemons were turned into lemonade by making it an old-fashioned pajama party. Lizzy suggested watching The Evil Dead, a horror comedy in her video collection. Reluctantly mom agreed so each had a task. Teresa fixed popcorn, mom got the rest of the wine, and Lizzy turned off all the lights. Didn't matter kernels fell in the sheets when mom's eyes were shut, there were no more tears, for now.

At the same time Lizzy had a sleep-over, Whende cruised above 39,000 feet on her way back to Africa. The cabin light was dim as engines hummed, only the small light above her seat was lit. Raising the shade, she peered into the darkness outside. In her time the voyage would've taken months to cross the Atlantic. Contacting Bennie was the right choice, and she was grateful Sonya hadn't been intimidated by a Queen's persona. Just one more reason Whende needed people unafraid to challenge royalty.

Sightseeing and food were on the agenda and now she could take a trip down memory lane. Wednesday afternoon the Queen visited a hole in the wall place next to the subway entrance at Saint Nicholas and 145th. Bennie had taken her several times for fish and chips while she was Linda. Being it was takeout only she wanted to experience placing the order at the counter once more. Besides, she could also squirt ketchup, tarter, and hot sauce the way she wanted. For that reason, two guards stood with her in line, one in front and one behind.

The Queen ordered fish, shrimp, and fries for everyone and went back to the car. Protocol dictates security eats at the Queen's table when they are honored for heroism. This time the Queen's table was in the back seat of a car double parked on the avenue. As if it were natural she placed the bag on the armrest and ate with a plastic fork as guards kept watch outside.

Before leaving Whende had to see the flat rock in the park. It was a place Bennie and his friends went as teens to smoke weed and sip Pink Champale. Without explanation she drew a crude map and sent a team to find the best path through Colonial Park Thursday morning. When they found it Whende was escorted from Bradhurst Avenue uphill behind the grounds of Colonial Pool. The rock was there but the vicinity was very dirty. There were garbage bags, overgrown weeds, broken bottles, used condoms and empty crack vials scattered about.

The last stop was Sherman's Barbeque a few blocks down the hill on Seventh Avenue. This time the Queen sent a car because the order was simple, a rib and spaghetti dinner with extra sauce. Now she went in the opposite direction to Riverside Park. It was a tranquil place with a great view where they'd walk Mister. Just Leah and the Queen took the short walk until surroundings were familiar. Back then while pregnant she, Bennie and Mister would face the Jersey shoreline watching ships pass under the George Washington Bridge.

So the Queen and Leah sat near the bike path to the right of the paddleball courts. Leah didn't possess the level of clearance for conversation about the past, so they sat quietly. Presently only a handful of people could address the Queen as Whende. Sonya, Jeff, little Calvin, and Bennie, and one of them was sick. She worried about Sonya every day and new technology could never replace face-to-face interaction. Sonya sounded weaker on the telephone and evasive when asked about her health. The thought of losing her adopted mother, sister and best friend caused her to leave abruptly.

Later at the hotel it was confirmed Bennie received a $500k cashier's check with a receipt for taxes paid on the money. It was more than the 270k she ran away with. In addition Bennie got her contact information and one more thing. Access to a 3-million-dollar zero interest loan with the first payment due 25 years after the first withdrawal. Whende could've given more but she didn't want to influence him with riches.

Apart from remnants in her basement chambers and stolen artifacts in museums, few places remained a queen could call home. This trip to America was reaffirmation of a past she could see, taste, and touch. So for her last day Whende went to Woodbridge NJ, past Tiffany's school, the library where Soriano kept eyes on her, and finally their old apartment. Joyful memories with Tiffany and weekends with Sonya were still here. This was her old palace now and she wasn't letting go. When she got back to the hotel she purchased the entire two story 70-unit housing complex.

Somewhat relaxed the Queen closed the shade leaving darkness on the other side. She accomplished what she set out to do despite a slight act of insubordination. In her father's time a guard would be executed for disobedience. In seven hours the plane would land and a decision had to be made. Certain aspects of humanity haven't changed with time. Love hate greed jealousy and desire to name a few. Without a king at her side some men behaved with hope of waking in her chambers. One more reason Lena would soon become the new Captain of the Guard. Finally the Queen reclined the seat unaware of more urgent matters to come.

Upon a Royal's return it's customary for servants, military officials, and family to witness the homecoming. Towards the end she saw Tiffany with Ms. Aquino at the entrance, but not Sonya, Jeff and Calvin. After being with Bennie she saw Tiffany had his hairline, cheek bones and the cadence of his speech. Before the question could be asked Tiffany told her mother Aunt Sonya wasn't feeling well. The Queen looked harshly at Ms. Aquino then hurried to the connecting corridor. Before going in she hugged her daughter tenderly, breathed deeply and went in.

It looked more like a private hospital room instead of a lavish suite. There was a heart monitor on the left side of an adjustable bed. On the right was a rolling tray table and a wheelchair folded in the corner. Sonya sat in a leather recliner drinking water with a walker in arms reach. In less than two weeks her condition worsened. She'd lost weight, her hair was thinning, and blotches were prominent on her face, neck, and arms.

"Baby let me talk to Auntie and I'll see you in a minute," said the Queen, watching Ms. Aquino and Tiffany leave.

"I know what you're thinking but I'm the reason they didn't say anything. I threatened to leave if anyone told you. I wanted you to focus and not worry about me and as you see… I'm fine. Please don't be mad my Queen," said Sonya humbly.

"I'll let it go," she answered tentatively.

"You promise?" said Sonya in a raspy voice.

"I promise," she answered taking a seat, "now tell me what's going on?"

Sonya put the water down and said, "my doctors tell me I don't have long Whende and…"

"No! there's something else we can do, just let me handle it," she said about to pick up the phone.

"Honey just listen! They've done all they can girl. If it wasn't for these doctors and nurses, I'd be dead already."

"Don't say that! Words have meaning!" uttered Whende as Sonya continued,

"Calvin got homesick so Jeff took him to his mother. He will be back on Tuesday."

"What can I do?" asked Whende with a comforting smile.

"I want to see the tomb of Jesus first. Then if it's the right time of the year there's a migration of Monarch Butterflies. Millions of them fly to one town in Mexico from as far as Canada. If it's too late, I want to witness the Aroura Borealis, the Northern Lights, and finally Mount Everest. Can you help me do that?" Sonya asked.

"Leave it to me," said Whende smiling before walking away.

When she returned all the arrangements were made. In less than two days they'd leave for a short flight to Jerusalem and rendezvous with Jeff. From Jerusalem they'd travel to Golgotha to see the tomb of Jesus. Sonya's 11-member medical team was notified of the trip, as were people under the Queen's influence living in the region. Afterwards Whende checked on how Tiffany handled these sudden changes. Naturally she tried being strong like her mother but death of a loved one would be a new challenge. Later Whende went to her quarters, buried her face between two pillows and cried. Then she composed herself, put drops in her eyes and spent the night in Sonya's room.

It was warm when they landed in Jerusalem and Jeff was waiting at the gate. The trip zapped Sonya's energy so they went to their accommodations to let her rest. In the morning, against the doctor's advice Sonya insisted on going. Not long after, they were in the city of Golgotha. Jeff wanted to take the wheelchair, but she insisted on using the walker. Slowly their group moved through a hundred sparsely spread people headed in the same direction. What he and Sonya didn't know was every tourist in the crowd had allegiance to the Queen.

Gradually they passed the Garden of Golgotha to the face of Skull Mountain. There Sonya saw a rectangular opening excavated into a solid rock wall. Along the bottom across the front of the opening was a wide groove also carved out. At first Sonya thought Jesus's tomb lay beneath the floor of a church but this place made sense. According to the Bible a stone was rolled in front of the tomb. The flat circular stone was gone but the track it rolled in was still visible. When Sonya's legs wobbled the wheelchair was brought up and she took a seat. Clearing her throat Sonya said, "this…has to be the place. I can see where a stone was rolled inside that track at the bottom."

"You know this was well after my time, but I'm told this is the place," said Whende staring at the entrance.

"Don't you mean to say before my time," Jeff said sounding amused.

"You're right Jeff, what was I thinking," said Whende after sharing a smirk with Sonya. Soon over exertion and heat had Sonya feeling worse, so they went back. In the morning Sonya was able to travel but lacked the strength to use the walker when they left.

It was obvious they weren't making the trek to Mexico so Whende created a magical moment Sonya would never forget. Whende brought the town of El Nevado de Toluca inside Sonya's villa at home. Millions of monarch butterflies were painstakingly painted flying and nesting in trees. A sun shined on the ceiling while the sound of Mexican music, and fluttering wings in the breeze played over hidden speakers. The collage was so large it stretched to each of Sonya's rooms. From that day forward Whende and Jeff would never leave her side.

In the evening Sonya woke to Jeff sitting on her left with Whende on the right flipping through the photo album. The unmistakable reality was her health was failing rapidly. Once the nurse checked her vitals and left, Sonya had a question.

"Whende...do you still believe in God and what's in the Bible?" asking after clearing her throat. Whende glanced at Jeff then back to Sonya and responded enthusiastically,

"Yes...now more than ever!"

"Girl how? Didn't you believe in more than one god?" asked Sonya confused.

Closing the album Whende pressed two fingers against her jaw finally saying, "How can I explain?" pausing before answering, "English words are not even two thousand years old. How many words are there for umm...the moon?"

"What's that gotta do with anything?"

"Well, I'm gonna tell you, in Swahili Mwezi is the word for moon. In Latin it's Luna. In my language we call the moon Iah. So, throughout the world the moon has been called many names, right?"

"Yeah, I get that...sooo," said Sonya waving her hand for Whende to continue.

"My point is it's still the moon. We called God Amun-Ra, but God is still God. It's the common beliefs that remain through time and culture. Believe in the Creator. Follow his instructions. Treat others how you wish to be treated. Have faith in a life after this one and be truthful, so your heart may be light as a feather on Judgment Day."

As they reflected on that idea she continued, "let me put it another way. To mature in understanding worship takes time. It can be years, a lifetime, or several lifetimes. God doesn't change; it is our perception or understanding that changes. Grows might be a better word. Take the age of the Calf somewhere in 2,500 BC. That ended and a new age of the Fish started around 30AD, the fish representing…Jesus. You've heard the references, fisher of men…two fish and five loaves," said Whende sitting back in the chair.

"Wow…now that's deep!" said Jeff waiting for more.

"Listen to this! Before I met Bennie an inner voice advised me. We call it Aahm the feminine part of Amun-Ra. In the age of the Fish Aahm is called The Holy Spirit, it's the same then as it is now just a different…" Whende paused.

"Name," said Jeff.

"Correct, which is why I easily accept Jesus, he's been around from the beginning," said Whende comforting herself with a hand on her chest.

"You know…I remember reading where Jesus says to…respect other religions. Its possible God is in all of them, or most of them," said Sonya with a dry cough. More and more her breathing became labored but she managed to say, "honey call the nurse…I need to use…the bathroom." Before Jeff could press the button Whende said sharply,

"Don't bother I'm here!"

"I didn't want to disturb you honey," answered Sonya feeling the hostility.

"Disturb me! Girl please I'm here," she said getting up. Feeling helpless, Jeff watched until the door closed behind them. After Sonya sat back in the recliner she said, "this is Friday night right?"

"Yeah baby," said Jeff wondering why it mattered.

"That means it's the weekend so we're gonna have some music and wine," said Sonya eagerly.

"Wine? Are you sure?" he asked.

"I'm damn sure, ya'll need to lighten up plus I need to talk to my girl so maybe you'll go run the trains," Sonya smiled knowing she wouldn't be refused.

"Alright," said Jeff turning to leave.

"Oh and don't forget the music…thank you, I love you."

"I love you too. Whende can I get you something?"

"No!"

The moment Jeff was gone Sonya looked at Whende and said, "You've done a lot for me but don't…act like my mother. We're not speaking now because…she can't forgive Jeff."

"I can't help it. You're struggling and he's walking around…it's wrong! He doesn't even look sick!" Whende said stomping a foot down.

"Whende listen…trust and believe Jeff tortures himself enough for everybody." Leaning closer Sonya said, "He already tried to kill himself because of this. Now I've forgiven him and…he's here because he…loves me, and I want him here."

"It's because of him I'm losing someone I…I love, and it makes me mad! It's not right it's just not!" Whende said shaking her fist.

"Whende I'm at peace…with this and…and I need you to forgive Jeff. Will you do it for me?" Sonya pleaded. With clenched jaws Whende found composure to say, "Yes I'll do it, you have my word."

"And you'll let him know he's…welcome here right?" Sonya said slurring a little.

"Yes…Jeff will be welcome my sister, and he'll have the best care when his time comes I promise," said Whende as if it took all her might.

"Thank you…I love you," said Sonya pressing the button to raise the footrest.

Jeff returned from the kitchen with wine, beer, and ice on a cart. Behind him a staff person brought a cart with baked chicken, steamed veggies, soup, sliced roasted lamb with potatoes. To change her mind towards Jeff Whende fixed his plate.

Sometime after Sonya said, "Jeff honey have a beer and play with the trains, or just relax. We gonna…talk and if I need you…I'll call you sweetheart."

"Sure, I'll do that," he said kissing her and taking two beers.

Whende put the cd player within Sonya's reach so they could hear. Sonya pressed play and said, "these small discs will replace records…you watch," then she made a toast,

"Here's to the butterflies."

"To the butterflies," repeated Whende.

As the music played Whende said, "that's good music, who is it?"

"Honey that's The Gap Band, yearning for your love," Sonya said moving to the music.

Before the song finished Whende asked to hear it again. When it was over she asked to hear it again, so Sonya set it to keep playing that song. "I'm happy you can remember…and I'm so glad…you picked the seat next to me in class," Sonya added, struggling to speak.

"You were in the front row," Whende said aware Sonya was having difficulty.

When the song started over Sonya said, "Sometimes I miss Linda."

"She's in here. All that matters is we still care about each other. I don't know what would have happened to me and Tiffany if it weren't for you," Whende said taking Sonya's hand.

"Honey you would've been…just fine, I'm sure of it! Oh…Linda was right-handed I meant to tell you," said Sonya taking another sip.

"I've always been left-handed."

"Listen…I saw it when we were…in the basement," said Sonya pausing to catch her breath, "Yup my girl was right-handed."

Later Whende helped Sonya into bed and continued conversing. Out of the blue Sonya said, "Bennie wants you back…trust me."

"How do you know?"

"Umm let's see…the man hired a detective and wrote a book to find you. Of course he wants you! You…tell me what's the problem?" asked Sonya clearing her throat again.

"I'm not sure I…love Bennie," she said as if unloading a heavy burden.

"What?"

After a shameful pause Whende said, "He had information from the future and I wanted it…so I lay with him. That's the truth," Sonya's mouth hung open before snickering, then she said, "Girl please…I didn't love Jeff at first. It had been almost a year, I needed some…dick!"

"Oow girl, you didn't just say that," giggled Whende.

"We tellin the truth…right? Hell our reasons don't always…make sense. I know women who did it cause…shit cause he was fine. He had good hair and they'd make a pretty baby. The nigga has benefits, sometimes it's revenge on another woman. So don't be so hard on yourself," Sonya said taking a sip and continuing, "So you remember having sex now?"

"Yes."

"So come on…what happened, how was it?" Sonya asked impatiently.

"It was the first time and I was nervous. He started suckling which was strange," Whende said raising the corner of her lip.

"Why was that strange?"

"Breasts are for feeding babies."

"Not anymore," she laughed and asked, "did it feel bad?"

"It felt…better," Whende responded bashfully.

"I know damn well it did," answered Sonya enjoying the moment.

Whende's eyes welled with tears when she said, "I love you so much."

"This is…like old times chillin in your living room. I love you too," Sonya said having difficulty speaking.

"Are you feeling alright?"

"It's been…hard to…breathe today," she smiled taking her glass for another toast, "To the butterflies."

"To the butterflies," said Whende bravely.

After which Sonya asked, "Sis…are you cold?" Without answering Whende put another blanket on. Before Whende could sit down Sonya said, "tell Jeff to come. I want to see him before…I" After Whende made the call Sonya murmured, "did I thank you…for my…butterflies?"

"You did sweetie," whispered Whende grabbing Sonya's hand. Not long after Jeff got to the room Sonya had dosed off. Neither Whende nor Jeff knew they'd heard Sonya's last words that night.

Later a nurse checked Sonya. After that the doctor came with two additional nurses. Jeff and Whende were asked to leave the room, so they waited helplessly in the hallway. When they returned Sonya had been washed and the linens changed. Because her condition worsened the heart and BP monitor were turn on. In addition, she received intravenous fluids, and had a catheter inserted.

The prognosis was tough to hear but Jeff held Sonya's hand and listened. Although unresponsive her eyes were open, and she wasn't in pain. The doctor said talking would help in her last days. Jeff told Sonya he and Whende weren't going away. He said Calvin sends his love and he misses her. Unable to think what else to say, emotion overtook so he stepped out. Jeff's sincere pledge caused all condemnation to fade along with any doubt of keeping her promise. Whende also told the doctor Jeff would make decisions for Sonya from then on. Hearing that, Jeff reminded the doctor of the DNR, so they disconnected the heart and BP monitor.

Saturday Jeff and Whende talked and so did Tiffany for a short time. Jeff read passages from the Bible and talked about the day they met. Soaking a small sponge, he let drops of water fall in Sonya's mouth, then applied Vaseline on her lips. While professing he was a better man and father because of her. He'd see to it her family and the charities named would be paid. Afterwards he and Whende opened the album seeing Sonya as a little girl dressed on Easter.

After Jeff left to take a break Whende brushed Sonya's hair. She considered sharing the fear of forgetting again, but quickly changed her mind. If Sonya was able to hear she didn't need added concerns. Before Whende put the brush away Sonya reminded her of someone. Whende told Sonya her cousin Mieythous kept a pride of trained lions as bodyguards. Mieythous's daughter Iruias discovered medicinal and practical uses from plants, herbs, fruits, and venoms. Iruias was a modern-day George Washington Carver and Sonya was her spitting image. Maybe subconsciously she sat next to Sonya for that reason.

Whende talked about an experienced seaman in charge of her father's fleet. Just a young girl when they met, he'd sailed the oceans in vessels over a hundred feet in length. After establishing a settlement of Egyptians to warm lands in the Gulf of Mexico he sailed north past Georgia. His crew discovered the Delaware coast covered by a mile high ice sheet, extending west inland to Illinois and to the north up to Canada. My people were crossing oceans when half the 13 colonies were under a mile of ice. Feeling agitated again, Whende took a seat just as Jeff came in. Neither knew Sonya had one last gesture of love to give.

Sunday morning on July 25th shortly after dawn Jeff went to Sonya and she was dead. He woke Whende who burst into tears after touching Sonya's still warm hand. They were sure but called the doctor to make it official. Finally the body was covered with a white sheet. Jeff quietly stared at the butterflies over the bed. He told Whende Sonya requested that her ashes be scattered in a small park on the Convent Avenue side of City College. Whende said she wasn't going, but he and Calvin always had a place at her table. The invitation caused Jeff's legs to tremble as he covered his face and wept.

Composing himself he said, "I dreamt about her this morning. I dreamt she tapped me on the shoulder and said I'm leaving. I looked at the bed and it was empty and when I turned back she wasn't there."

"Jeff…I dreamed about her too! I was sitting in our class. She came in, and I was about to ask what she was doing cause I knew she was sick. She grinned then you woke me," said Whende baffled.

"Wow that's…I can't believe it…wow!"

"How did she look?"

"She looked…peaceful…content…she looked…good," he said seeking words.

"She did. So what was she wearing?"

"I think you call it a jump suit like something from the seventies and," he and Whende said at the same time, "green with tan squares!"

"Wow…she said goodbye," said Jeff scanning the ceiling. Whende looked upwards as if Sonya could hear her thoughts. I'll keep my word. He is my family.

Five days later Jeff was back in their Jersey home holding Sonya's ashes against his chest. He put the urn on the table and sat. In this seat over smothered pork chops with mashed potatoes he made a confession.

Leaving the urn in another room Jeff toured the house ending in their bedroom. In front of her walk-in closet he wondered why women need so many shoes? None of it mattered anymore. Not the private jets, the chauffeurs, or the money without Sonya. The challenge was to do better and fulfill her last wishes. Except for ten million in donations and gifts to certain co-workers, she left Jeff everything.

Sunday, one week from the time Sonya died Jeff was in Harlem on Convent Avenue near a tree. Holding the urn above the roots he circled the tree sprinkling her ashes. A breeze caused some to stick on his pants below the calf. Jeff made no attempt to brush them away, instead he took it as a final sign of Sonya's forgiveness.

In another part of the world, meditative grief, senseless loss, and revenge lingered within the palace. All the power, wealth and influence couldn't break death's grip. It was seventeen days Sonya had been dead. And with Jeff and Calvin gone there were fewer places at the Queen's Table. In loneliness Whende bore a silent rage capable of slaughtering nations. To channel her anger she revived her combat training and study of history. Countless revolutions and inspiring words from brilliant women and men solved nothing. Every righteous movement is systematically sabotaged from within, from outside or both. New strategies were essential to combat power capable of destruction with the push of a button. A trusted king was essential to keep absolute power from corruption, and Bennie hadn't called.

Twenty-two days ago Whende said goodbye to Tiffany's father, and he hasn't called. The check was cashed but not a cent of the three million dollars was touched. With one call she'd know if Bennie had changed his mind and gone back to Lizzy. If that happened Sonya would be the only reason to move on. Life is meant to be enjoyed and the one constant is death. Whende wasn't going to wait for Bennie much longer. A queen is not put on hold indefinitely. As if Linda was talking to Sonya in the Woodbridge apartment she spoke aloud, "I've crossed thousands of years to wind up in fuckin baby momma drama!"

Chapter 19

Nighttime reflections fell as familiar drips of torture on his brow. One step forward two backwards. Happiness a myth and sleepless nights became the rule. What happened to the guy who believed he was being forged for a purpose? He was back at the starting line going nowhere.

Bennie's problem was that he required stillness while at the same time feeling obligated. Unintentionally Lizzy's heart was broken. The flip side was Whende's plan for change gave him serious concern, so he shut down to protect his sanity. Outside the front door where he and Lizzy sat was no longer sacred, it was a house of detention. Lizzy's belongings were unmoved like the pictures of Tiffany still in the living room.

Lizzy deserved more of an explanation, but he couldn't chance looking into her stunning eyes. The fears she'd take him back and he'd never leave. Bennie wouldn't contact Whende because one, she was living evidence of the unbelievable. Two, how could he be an example of a father the way he'd treated women? Two weeks ago Bennie dreamt about women sitting at this conference table with a little girl at the head. Each gave intimate details, and how they got their walking papers. He yelled for them to stop because little girls shouldn't hear such things. The next morning Bennie thought after these many years Tiffany might be better off not knowing her father.

August 5th Bennie was preparing payroll when Ronald came to the office. The once best friends had ceased social contact, so Ronald must've forgotten something. His first words after closing the door were, "Kayla's marrying a white man!" Apparently, Ronald met Aaron last weekend at Kayla's. He'd gone unannounced again expecting she'd finally give in and have sex. Ronald ended up disappointed. The next day over the phone Kayla told him she was studying to be a Certified Public Account and was engaged to marry Aaron. Together they'd open an office and move from the city by next summer.

Bennie had no choice but to listen while Ronald paced. Why was it a problem when there was no future with him? Bennie thought it was nice but asked, "she's gonna let you see Ronald Jr., right?"

"Yeah…whenever I want, that ain't the problem," he said leaning over the desk, "I don't want some white dude raising my son! I'll take her ass to court, watch," said the man who hasn't changed one of his son's diapers. "I was gonna let Aaron know Kayla stripped but he knows," said Ronald indignantly.

Checks weren't getting done with Ronald stifling the atmosphere. Consumed with Ronald's bullshit Bennie put down the pen. He imagined standing face to face telling Ronald he'd fucked Kayla too. Hell Ronald had a wife, what could he do about it? Those words on the brim of Bennie's lips like a cup about to overflow.

"Yo Ron…how long we known each other?" said Bennie gravely.

"A long time. What's up?" said Ronald skipping the usual answer. After a pause Bennie said with a grin, "Ron…I'm getting out. You can buy my share at a discount. If you can't I have a buyer," Ronald was speechless, so Bennie continued,

"I'd rather see you keep everything we built so think about it, cause I'm out buddy."

"Ben you sure? I mean what happened?"

"Nothing happened, it's time that's all, and I have no hard feelings," said Bennie leaning back.

"So you and Lizzy are gonna do what?"

"I don't know yet, but I'll call you next week so think about a price."

Inadvertently Ronald left Bennie with a unique perspective on friendships, like seasons they don't always last. The days of basketball, cards and hopping the turnstile were gone. Smoky, Michael, Diana, and Luther went their separate ways. If the guy watching the funeral in Cooley High could leave, so could Bennie.

A new revelation became the reason check writing ceased and not Ronald. For years Bennie wished to be a father, but he was allowing that opportunity to pass. If anything he learned today it was stop running from uncomfortable situations. Failing Lizzy was an open wound on his heart that needed healing, so he called hoping to leave a message, but she answered. After Bennie's desperate pleas Lizzy agreed to talk when she got home from work.

Lizzy got home and put an unopened bottle of wine on the counter next to the phone base. It was going to be one or the other and she chose the phone. Lizzy extended the cordless antenna and dialed without first announcing herself. She heard hello a few times then Bennie said, "Lizzy...Lizzy is this you?"

"Yeah."

"Thanks for calling...how are you?"

"Whataya want?" she said sadly.

"Lizzy let me say this and I won't bother you again." Because she stayed quiet he continued, "I know how all that stuff looked but I never tried to hurt you...and I never cheated on you Lizzy, that's the truth!"

"If that's true...so why'd you lie to me?" she asked sounding offended.

"Because I thought I was losing my mind. I...I didn't know how to tell you cause it sounds unbelievable. Lizzy I saw Whende and the next thing I knew I was on the floor and the ambulance was there...I passed out! I saw a Jane Doe file with pictures of corpses."

"You know, I think I could've believed you but here's what you told me. I am...where I say I am. Remember that shit! But you were where you said you were alright. Coming from her hotel room...in a limo. Bennie you must think I'm stupid. Why you had to go see her in a limo huh?" said Lizzy as her right leg jittered.

"I didn't order a limo...she sent it," he said with instant regret.

"Ohhh...sheee sent it...nice of her," said Lizzy cynically. In desperation Bennie said,

"Lizzy let's suppose for a minute I'm telling the truth and..."

"Her scent was on you mutherfucker! Yeah her scent...it was in your damn clothes! You gonna tell me I didn't smell her on you?" she shouted. Bennie kept quiet so Lizzy relaxed, finally asking, "did ya ever really love me?"

"I did."

"You did. You did...did. You need to leave me alone you understand?" she whispered pushing the antenna back inside the phone.

Months before she eagerly shared details as if theirs was the greatest romance ever told. From meeting at a museum to moving plans and starting a family. The window for reconciliation was still open if Bennie called to rephrase.

Holding the phone Lizzy made her way to the couch. She and mom shared a common heartbreak. Mrs. Winters over a first-time lover; Lizzy over a first idealistic experience with an engagement ring. The first to consistently open doors and pull out her chair. He was the first man to feed her chocolate covered strawberries in the bubble bath and lick the juice from her lips. For weeks she hoped, but now without question it was over. His last words were "I did," and not "I still do."

That night if Bennie wasn't pacing the floor he tossed in bed, but Saturday morning he called the number Whende provided and left a message. Afterwards he took Mister for a walk and the moment he returned the phone rang. Her name was Angelica Seale and she addressed him as Mr. Reeves. After saying what he wanted Angelica asked him to hold on. She came back to say he'd receive a call from Queen Sakatet at 9pm his time. Thirteen hours later Whende called but he couldn't recognize her voice.

"Is this you Whende?"

"Yes."

"It's the first time we talked on the phone so I couldn't recognize your voice," Bennie said timidly. After a period of silence he said, "I need to meet my daughter."

"That will be fine…Angelica will make arrangements. It's best not to tell Tiffany you're her father right away. Maybe a few days after you get here," Whende said nonchalantly.

"Um…sure Whende ahh…see you soon," he answered, embarrassed.

"Alright," she said ending the call.

Thirteen hours to wait for a minute conversation seemed unusual. Whende didn't sound excited, she didn't refer to him as her king, or use his name once. Maybe she had second thoughts because he didn't reach out sooner. Before Bennie could think hard Angelica called to discuss a possible itinerary. Once again referring to him as Mr. Reeves, she would have his private plane ready to depart any time after Monday with eight hours' notice. Before the discussion ended Angelica clarified the scope of her duties. She'd arrange all aspects of travel, security, a barber for his locks, wardrobe, legal representation, storage of his car, plus upkeep of his home and business interests. For now Angelica needed to know was he taking the dog? Instead of answering that he had a more pressing question. Bennie explained a plan to sell his share in the Kleenit Laundry business and could she be of assistance. Angelica said she'd have the best options when they spoke on Monday.

Oddly, torturous thoughts weren't interrupting sleep tonight; it was revelations. At the risk of feeling like a bitch, Bennie was pissed Ronald hadn't called. Apparently, he was more concerned about Kayla than brotherhood, and twenty-five years of their history didn't matter. Thrills hopping the turnstile when the train came. Laughing until their sides ached. Copping a tray bag of weed and hearing Summer Madness and Voyage to Atlantis over the radio. Suddenly Bennie sat up, tilted his head to one side at the thought. He and Ronald were the last buddies from the stoop going through a friendship divorce.

As Mister's head turned Bennie imagined the dog called him a bitch ass. "What…you callin me a bitch ass…for real? That's what you're thinking," said Bennie aloud. Mister watched a bit longer then put his head down. Okay so why wouldn't a guy call his married friend to let him know where their favorite stripper was working? He could've gone alone but it's more fun with your friends Bennie thought. Hell as kids they'd stand near the door of the bar on 145th for a peek at the women inside. The fact is Ronald needed no encouragement to cheat on Lorraine.

Because Bennie was being honest an inner voice as real as his own said, "a real friend would encourage Ronald not to go, but you wanted to get even with Lorraine." It was a moment of clarity followed by shame. If you know your friend is an alcoholic don't meet at the bar. Understanding he could have been a better friend, Ronald would get a larger family discount, but the divorce was moving ahead. So Monday morning Bennie told Angelica Mister was going with him. Also, he instructed her to contact Ronald. If he could manage the "For Old Times Discount Price" fine, if not she was to find another investor.

About noon Bennie got a call and let the machine answer. It was Ronald sounding disturbed, wanting to talk about the sale. Not long after he called back, and Bennie answered.

"Yo Ben, a woman name Seale says she's working for you and you're selling out?" he asked.

"I'm getting out yeah."

"Dude…you could have said something," Ronald said sounding hyper.

"Ron, I told you I was selling Friday."

"Yeah well, I thought you were just…just talking," he said. The final straw was hearing Lorraine in the background.

"Ron listen, let your lawyer look at what I proposed. You can be the sole owner with a small amount down with monthly installments until the balance is paid. It's more than fair so sign the papers dude! But I'm out! You hear me Ron, I'm out!" said Bennie firmly. Lorraine was in the background saying she knew this was going to happen. When Ronald didn't speak Bennie said, "Ron…I gotta go. Bottom line, you can have all for yourself or take a partner, it's up to you buddy. You hear me?"

"Yeah," said Ronald ending the call.

In less than 72 hours Bennie's stress from avoidance to some extent was relieved. He put the phone down and breathed a sigh of relief as the dog's head tilted. Mister was right again; he had been acting like a bitch ass. From this day Bennie wasn't going to languish with challenging issues. Whatever was going to happen was going to happen. Inaction is a waste of time. A season that lasted for many years between best friends was over. At least the divorce didn't end with a restraining order.

Thursday evening Bennie dressed in a brown suit leaving the two top buttons open on his way to the airport. The driver was a man and the woman sitting in the back was Angelica Seale. She was the driver who took Bennie to meet Whende last month. On the way Angelica talked of the ways Ronald's deal could be structured. He'd refused them all including the no money down offer. Reluctantly Bennie sold his interest to an investor from Spain.

Inside the airport away from the passenger terminals was a fenced in dog park where Bennie took Mister. Afterwards they drove inside a cargo hanger, stopping close to the steps of the plane. Before getting out Bennie signed the papers and boarded. The flight attendant led him to the seating area. Behind that was a long couch which converted to a bed. While Bennie looked at the menu, the captain introduced himself and headed for the cockpit. Mister relaxed on the couch when the attendant asked if he was ready to leave.

Cruising for the first time higher than commercial flights Bennie saw the curvature of the earth. Even at that altitude regrets found their way. His hope was at the end of their talk he'd get Lizzy's forgiveness. Instead Bennie lied again when he pretended not to love her anymore. He honestly believed it was kinder to let her go now. There were bound to be more questions, and the truth would sound like a lie anyhow. On the other hand, what would have happened if they were married with children and Whende showed up, what then?

Meanwhile Mister relaxed allowing the crew to pet him periodically. But halfway through the flight regret followed from the lives Bennie left behind. He and Ronald were friends so long they called each other brothers. A buddy who stepped in when no one else would. It was Ronald who fed Bennie after he hadn't eaten in several days. Then there was Kayla, she was a good woman too. So she stripped for a minute and quit that life. Ronald wasn't marrying her, why shouldn't Kayla marry a man who loved her even if he's white.

Sometime later Bennie requested a vodka martini. He reclined then stirred with an olive pierced straw and had a sip. Come to think of it his fake aunt wasn't so bad either. In her own way Thomasina kept him from losing his mind. She'd sing naked to Prince's Insatiable holding a forty-ounce of Old English as her microphone. Every time the song ended, she asked to hear it again. Thomasina could let go of a bad situation as if it were a hot potato in her hand.

After the last sip and olive Bennie had a sobering thought. He'd known Ronald for almost thirty years. Kayla more than a year, and Lizzy almost a year. Whende the queen with memory intact he'd known less than two weeks. Even he and his serial killer girlfriend were together more than a year. What if this reunion was the biggest mistake of his life? Bennie had the cabin light dimmed, took a seat by Mister, and stared at the darkness out the cabin window.

With the time change the plane landed after 4pm Friday. It looked like the people who guarded Whende at the park were outside the plane. Once Mister finished a short walk they were on the way. Just before the door closed Bennie was handed a sealed envelope. The note was from Whende which read, "Remember you are a friend. Tell no one who you are." As they traveled Bennie tried reading between the lines. Remember you are a friend. What is that supposed to mean? He flipped the paper over and back again. Being a woman's friend could mean several things. It could be either you were getting in, or you didn't stand a chance of getting in. So which friend was he?

He read the note four or five more times until the car slowed down. "We must've arrived," Bennie thought as his heart quickened and hands began to sweat. Men played drums as a group of men and women formed a gauntlet to the entrance. Ms. Aquino greeted them and led the way inside. Mister tried pulling away, but Bennie held tight to the leash. It resembled Whende's home thousands of years ago except for wall sockets and light fixtures. Mister's nails scraped the smooth floor while his stubby tail wagged like a windshield wiper on high speed. He'd caught her scent and tried to run ahead. Bennie heard Whende say, "Let him go."

Like the telephone conversation days prior Whende spoke a tiny bit. She was more interested in playing with Mister. "I'm glad to see you," she said and with a nod she continued, "You must be tired. Ms. Aquino take our guest to his quarters. I'll keep Mister this evening, and we will speak later."

"Sure, see you then," said Bennie as if he didn't care. While a man motioned him to follow, Bennie noticed Leah close by. From there he was taken to where Sonya and Jeff stayed months ago. The space had been redecorated, and the butterflies were gone except one above the doorway. After the man left, Bennie got a bottle of water and thought about what just happened. Whende didn't quite give him the cold shoulder, but something was off. She called the dog by name but didn't mention his, and why wasn't his daughter there?

It just so happened Bennie never saw Whende until the following morning. The reason being he'd only slept two hours Wednesday and was up early the next day. By evening Friday after landing and settling down jet lag crept in. Bennie meant to lay across that spacious bed just a minute never expecting aromatic linens could induce unwilling sleep. It was Saturday morning when Bennie woke in the same clothes he arrived.

Not long after Bennie wandered the halls until given directions to a high school sized gym. At one corner two women sparred atop a padded area with head protection, and open fingered fighting gloves. As he moved closer the ladies paused like lions spotting an injured buffalo. Mister ran to Bennie wagging his stubby tail while Whende removed a mouthguard and said, "Did you rest well?"

"Yes, yes I did," he replied not knowing how much to say in front of Leah.

"Good, we'll catch up this evening at dinner," Whende said dismissively. Before Bennie could say another word Whende said, "Mister sit!" Hearing that, the dog left Bennie for his spot by the edge of the mat. As Bennie left, Leah revealed a slight hint of desire and paid a price. Whende replaced the mouth guard then slammed Leah fiercely to the mat. "That's all for today," the queen said stepping over Leah.

Inside her chambers Mister watched Whende the way he'd watch Bennie for signs of distress. She stood on the balcony realizing what just transpired. Her irrational reaction could've broken Leah's neck. Sonya was still right even from the grave about human nature remaining constant over time. From the dawn of humanity sadness and laughter existed. Sexual desire absent love occurred, and jealousy was still unpredictable.

In his room Bennie imagined the women scuffling in their spandex and sports tops. Strangely Whende's combat skill made her desirable. Minutes later he got a call from his concierge Bassaw. It was Bassaw who led him to Sonya's old suite when he arrived. Bassaw was brown skinned, in his fifties, immaculately dressed, close cut hair with a full beard. When Bassaw came he ordered Bennie breakfast. Soon after, racks of clothes came and Bassaw proposed wardrobe ideas for the coming days. Between sips of coffee Bennie was custom fitted for each garment. Immediately after he went to the lower level of the suite where two women washed, oiled and retwisted his locks. About that time the queen called and Bassaw relayed her message. Dinner was at the Queen's table at 6pm.

At the concierge's urging Bennie wore a tan silk shirt with dark brown stitching accentuating the collar and sleeves. His pants and sandals matched the brown in the shirt and the finish was a simple necklace made of polished onyx beads. The ladies twisted Bennie's locks in a way making the length longer. While Baasaw brushed lint from a pant leg Bennie felt confident he'd never looked this good. The only thing missing was some funky walking out the door music. Just before time to leave he wondered would the night end with sex like the first time they met.

Now he followed Bassaw past statues of people chiseled in stone and some marble when his concerns grew. Turning right at the end of the hall Bennie wondered how Whende accumulated this wealth in such a short time? He remembered what she said back at the hotel about confronting wrongdoing. The audacity to think she, a black woman, could change the world. A few steps later Bennie questioned himself, what if she could?

Eventually they stopped in front of tall double doors. Bassaw pushed them open and closed them leaving Bennie alone. What kind of game is this woman playing he wondered? There not even a glass of water on the table, and that's when Whende came in. Casually dressed in fitted blue jeans with a white button-down blouse, but her hair was his focus. Her crown was simply six thick Goddess braids flowing past her shoulders. It was as if she went out of her way not to look like the royalty. Smiling she said, "I have a better place prepared for us. We'll eat and talk there." After taking her extended hand she led him to a smaller room with a table, two chairs, and two place settings.

"What are you drinking with your dinner?" she asked.

"Water's fine," he answered watching her fill both glasses.

"Please sit," she said removing the dome shaped metal covers from the plates as if it these simple acts were new. Bennie reached for the water while watching her suspiciously. Whende sat and breathed so deeply it caused her back to straighten and said,

"Bennie…nothing's changed. I stand by my word but I…we…we need to be sure…right? I'm being careful so I sent Tiffany away just for a few days you know, so we could…talk."

"So she's not here?" he asked disturbingly.

"No, but you will see her. I swear by it!" she said solemnly.

"I get it, it's an awkward situation." Disappointed, he put his hand under his chin and looked away momentarily. When their eyes met again Whende had "the stare;" the look women give then say nothing. Terri's came before they went to sleep. Kayla's, he thought probably had to do with love, while Lizzy's had to be about trust. One thing they all had in common was he never knew for sure. "I want you to see something… come!" she said getting up.

During the walk through the palace to the underground vault Bennie got another perspective on its dimension. Inside they passed items until Whende lingered at one table. She touched the cheek of a face carved in stone with her palm and said, "This was my father and that's my momma.

"Folks would say you look like she spit you out. That's a way of saying you look very alike," he clarified. Afterwards they wound up in front of a door with a keypad. Whende entered the code and went inside. She stopped in front of something tall covered by a white sheet. Bennie looked down at the wooden legs carved like lion's paws and his heart began racing. "Is this what I think it is?" he asked.

"Uncover it," she said enthusiastically. Gingerly he removed the sheet careful not to snag it and was flooded with memories.

As a child the first time Bennie saw a picture of The Great Pyramid of Giza in The World Book Encyclopedia, he dreamed of going there. With the return of Halley's Comet in 1986 he went. While there he visited an antique shop and met an old woman who seemed to be expecting him. Bennie saw what he assumed was a flat hourglass with dark grains of sand five feet high. For some reason he purchased the Obeni along with a chilling story behind it.

Candice Ali, the old woman, told her granddaughter Farisha to lock the front door while inviting Bennie to the kitchen. Candice said The Obeni took her father in 1910 when she was just a child. The sand inside was transparent and her father was inside and spoke to her. No one believed the little girl's story despite weeks of searching for her father's body. The Obeni was delivered to Bennie's room the following morning, and he believed it because Whende was speaking to him. She explained the particles came from larger fragments of a collision between two comets. Yemot's comet came every 76 years, but a guy named Halley named it after himself.

Many thousands of years ago Whende walked by a pool behind her house only to see the rippling image of a Bennie in the water. At first, she believed it was a spirit named Muadie, or in English, Squiggly Man.

With further dialogue Whende realized Bennie had one of four Obenies used as an entryway through time. Working only after sunrise and while Halley's comet is between the earth and sun. For some unknown reason Bennie and Whende were able to understand each other until he went into the Obeni. Once he was back in Egypt with her the language link was severed.

It was supposed to be a one-way trip for him so he could use knowledge of the future, but it didn't go as expected. Both he and Whende wound up back in his hotel room. Bennie was able to remember, but Whende suffered from a form of paralysis, and loss of memory as well. Believing her condition was permanent Bennie took her to his home to care for her. Now seven years later they were reunited at the same time, and in front of the Obeni.

Whende gave Bennie a box to open. Inside was a disc made from a larger fragment that fit into a slot on the top of the Obeni. Without this key of sorts the portal wouldn't open.

"This is it," said Bennie feeling it with his thumbs, "you know…I thought I'd lost my fucking mind…I did! And when I made you run away I,"

"It wasn't your fault," she interrupted.

"How many times I…I tried telling myself it was a…a hallucination," he said straining to speak.

"No, it happened. Kfaru the captain of the guard was going to have me killed and assume the throne, but you came back and saved me," Whende said placing her hand on his shoulder. Bennie stared at the grains behind the glass of the Obeni looking higher to the empty slot where the disc belonged. "You and I could tell a tale no one would ever believe," she said watching his reaction.

"You're right. If it didn't happen to me I'd never believe it," he said continuing to look over the Obeni.

"And I want to thank you for taking care of me when I wasn't myself. You came back for me like Shaft in the movies," she said grinning.

"What you know about Shaft?" he asked surprised.

"Shaft…don't talk about Shaft…shut ya mouth. Listen baby I been catching up on stuff, trust me, but really, I never got to say thank you" she said leaning closer.

"You're welcome," he said gazing at her.

"So what ya been up to or better yet what are you thinking right now, tell me?" she asked clutching his hand.

"It's funny you ask; I was thinking two things. Why women ask what we're thinking. The other one was sometimes you sound like Whende, then you sound…I don't know…regular," said Bennie trying to explain.

"Regular…honey ain't nothing about me regular!" she answered with a bit of arrogance. This was no time to act like a wuss, so he raised his voice a bit, "Then how you want me to say it?"

"Calm down man I get it. I'm who I was when you met me, and I'm a girl from Harlem who lived in the Bronx, and moved to Jersey baby," she said lightening the mood while being direct, "but seriously what do you think about us, tell me?"

"How do I say this?" he wavered.

"It's okay just tell me," she said reassuringly.

"See it's that…that right there! You never talked like that. What if you think I'm your brother. The look on your face after we kissed and you left, I can't let that happen again…no, no way," said Bennie shaking his head. Gripping him tighter Whende said, "It's not gonna happen and here's why. I know who I am, and I know who you are! You're the man who taught me English. Who took me inside the park, sat me on a big rock, and let me tell you it's nasty over there now, and told me I was having a baby, right?"

"Yeah?"

"When I did remember, which I'll tell you about that another time. By the way your book "Tales of the Obeni" filled in the blanks."

"You read it?" he interrupted.

"I did. You wanted to change history with knowledge of the future, and I'm ashamed to say it's why I went to bed with you. I wanted to know what you knew and I'm sorry for that. We had a…a what ya call it, a one-night stand," she said nudging him with her elbow. Bennie smiled at her effort to be funny before she said, "And we have a beautiful child, smart like her father."

"Thank you."

"You still hungry?"

"Naah."

"I think our first date went well," she said standing up. Her breath warmed his neck as he pulled her closer. "You shouldn't sleep alone tonight. I'll come to you within the hour," she said peeling away.

"Sounds good."

"Oh! I forgot to say, you look real good tonight," she said walking ahead with slightly more movement in her hips.

At the suite Bennie kicked off the sandals, removed his pants and shirt, rolled those clothes in a ball and tossed it in the closet. He gargled then watched himself in the mirror. He thought about lying across the bed, but it was too presumptuous, maybe later. There was a CD of Anita Baker, so he played it while turning some lights off to create a welcoming atmosphere and waited. Whende knocked but she wasn't alone.

"Mister…go on," she said as the dog walked past.

"What…I thought you were…" he said pausing.

"Oh, you thought I was…no not now. We have more to consider but it feels good to know you still desire me. When I'm ready to receive you, you'll know," she said kissing him lightly on the lips. Bennie watched Whende leave, having no clue their second date would resemble the meeting between the Queen of Sheba, and King Solomon.

In the morning Bennie went to the room behind the double doors to meet Whende. For hours a corporate board meeting of sorts took place with questions, reflections, and intentions. With a stack of books in arms reach and water by her side, she urged him to sit and went back to reading. Her braids were out so all the hair was stuffed under a twisted head wrap. Whende closed the book and held her hand on the cover as if the words were being absorbed. They were slave narratives from the book Bullwhip Days, and that's where her lesson commenced.

Whende asked Bennie if her intellect was still attractive to him and if so, they had to write this phase of their story together. Because he'd written embarrassing moments about her and others, he must do the same about himself. No doubt this moment she spoke as Queen Sakatet, and it wasn't a request.

She placed the book near the rest while telling him what she'd read. It was a slave woman tied to a tree being whipped by her Misses. This slave said it was the worst whipping she'd ever gotten. Basically, this black woman told the Misses if the situation were reversed, she'd never treat her this bad causing her Misses to stop. For this and other reasons, Whende would adjust her plans for worldwide retribution. Whether Bennie was ready or not she'd explain with historical facts and common sense.

Whende said violence, injustice and devastation will spread like the universe. She was born when 96% of people on Samae, an ancient name for earth, were dark skinned. A question to Bennie was did he know if he knew Homo Sapiens first walked in Africa, what she called Alkebulica. When he agreed she tied that fact to the story of Moses, a Hebrew mistaken for an Egyptian. Finally conveying she was Egyptian which meant Moses looked like her family, not Charlton Heston. The entire Bible was written about cities within Africa, and who was responsible for bringing the written word to the masses? King James, a Black king.

Before going on, Whende shared the story of a man from the book she'd put aside. His thumbs were cut off for learning to read and from there she pivoted to the Bible posing a question without requiring an answer. If Jesus was a man of color who couldn't be told apart from his disciples, it would make Judas a Black man who betrayed him.

Letting that sink in she went on to the Black people who killed Malcolm X. Pressing on according to Steve Cokely, Jesse Jackson would show up for meetings he wasn't asked to attend. Cokely said with some documentation Jesse pointed in a direction away from the real killers of King. Whende told Bennie she read "I Know Why the Caged Bird Sings" and spoke about the Black man who raped young Maya Angelou. The point being made was African people were quite capable of aiding in their destruction.

For that reason, she'd alter her original plan for violence acknowledging all the so-called races were her descendants. Intrigued, Bennie asked for an explanation which wasn't complex at all. Exercise or absence thereof are human physical changes promptly visible. Overeating, or lack of food, was another of her many examples. So it was reasonable for skin color, noses, lips, and hair to have everything to do with climate, diet, and territory, bringing her to the next point in her lecture.

As a royal duty and the oldest matriarch of humanity Whende searched for solutions. The question, what role did her ancestors play on the road to fratricide, and when did it start? For that reason, Whende wouldn't seek justice by murder, at least not right away. She was concerned about a greater issue that scared her more, annoying Samae. Whende said if humanity continues deforestation, contaminating the water and air, the spirit of earth itself could shake us off like dust.

Continuing to snack on fruit and wine he noted Whende wasn't speaking with mannerisms of a modern woman like before. Deciding this encounter was adequate she sat back in the chair to say, "Our conversation went well, and I enjoyed our time together. It's why I became so fascinated with you."

"Honey I could listen to you for hours," he said placing his hand on top of hers. She responded by caressing the side of his hand with her thumb and said, "I know what you're thinking Bennie."

"Do you? So what happens now?" he said grinning as if they were going to have sex.

"Tomorrow we'll talk about you and me. What you want…and what I expect from my king," she answered hopefully. Like an executive concluding a board meeting, she crossed her arms and sat back until he left.

Back in his quarters there was nothing to do but contemplate what went down. Not only was Mister gone, Bennie felt dismissed and alone. She knew what he needed, and she seemed ready too. Instead Whende toyed with him. She had the nerve to order him around and for that she'd pay. He'd act as if it didn't matter one way or the other, but when it happened, he'd be the one doing the teasing.

At night his thoughts became drips like old times keeping sleep at bay. Bennie respected her disregarding vengeance to work on a different strategy because the people of this world were her family. Like Malcolm X, self-defense stayed a priority with apology. He learned the impact Sonya had on her life and how she died making her insistence on him having a negative test.

There was so much to learn Bennie's chest was tight with doubt. Whende said it was imperative he learn the politics of being king plus speak and read Egyptian. When her father was Bennie's age he fought alongside his men. So, Bennie needed to possess a high level of combat skill which she'd teach privately. Finally arranging for him to beat down one of the guards so the rest would respect his authority. Was he sure he wanted to be a father when some Black men chose Atari over changing a diaper?

Whende spoke of subliminal messages written by Hollywood directors starting from "Birth of a Nation" to present day sitcoms. She felt the way he did about Good Times; it was funny at first until you analyze the premise. A Black family of five in an apartment who couldn't pool their money to make a better life. Ain't we lucky we got' em. It wasn't smart for George Jefferson to leave his home to pay rent on a deluxe apartment in the sky.

Bennie turned over to think of something else, but it was no use. Shortly before the 1400s a blatant and subliminal assault has rained down on mostly people of color, the poor, and women. The chains disappeared but if the profits from ideas and labor aren't distributed fairly it's still slavery. Whende predicted it was going to get worse but that wasn't what bothered Bennie. He'd gone along with the program for years, but she came to her right mind and was ready to act. Was he ready to match this woman's courage and honesty?

Another quality Bennie admired was her candor. From their first encounter in 1986 Whende answered his questions honestly without hesitation. Today he found out her father was a combat leader. Not only must Bennie learn to speak and write her language, but he also needed battle training equivalent to hers. Would he be the man she was expecting and a good father? It was turning out to be another sleepless night like so many others.

On the other side of the palace Whende was fidgety in bed as well. Bennie's willingness to listen for hours had been an aphrodisiac. Without him noticing she'd glanced at his shoulders, lips, and locks only to imagine their bare skin against each other. Now alone the urge to be with him mixed with many questions.

The man she desired was less than four generations from being a slave himself. How much of that mentality remained? Could he reject that ingrained mindset to accept freedom? It would be the first time a captive chose to stay.

As her king he'd become the richest man in the world. Unlimited resources and influence will eventually divulge Bennie's actual nature. Could he become far worse after taking control? Will he ask her to shave her underarms? Would she be enough to satisfy a modern man, or would his eyes wander? Does he still think about Lizzy? Will she have to use relaxer in her hair to be more pleasing, or will he find her scars revolting?

Whende relaxed until the questions subsided. Later a memory of his lips on her skin brought back a conversation with Sonya. She was right; breasts weren't just for babies, and before she could stop her feet were on the floor. Exerting pressure with her hands Whende kept those knees together. All she had to do was throw caution away and have this need satisfied, but critical topics hadn't yet been addressed. With a hard gulp she laid back down and prayed Bennie's test came back negative.

Early in the morning Whende called in a tone Bennie never heard. It was a voice stuttering with timidity and submissiveness. She admitted her thoughts were of him last night and asked did he think of her. When he said he did she sounded relieved. After the morning workout she requested their next date be in his suite. Whende was leaving the arrangements to him, even the time she should come. Not to seem desperate Bennie waited several seconds before saying any time after 4pm. As soon as the call ended, the phone rang only for Whende to say both of their tests were negative. Stevie Wonder could see this was a signal. She was leaving everything to him, so they were damn sure having sex tonight.

Meanwhile Leah entered the gym like a shy little girl. Today Whende wanted to punch and kick the heavy bag instead of sparring. Once sweat flowed Leah broke the silence by asking had she unknowingly angered the queen. Instead of an answer Leah got a sincere apology for the other day followed by their twenty-lap run around the gym.

Bennie began mapping and strategizing after the second phone call. The menu should exclude foods that cause bad breath or gas like beans, broccoli, garlic, and onions. Whende wasn't coming here to talk not the way she sounded. She played her game. Now it was his turn. With years of accumulated knowledge, he'd take the pawns and have this queen tonight. The CD player was programed with Anita, and this new group called Next. They'd dance to "Too Close," and while they were up slow dance to "Cozy." Chaka's "Sweet Thing" was good as they talked, and when all that was said, some Luther.

Continuing preparation, a crucial detail needed to be worked into his strategy. Bennie had ideas of making low interest mortgage loans and scholarships to HBCUs. They're making cameras small enough to catch corrupt individuals in authority. The CIA and FBI use those tactics; now it was time to turn to tables and level the playing field.

With strategic ideas and Whende's fearlessness they just might be able to do it, and then came a knock at the door.

So not to appear anxious Bennie waited with his hand on the knob. Gradually he opened the door and one word escaped his mouth, "Daaaamn!" Whende was indescribably beautiful. With barely any makeup her coco skin gave an elegant luster. Her hair was as perfect as her ears. In a silk dress the color of gold if Whende had feet he wouldn't have known. All the hours of prep were worth the gaze in his eyes then she asked, "Are you going to invite me in?"

"Of course…come in." Stopping just long enough to kiss him before passing by. Bennie watched a Queen's stride like a slow-motion movie before closing the door. Her fragrance beckoned him to follow. So absorbed Bennie never noticed the small overnight bag she placed by the foyer. "I like what you've done with the place," she said jokingly as he came closer.

"Thank you, I had some help," said Bennie gleefully.

"I meant to tell you yesterday, your hair has grown nicely. I like it, and you have a beautiful smile" she said twirling two locks between her fingers.

"Thank you," he said placing the other hand on her waist.

"What made you grow them?"

"I always wanted to, so I did."

"Okay there was something else. Last night was our third date not our second," she said squeezing his shoulder.

"How do you figure?"

"Well, you remember our first meeting. We made love and it almost happened again last night."

"Really?" he said kissing the corner of her mouth.

"Ooooh yes…I was this close to coming over," said Whende holding two fingers apart.

"What stopped you?" he asked, kissing the opposite side.

"I knew we had more to talk about before…you know," she said feeling his heartbeat with her palm.

"You're right. Let me tell you what I've been thinking about. Make yourself comfortable," he said, thinking how strange it was to say when everything belonged to her.

Whende sat on the couch while Bennie poured glasses of iced tea. He placed hers on the end table then asked, "How are you?"

"I'm good as you can see," Whende answered assertively.

"No! I mean how have you been? You said you lost someone. What was the name?"

"Sonya…her name was Sonya," she said with a painful pause.

Bennie waited until Whende shared how close they were and how she felt alone after her death. He learned how Sonya watched over her all those years. Lastly Sonya taught Whende forgiveness by showing it to the man who gave her the virus. It was one of the reasons Whende put plans of carnage aside. About the time her voice started cracking she went to the bathroom to compose herself. In her absence he realized she'd never laughed or cried in his presence.

Whende returned wanting to change the subject so Bennie shared thoughts from last night. He talked about building Think Tanks comprised of the brightest intellectual minds in the world. The Tanks would focus on tech, medicine, clean energy, plus legal and financial affairs. She was intrigued so he resumed.

Bennie touched on reeducation for every age and racial group tying his point with of all things, Holocaust survivors. It's inconceivable those Jews would ever let their children be taught by the Nazis who tried exterminating them. So why do black people turn their kids over to former slave owners to be taught? A new and innovative form of schooling was required, but competent teachers weren't used.

What Bennie proposed aroused Whende which was the intention. She kicked off her sandals and sat cross legged exposing more of her inner thigh. While he continued, she nodded in agreement, periodically taking peripheral glimpses of his crotch. Later she rested a hand on his and the conversation turned extremely serious.

"From this moment I speak truth to you," she said solemnly.

"And so will I…I promise," Bennie said noting the ocean blue color of her nails matched the stones in her necklace. What Whende said next came from hearing Black women disparage Black men calling them dogs and useless children.

"I want you to know I need you and I believe you will rule with the wisdom of Solomon. And we will grow old together," she said. With her next breath she was about to ask was he over Lizzy. Tenderly Bennie said, "I love you Whende."

"Neia abeir Bennie ent nench nirainta," Whende whispered, "I love you Bennie, with all my heart."

A heartfelt embrace was disrupted by a knock on the door. Bennie wheeled the cart inside and set the music on play. Coaxing Whende to her feet they had a first dance to tender melodies. Her fragrance was pleasurable and familiar. They explored each other. It was about to happen midway into "A House is Not a Home." Whende stepped back, snatched her bag and went to the bathroom. "Luther never fails," said Bennie to himself.

While she was doing whatever, he dimmed some lights and took off his shirt. Bennie envisioned walking her to the bedroom. Hell, they might end up on the couch or right there on the floor. Rubbing his hands together he thought of kissing her ankles and working north or starting from New York to Virginia. Whatever happened she was going to have her socks knocked off.

Inside the bathroom perceptible aging peered from a mirror with tiny wrinkles of stress. Whende was still a young woman, but the years were beginning to show. Changing into something more revealing, she was convinced Bennie would make a good father. Every question posed had been answered and with her guidance he would become a great leader. Satisfied there was no mistake, she took a ring from her bag, placing it on the sink. Remembering the intensity of their first night together, Whende was finally ready.

Seconds passed before Whende came out to Bennie lounging on the couch. She went to him slowly like a bride down the aisle standing within reach. Her gown tied loosely at the middle and a shorter garment underneath. The material so sheer it was like looking at her naked body through fog. Just when he had asked her to model, she asked, "what happened to the music?"

"I just want to hear you…nothing else," Bennie said reaching after the familiar feeling of excitement developed.

"I have something for you."

"I'm ready Whende," he said reaching for her.

"Wait! It's my father's ring," she said placing it in his hand. The top of the ring was a flat circle with three ridges on top. It was the shiniest most unique piece of gold he'd ever seen. Whende moved close so their legs touched. His pinky was too small, but it fit the left-hand ring finger perfectly.

"You said this was your father's ring?" he asked looking up at her.

"It was…now it belongs to you. All that you see…belongs to you my love…my king," she said twiddling the tie of her outer garment.

Normally he'd be ready to receive loving, but the weight to the ring withered his excitement. With this new responsibility came tension and Bennie wasn't focusing on the task at hand, but Whende wasn't hesitant. She removed the first garment and straddled him on the couch. He squeezed those cheeks as they kissed but couldn't get out of his own mind. In an earlier conversation the fate of an insubordinate guard was left for him to decide. The usual penalty was death so would it be weakness if he let the man live?

Wet kisses, fondling, and dry humping changed nothing. Bennie was nervous like a guilty man walking into a police station. Soon she'd know something was wrong and what would she think? Stalling for time he coaxed her to the bedroom all the while wishing he'd let the music play to drown out these thoughts. One thing hadn't changed, Whende was gorgeous and her kisses sweet. Undressing each other Bennie left a tingle and things began to happen. It had been months since he'd had sex. Ultimately, he found his way inside the queen's chamber, and it was good, too good. "Yes…yes my king…yes," said Whende in his ear. There was nothing Bennie could do. It was over in less than sixty seconds.

Chapter 20

What ended abruptly earlier was overlooked and they'd spend the next two days at each other's side. Absence of tension they shared beliefs, emotions, spooned, made love, slept, ate, and made love again. There came an instant of belly aching laughter when he told the shortest joke in the world. There was a lion…around. In silence Whende waited and when she didn't get it he said, "lying around, get it…lying…around!" It was solely his serious expression that made her burst into laughter. She'd compose herself only to see his expression and laugh again. Another first added to an unforgettable night.

That first night if they weren't listening to music, they were on the balcony peering up at the stars. She spoke of her mother dying shortly after her birth. How she'd have conversations with a stone bust of her mom Queen Kymeka. She went on about losing Sonya to the virus and the ensuing loneliness. It was clear Sonya was more than a friend and when she strained to get words out, he held her.

Ronald was alive, still Bennie spoke of loneliness and losing a close friend over bullshit. It was always his hope the fellas from the block remained close and their offspring would do the same. Long before Bennie left it was clear that wouldn't happen. Later he confessed his role in the damage to their friendship. They talked about the insanity of using nuclear weapons and Whende seeing the Blue Pearl photo, earth taken from space. She said the world was like a huge fish tank and humanity was fouling the waters. Affirming faith in God the Creator she said He will not change, it's our perspective of Him that changes. Bennie wouldn't understand what she meant until years later.

The next day their discussion was on Ralph Ellison, Nicki Giovanni, Sojourner Truth, and Bennie's parents. This evening she rested her head on his chest while he caressed her hair, she had a question. Did he like her hair? His answer was he loved it! He could run his fingers through it and massage her scalp. Whende didn't understand the statement but would in time.

Drowsiness came followed by contagious yawns. Bennie kept touching her hair and she went to sleep on his shoulder. Once Whende turned over the snoring began. A cross between smacking lips and pig grunts. When it was no longer amusing, Bennie sat in a lounge chair near the bed. Eventually he'd go to the balcony and look at the night sky.

Whende had advice about leadership and some he'd find useful. It's a short path from insubordination to insurrection, she warned. It was crucial to deal publicly with the guard, but death for disobedience was too extreme. Bennie believed detention, a jail of sorts to serve as a warning was better. If he put his plan for the guard into action it had to work. At the same time Bennie had a warning. Every organization Black folk created was infiltrated and sabotaged from within. It was remarkable this secret lasted so long.

There also came another revelation different from the night before. In the same way her speech pattern fluctuated from royal to modern, so were her moments. Nobel Whende's body rippled as if floating on calm waters. Concluding with a deep exhale after each wave. So refined you'd think nothing happened, but the other woman wasn't restrained. Tonight, a section of the palace may have heard the yeahs, the that's it, and the don't stops.

Against the stone guardrail stale beer and exhaust fumes were a thing of the past. Bennie touched the top of the ring spinning it on his finger when she came out. The woman who fought like Tyson days before trembled in his arms from a nightmare. Whende dreamt some woman tried drowning her in a tub. Oddly she described Terri catching her in the bathroom at Bennie's house in Harlem. Was it a flashback, or did it come from reading his Obeni book? She asked the name of the lady who poured liquid soap in his fish tank. Hesitantly he said her name was Terri and she had been murdered years ago. Quickly Bennie told what he knew of Terri's murder spree. When he finished, Whende was about to ask about Lizzy but didn't. It wasn't until a tiny sliver pressed through the bottom of a dark horizon did Whende finally settle down. Eventually they went back to bed sleeping a few hours till morning.

When they were ready to leave Bennie was taking Mister for a morning walk. Whende had responsibilities so they'd meet back in a few hours. As she went to the door to leave Bennie, got startling news. Tomorrow afternoon Tiffany will be back. Now he's the one nervous and stammering. He couldn't believe she'd say that and leave so Bennie had questions. What was the plan? What should he say or not say? Did Tiffany know about The Obeni? Amused, Whende said Tiffany saw the Obeni and was told what it did. To her it was a child's fairytale like Santa and that's how they left it. The plan was she would introduce Bennie and back up what he says to Tiffany. Whende cautioned their daughter was intelligent for almost seven, so don't make his story sound unbelievable. Before he could think she kissed him and walked away.

The older you get the faster years flow past. It was like yesterday Bennie held Tiffany in Harlem Hospital after Whende gave birth. He almost blurted out in front of the nurse and Linda he had a daughter. A hasty lie they were siblings to get her passport caused sleepless nights for years. The last time Bennie saw the baby she was four months, now she'd be almost seven. Unlike how time dragged in expectation of Whende spending the night, the call to meet Tiffany seemed almost immediate.

By now Bennie knew his way around so no escort was needed. At first sight Tiffany had his mother's eyes. "Tiffany…there's someone I want you to meet. This is Benjamin Reeves," Whende said happily.

"It's nice to see you."

"Hello Mr. Reeves, it's nice to meet you too," said Tiffany. Her voice is concise and authoritative like her mom. Unpredictably like removing a band-aid Whende said,

"Mr. Reeves came all the way here just to tell you something important."

Trying not to sound nervous he said, "I'm…your father."

Tiffany stepped toward her mother and said, "My father is dead." If he was going to take charge, he may as well start now. Bennie gestured for Whende to wait and said,

"She thought I was, but it was a mistake. It's not her fault. And I didn't know about you…I mean I didn't know how to find you…you all. I thought you were…" stopping himself from saying dead.

"Your father didn't know where we were baby. We moved and he's been looking for us all this time," said Whende quickly.

"Mommy you didn't know where he lived?"

"Baby you remember mommy couldn't remember."

"I thought we were running away from him. I heard you and Auntie talking one night and you cried," said Tiffany searching for the truth in her mother's eyes.

"No baby I wasn't afraid of your father. Believe me…he's a good man."

"How about we shake hands first."

Tiffany held his hand with a hint of delight.

"We'll take it one day at a time. Is that alright with you?"

"I guess," she said after mom's approval. Tiffany came for a hug, Bennie was reluctant to give for fear he'd never let go. He settled for a short one before pulling away and asking,

"Now I have a question for you. Can you skate?"

"Sure can and I can skate backwards! What about you?" Tiffany said smirking.

"I fell when I was a kid and never tried again, but it looks like fun."

"We skate in the gym and it's sooo much fun!" she answered.

"I fell when I was your age and never tried again, but you're right it looks like a lot of fun. I saw people skating outside at Central Park and I wished I could do it," he said somberly.

"I could teach you," she said looking at mom again.

"You would? Thank you…the three of us could do it together!" he said as his daughter's smile grew.

"It's a perfect idea," said Whende.

Bennie leaned closer and said, "I'm glad to be your father." All at once Tiffany dashed to hug him again. A few moments are defined as your happiest, now he had two. The first when he saw this newborn, and right now. With closed eyes he hugged back restraining tears. Only her mother saw one tear which he quickly wiped away. A family reunited today remained together until late evening. Finally in the solitude of his room Bennie cried with joy.

Every week after, he'd encounter the so-called expanding weight of one who wears the crown. Each morning Whende spoke to Bennie in her ancient tongue. There were daily surveillance reports on persons of interest. Legions of men and women under his command. Statements showing their wealth topped Mansa Musa, an African king from the 12th century reported to be the richest person to ever live. Bennie could spend a billion a day for the rest of his life, but money didn't matter.

He was determined to make up for everyday away from his child. If they didn't eat breakfast, he'd always make it for dinner. There was time for a skating lesson with Whende and Tiffany. They rolled around the gym to a playlist Bennie had made for the occasion. When he fell, Tiffany came over like the calvary and called him daddy for the first time.

Several weeks passed and Bennie began calling Whende during night. Not to have phone sex like new couples, but to share potential ideas.

Mister's behavior changed during that time. Like he caught a whiff of Whende in the car months ago, he remembered the scent of her baby becoming her new bodyguard. At night he'd sleep in front of her doorway, so you had to step over him to enter. And if his bed was moved, he'd drag it back to the same spot.

Additional disclosures came towards the end of August with Tiffany's guardian Ms. Aquino. Unknowingly, Bennie spoke to her several times on his first trip to Cairo in 1996. At the time Ms. Aquino disguised herself as a maid. Normally she'd be in the hall when he came and went. One day he asked if she ever took a day off? She'd simply say in broken English, "room clean you want?"

There was also Mr. West who got Bennie out of jail for hiding in the Cairo Museum after hours. It was Mr. West again who arranged for Whende's passport, and private jet so Bennie could take her to the United States. Mr. West and Aquino weren't the only people in this weird reunion. The doctor who gave Whende the first vaccinations years before was on Sonya's medical team. Over the years there were dozens of people rotating around so Bennie never knew he was being watched. Now all of them were under his authority.

New responsibilities softened Bennie's criticism of President Clinton and other leaders. His insomnia returned not from past shame, but from encouraging predictions. Adding to sleeplessness was comprehending how this woman would trust him so much? His faith allowed women keys to the crib, but not credit cards and passwords. Now with limitless wealth he wasn't thinking of expensive cars, giant yachts, and super models. For Bennie it was about demonstrating competency to lead.

Whende was grateful Bennie took his role seriously. She was tolerant of night calls to share ideas, but he was forgetting something. So next time Whende hinted she'd come see him and he totally missed it. After dinner they would kiss, and he would leave. The next night he called to say he was scheduling Judo and kick boxing three days a week for two hours. A few days later he called about alternative energy and investments in the media. Yawning, Whende asked when they were going to speak to their child about sharing the bedroom. Bennie agreed while not sounding enthusiastic. Why didn't he want to be with her again? Not long after she bid him a good night and hung up the phone.

By mid-September the weight of the crown grew with bruises from training. Added were the usual reports, skating, and evening dinner. Whende kissed his cheek after dinner and followed that up with a look.

Had Black women used it to make men crazy since time began? So Bennie said, "what?"

"Nothing," she said continuing the stare. as if there was more.

"No...tell me...what?" thinking Whende found an idea worth discussing.

"It's nothing," she answered leaving him standing there.

On the other side of the palace Bennie tried making sense of the look while going over tomorrow's schedule and paperwork. Fidgeting with what was now his ring he went over a new checklist. He was devoted to this dynasty, to Whende, and his child. He confined the defiant guard for a year instead of taking his life. He was strengthening his body and focusing not to slip back to uncaring ways. Still thinking what more could be done, he got into bed. Finally it registered, an assignment overlooked, a house call.

Bennie freshened up, went to the other side of the palace, and lightly knocked. He asked Whende if Tiffany was asleep in the adjacent room? Hearing a yes, he kissed her at once. Forgetting to close the door she took him to her room. Hungerly, they kissed before forcefully pushing her backwards on the bed. There was no questioning her look as they undressed. There'd be no quick finish tonight. Grabbing her ankles, he pulled her to the edge of the mattress. Just before linking he said, "Neia abeir."

"I love you too," said Whende. She tried pulling his arms, but he remained slightly distant. This wasn't the deep connection she recalled.

"Come on!" Whende said.

"Shuuu...I'll get there."

This dynasty wasn't going to fall because he paused appointments to spend time with Whende. In some ways it was more important emotional needs were met. Money can't buy love, and the love of money can be the worst addiction. Whende put him in charge so the next morning he spoke with Tiffany at breakfast. Bennie said he loved her mother and for lack of a better phrase they were getting married. Taking a chance he asked permission and Tiffany gave it. After which he announced he'd be with her mom at night in the next room. That same day Bennie moved a few items while Whende met with the architect to redesign the space. After dinner he sat by Tiffany's bed with Mister close by until she was asleep.

You quickly learn a person's nature when sharing the same space. Are they restless, temperamental, or just distant. Whende's perspective of the world in this time was unique. She was a 34-year-old Black woman born thousands of years ago in the time of Pharaohs. Now she'd seen photos of Earth taken from space and craters on the moon. Horse-drawn chariots and torch lights were no more. News took months to travel, now misinformation can go around the world in a matter of seconds. Back then the entire population was over three million, now in 1993 it was five and a half billion people. Pollution and disregard for the Earth, which she called Samae, frightened Whende. Comparing humanity to parasites Samae could just shake us off.

With pure transparency Whende confessed to grappling with two personalities. Remembering Sonya had her speaking as Linda. The thought of her real family caused her to behave royally. With that Whende placed her hand on Bennie's cheek, looked him in the eyes and said, "I should tell you why the captain of my guard Kfaru wanted to kill you. The night I was going to offer myself to him he spurned me for my hand maiden and I…I waited for him to leave and I…killed her. In the morning I saw your image in the water of my pool. I thought you were a spirit come to judge me. So when Kfaru found us in bed he wanted you dead. The only way I could save you was by saying I'd do it."

"What the fuck?" he thought to himself. Even then murder and jealousy were accomplices. He wouldn't think of asking was that the only person she murdered. Hell, Whende could take him out with her bare hands, and he couldn't stop her. "I want you to know I am sorry for what I did, and I wouldn't do it again except, you know…self-defense, or someone's after my family…you know," she said seeking compliance.

"Okay," said Bennie slowly looking away.

"And if you're wondering…that's your child. You're the only one I've been with," she said intently. Without responding, Whende pulled his arm around her waist spooning with him. "There's one more thing you need to know," she said calmly. Holding his wrist tightly she took the deepest breath and released it.

"I can't have any more children," she said regretfully.

"It's alright," he said instinctively holding her tight. They lay in silence for a while and after Whende yawned she said, "I've got a few ideas for the new book and maybe a title. I used to write. Well the scribers chiseled what I told them but it's the same."

"Another book might bring us unwanted attention," said Bennie sounding reserved.

"I mean who's gonna believe it…nobody. Besides, we don't have to stay in this palace, there are others…okay?" said Whende, like he had no choice.

"Sure, sounds good," he replied cautiously. The following week he doubled his workouts. Whende lay still wondering what he thought. Soon she'd tell Bennie the most difficult confession but not tonight.

Every few minutes Bennie moved away until he lay on his back predicting sleeplessness. He could deal with no more children, but that murder bomb she casually dropped was different. What were the odds he'd fall for another killer, unfuckingbelievable, that's what they are. He'd accepted her father's ring, the money, the title, and that ass. There was no getting away. This was reminiscent of the day Terri asked, "are you sure this is what you want Bennie?" The difference was a child was in the mix. So as Whende snored, one word became the latest drip pounding his skull. Un-fucking-believable, un-fucking-believable, un-fucking-believable, un-fucking-believable!

Morning came with Whende's expressionless gaze upon him. He wondered how long she'd been watching him. It was reminiscent of Terri's behavior and a bit creepy. In the middle of him stretching she asked if he loved her. After a reasonable delay Bennie said yes. Whende head rested on his chest for a bit then she got up as if last night's confessions had no significance.

During breakfast while Whende spoke with Tiffany Bennie sought justification for the crime of murder. He reasoned the hand maiden's death occurred thousands of years ago. It wasn't like she killed her yesterday and the body was hidden in a closet. What mattered was she was sorry and wanted to change. He drank some water, kept eating and recalled an earlier conversation. It was Whende who rejected his ideas for reprisals against the Klan. Her response was they can't kill everybody. So by evening lying side by side Bennie made peace with it.

Whende broke her routine for the next couple of days. She didn't go to the gym or do the customary hours of historical research. Instead, she took a breather and listened to a playlist Bennie compiled. The list was entitled "Chillin," comprising select tracks of Earth Wind and Fire, Steve Wonder "Innervisions," Ronnie Laws, Frankie Beverly, and The Isley Brothers ending with Ramsey Lewis's "Sun Goddess." Whende listened to those tracks until she knew them, especially "That's the Way of the World."

During that time a non-sexual intimacy surfaced when couples stay together begging the question, was it always like this between men and women? For instance Whende prepared her hair before bed tying it up with a scarf or wrap. She'd remove a small amount of makeup and sometimes tend to her nails and feet. A surprise came while Bennie brushed his teeth and Whende came in to use the toilet. He took it as just another couple's sign.

One night he left the bathroom Whende sat in a chair scraping the dead skin from the sole of her foot. Suddenly she sparked a conversation about branding slaves, tying that into Blacks obsessed with brand names. Her theory that freed people could use their money to brand themselves was jaw dropping, but there was more. Whende had one last confession worse than murder, as far as she was concerned. She stopped tending to her foot and let out a deep sigh. Bennie noticed as queen she spoke with authority. Only when the two personalities conflicted would she stutter.

"There's…there's something else I never told you about…about your rights as king. I…I can't give you more children. Sooo…so it's your right to take…to take another. Please don't choose any women in the palace," said Whende refusing to look at him. Bennie first thought was to say he'd had his share of women plus two more guys' share. There was nothing new left to do at this stage in life. His focus was on more important matters, so he said nothing. When she looked up he replied, "Okay."

"What?" she answered. Bennie pretended to forget something in the bathroom and left. Soon as he came back she said, "So you want…more children?"

"Well let's see," he answered getting in bed, "just to be clear, do you mean artificial insemination, or can I do it the natural way. What are my choices?" Before Whende could answer he laughed and said, "I'm joking with you baby. For real…I'm just messing with you."

"You don't want more children?" she asked, not observing the humor.

"Our child is enough sweetheart," he said caressing her shoulder.

"You're sure?"

"We could always adopt."

"Sooo…you were toying with me?"

"Whende you shoulda seen ya face especially when I said how, artificial insemination or the natural way," he said grinning, "you are enough sweetheart." Bennie leaned in for a kiss and she backed away.

"I see my king's got jokes," she said heading to the bathroom.

That night Whende's competitive nature demanded recompence for his humor, coming back with a plan. She'd sprinkled that fragrance from their first night together and got back in bed. Pausing between kisses she went down to his navel, stopped and grinned. Before Bennie said anything she laid on top of him. When he urged her into position Whende resisted, allowing just enough distance to avoid connection. Her aim was to tease him to the brink. In desperation Bennie said, "Come on now!"

"Don't worry, we'll get there," she answered. Tonight, her hand was over his mouth keeping him quiet. At the time of her choosing he was allowed to release. Later while he slept Whende thought about what Sonya use to say, "sometimes payback is a bitch."

In the second week of September Ms. Seale spoke to Bennie from his house in Harlem. She called to say some neighbors stopped by concerned they hadn't seen him. His answering machine tape was full, so she replaced it with another. Bennie knew he had to go back but lost track of time. No one was going to pack things for him, so he'd let her know when he'd be there. It was before hanging up Ms. Seale told him the mail was piling up and he had a letter from Elizabeth Winters. Later that day Bennie told Whende he needed to return and mentioned the letter just in case she already knew. Immediately Whende said she was going too.

Arranging an itinerary was easy, Bennie and Mr. West just looked at the calendar. Mr. West believed two weeks should be enough time. Bennie and Whende could spend time at the house and maybe go back to that rock in the park. Whende needed a day or two to see Jeff, and his son Calvin in New Jersey. A day for Bennie to visit his sister Demetrice in the Bronx, then grab a calzone from the pizza shop. He also wanted to talk to Ronald alone.

Mr. West stopped taking notes to ask a specific question, in preparation for their trip. What level of surveillance was Bennie requesting and on who? Top level monitored movement 24 /7, reports on credit, bank account balances, and a wiretap. His reply was to just advise when Ronald was without Lorraine. After the meeting Bennie couldn't help wondering what level Whende used before contacting him? Two days later Bennie and Whende landed at Newark Airport and had their first heated argument.

Apprehension was building up like a misused pressure cooker before they even boarded the plane. Bennie felt it building because Whende questioned the travel plans periodically. Once after the bags were packed, before they took off, and again during the flight. Always the same question, was there anyone else he wanted to visit? Bennie mentioned checking on Chris's wife Danielle who'd gotten HIV from her late husband. Whende continued looking out the window never saying anything. If Bennie asked a question, she gave one-word responses, yes, no, or you tell me!

The plane landed in Newark Airport Monday the 13th of September and they were taken to a magnificent property in Montclair, NJ. Once they were alone, Bennie was going to find out why she had this funky attitude. Finding anything to keep busy Whende walked from room to room. At times she'd spoken to the staff harshly and he wasn't gonna stand for it.

Bennie never hit a woman in his life, but a question arose. Could a man use self-defense against a professional female fighter? At least if he got his ass kicked Tiffany wasn't here.

Exercising King status, Bennie called to Whende adding bass and volume, in a way that wasn't a request. She came slowly sitting next to him. He began talking about the vows of honesty they made. Bennie said she and their child were more important than wealth and influence. Whende softened only to ask was he thinking about seeing the dentist? He said no and didn't understand why he got a letter, but he would let her read it. Then he took Whende's hand saying she'd trusted him with the least. Why is it hard to trust him with her heart when she was enough?

Whende referenced Denzel having several women in "Mo Better Blues." Bennie quickly reminded her that television and movies are fictitious, even at times the news. Allowing it to sink in he told her Ozzie Davis played a drunk. In real life he and Ruby Dee have been married for over forty years. They continued talking but before going to bed Whende said Bennie had her total confidence. Shortly after 5am in the morning Bennie got a call and left.

Tuesday Ronald sat in the office after assisting early customers with a temperamental machine. Nothing was normal after Bennie sold out. His new partner and Lorraine got into an argument the second day over the soap and fabric softener dispenser. As weeks passed Ronald regretted letting Lorraine talk him out of that offer to be the sole owner. He'd upset Kayla so much she took him to court and was granted 3,300 dollars support a month for Ronald Jr. That was the check he was writing when there was a knock at the door. The office monitor showed a person Ronald didn't want to see. By now Bennie had been away five weeks but Ronald opened the door.

"What's going on Ron, how ya doing?" asked Bennie optimistically. Ronald stood in silence with a raised eyebrow.

"Dude…you gonna let me in? I wanna talk to you," Bennie said gesturing to go inside.

"What do you want?" said Ronald folding his arms.

"Yo Ron…how long we known each other?" asked Bennie sincerely.

"Whoa…it's too late for that. I remember everything!" said Ronald indignantly. Bennie was about to remind Ronald of a few things then changed his mind. To think on the ride here Bennie was going to buy the new partner's share and turn it over so Ronald owned the business outright. But fuck that, he thought, turning to leave. On the way were two familiar faces folding clothes in front of the dryers. It was the man and woman from Saint Nicholas Park the day he and Mister waited for Whende. They watched Bennie walk past barely made eye contact, but he was sure they were the same couple.

From there they drove up Sugar Hill towards Bennie's house. When he got to the top of the stoop Ms. Seale greeted him. Once inside he immediately noticed some changes were made. The wooden staircases and banisters were cleaned and polished. The linoleum he knew as a child was now dark wood. All the carpet was replaced including the appliances. What Bennie couldn't see was new plumbing and wiring behind the walls. Only the living room and kitchen furniture were new and the old was put in storage. All these improvements, Ms. Seale said, were a gift from the Queen Sakatet. After a brief walk through, Ms. Seal gave Bennie a stack of mail held by a rubber band. Right now, he just wanted to listen to the messages, so he left Ms. Seale and went upstairs. The light was blinking meaning the messages weren't played so Bennie sat on the bed to listen.

The messages began from the day he left with Ronald asking for a postponement of the sale. It was him again saying the same thing but slightly different. The third was Ronald asking Bennie to pick up. Once the sale was final Lorraine left a message of the usual complaints. This time her words couldn't leave pressure like a migraine. Bennie was a runaway in a free state refusing to return. The other messages weren't as important as the one not left. There wasn't a message from his sister Demetrice. Bennie left her a message before leaving overseas, and she never returned his call.

Moving on he searched through the mail until he had held Lizzy's letter. What was left for her to say? She'd done everything right and still got her heart broken. Bennie sat on the bed massaging his temple. If it were any of the other women he could read the letter, perhaps laugh, and throw it away. Unfolding the paper he saw there were just a few lines.

Dear Bennie,

I was going to ask if you ever loved me? In some small way I know you did but it wasn't

enough. I want you to know it's taken a lot, but I forgive you. Please get help for yourself.

I wish you well. PS. I couldn't keep the bicycle, so I gave it to a patient. Have a great life, Lizzy.

This time he read it imagining Lizzy's melodic voice. Her words carried no sting or solace. His only thought was when she bought a new mattress it would be for a better man. As far as keeping the letter for Whende, Bennie changed his mind and tore it up.

Later in the living room Bennie instructed Ms. Seale on the items to send back when the trip was over. Tomorrow he'll return with the Queen for important papers, photos, and family heirlooms. Then he told her he was leaving. Truth was Bennie wasn't finding peace in his childhood home. Memories were vivid like watching ghostly figures moving about. In that corner was the 50-gallon fish tank Terri poured soap in the first day she found Linda here. Bennie could see the fish dying slowly in the milky water and Terri walking out the door. On this couch he'd rubbed Lizzy's feet and that relationship was toast. But the most awful recollection came from the mirror in the hallway behind him. It's where Whende embraced him, reverted to Linda seconds later, and fled in the morning with Tiffany. All those recollections were past, but the discomfort was fresh.

Bennie decided to go to the Bronx for calzones and head back to Jersey. Before the car left Ms. Seale gave him a small ring-sized box. Inside was a 32-caliber bullet and he knew it came from the wall adjacent to the kitchen. In fifth-grade Bennie's classmate Christopher spent the night. Dad had a habit of leaving his Colt on the stereo while making breakfast. Suddenly there was a shot and when Bennie turned around, he was staring at the barrel of his father's gun. That bullet left a small hole in the top of the wall. Now after more than twenty years he had in his hand the bullet meant to end his life.

Wednesday Bennie and Whende avoided the morning rush and went to the Brownstone. Because they were together their motorcade was seven cars of different makes and colors. Leah was up front by the driver listening in her earpiece while speaking occasionally into a mike in her sleeve. The queen leaned against Bennie with her hand on his knee. They were allowed to exit the car when the sidewalk was empty. Bennie's heart began racing the instant they went up the stoop. Ms. Seale held the door with Leah the last to enter. Whende told Leah to wait outside while they were in the alcove, and Ms. Seale to wait in the kitchen. Once they were alone Whende looked into the hallway mirror. Bennie became trapped in his vision of yesteryear. She was going to turn away, look at him, and forget all over again. Seconds felt like minutes. Whende touched his cheek leaning in for a kiss and he withdrew. "It's alright my love…it's me I know who I am," she said reassuring him.

Whende's first stop was her old room on the next floor above. Everything she left from her crayons and coloring books to advanced mathematics. In the closet was a box of toys and black dolls she played with. On top of the dresser was a picture of her and Sonya and one of her, Bennie and Tiffany at three weeks old. Suddenly it clicked why there wasn't one photo of her and Bennie as children or with their parents. Everything Whende saw and touched stirred a memory, and stress for Bennie. From the hall Bennie said he was going to the backyard leaving Whende to reminisce. He saw Ms. Seale in the kitchen and changed his mind. He stood outside at the top of the stoop which turned out to be worse.

It wasn't that Bennie and Lizzy ate Chinese food here, but what he told her here. I am…where I say I am. Suddenly he walked down to the sidewalk and kept going. Leah exited the car, catching him. "Sir! Where are you going?" Leah asked, cutting him off.

"I'm gonna go up the street."

"Sure that's fine. Station two and three, you're up," said Leah into her sleeve. In seconds eight or so security personnel took positions ahead, behind and across the street.

"Tell the Queen I'm going up the block and I won't be long," said Bennie turning and walking away.

As he got closer to the corner of St Nicholas, Bennie caught a welcoming aroma of fried fish. Because he and Whende ate it together years ago he decided to take some back. Security took positions in front and behind him in line, while two cars from the motorcade parked close by.

Leaving Famous Fish with food in hand Bennie saw Dennis Palmer. He and Dennis were classmates in high school until Dennis dropped out. After high school Bennie gave him a job in the laundry. Dennis was late every day if he showed up at all and was let go. When he got out of rehab Dennis did odd jobs around the neighborhood, even washing Bennie's car occasionally. Today Bennie granted his high school friend a favor and changing Dennis's life forever.

Dennis asked for help getting to Augusta, Georgia to see his Great Aunt Little Mama. She was 99 years old and wrote to him twice. There was a family legacy to urgently pass on. Bennie was about to say no but something about Dennis was different. He asked for help without mentioning money so Bennie helped. He gave Dennis Ms. Seale's number with instructions to call in an hour.

By midafternoon the motorcade headed back to Jersey with two items Whende wanted. One is a picture she painted of The Pyramid of Giza after waking from a dream. Strangely she envisioned smooth marble covering the blocks, so it radiated light from the sun's rays. It should've been a clue her memory might return. The other item was Bennie's mother's Bible which she kept on her lap.

On the way back Leah said Tiffany's flight was two hours away. Since Whende was queasy that morning Bennie would meet them at the airport. On the way he told Leah to arrange a trip to the amusement park on Friday. Thursday he would spend with Mister while Tiffany got over jet lag.

On Friday they were at Six Flags Great Adventure when the gates opened. Today would be a stress reliever. He even caught a few smiles from security who blended in with the rest of the crowd. Whende, Bennie, and Tiffany went on the teacup ride first. When it was finished Tiffany said it wasn't thrilling enough. She was tall enough to go on the adult rides, so Bennie let her pick. At one point it was comical seeing security reluctantly on the Looping Starship, and the Scream Machine.

Early Saturday Ms. Seale had an update on Dennis Palmer. She got him on a bus to Augusta with an open return ticket. Dennis arrived Friday evening and met with his family. That same day the motorcade went to Harlem so Tiffany could see the house where her mother grew up. At some point they'd tell their daughter what really happened. The next day they went to the old apartment in Woodbridge, New Jersey. Like Tiffany walked through the house in Harlem, Bennie saw where Tiffany and her mom stayed. Sightseeing continued with a drive past their old church in East Orange, the library Linda worked in with Mr. Soriano, and lastly Tiffany's old daycare. On Monday they visited Calvin and Jeff at their home. While the children were occupied Jeff told Whende his friend J-Rock died last month.

Most of those days they ate from both of their favorite places. Whende took Bennie to a spot in Jersey called Jimmy Buff's for hot dogs. One day they had White Castle burgers. Another time it was ribs and spaghetti from Sherman's Barbeque on Seventh Avenue, and more calzones from the Bronx.

The Saturday before Tiffany left, she and her mom went to The Metropolitan Museum of Art in Manhattan spending most of the time in the Egyptian Exhibit. Bennie waited outside because it was a reminder of where he and Lizzy met. Afterwards they went to a section of Central Park closed off for skating. Like the amusement park, security who could skate had to participate. It was also a chance for Whende to witness different races of people coming together to have fun.

It was almost two weeks since they arrived. Tiffany, Mister, and Ms. Aquino were gone, but there was one more place to see. On a cool Thursday afternoon, he and Whende stood by a black iron guardrail in Riverside Park gazing across the Hudson River. Behind them was the bench he sat on before going back to Kayla's apartment. New Jersey was across the river, with the George Washington Bridge in the distance to the right. It couldn't get any better than this, he thought pointing to the tugboat. "Hey Whende…how you feeling?" he asked abruptly.

"My king my stomach's been acting up, but it gets better during the day."

"It's all the different foods and that's my fault. I wanted to have this stuff while I was here…sorry."

"You can always have it shipped cold, or just tell our chefs to figure out the recipes."

"Yeah, it's not that serious, but back to you. How many days you been dealing with your stomach?"

"About a week," she answered leaning on him.

"You told the doctor?"

"Yes, I had an exam, it's not exactly my stomach" she answered hesitantly.

"So…what?"

"I'm…I'm pregnant. They told me I couldn't, but I am," said Whende not knowing his response. Bennie looked over the water, turned to her and said, "it's a boy."

"It's too soon to…"

"Honey…it's a boy. I'm telling you it's a boy!" he said eagerly, "Let's see I need you to help me with names. I want Tiffany's new name to reflect kindness and wisdom. Our son's name should be something like… like um Adam, the first man! Yeah something like that and I gotta choose a new name for myself."

"Yes that's right my king," she said lovingly.

"One more thing. I want you to call me something other than king when we're alone."

"Yes my…my man…my love. Sonya would say you got up in there and knocked the kitty back in shape," she said amusingly. They looked out across the water and shared the first public kiss. Then Bennie said, "Baby…let's get the hell out of here and go home."

There was a surprise waiting for Bennie when they got back. Like the Brownstone, Whende had what will now be The Royal Chamber redecorated. Artwork of Bennie's father was hung throughout, and his clothes were in a closet the size of two rooms. The new bathroom shower was the largest he'd ever seen with six different nozzles.

The baby was due in May between the 13th and the 23rd so Whende stopped combat training. Instead, she walked around the gym and used the stationary bike each day for an hour. She never smoked but let go of the wine. Most of her time went to research and making notes for their book.

Bennie continued working out and reading intelligence reports. He wanted someone at the FBI willing to expose corruption and there were six prospects. If the government was willing to spend tax dollars to eliminate King, and Malcolm why not the KKK and white supremacists' groups. He knew why, but needed Whende to understand the current power structure. Rather than allow fairness and happiness for all, some would see the world destroyed.

While that was happening, Bennie decided to name the baby Atum, Egyptian for the first man. Tiffany would be called Kymeka after Whende's mother, and Bennie chose the name Kefieous.

One night on the balcony watching a full moon they talked about the problems of the world. Bennie wondered if Farisha Ali's grandfather changed history when he used the Obeni in 1910. Whende thought their grandchildren could use it again when the comet came in 2061 or make matters worse.

Whende prophesied of a time when lies become more abundant than truth. That every lie spoken from every mouth remains in the air from the very first one. They collect like droplets that saturate clouds and form hurricanes. Like a bucket that finally overflows all those lies will unleash a storm and end the world. Bennie thought how his recent lies to Lizzy added to the that overflow.

But there was always hope. Whende asked for trust that she knew the strategy of warfare taught from her father. Still the Obeni could be used over and over and there would still be good and evil, truth and lies. The plans God has can't be undone. All we can do with the time we have is try to make this world a better place.

Weeks later while Bennie was studying Whende's painting of the Giza Pyramid he had a recollection and said, "I forgot to tell you I had a premonition about the Pyramid when I was a child. I see myself touching it and something's supposed to happen," he said.

"What do you mean touch it?"

"I always felt I had to touch it?" he repeated.

"Touch it where? Just tell me everything," she said impatiently.

"I'm supposed to touch the left side of the Pyramid facing the back of the Sphinx. I place the palm of my left hand on a stone with my fingers spread apart. And I should be bending slightly to the left when I do it."

"And what happens?"

"I don't know…something is supposed to happen."

"I've had the same vision as a child to touch the side facing the back of the Sphinx but on the right side of the Pyramid with my right hand open like you said," she answered then put her hand over her mouth.

"Did you do it?"

"No because in my vision I was touching a stone block and in my time the Pyramid was…" then Bennie finished her thought, "Smooth…it had smooth marble sides like the painting made."

"That's correct so I never tried, but I felt like something was gonna happen when I did touch it," Whende answered.

"We're gonna do it tomorrow. Your vision was in the daytime, right?"

"Yes."

"Yup we're going tomorrow," he said making a call to Leah.

On the way Bennie wondered was this the time and place he fit. Could this be the reason he was forged and toughened for? In the afternoon a falcon perched on a stone of the Giza Pyramid watching their approach. Until you see what Whende called the Pyrka, its magnitude can't be portrayed by a picture. The Pyramid could take your breath away standing as the tallest man-made structure until the early 1300's. Aliens didn't make this; it was black people in Africa.

Whende let his hand go and they walked like cowboys about to duel in a western movie. Bennie went left stopping when he reached the corner. At this distance it was like watching Whende at the opposite end of a football field. She waved as if giving a signal. Bennie picked a stone block, leaned over, and placed his left hand on it. Now they couldn't see each other but he kept his hand still.

Ten minutes and nothing. They touched again and again and nothing. In Bennie's vision he didn't see anything special, he just touched the stone. Maybe it was the wrong day, or the wrong time of day. After an hour of trying they met near the center of the Pyramid. That's when the ground vibrated, and thunder was heard in the distance. After the falcon took flight a flat plate-sized stone dislodged from above breaking on the ground a few yards away. Bennie went for the large piece while Whende searched the ground. The stone was carved with hieroglyphs which Whende tried to translate. "This is language older than me. I believe it says there's a fifth Obeni with directions to find it," she said alerting Leah to come. Whende told her they were leaving, and the ground had to be searched for a missing piece.

At the car Whende had the liftgate opened and placed the pieces on a towel. Gently she positioned a smaller piece by the broken end and began deciphering. "Right here it says there is another Obeni. It works with any comet passing between Samae and the Ra, the Earth and Sun. It's buried…there's a piece missing," she said stopping her finger on the crack, "we have to find it!

The end?

Made in the USA
Columbia, SC
08 September 2023

22618472R00207